afterparty

Also by Ann Redisch Stampler

Where It Began

afterparty

ANN REDISCH STAMPLER

Simon Pulse
New York London Toronto Sydney New Delhi

SIMON PULSE

An imprint of Simon & Schuster Children's Publishing Division

1230 Avenue of the Americas, New York, NY 10020

First Simon Pulse hardcover edition January 2014

Text copyright © 2014 by Ann Redisch Stampler

Jacket photographs copyright © 2014 by Getty Images (front)

and Thinkstock (spine, back, and flaps)

Jacket design by Jessica Handelman

All rights reserved, including the right of reproduction in whole or in part in any form.

SIMON PULSE and colophon are registered trademarks of Simon & Schuster, Inc.

For information about special discounts for bulk purchases, please contact

Simon & Schuster Special Sales at 1-866-506-1949 or business@simonandschuster.com.

The Simon & Schuster Speakers Bureau can bring authors to your live event.

For more information or to book an event contact the Simon & Schuster Speakers Bureau

at 1-866-248-3049 or visit our website at www.simonspeakers.com.

Interior design by Mike Rosamilia

The text of this book was set in Adobe Caslon Pro.

Manufactured in the United States of America

2 4 6 8 10 9 7 5 3 1

Library of Congress Cataloging-in-Publication Data

Stampler, Ann Redisch.

Afterparty / Ann Redisch Stampler. — First Simon Pulse hardcover edition.

p. cm.

Summary: Tired of always being the good girl, Emma forms a friendship with fun and alluring Siobhan. But Siobhan's dangerous lifestyle becomes more than Emma can handle.

ISBN 978-1-4424-2324-4

[1. Conduct of life—Fiction. 2. Friendship—Fiction. 3. Peer pressure—Fiction.

4. High schools—Fiction. 5. Schools—Fiction. 6. Single-parent families—Fiction.

7. Los Angeles (Calif.)—Fiction.] I. Title.

PZ7.S78614Aft 2014   [Fic]—dc23   2013029008

ISBN 978-1-4424-2326-8 (eBook)

For Rick, Laura, and Michael,
as usual

afterparty

It is not the ending I expected. The free fall from the roof and the torn green awnings. Her body landing in a heap at the foot of a hydrangea bush. The hedges lit with pink Malibu lights that glint off the sequined skirt, the blouse half open, and her pale hair.

The thud, the doorman running down the sidewalk, and then sirens and more rain.

Siobhan the Wild and Emma the Good.

I was the good one . . . maybe not so much.

Poor Siobhan.

She could batter mean girls with a field hockey stick and make it seem accidental. She could break your heart and make it seem accidental.

And then she couldn't. Then she was gone.

Maybe.

Maybe she is only temporarily asleep—but more likely, she is only temporarily alive.

Hanging on by her fingernails is what they say.

The wild one is gone and the good one . . . isn't good. Because good girls don't usually wear long sleeves to cover where their best friend's fingernails scored their forearms. Good girls don't usually slip out their bedroom window in a silver dress and taxi to the Camden Hotel late at night.

Good girls don't usually kill their best friend.

PART ONE

CHAPTER ONE

THE BEACH CLUB WHERE WE LAND OUR FIRST DAY in L.A. is all white and sun-bleached, with striped awnings and a platoon of valet parking guys in shorts and starched safari shirts, like privates in the tap-dancing division of a silent movie's tropical army. The sky is dazzling blue with a faint grayish haze, a smudge all along the horizon.

My dad thinks it's some smog-like form of breathable dirt.

I think it's the edge of Paradise.

On the drive from the hotel to the beach, I start counting palm trees, but there are so many, I lose track. Then I count cars so low to the ground that you could use their hoods for coffee tables, and then landmarks that I've seen in movies. The pink-and-green façade of the Beverly Hills Hotel. The gates of Bel Air. The Ferris wheel on the Santa Monica Pier.

My dad says, "We're not in Kansas anymore."

Although you wouldn't know that if you looked at us.

My dad is in creased khaki pants and a blazer and a white shirt and cuff links. I had to fight with him to leave off the tie because, seriously, it's a beach party at a beach club at the *beach*.

I am wearing a sundress that is saved from intolerable dowdiness only by the fact that it's vintage. (Hint: If your dad insists you wear skirts that are several inches longer than any skirt worn by a girl who wasn't Amish since the nineteenth century, go vintage.)

Cinched waist, wide belt, Audrey Hepburn flats, and big cat's-eye sunglasses.

I say, "Best city yet. So far."

We have spent almost my whole life wandering all around the North American landscape like a tiny band of lost nomads from the icy North, pausing at medical schools that needed a visiting professor, my dad, who could work on their research grants, and then pack up and leave. Dragging his kid behind him.

Until now.

My dad says, "Ems, are those polarized lenses? Blue eyes and sun don't mix."

I say, "Dad. Of course they are."

Welcome to California.

I have been here for less than twenty-four hours. I am sitting in the backseat of a limousine behind a driver in a jet-black cap who drives too fast. I am dressed for 1958. And already I am telling lies.

We head down a sharp incline at the edge of a bluff toward the beach and up the coast. I can't tell if we're in Santa Monica or Malibu or some other sunbaked city that I've never heard of.

I start counting cars with surfboards strapped on top of them, and cars with surfboards sticking out of hatchbacks. I start counting cars with out-of-state license plates, with drivers who look ecstatic to be here and not there when we pass them.

I am counting license plates because I don't want to think about whether there's some way my dad can check out if my sunglasses really are polarized.

I am trying to think about all the seagulls here and all this light instead.

How I'm wearing coconut oil instead of dermatologist-approved number 50 sunblock so I can get tan during the last remnants of afternoon sun at this beach party.

I feel very princess-y in the back of this black car. The valet and the driver and my dad all lunge to open my door.

My dad wins. There's not a minute that he isn't trying to take care of me. Sometimes maybe too much, but still.

We are here because the head of the Albert Whitbread Psychiatric Institute dropped dead on the last day of July, by the side of the road, on his annual bicycle trek through Provence. The Institute started trying to hire my dad to replace him when his corpse was still in a cooler in France. My dad has spent the month of August trying to decide whether to sign the contract sentencing him to five years in Sodom and Gomorrah, which, if you're not up on your Biblical trivia, were the ancient prototypes of Sin City.

Usually I am the person protesting the move while my dad tries to explain why moving from Montreal to Toronto to St. Louis to Philadelphia to Baltimore to Washington, D.C., to Chicago in the space of ten years is a good thing.

Not this time. This time I want it.

We walk under a striped awning toward a cluster of white clapboard buildings between the parking lot and the sand.

My dad brushes sand off the cuffs of his pants and gestures toward the club, where, I can tell just by the way he's frowning, there's way too much perfectly tanned skin and visible fun. He rolls his eyes "Would you say this is more killer or more gnarly?"

I say, "Dad, I love you, please don't get mad at me, but if you want these people to hire you, you can't say those words out loud ever again."

I don't know when people actually said "killer" and "gnarly," but I'm pretty sure my dad was in Quebec, speaking French, back when they did.

My dad says, "Let's not get ahead of ourselves. I have to decide if I want them to hire me."

This would be the whole rest of high school in one place, and the place would be *here*. I have already decided.

Beyond the giant wooden deck of the main building, there are pools and shuffleboard and rows and rows of beach chairs, studded with giant striped umbrellas that skirt a lagoon on one side and go straight down to the surf on the other.

Kids my age seem to own the chairs and the fire pit and the snack shack by the lagoon. My father makes me promise that I will not, under any circumstances, even so much as dip my baby toe in that lagoon, which he is pretty sure is formed from toxic runoff from a storm drain.

"What if my hair catches fire from a rogue tiki torch?" I say.

"Ems, I'm sure there's a highly trained staff of lifeguards with fire extinguishers if that happens."

"Just so long as I can swim in the ocean when we move here."

"*If* we move here."

A hostess in white linen leads us to wicker club chairs on the deck next to Dr. Karp, the head of the Albert Whitbread Institute board of directors, and his wife, who are mounting a campaign to convince my dad that Los Angeles, far from being Sin City, is actually a lot like Heaven. Only with a beach.

It is hard to tell from here if all those kids are hanging on the outskirts of the beach club willingly and are having a wonderful time (in which case we should move here and join up immediately, despite the toxicity) or if they've been dragged here under protest to keep them penned up and away from the un-rich.

The piped-in music plays "I Wish They All Could Be California Girls," followed by "California Dreaming," a version of "Hotel California" with marimbas, and "I Love L.A."

All I want at that moment is to be a California girl leading a normal California life, sitting by the lagoon, drinking, all right, a bottle of root beer, with my magically transformed California dad, who has become completely okay with me engaging in normal California teen activities.

For my whole life, I was *that* girl. The girl who wasn't allowed to watch PG-13 movies until I turned thirteen—which made sleepovers tricky, since if I couldn't, nobody else could. The one time I broke down and watched the forbidden movie, and my dad found out, I basically spent the next two weeks in my room, nodding my head during long, heartfelt talks about how disappointed he was, and didn't I have a moral compass?

It wasn't a ploy or a trick or a parental manipulation, either. The thought that I might not be Emma the Good filled him with woe. I cried so much that he made me crème brûlée with a burnt sugar crust, and I sobbed the whole time I was eating it.

By the time we hit Chicago, the only kind of coeducational activities that didn't leave him in a state of overwrought parental panic were rehearsals of the Chicagoland Youth Orchestra.

Yet here we are.

Here I am, the girl who has been craving sugar all her life, in Candy Land. Here I am, standing on the exact sandy spot where I want my life as the girl previously known as Emma the Good Girl to begin. Here I am, sliding the sunglasses into my bag after I look at all the other beach club kids and see that cat's-eyes aren't an Audrey Hepburn kind of fashion statement at all; they're just weird.

Mrs. Karp, who keeps putting her hand on my arm when she talks, says, "Your daughter is so lovely. I'll bet you have to beat the boys off with a stick."

Not that he wouldn't, given a boy and a stick, but this is the completely wrong direction for the conversation to be going. In fact, two boys standing in line for the bar at the edge of the deck are at that moment checking me out. At least they are until my dad gives them a look suggesting that unless they avert their gaze, they won't live long enough to put their shirts back on.

Mrs. Karp tells me how much I'll like California, oblivious to my dad miserably trying to get the sand out of his shoes.

"But really, a new school that's already started?" my dad says. "During junior year."

"But school doesn't start for days, and I'm a really fast packer!" (Also a highly experienced packer. I could be out of Illinois in forty-eight hours.)

Mrs. Karp pats my hand and says, "Isn't she precious," as if I weren't actually there.

Then Dr. Karp tells my dad how he's also on the board of Latimer Country Day, where half the kids at this very club (kids who appear to be drinking beer and hooking up in broad daylight halfway across this crowded strip of ritzy beach) go to school, and moments from now, I, too, could be attending.

I am quite certain my dad is appalled at the thought of me having anything to do with these kids. Every time Mrs. Karp offers to take me down to the lagoon to introduce me to some kids my age, he shoots me a don't-you-dare look and I end up ordering more lemonade.

My dad sighs, "You'd probably have to drive a car."

The prospect of spinning out down the beachfront highway, behind the wheel, windows down, completely free, makes me almost die of longing. I start wondering if there are GPS bracelets you can clamp on your kid's ankle, but I'm pretty sure that if you could buy them, I'd have one already.

I say, "I wouldn't mind driving."

My dad, who generally manages to walk the fine line between oppressive dictator and overprotective good guy, smiles. He says, "I thought you might have that reaction."

It's getting dark, and after hours of observation, I want to go sit with the kids. A lot. Even though I am wearing a polka-dotted dress with a circular skirt that falls three inches below my knees and they're wearing almost nothing. Even if I end up next to the girls who came up onto the deck to moan about something to their mothers and gave me a who-are-you-and-what-are-you-doing-here once-over on their way back to the sand.

Not a chance.

We have reservations in the dining room, where the waiter hovers over us, keeping our water glasses perfectly full and whisking away the appetizers like a magician before bringing even more food. Of course, Mrs. Karp has long since given up on trying to maneuver me across the sand to meet other kids. She has practically given up talking to me altogether, ever since she kept trying to shove surf 'n' turf down my throat over my (extremely polite) protests. Then she clammed up, horrified that maybe she was trying to force lobster on a kosher person who can't actually eat shellfish.

I am not a kosher person. It isn't even clear if I'm a Jewish person. My dad claims he wants me to make spiritual decisions when I hit adulthood. I just don't like lobsters. They're like giant bugs that stare up at you from the plate. I keep telling her that it's okay, but Mrs. Karp looks stricken, even when my dad reassures her that we left all that (kosher food? religion? all vestiges of our past life?) behind in Montreal.

I am starting to feel as if I'm a walking, talking motherless-girl vacuum that nice women who so much as spot me across the room are inexplicably drawn to fill with helpfulness and insects of the sea.

I wander off in search of the ladies' room, in search of five unsupervised minutes during which I plan to chew some contraband gum, which my dad thinks is a disgusting and therefore unacceptable habit. I am visualizing a moving truck carting our stuff across the Rocky Mountains.

When I see him.

The guy is in a gray Latimer Country Day football tee, worn almost to transparency, and tight but not disgustingly tight jeans, ocean-soaked around the ankles. I am at a dead end in the maze of hallways and unlabeled doors where the ladies' room is supposed to be.

The guy has a corkscrew and two wineglasses dangling from his fingers. He has a face you could draw from memory a second after you first see it, a line drawing of hard-edged, witty symmetry. He looks like an underwear model who also attends Yale, and is deeply amused by the world but not so much so that you're distracted from the cheekbones, or the eyelashes, or the long upper lip, or the mouth.

The mouth.

There is a bit of toasted marshmallow at the corner of his mouth. Which he licks off.

He says, "So. Were you looking for me?"

I watch his tongue trace his lower lip, possibly in search of remnants of marshmallow and possibly flirting.

He has the best hair. Light brown, shiny, slightly spiky from having been in the ocean recently enough to still be damp and only just shaken dry.

He says, "Did I miss something?"

"What?" I am leaning against one of the unmarked doors, which is cold and slippery, as if it's sucked up all the air-conditioned air and left the hallway balmy.

He says, "You're looking at my mouth."

I am.

I say, "Marshmallow."

He tilts his head. He is bemused, and also gorgeous.

I say, "I'm trapped up here in the dining room with surf 'n' turf, and I want marshmallows."

He says, "Poor you. Avoid the clams. Unless you like rubber. You could stick them together and use them for handball."

I say, "Not my game."

He rests the back of his head against the wall opposite, but it's a very narrow hall. "What *is* your game?"

Oh God, a line! I've been here for less than twenty-four hours, I'm just wandering around looking for a quiet place to chew a stick of gum, and I'm two feet away from a tan guy who is feeding me a line.

The guy leans forward. He smells like salt water and smoke from the bonfire down by the lagoon. He slips the hand that isn't holding the corkscrew and the glasses into the small of my back and then he pauses, and I smile, and he's kissing me.

Welcome to California.

I do not hook up with random guys in prep-school tees, and

I don't flirt, and I don't kiss them back—not that I've ever had the opportunity to kiss them back—and I don't put my hand on their shoulders in tacit acknowledgment of how much I want to be doing this strange, random, surprising thing.

There are footsteps, but he doesn't stop until he's finished kissing me. Doesn't look back at the blond girl in the black bikini top and sarong who is looking at me over his shoulder. I didn't know that people even actually wore sarongs. It might just be a really well-draped beach towel.

She says, "Right. Well, don't get any ideas about sister-wives, jerkoff. Just give me the corkscrew."

He is smiling, apparently capable of smiling intensely at two girls simultaneously.

I would jump back, but I'm already pressed against a closed door. I say, "Oh God, is this your boyfriend?" She looks as if he'd be her boyfriend. She is wearing a thin chain with a tiny diamond every few inches that is pooled between her breasts, and she has the same wet hair and the same potential for a lucrative career modeling tiny pieces of lingerie while glaring.

She says, "You can have him. He's a shit kisser, anyway." She hooks a finger through his belt loop and pulls him away, down the hall.

I go back to the dinner party, but it's hard to pay attention.

Three weeks later, we live here.

CHAPTER TWO

I HAVE STARTED AT NEW SCHOOLS ON DAYS THAT
weren't the first day often enough to know the drill.

This time I wake up in a Spanish Colonial house covered
with night-blooming jasmine a half mile above the Sunset Strip.
At night, we see its colors filtering skyward through the pine
trees in the canyon at the edge of our backyard, spotlights sweeping the too-bright sky. If I open my bedroom window, I hear traffic and coyotes and wind.

In the morning, my room smells like fresh paint and the aroma
of my dad baking me pumpkin bread in his belief that motherless
girls need fathers who know their way around a mixing bowl.

He pulls my uniform out of its box and rubs the fabric of one
more plaid pleated skirt between his fingers. The other Lazars—
the ones who, unlike him, did not go to medical school and then
scandalize Montreal by marrying the spectacularly wrong woman
and producing me—are the kings of Canadian imported silk.

He says, "I've never felt so much synthetic. If someone flicks a live ash, your skirt will melt off."

I imagine myself standing skirtless in a puddle of navy blue and burgundy. You can guess who I imagine flicks the ash. (Hint: He is wearing a worn-out Latimer football tee.)

My father, gazing at me slouched in the doorway in the stiff white blouse and dinky little tie, as I pin up my hair, says, "Ems, you look just like her."

It is the first time he has mentioned her—She Whose Name Shall Not Be Spoken, the unmentionable junkie otherwise known as my mother—since Baltimore, two cities ago.

And it's not that I haven't been waiting for an opening to have this conversation with him since Baltimore, because I have. It's just that I'd like to make it to my first day of school without snot and mascara streaming down my face.

I pretend that I am suddenly fascinated by our neighbors' English bulldogs, Mutt and Jeff, who have tunneled under the fence between our houses and are currently wagging their stubby tails and panting, noses to our French doors, watching us.

My dad grabs the backpack he has filled with brightly colored plastic school supplies, well suited to the carefree twelve-year-old I never was, and we wind down to Sunset, past the flower beds on the median strip at Sunset Plaza, past the Viper Room and the Roxy, back into the hills toward Latimer.

We can see the ocean dead-on from the parking lot despite the gray-blue haze.

The landscaping belongs at a luxe tropical resort (not that

we go to luxe tropical resorts: we fight off bloodthirsty Canadian mosquitoes in a cabin in Quebec near Lac des Sables; we take nature walks in the hills, facing due north, away from Montreal).

The buildings are palatial, the pathways wide and curved and swept immaculate.

And in the middle of all this, there is a sign pointing to the stables. The *stables*?

I was prepared for swank, but not this level of swank. I panic, but now that we are (sort of) Southern Californians, my dad shows no inclination to protect me from all this K-12 ocean-view opulence. He half drags me down the perfect path toward the awe-inspiring administration building.

Our hands are shaken firmly and repeatedly by well-dressed Latimer administrators, juggling the words "welcome" and "elite" and "fit right in."

I am sent off to get my student ID photo taken in the student store, which has Latimer-logo clothes, school supplies, and every kind of ball, oar, paddle, fencing jacket, and athletic headgear known to man.

A girl in riding clothes—boots no doubt sewn together by Italian shoemakers while her calves were encased in the cordovan leather, and jodhpurs so tight across the back, you have to wonder how she got her thong so lined up with the seam—is complaining about the brand of saddle soap and the fact there hasn't been any mink oil for her bridle for a week.

The kid behind the counter keeps trying to end the tirade by offering abject apologies, but the tirade is endless. When there's the slightest pause, I say, "Excuse me, is this the right place for the photo?"

The girl turns on her heel (literally); she pivots toward me. She says, "I was talking about my *bridle*. So unless you have something to add . . ."

I suddenly recall why girls without Miss Teen Universe potential should never be the new girl. Then she does a double take and looks me over in a horrified state of disbelief.

She says, "Didn't you, like, babysit the Karp brats at the beach club?"

I am about to descend into my own state of horrified disbelief, but even though she is tall and blond, she is not the girl in the bikini top. I say, "I was having dinner with the Karps."

"I'll bet you were," she says. "*Anybody* can go as a guest. Barbeque Wednesday is turning into freak night. But who knew Latimer was slumming it too?"

I am standing there, counting the number of maroon balloons floating upward from the WELCOME BACK, LATIMER LIONS! banner. So much for a fresh start with boys in it, and maybe some friends who don't remember me with knee socks covering unshaved legs through middle school.

A girl behind me says, "Who *are* you?"

I'm afraid that she's talking to me, but she's not.

The girl in the equestrian cat suit doesn't take her eyes off me. "Here's a tip," she says. "This is *Latimer Day*. You might want to stop interrupting people like you do at Walmart, or wherever you got that cheap barrette. You might want to lose the tacky vintage thrift-store look and get over yourself." She pats my arm. I want to hit her, but more than that, I want to not cry. "There, there. There's always Halloween."

I am not even fully enrolled yet, and it's starting.

"And here's a hint for *you*," the voice behind me says to Equestrian Girl. "You might want to get some pants that fit so the cellulite in your butt doesn't show. And you might want to bone up on cheapness, because, guess what, you dress like a hooker with a trust fund."

The kid behind the counter is frozen in reverential awe and wonder.

The voice behind me asks, "So where's the transfer photo place?"

I turn around, and there is Siobhan.

Only without the sarong or the bikini top or the necklace with the tiny diamonds. Without her index finger hooked through the belt loops of a guy's pants.

She says, "Hey, sister-wife."

She is blond and slouchy and tapping her foot. The sleeves of her jacket are pushed up almost to her elbows; her hair is coming out of the wood bead bracelet she is using for a rubber band; and her socks are pushed down to the rim of high-top sneakers that are not, strictly speaking, part of the uniform.

She doesn't look messy; she looks perfect.

I wait for her to slink away in search of someone cooler, but she doesn't. She stares down at my feet, in pointy black Mary Janes from the fifties and frilly white anklets that are, in fact, part of the uniform if you're in K through 3.

I say, "Listen, at the beach, if that was your boyfriend—"

"Not. At this very moment"—she looks at her watch, which is wafer-thin and stainless steel and Swiss—"he's probably playing two or three other girls in college somewhere. His loss."

It feels more like my loss. I have been waiting for him to come jogging up from the gym in that old T-shirt, or brush against my entirely synthetic navy sweater in the hall.

I say, "Admit he was a really good kisser."

"Ooooh yeah."

We head into the exceptionally green quad that smells like freshly cut grass. We have linked arms. People heading in the opposite direction have to go around us.

"Thank God, another human," she says, pressing her arm against my arm. "All the clone girls here have fruit-scent lip gloss and headbands. Jesus. It looks like they all just sucked on the same lollipop."

"Headbands?"

"Exactly. Where were you when school started? I was in Africa. You're not from here, right?"

As it turns out, she was in Africa because her mother, Nancy, and Nancy's flavor-of-the-month husband, Burton Pratt, were carting Sibhoan around Zimbabwe on an arguably educational safari, and her mom doesn't believe that school should interfere with pretty much anything.

"I'm from Montreal," I say. "Kind of. I haven't been there since I was five."

"*J'adore* Montreal! You speak French, right?" We walk past

the administration building, where we're supposed to be, toward a wooden bench that backs onto a hedge of red hibiscus. "I hate it here," she says. "I just got used to some crap school in New York and now my mom's squeeze wants to be in Hollywood and I have to go to school with nasty clones in headbands."

"He's an actor?"

"He's too old to be *anything*. But my mom used to live here. She says L.A. is boss. *Boss*. Who even says that?"

So far, this is the main thing we seem to have in common, our parents' use of outdated vocabulary. That and the ability to speak French. And kiss the same boy.

I say, "I'm not too optimistic about *Latimer's* bossness. But my dad says I catastrophize."

"No way," she says, tightening her grip. "This place is the cradle of catastrophic boredom. Look around."

But some of us are not bored.

Some of us are saved from the scourge of catastrophic boredom.

By her.

CHAPTER THREE

THE QUAD EMPTIES SLOWLY. I HAVE NEVER SEEN so much blondness, or a school with students so unconcerned about getting to class on time.

I say, "Eventually, we're going to have to do this." I am likely the world's expert on knowing what I have to do and doing it.

She says, "Yes, Mommy." But we don't get up.

Siobhan tears off a hibiscus flower and lodges it behind her ear, the side of her face shadowed with red petals. Then she takes the barrette, mother-of-pearl, from Montreal, out of my hair. Bangs in a state of droopy tendrils fall over my forehead and ears, leaving the ballerina bun moored at the nape of my neck.

She says, "You can thank me later."

Miss Palmer, the guidance counselor, doesn't seem at all perturbed that we're an hour late and don't have the ID cards she sent us to get. She delivers an unsettling pep talk about how wearing the Latimer uniform means we're the best of the best of the best (as stated, in Latin, on the school crest), marches us across the quad to a building modeled after a Greek temple, only with air-conditioning, and ditches us inside the carved door of our French class.

Siobhan whispers, "I already speak French. You'd think they'd ask."

"*Bonjour*, Siobhan Lynch *et* Emma Lazar." The teacher, M. Durand, is an authentic Frenchman, slightly graying, slightly put out to be here. He looks us over with an unabashed stare and asks for two volunteer hostesses to show us ("How you say?") the ropes.

The girls in the front row are busy examining their fingernails, the wood-grain surfaces of their desks, and the floor. Equestrian Girl from the bookstore rolls her eyes so far back in her head, it seems that our mere presence in her lair has precipitated a seizure. Nobody raises her hand to volunteer.

Siobhan twirls a lock of hair around her index finger and glares at *la classe*.

"No worries," she tells M. Durand. "*Je m'en fous de* hostesses." Roughly translated: I say screw you to the hostesses.

She really can speak French.

M. Durand raises one thin black eyebrow.

"Emma and I will show ourselves around," Siobhan says in French spoken so slowly that even first-years could follow. "We could, no doubt, show you one or two things." (There is no perfect translation, but it is so suggestive that M. Durand turns crimson all down his neck.)

"Oh, and *Monsieur*," Siobhan continues, "*s'il vous plaît*, assure these girls that even though Emma and I are *un peu* intimidating, we hardly look down on them at *all*."

The entire front row looks up. It's like the Wave people do at baseball games, only with bobbing headbands sparkling with a dizzying array of tacky rhinestones.

A boy leaning against the window turns slowly and looks at me, nodding in almost imperceptible approval.

Dylan, but I don't know that yet.

And I full-on smile back.

Welcome to California, land of boys. I have just dissed an entire class that no doubt thinks I'm smiling about how much I look down on them by beaming at one.

He is worth beaming at.

I distract myself by cataloguing concrete details: hazel eyes, that wide mouth, slightly long brown hair, unbuttoned cuffs, his right arm hanging over the back of his chair. The wicked laugh he swallows just before the point he'd have to have a coughing fit or leave the room.

He looks as if the uber-prep clothes blew onto his body by mistake when he fell into a wind tunnel on his way someplace a lot more interesting. Which could explain why his hair is mussed and his shirttail has escaped from his pants and why he isn't wearing socks.

He is the most attractive person I have ever seen, with the possible exception of Siobhan and the guy at the beach club, who was more of a fleeting mirage in the sad, overchaperoned desert of my life than an actual person.

At Latimer, on the other hand, I am surrounded by all manner of boys. And it's clear that even in a lush forest of boys—their minute differences, the rich variety of their faces and shoulders and hands, emphasized by the fact that they're all wearing the same thing—this is *the* boy.

It occurs to me that if I don't stop staring at him, if I don't suppress my desire to follow him out of the room and basically anywhere, he will probably notice.

"That was beyond good," I say to Siobhan when we are sitting in the empty cafeteria after French, when I'm supposed to be in Math and she's supposed to be in Econ.

"And it's going to get better. I hold on to grudges for an unusually long time."

"Remind me not to get on your bad side."

"How could you be on my bad side?" she says, wide-eyed. "You're my best friend in America. Aren't I your best friend in America?"

I have several semi-friends scattered across North America, in cities where we lived when I was little and you make friends fast. They post sneezing panda videos on my Facebook wall and send chain letters threatening doom.

I say, "Yes."

Eventually Miss Palmer finds us, draws us a map of where we're supposed to be for all of our classes (just in case we'd planned to spend the whole rest of the day eating frozen yogurt), and shepherds us to PE.

Siobhan and I have checked our schedules, and we have four classes together, but PE isn't one of them. I say, "Miss Palmer.

I don't think I'm supposed to be in PE. My schedule says 'PE Alternative Dance.'"

But apparently I'm trapped playing field hockey until I'm assigned to a ballet class.

"No worries," Siobhan says when we are rifling through the leftover gym clothes they lend people who need them. "I'll get us out of this."

First, she tries to convince the teacher we can't run around because of our periods.

"We're synchronized," she says. "It's a scientific fact that best friends synchronize. You can look it up."

"Suit up," he says.

"This would *never* happen in Italy," Siobhan says, ostensibly to me. "I lived in Milan before New York. There are old ladies who think you shouldn't take a *bath* during your period in Italy."

Mr. Tinker points to the hockey sticks.

Naturally, nobody wants us on her team. They stand there, leaning on their sticks, ignoring us as much as possible given that we're ten inches away from them. When Mr. Tinker blows his whistle, we go trotting after them, trying to blend in. Thirty seconds later, Siobhan is on the ground and you can't even tell who put her there, which girl is saying "whoops" over her shoulder.

"Whoops?" Siobhan says, rubbing her thigh. "Really?"

Siobhan, it turns out, is the poster girl for "Don't get mad, get even." Or, more accurately, "Get mad *and* get even." Soon, half the girls on the field would have bruised ankles and battered shins if they weren't wearing monster shin guards.

Equestrian Girl, who has been slashing her way up and down the field, cornering the little ball and slamming it into the goal, plants herself in front of us.

She says, "What the hell." It isn't even a question. "Did somebody forget to lock your cage?"

"I'm sooooo sorry," Siobhan says. "Maybe I'm swinging too wide."

The girl snorts, a horse's whinny kind of snort, appropriate because it turns out she's the queen of the eleventh-grade horsey girls. "Right," she says. "Well, I'm Chelsea Hay, and you can't just do whatever you want."

Siobhan says, "Watch me."

The whistle blows. I careen, half pushed, half stumbling, into a petite girl who elbows me as if I'd jumped her. Chelsea takes off with Siobhan at her heels, swinging (maybe at the ball and maybe not) and yelling, "Take that, bitches!"

Mr. Tinker blows his whistle until Siobhan can no longer pretend she doesn't know it means she's supposed to stop trying to shed blood.

"I don't know what you did at your old school," he says. "But at Latimer, we don't swear at our teammates."

"They're my teammates?"

Mr. Tinker rubs his shaved head. "Do you play lacrosse?"

"Eastside Episcopal," Siobhan says. "Boys' team."

"Varsity tryouts," he says. "Tomorrow. Give me that stick."

CHAPTER FOUR

"SO," DYLAN SAYS ON THURSDAY, WALKING PAST my desk in homeroom. "I hear you're violent for a ballerina." You can't tell from his face or tone or posture if he thinks this is a good thing or a bad thing.

I say, "Not a ballerina. The bun is for PE Alternative Dance, not actual ballet."

When he rests his hand on the back of my chair, there's a chill at the nape of my neck under the ballerina bun, in the same general category as tingling, or a cold wind, or waves of high-frequency vibration, or possibly lust.

"I heard you got a lot of help slashing from your friend over there."

Dylan nods toward Siobhan, who is sitting at her desk admiring her manicure, full-on lacquered gold in a room full of frosted pastels studded with small yet hideous jewel stick-ons.

"I don't know what you heard, but all dismemberment was purely accidental."

Dylan is too deadpan to smile, but the corners of his mouth do a little twitchy thing that's just as good. "So. Did you grow up playing ice hockey in a Canadian street gang, or do you just have a bad temper?"

In actual fact, I grew up eating homemade pie and watching wholesome teen movies from the 1980s where the worst thing anyone does is wear criminally gigantic shoulder pads.

"Bad seed," I say.

"Maybe you should ditch the field hockey and stick with ballet. I play for their performances—orchestra does. Seems like a more stable gang of thugs."

"What do you play?"

"Violin. Third chair, not exactly stellar. Only class I can stand to attend on a regular basis this year."

"You're making me regret giving up cello." And not for musical reasons. "I love the music, but I suck."

He says, "You'd fit right in."

"Anyway, thanks for the advice. I always keep my eye out for bands of thugs. Coming from a Canadian street gang and all."

Dylan shakes his head. "You know what they're going to do to you, right?"

"What?" I say. "Embarrass us in front of the whole French class. Knock us down when we try to be on their lame field hockey teams. Not talk to us. Avoid us. Sneer when I talk in class. Stick needles in my eyes."

"All of it," he says.

This is not an incorrect assessment of the situation.

Siobhan and I are a two-girl island in a sea of bobbing mean girls.

I get into (somewhat remedial) ballet that meets just before lunch, and the girls tend to eat together. But in a room of stick-thin, aspiring ballet girls, I'm the Sesame Street, one-of-these-things-is-not-like-the-others, doesn't-fit-in one who eats actual food. Because the ballet teacher here pitches a fit whenever anybody jiggles, even if they're only there to get out of field hockey.

I am not giving up food.

Siobhan, who is apparently the most terrifying lacrosse player in the history of girls' lacrosse, has teammates swarming her (grateful she has saved them from a season of endless defeat), but she says they're all hormonal.

And boys.

She could be eating lunch daily with the football guys at the picnic table the unattached ones—the ones who don't spend lunch making out with their girlfriends in between huge bites of burger—like. They go, "Hey, Siobhan!" and then, as an after-thought Siobhan insists is not an afterthought, "Hey, Emma!"

Within a week, she is playing midnight touch football with them, climbing the fence and evading Latimer security. And I, Emma Lazar, Canadian good girl, am eating lunch with the Latimer Day football boys.

Dylan is never around at lunch.

Siobhan says, "Who are you looking for? Not that jerk from

the beach club. I *told* you he's not here. You should listen to me."

I say, "No," because I'm not. I don't say who I *am* looking for, as this would involve pointing at Dylan and gnawing on my arm to keep from saying something truly embarrassing.

"Guy's an arrogant dick," she says. "Guy can't go on a simple corkscrew run without sticking his tongue down some handy skank's throat."

"Making *me* the handy skank?"

She says, "How do you know how many other girls he kissed on his way to the maître d'? How do you know if he even kept it in his pants between the beach and the clubhouse? Oh, that's right. You don't."

"How do *you* know I didn't captivate him with my charm?" I don't actually think this is what happened, but the thought of him kissing his way up from the beach, his lips landing on mine just because they were there, is not my memory of choice.

"Your charm and that dress. I love that dress."

The football boys, catching a snippet of a conversation with "not keep it in his pants" in it, are suddenly attentive.

The mean girls walking past our table take note, but what are they going to do, dump their Fiji water down our backs?

"Us against them," Siobhan whispers. "We win."

In Math, Dylan walks past my desk even though his desk is in the farthest back corner, by the door. The blazer hanging off one shoulder brushes my arm, smooth and alarmingly electric for navy blue gabardine. "So. Any needles in the eye yet?"

I say, "I'll let you know. If."

"Not if. When." He writes his number on a slightly used Post-it and sticks it on my sleeve. He says, "Text. They don't confiscate cell phones. They say they do, but they don't."

I type his number into my phone.

I do not pay attention in class.

I feel an astonishing absence of guilt.

CHAPTER FIVE

IN MY DEFENSE, EMMA THE GOOD DID NOT SLIDE easily into the realm of the formerly good. I was not a complete scourge-of-God liar leading a fun life of deceit from the moment of the magic kiss.

Because, at first, my life of virtue remained stunningly intact. The extent of my evil was the sunglasses mini-lie I told my dad, and the completely false claim that the only makeup on my face was the slightest faint hint of mascara. And, all right, every word I said (and didn't say) about Siobhan and pretty much everything we did, other than study.

In the Emma the Good column, I finish all homework and commune with my dad's pick for my best friend in L.A., Megan Donnelly. It's lucky that Megan and I like each other because we're like the arranged marriage of kid friendship. It's not her fault she's the prisoner of her exponentially more clueless dad and overly attentive mom, goes to school in a convent even though she isn't, strictly speaking, Catholic anymore (although she has yet to share her lack of religious conviction with her parents), and spends all her time studying, going to church, and attending uplifting cultural events.

My dad achieves a state of parental bliss at the Donnellys': While other parents worry that their kids are having lots and lots of unprotected sex, Megan's mom worries she'll drink beverages with artificial sweeteners.

Something about rotting your cerebral cortex.

"Just drink the apple juice and don't ask," Megan whispers. "You really do not want to know."

If you line up Megan, whose idea of teen rebellion is talking to Joe, a boy she never ever gets to see in real life, on her cell phone, with Siobhan, whose idea of teen rebellion is teen rebellion, it's hard to tell that they inhabit the same century.

Also in the good column, all the way on top, I cart sacks of brown rice around and teach eager eighty-year-olds (and kids who only know how to operate, say, late-model Macs) how to log in donations on the world's oldest, slowest computer at the food bank where I volunteer—the place that my dad, in a giant breach of good-father decorum, slips up and calls Temple Beth Boob Job.

Obviously, this isn't the name of the temple: It is Temple Beth Torah, and the core of its existence is repairing the world, one grocery bag at a time.

It is not a bad place.

Except the young, girly rabbi is too friendly. I'm pretty sure it's because my needy-motherless-girl flag is flying and she wants to share how to knit sweaters and the mysteries of tampons. (Hint: motherless, not needy.) But I think she catches me admiring her kippah, which is made of silver filigreed wire, as if a highly disorganized spider spun a skullcap that caught tiny pearls. Just as she's telling me how welcome I'd be in levels of the temple higher than the basement where the food bank is, say in youth group, where I could be part of my own *little community*, my dad—who volunteers himself every couple of weeks, partly to help heal the world and partly to check up on me—bundles me into the car and starts making cracks about the place.

"Our community isn't *little* and it extends far beyond the walls of this temple and all these reconfigured breasts," he says. *"Entendu?"*

Overlooking the fact that every Friday night, he makes Shabbat dinner. I light candles, he blesses me, and we eat an exact replica of the giant Moroccan Sabbath meal my grandma Bella—whom I barely remember—no doubt cooks each week in Côte Saint-Luc, just north of Montreal. During which he drills me with the tenets of Judaism he approves of, his favorite being *tikkun olam*, repairing the world, into which feeding the hungry falls. And somewhat *lashon hara*, which boils down to no mean gossip, his free pass to establish a vast list of important topics that he won't discuss.

All of which we pretend never happened because, in another never-to-be-discussed fact of Lazar family life, my dad is off organized Judaism, religion in general, and all members of the Lazar family (religious or not) in Montreal. Which is so far from an approved topic for dinnertime chatter that you have to wonder if my dad ever thinks about it anymore.

When we are driving home from the food bank, I go, "Dad, so if Rabbi Pam asks what religion I am, what do I say?"

He says, "She asked you that?"

"No, but the thing is, we're bagging groceries in a *temple*."

"Would you prefer a church?" He sounds flustered, as if he's beating himself up for committing a child-rearing blunder. "I could find you a church."

Not find *us* a church, find *me* one. Raising the question of whether he thinks of me as the same religion as the rest of the Lazar clan, or, for example, as him.

I say, "No! Dad! This is fine. I like Beth Boob Job."

"Ems!"

"Don't look at *me*. *I'm* not the one who made the inappropriate comment in front of *my* impressionable kid."

My dad fake-slaps at my jeans. He says, "Enough. You're a good kid, but enough."

But before long, when you add up the number of hours I spend as a paragon of virtue in the basement of that temple, it turns out to be the exact number of hours I feel as if I can still claim the title of Emma the Good, figuring out how many cans of tuna I can give people, whether there are enough boxes of dried mac and cheese to go around.

Siobhan says, "You spend *every* Sunday sorting rice and beans? You can't come with me *once*?"

Siobhan spends her non-lacrosse Sundays at her stepfather's country club, flirting with Wade, the junior tennis pro, who goes to UCLA. This drives her mom up a wall as apparently her one and only rule for Siobhan is No Older Guys. Her strategy when driven up a wall is to try to distract Siobhan by taking her shopping and burying her under the entire contents of Kitson.

"Win-win-win," Siobhan says, cracking open her uniform blouse to reveal a new black camisole. The blouses are the thickness of plastic picnic tablecloths. The black doesn't show through.

She says, "I still don't get it. Why doesn't your dad write your food place a check and just be done with it?"

Megan Donnelly says, "He offered to find you a *church*? Maybe he's giving you a choice. Unlikely, but consider. If my parents gave *me* anything resembling a religious choice, I'd throw a party."

We're sitting on Megan's bed, eating my dad's fudge brownies that I had to sneak in because her mom thinks pastries are a public health menace.

I say, "Or maybe he just doesn't want the spawn of Satan in his club."

I'm talking about my mom, and Megan knows it.

Megan says, "She wasn't Satan! My dad says your dad was so in love with her, he couldn't even think."

"Meaning he was thinking with . . . you know."

Megan, who is the nicest, but not the most experienced, person you could ever meet (even compared to me), says, "No, thinking with what?"

I say, "Nothing."

Seriously, would Emma the Good corrupt Megan Donnelly?

Every time we go over there, Megan's parents, my dad's friends since medical school, make him look like an irresponsible, anything goes–type parent. Before we escaped to Megan's room with the contraband chocolate, the dinner table talk involved how her mom spends her nights in the ER, cleaning up the alcohol-poisoned, bloodied, car-wrecked, controlled-substance-ingesting teen wreckage of other parents' failure to recognize the dangers of urban life. Then we listened to her dad complain about how minors can get condoms at twenty-four-hour drugstores.

On the drive home, my dad says, "There's a revelation! Compared to Edgar Donnelly, I'm the groovy dad."

I am practicing driving my dad's car through the winding streets near the base of Griffith Park. Which is why all I'm thinking about is not hitting other cars. I say, "I hate to tell you, but you can't say 'groovy.' Were you even born when people said that?"

If I'd been looking at him instead of the road, I would have stopped there.

I say, "Also. You're the total despot dad. Edgar is just a whack job."

"I'm a *what?*"

"Sorry! That was a completely bad joke. Sorry!" I accidentally slightly swerve the car across the dotted line that runs down the middle of the street.

He says, "Pull over." Which I do.

He says, "A *despot?* Is that what you think?"

I have made my dad miserable again. I say, "Of course not! We've been at the Donnellys' too long! *I'm* the one who's *allowed*

37

to joke around. *Megan* is the totally oppressed one who will no doubt run away and go to stripper school if you don't make Edgar see reason."

He says, "Good save."

He pats my shoulder. He says, "I'm proud of you, Ems. Don't disappoint me."

I am determined not to. Emma the Good. Emma the, all right, considerably less than good. Every cell and eyelash of me is determined not to disappoint.

Meaning: He can't find out. Anything. Ever.

CHAPTER SIX

ON MONDAY, GOING INTO HISTORY, DYLAN WANTS to know if I had a nice weekend.

"Hey, Bad Seedling," he says, "what do Canadian ballerinas do in L.A.?"

I say, "It's just *PE* ballet, not *actual* ballet."

"Hard to picture you doing jumping jacks in toe shoes."

"Visualize my father taking me to concerts at UCLA. Visualize me listening to three hours of Brahms."

Chelsea, who just won't give it up, says, "So that's where people who don't get invited to parties go. What *do* they do for fun, I wonder?"

"How do you know if she goes to parties?" Siobhan says, dropping her notebook on her desk.

"Answer the question," Chelsea snaps. "Did somebody invite you to a party somewhere in civilization, Emily?" She turns to Siobhan. "Maybe you can get yourself invited if you rub up against everybody on the football team enough—I hear you're very close to groping *all* of them—but Miss Thrift Shop here?" She looks me over, and recoils. "I doubt it."

I say, "It's *Emma*."

Dylan holds up his hand, to no avail.

Chelsea says, "Even Dylan Kahane thinks she's seedy. And he sleeps in his clothes." As if he weren't there to hear her dissing him.

"*Seedling*," says Arif. Arif Saad is the English-accented, creased and pressed, Saudi Arabian foil to Dylan's casual insubordination. They are a matched pair of opposites. "He called her 'seedling.' Friends often call each other by terms of endearment. Something you'd know, Chelsea, if you were more endearing."

Chelsea mutters something about a camel and starts to walk away. Arif puts his hand on her arm. He says, "Repeat that."

Chelsea just looks at him.

"That thing about the camel. Repeat that."

Apparently Chelsea *can* be stared down.

Apparently Arif, once provoked, won't give it up either.

"A point of clarification," he says. "Was I the camel or the camel *jockey*? Or was I having sex with the camel? Or was that *you* and your maggot of a horse?"

There is a sharp intake of breath from Chelsea and everyone else.

"You aren't going to repeat it, are you?" he says. "Unfortunate. Because I'd so enjoy a written apology."

Dylan says, "Don't pout. Maybe next time."

Chelsea storms off, but doesn't open her mouth.

I turn to Arif, who sits behind me. I say, "Thanks. And sorry."

"My pleasure. His seedling is my seedling." He looks over at Dylan, who is turning toward his seat in the back, snickering. "Oh no. 'Seedling' wasn't offensive or sexist or degrading, was it?"

Dylan swings around and smacks him on the back of the head. You can tell that they've been hanging out together since forever.

Arif says, "I'm going to sic my camel *and* my falcon on you."

Dylan flips him off and Arif responds in kind, except Dylan is nowhere near his seat, whereas Arif is sitting down with his notebook open.

"Mr. Kahane," Mr. Auden, the AP European History teacher says, coming into the room. "Again? And Mr. Saad, not what I'd expect from you."

Dylan says, "Heading to my seat."

"Or you could leave now and save us the suspense of wondering when you're going to disappear." Mr. Auden sighs. "What I wouldn't give to have your brother back in my class. You have no idea."

Dylan flinches. Then he says, "Okay," and walks out the still-open door. Illustrating the idiocy of Latimer's policy that skipping out on its magnificent educational offerings is its own punishment, a free pass for constant cutting.

Over my shoulder, I see Arif put his head down on his desk.

Lissi Kallestad, completely oblivious, waves her hand, flashing the bracelet on which her family motto, "Strive, strive, strive," is engraved in Norwegian. "Mr. Auden! Mr. Auden! Is there extra credit for chapter four?"

Chelsea says, "Extra credit for shutting your mouth."

I say, "Leave her alone." Reflexively and without thinking. Oh God.

I feel a buzz in my pocket and check my phone under my desk.

> **Dylan:** Seed. How are your history notes?
>
> **Me:** I noted your departure.
>
> **Dylan:** It's my signature move. Notes?
>
> **Me:** I take OCD notes. With footnotes. You still want them?
>
> **Dylan:** Afraid so. Maybe for more than today. I don't think I'll be there much.
>
> **Me:** That was pretty rank.
>
> **Dylan:** O the horror. I've got better things to do.
>
> **Me:** Who doesn't?
>
> **Dylan:** Remain seated. Resist impulse to flee. Take good notes.

When I'm anywhere near him, even by electronic proxy, even when my texting fingers are hovering three quarters of an inch over his words, I have to resist any number of impulses. Fleeing is not one of them.

CHAPTER SEVEN

IT WOULD MAKE LIFE A LOT EASIER IF I WERE THE kind of bad seed with a hard, protective shell and thorns that leave splinters if you try to crush them in your hand. The kind Chelsea wouldn't mess with.

But in the absence of a shell, there's Siobhan.

"We should burn her at the stake," Siobhan says.

We're reading *Saint Joan* in English class, and Ms. Erskine insists that what happened to Joan (hint: she pissed off all the important men in France and then they burned her at the stake) is the perfect metaphor for the fate of women in the cruel, cruel modern world. Discuss.

A large number of boys grab hall passes and don't come back. Dylan is out of there in five.

And every time I speak, Chelsea mimes an imitation of me with the added touches of protruding tongue and hands clenched like two claws in rigor mortis.

Kimmy, the horsiest of horse girls, mouths, "Stop it, Chels," but Chelsea doesn't stop.

I try to gut it out, but I choke on my words. What I was trying to say about the Bishop of Beauvais is lodged in the back of my throat, like a mouthful of gristle.

"My *horse* has more interesting things to say," Chelsea mutters after class, falling into her little brigade with Mel Burke and Lia Graham.

Siobhan keeps saying that it's going to get better, but I don't believe her.

For me, better is when Sib and I are alone together somewhere else. When we're sitting in the screening room at her house, semi-watching a French film *Paris Match* said was stupendous, which I guess it is, if you like attractive naked people who can't act.

Siobhan is trying to get her laptop to Skype-connect with William, her best friend on all continents except North America, where I am the reigning best friend. She can see him, but there is no sound.

Whenever I look away from Siobhan's laptop to the movie screen that spans the front of the room, I get an eyeful of full frontal nudity.

Siobhan says, "You need a drink, right?"

I say, "Thanks. I'm fine."

"Oh Jesus, don't go all American on me. Montreal is practically France. Say you haven't been guzzling wine with dinner since you were eight."

All right, I have, liberally cut with water, but I am unprepared for high-octane vodka in orange juice.

"Better, right? Wait!" She lunges for her laptop, which has started to make dial tone noises. "William! Where the fuck are you?"

Siobhan and William are bound by years of little-kid pacts. It is difficult to reconcile her stories of their childhood—jumping into fountains in Milan, riding scooters down staircases at his country house in Umbria—with chain-smoking, insomniac William, who is always up no matter what time it is in Switzerland. His boarding-school buddies, half passed-out, dispense crude comments in three languages in the background.

Siobhan and William have pacts from when they were twelve to get married at thirty and become gamekeepers in Africa, pacts filled with adventure and secrecy and a long-remembered rush that will keep them friends forever.

"A gamekeeper?" I say when she tells me about it.

Siobhan says, "It's a pact. We're stuck with it."

Then, over the din of the grunting French actors, Siobhan screams, "Fuck this laptop!"

William's face freezes. The connection turns to static and then silence. William's image, heavy-lidded eyes staring straight out, fades to grey.

"You want a pact?" Siobhan says. "Let's mess with Chelsea. Let's mess with her creepy horse. *I'm Chelsea and Sir Galahad only performs for meeeee.*"

Of course I want a pact.

She says, "Can you ride English?"

It's hard to tell, sitting in the half darkness of the screening room, if what we are planning is adorable teen hijinks on the order of pasting a mustache on the statue of Charles Emmett Latimer in front of the administration building, or more of a late-night felony by reckless rich kids with no morals, conscience, or sense.

I come down on the side of hijinks.

Which is how I find myself in a basic black breaking-and-entering outfit when my dad thinks I'm sleeping over at Siobhan's house so we can practice our Joan of Arc oral report and get up early to wrap each other in tinfoil suits of armor. I have never done anything remotely like this, told my dad a lie of this magnitude to cover up something that is no doubt fourteen kinds of illegal, and also kind of wrong. But somewhere between trying to talk myself into the idea that this is hijinks and ordering myself to bail, I climb over the stone wall near the dark paddock.

"How long before Security shows up?" Even fortified by brandy that Siobhan claims is good for quelling fear but seems to have left me slightly uncoordinated, I'm pretty sure we're doomed.

"Get a grip, grasshopper. They're playing cards in the gym."

"How do you even know that?"

"Midnight football," she says. "Remember? If you'd give up the boo-hoo, Daddy-I'll-be-sooooo-good shit, you could be tackling Ian Heath."

"Wow, I could be hooking up with a functional illiterate."

"Or Sam Sherman. You could be hooking up with him. Football *and* he's the only guy in Mara's so-called band. Man of your dreams."

"Could we possibly concentrate on what we're doing? I haven't ridden since I was six."

She pulls open the unlocked double doors to the stable. "We are so in."

I am staring down Kimmy's horse, named Loogie by her brothers due to his giant, snotty horse nose, at least eliminating the pretentiousness factor. Loogie stares back in round-eyed confusion.

"You *said* you wanted a horse that's a big puppy," Siobhan says. "Do you need a leg up or what? Shit. I hope I remember how to tack them up."

But she does it, perfectly.

Also, it turns out, you don't forget how to ride a horse, especially the part about how you'll fall off if you aren't gripping with your thighs. Which I am, hard. But heading onto the trail that leads away from school, through the dry creek bed, through rustling leaves and confused birds that chirp in the dark, I get what the horsey girls have been going on (and on and on) about.

"Best pact ever," Siobhan says, even though Chelsea's horse, Sir Galahad, looks like he bites and keeps wiggling his horse butt as if he wishes she'd fall off. "Cool, huh?"

"Beyond." I want to whip off the black breaking-and-entering ski cap, shake loose my hair, and canter. "Doesn't it make you kind of want one?"

"Hello. It's me. If I wanted one, I'd have one."

It's true. I can see her going, Hey Marisol, let's fly down to Kentucky on Sunday and get me a horse. And Marisol, the housekeeper who is always there when Siobhan's parents are away doing whatever they do, booking the flight.

"You're just down on horses because Galahad is nasty and Loogs is Mr. Cutie."

"Don't go all horse whisperer on me," she says. "They're just buff cows you sit on. All I want is one little video of Galahad going over a fence with me on his back. He only *performs* for you, Chelsea? We'll see about that."

"Siobhan, *no*! Security will be down here in ten seconds if you turn on the lights in the paddock."

"Boo! Hiss! I'm trying to cheat with Galahad and you're spoiling our special moment." Siobhan waves her cell phone at me, but I don't take my hand off the reins.

She chucks it at me from a foot away. We hear it hit the ground.

"Shit!" Siobhan says.

We hear Sir Galahad crushing what turns out to be the plastic case. Siobhan dismounts and gets her battered phone, scooping up shards of the gold plastic case from the walkway just outside the stable.

She says, "Don't freak! It's not like it's purple and my name's bedazzled on it or anything."

"I'd be just as happy not to get my name bedazzled onto a police report!"

Or whatever kind of document wrecks your permanent

record when you leave evidence of horse rustling strewn all over
Latimer.

"Kill the mood, why don't you?" Siobhan snaps as I slide off
Loogie's back onto another plastic fragment that crunches under
the heel of my boot.

"So," Dylan says when he's standing by my locker, waiting to col-
lect my notes. "Get much work done last night?"

I say something that sounds a lot like "gark."

He says, "I heard somebody went riding."

"Really?" I deserve the Oscar for best performance by a girl
pretending not to jump out of her skin. Not just because he *knows*
but because what if the idea of criminally insane girls is a turnoff
for him, not unlike all other boys in their right minds?

"Kimmy is pissed," Dylan says. "McKay bawled out her and
Chelsea for not grooming their trusty steeds after they rode them,
and Siobhan's trash-talking Galahad. So I'm thinking, Hmmm. I
didn't know you rode."

I haul Siobhan to the bleachers at the end of the field. She is
abnormally serene.

I say, "Excuse me, was this a pact to get expelled? Because I
missed that part."

"Stay calm. Surrender sharp objects."

"Sib, this could mess up our lives!"

"*I'm* messing up your life? Because your life is *sooooo* perfect
without me? Your life *sucks* without me."

"Not what I said."

"Calm down," she says. "Chelsea thinks it was some guy on the soccer team who likes her. Nobody knows."

Except that when I'm standing there in the carpool line, Dylan comes up behind me and hands me a neatly folded napkin with a rubber band around it and a big piece of Siobhan's gold plastic phone cover in it.

He says, "Next time, try not to leave a trail of bread crumbs."

First pact, and I have fallen off the Good wagon.

CHAPTER EIGHT

YOU'D THINK IT WOULD BE A GIVEN THAT MESSING with Chelsea wouldn't include letting her know we did it. But Chelsea thinks it's proof that boys will go to any length to get her attention. She's *happy* about it. Which is so not the reason we borrowed her horse.

"Don't you want to see the look on her face?" Siobhan says. "If she *knew*."

"I would love to see the look on her face. But not as much as I don't want to get kicked out of Latimer and grounded for all eternity."

"Boo-hoo," she says. "I'm bored. Let's go play at Century City."

Usually, we go to Century City after playing dress-up in her mom's closet. Which is the size of my house.

Back in the day, when naked ladies were found in magazines and not online, Sib's mom, Nancy, was crowned the best Miss February ever. Posed across two full glossy pages, she was billed as a sharpshooting, baton-twirling Texas cowgirl, with sparkly red cowboy boots, a Winchester, and a small quantity of strategically arranged red gauze.

She was already pregnant.

When Nancy showed up, still gorgeous, at a Playboy Mansion charity event a few months later, with the highest, tightest baby bump ever, someone from a porn channel stuck a mike in her face and asked what she'd been doing. She snarled, "I'm writing a memoir. I'm writing how to be pregnant and sexy, see?"

Two ghostwriters later, *Pregnant and Sexy* was born. So was Siobhan. Followed by *Sexy Mom*, *Sexy Mom at the Office*, and a host of other bestsellers that make Siobhan cringe.

Nancy's taste in clothes still involves the absolute minimum of cloth.

Siobhan says, "You can't wear *that*. That's what she wore to church on Christmas. I'll pick."

Nancy has thirty-one pairs of sandals, each one high-heeled, with delicate thin straps and ties and buckles. I've tried on all of them.

My dad thinks malls are playgrounds of sick, unfettered materialism, thus eliminating any possibility that he'll stumble on me teetering around in these sandals and small dresses while Siobhan screams at men who leer at her (this is the rule: they have to leer first) in languages other than English. Eliminating any possibility that he'll see her poking me and saying, "Your turn, babycakes."

"In the first place, no one is leering at me," I tell her. "And in the second place, no."

We are sitting on a wicker couch near the bar, sipping wine a guy in a turtleneck sent over.

Siobhan says, "Look at that one in the Ultrasuede blazer. Gross. He is completely leering."

"Not at me. You might have one or two Miss February genes I didn't get."

She uncrosses her legs and extends one foot in front of her, rotating it as if she's checking out whether her ankle works. A middle-aged guy in a sports coat looks her over. She lifts her glass and shouts something angry at him in what sounds as if it might be a real language, but isn't.

"There," she says. "Isn't this so much more entertaining than if we were at French Club listening to those brats massacre French?"

The chasm between who I'm supposed to be and who I actually am, between Emma the Good and this person my dad *cannot* find out about, is growing daily. Siobhan is getting impatient that I won't play more games with her, but even here, in the land of the impending earthquake, the ground can only fissure so fast.

I say, "I want to play, I do. Theoretically I get it, but I lack the skills."

"You lack yelling-at-pervs skills? How can you walk down the street without yelling-at-pervs skills?"

I try to explain how I've spent my life chained up and left to rot without sounding geeky.

Siobhan says, "So basically, you're like this inherently cool person who got corked in a magic genie lamp for sixteen years?"

She seems more intrigued than upset. "You can be my science project! We can *slooooooowly* raise your body temperature and ease you into the twenty-first century."

"There aren't a lot of outlets for coolness in a magic lamp. Just saying."

She says, "People think you're cool. And not just because you're with me."

Whenever Siobhan comes up with one of these completely untrue reassuring assertions, I want to invent an un-cheesy substitute for the matching friendship necklace and slip one underneath her pillow.

CHAPTER NINE

PEOPLE DON'T THINK I'M COOL. I ACTUALLY CHECK out French Club and Lia looks away, as if she's searching for a rock-hard, day-old baguette among the fake-French snacks so she can chase me with it.

Mara, maroon-haired and infinitely cooler than Lia will ever be, says, "So what if sign-ups are over? Why can't you let her in?"

Lia makes a disgusted noise, aimed more at Mara than me. She sits down on a table directly in front of Mara, her butt on Mara's notebook, blocking her altogether.

But the next day, when I take a chair next to Mara in the student lounge, thinking to bond over vintage hair clips, admiring her orange Bakelite bracelets and her Felix the Cat ring, she won't even talk to me beyond monosyllabic frost. She swings her head around, facing away from me so fast, my face is slapped with a hank of maroon hair.

Arif, getting Orangina from a vending machine, watches her slouch away.

I say, "Wow. Was it something I said?"

Arif shakes his head. "She's a bit prickly. The Global Studio scandal? That was her father. Lost the spread in Bel Air. Had to move to the Valley."

"*That's* why Lia treats her like dirt?"

"Don't worry about her," he says. "She still has the Beemer. It was rough for her last year, though. The pony pals wouldn't let her forget it. Latimer has an obsession with good families—no one will utter the word 'class,' but you know what 'good family' means—and when the mighty fall . . ."

And I feel bad for her, I do, but mostly what I feel is even more doomed. At least her father's scandal was a good-family kind of one—a glam studio power grab he lost. (I looked it up.) The kind without a junkie in it.

What if everyone knew about *me*? No palace in Bel Air, no Beemer, no horse, *and* my mom?

After school, I sit in Siobhan's screening room, munching a day-old Taco Bell burrito, grateful as hell. She punches the remote and the screen fills with sheets of rain pounding the window of what looks to be a Parisian bedroom.

I say, "Bad French movie?"

She says, "I *know*. That one from yesterday? I watched the ending last night and they all said haute-pretentious things and then they got *shot*."

"Thanks for finishing without me!" I say, not entirely upset that I don't have to slog through any more haute-pretension. "You want to watch another Bogie and Bacall? Or *Roman Holiday* or something?"

"You just want to watch that old stuff for the clothes. Let's get out of here."

I look at my watch. "Dinner."

"So what if you walk though the door five minutes late?" she says. "Is he going to scalp you?"

"That would be a yes. We won't even have time to get dressed, and I'll have to go home."

"Come on!" she says. "Let's play. You know you want to."

"Why do I want to again?"

Siobhan sighs. "Because when these asshole boys figure out their dicks mean more to them than what freaking Chelsea thinks, they're going to want to go out. With *us*. And when they do, you should know how to talk to a guy without fainting."

"Sib!"

Two girls are going at it on screen, making alarming noises.

"Don't be so literal." She twirls the ends of her bangs. "By 'dick,' I don't mean dick. You know what I mean."

"The 'go out' part? We'll have to drug my dad first."

"Jailbreak!" Siobhan says.

I'm kidding, but I can tell she's not.

She says, "I don't even feel like playing dress-up. I'm so bored. Let's just go."

We leave for Century City dressed as ourselves, following the ritual consumption of champagne with Cheetos. ("It's champagne," Siobhan says. "It has an alcohol content of like zero point zero. And"—she holds up a Cheeto—"it's not like we're drinking on an empty stomach.") This puts me, somewhat buzzed, in a well-preserved fifty-year-old swishy skirt and a beaded sweater and pink flats, and Siobhan in a mini and the black camisole and diamonds. We sit at the outside bar drinking tomato juice with celery sticks popping up over the rims of the glasses because, when we go dressed as ourselves, Siobhan's fake ID is useless.

"Watch this," she says. "New game. It's called shock-the-dork."

She walks over to two middle-aged guys who look a lot more clueless than the ones she usually likes going after. She waves a cigarette at them; they grope for their lighters, matches, whatever it takes to keep her happy. She's all giggly and girly until one of them offers her another drink and she shrieks, "No! I will not meet you in your hotel room! I'm sixteen years old! What's wrong with you!"

The men throw money on the bar to pay for their half-drunk drinks and sprint toward the escalator.

Siobhan turns back to where I'm sitting, on the verge of breaking my tomato juice glass with my bare hands by squeezing it so hard. I stare at the place where the two guys turned the corner and disappeared, and there is this moment of intense relief that there's no sign that they were ever here.

I wonder if the shocked dork was supposed to be them or me.

Siobhan says, "Now I'm not bored. Are you bored?"

I take another sip of the fake Bloody Mary. I say, "I seriously don't *ever* want to play this game again."

Siobhan looks as if she's going to say something, but then she doesn't.

I say, "Is there some way you could get me a real one of these?"

Siobhan says, "No, but he could," and walks off in the direction of a guy in a Cal T-shirt.

My dad says, "You're late."

Fourteen minutes late from an afternoon I wish had never happened.

I say, "It won't happen again."

My dad looks at me quizzically. This is never good. He says, "Ems, have you been drinking?"

I'm trying to set the table. A wineglass crashes into the salad bowl. The crystal rings for an eternity.

"Of course not!" I swear, all I'm thinking about is the virgin Bloody Mary with the celery stalk—not the champagne and not the real Bloody Mary and not the fact that I've been drinking.

My dad crosses his arms across his chest.

I feel my cheeks beginning to go red. "I had a glass of champagne."

"You've taken to drinking *and* lying to me?" This in French, connoting a meltdown.

"Dad! No! I think of drinking as, you know, a bunch of kids getting smashed. I mean, we have wine at dinner." I nod toward the uncorked burgundy on the dining room table as deferentially as humanly possible while buzzed and being yelled at. "It was a glass of champagne."

"Siobhan's parents served you alcohol?"

"No! We were just"—I grope for something credible and redeeming—"celebrating something." Something parent-friendly. Something believable that nevertheless didn't happen. "Siobhan raised her Econ grade to A. Her mom went . . ." I grope for a polite synonym for "apeshit" that isn't also a synonym for "crazy," a word he's sensitive about.

He nods toward the landline. "Get Siobhan over here."

I think of Siobhan stretched out by the mall bar, crossing and uncrossing her legs as some middle-aged guy in a fake-suede blazer looks her over. I think of her lifting her glass and shouting something angry at him in Portuguese. I think of her in four-inch heels, sitting in my living room pretending she doesn't speak English.

"Now?"

Yes, now.

I panic.

My dad has tried to get Siobhan and her family over before. And, okay, what I told him can be dressed up, spelled out in letters made of butterflies and emblazoned in fancy needlepoint on little velvet pillows, but the bottom line is: I straight-up lied.

I told him the (completely fabricated) story that Siobhan's mom rarely let her go out, where there might be R-rated DVDs, bad language, dangerous pit bulls, and unlocked guns lying around. I sent her entire family on (imaginary) church junkets to Tijuana to build (also imaginary) orphanages. I enrolled Nancy in a (fictional) Italian cooking class where she spent weeks gathering wild herbs in Sicily.

Let me pause here to say, no matter what my dad is worried about, I do not lack a conscience, or a rudimentary concept of right and wrong, or an at least minimally functional moral compass. I could tell, as all these untrue sentences came cascading out of my mouth, that the needle of that moral compass was pointing toward *wrong* and *untrustworthy* and *bad daughter* and *overall bad, dishonest person.*

But how could I tell him the truth without his head exploding?

I dial Siobhan with blood pressure that's highly elevated for a girl who doesn't run marathons or do massive amounts of cocaine.

I try, unsuccessfully, to sound normal. I say, "Hey, Siobhan."

She says, "Hello?"

I say, "And congratulations again for that A. Way to go."

She says, "Have you been smoking something?"

I say, "Yeah, we're eating in a minute too. And I wanted to ask, do you want to come over tomorrow?"

"You're shitting me."

My dad mouths the words "Family Game Night."

I say, "Family Game Night."

"Oh. Is this a hostage situation? Does someone have a knife to your throat?"

"Something like that."

"Cool. Sure. Family Game Night. Are you okay? You sound kind of slurred."

"Yeah! My dad thinks so too! He can't wait to meet you."

"Shit."

I nod to my dad. I say, "Tomorrow."

He says, "Good. I'll be sure to lock up the assault rifles and pit bulls."

CHAPTER TEN

"HOW COME HE WOULDN'T THINK I'M YOUR PER-
fect friend, anyway?" Siobhan says over a spiked Big Gulp in her
kitchen after school. "Don't you think I'm presentable?"

"Of course you're presentable! It's just . . . I don't know . . . he
wants me to be more like Megan. Which means maybe *you* could
be more like Megan. Just for tonight."

Siobhan and Megan met once during my effort to make the
pieces of my life converge over a pedicure. Megan thought Siobhan
was too wild of a wild child. Siobhan thought Megan was suffer-
ing from metastatic dullness and I was lucky to have Siobhan at
Latimer to save me from succumbing to the same sorry fate.

"Siobhan, *promise* you'll be good."

But when she's sprawled in my living room, fifteen minutes
into Family Game Night, it's clear that Siobhan being good isn't
that good.

The evening starts with me and my dad playing French

Scrabble before she arrives. We're eating his potato cheesy puffs, the perfect food, crunchy and gooey and somewhat addictive.

He says, "We'll switch to English when she gets here."

I say, "We might not have to. Her French is great."

My dad heads into the kitchen, humming, to get another bottle of Pellegrino. He calls back, "Don't you steal my *x* when I'm gone, *ma princesse*, or I'm impounding that zed."

"I'm hiding it right now! You'll never find it!"

My dad cackles, "Ve have our vays," in a mad scientist accent.

I yell, "Child abuse!"

My dad cackles some more.

I get maybe a half hour of him not worrying about being a good example, not worrying about me, not worrying about how, if he doesn't stay on top of things, I'll go from perfect to degenerate in three seconds flat.

Then Siobhan knocks on the door, and he starts worrying again.

It would probably help if she hadn't fortified herself with a whole lot of vodka and orange juice before she got here. Or if she weren't sharing tidbits of random information, which start off great before swerving toward the parental terror zone.

For example, given that she speaks many languages, she wants to become a translator at the UN. This sweeps the tension off my dad's face like a giant windshield wiper. Until she adds, "And then, if the delegates get testy, I can screw with their negotiations."

There is a gasp he doesn't even try to hide.

Then she jostles the table and catches her Scrabble tiles in flight, one-handed, as they pitch toward the floor, demonstrating how she can play lacrosse, all right, slightly impaired.

She says, "I might not have the patience for Scrabble. I might have ADD."

I say, "But you don't take anything for it." Big mistake.

"Don't like the pills. Can't eat, can't sleep, bags under the eyes."

My dad is switching rapidly into doctor mode, getting his game face on.

"But not everyone feels that way," Siobhan says cheerfully, "so I sold them."

"You're selling Adderall?!" my dad says.

I am one hundred percent certain I would know if Siobhan sold pills, if her Econ project involved marketing pharmaceuticals. My dad, on the other hand, looks completely unnerved at the possibility I'm hanging with a drug dealer and future obstacle to World Peace.

"No worries," she says. "Long time ago."

I kick Siobhan under the table. Hard.

"Whoa!" She kicks me back. "Just kidding. I have a very dry sense of humor."

We play out the rest of the game very, very fast in almost absolute stone silence.

When we finally decamp into my bedroom, behind a closed door, Siobhan starts giggling, rolling around on my bed hugging a pillow.

"That went well," she says. "But he still loved me, right?"

I don't even know what to say.

"Stop looking at me like I run a *cartel*!"

I say, "Sib, you don't do drugs, right?"

Siobhan throws the pillow. "Right, because vodka in a Big Gulp is the gateway drug to *more* vodka in *bigger* gulps. And you're asking me because . . ."

I shrug.

"Because I was a screwed-up *twelve*-year-old?" she says. "Have you ever *seen* me take drugs? Do I have sacks of drugs lying around my bedroom? Oh no, is it the Oxy I put in your orange juice? Because sixth grade, it was the third stepfather, the pervy one she ditched in two weeks, *and* we moved back to New York *and* Nancy started dating freaking Burton *and* she tried sending me to freaking boarding school. So I had some extra pills. Get over it!"

She is picking up and putting down everything in my room. The silver brush and comb from Montreal. The small framed photo of my mother with me as an infant in a pom-pom hat. Snow globes from every city where we've ever lived.

I want to scream, "Don't touch that!" every time she picks up something else, I want to scream until I don't feel anything but the vibration of screaming. So it's not like she's the only screwed-up person in the room.

My dad keeps knocking on my bedroom door, offering us snacks, I'm pretty sure so he can make sure Siobhan isn't shooting heroin into my veins. When he leaves for a night meeting at

Albert Whitbread, he kisses me on both cheeks at the front door, looking toward my bedroom where Siobhan is sprawled on my bed, leafing through my collection of *Vogue Paris*.

He squeezes my hands, and even with my eyes closed, I would know these squeezes were a warning.

He says, "She's out by ten. And don't leave the house."

CHAPTER ELEVEN

YOU KNOW HOW IN THE MORNING, EVERYTHING IS supposed to look all shiny and better? It doesn't.

My dad makes waffles with blueberry smiley faces, like he did when I was seven. I'm pretty sure this is because (1) he wishes I were seven and (2) he wants me in the best possible mood so he can tell me that following our (trashed) Family Game Night, courtesy of my (trashed) best friend, he wants me to stay home more. I am not supposed to mistake this for being grounded; it is intended more as extreme family bonding. Or of me bonding with the inside of our house. Or of me bonding with anybody other than Siobhan.

And I understand his concern, I do. He's not being mean, he's being worried. I get that. But people change, right? She was a wrecked twelve-year-old, but it's not like she's still in that same wrecked place. Not everyone who screws up is doomed to be, well, doomed forever, right?

I wish I could explain this to him, but he's so shaken up, I'm afraid if I add even one tiny sliver of unpleasant information, it will be the straw that got the camel sentenced to fifty years to life in solitary.

So I eat breakfast and I don't say a word. Which, just to be clear, is not the same thing as lying. It's more like not being argumentative. Not being confrontational. Not being completely stupid. Not being completely honest.

By the time he drops me at school, I feel so wrung out from the past two days, I just want to sit under a tree. Alone.

Dylan, walking up from the parking lot, says, "You look wiped. You liberate more quadrupeds last night?"

All right, possibly not alone.

I say, "You torment any bipeds? Other than me."

Dylan tsks. "Somebody tormenting you, Seed?"

I pull a tiny pumpkin bread out of my backpack and break it in two. It's difficult to think of my dad, who baked this still-warm pumpkin bread and tucked it into my pack, as the tormentor.

Dylan says, "You bake? If you baked this, forget school and open a bakery."

"My dad."

"The man's a baking genius."

I am in such a state of pathetic reverie, I am actually marveling at how the crumbs of pumpkin bread that fall onto his white shirt before he flicks them off match the rusty brown flecks in his eyes. I am watching him push his hair behind his ear and actively holding myself back from touching that hair. I am speaking to myself in command sentences: Do not touch hair. Keep breathing. Say something conversational.

I say, "The man seems to be threatening some form of benevolent house arrest. Eating baked goods may soon be my sole form of recreation."

I realize that we are drifting toward the quad while everybody else is drifting toward class.

"That doesn't sound so benevolent."

We're sitting on a bench, out of sight, behind the library, but I have no idea how we actually got here.

I say, "It's my own fault. I virtually waved a Bloody Mary in his face. Then I waved Siobhan in his face."

"And people come down on me," he says. "One whole Bloody Mary and Siobhan."

"Do you enjoy making fun of me?"

"At least I have the sense to drag home a respectable friend."

I say, "Not all of us get to have the secretary general of the UN as our best friend. I heard he's already taken."

Dylan laughs, an outright laugh.

He says, "Gotta go."

I start to say something, but he's already half sprinting across the quad, and not in the direction of class.

"Tell me," Siobhan says when we're standing outside homeroom. "Am I an honorary Lazar yet?"

I shake my head.

She claps her hands over her mouth with sort of fake amazement, but sort of not. "Was I a shit Bo Peep? I didn't get you in more trouble, right?"

"Here's a helpful hint. In general, the sheep shouldn't be cooking meth."

We are walking toward the wooded hillside that forms a semicircle behind Latimer. We've been cutting junior class assembly, anything related to pep, and the occasional boring class on this hill since we figured out Latimer's completely lax attendance policy.

When we are lying in a stand of twisted scrub oak, Siobhan says, "That girl in the picture with that baby is your mom, right? What is she now, like thirty?"

Oh.

It occurs to me that in addition to not telling Siobhan about the extent of my geekiness, the fact I like Brahms, and my irrational devotion to Dylan Kahane, I might have skipped the story of my life.

I mean, she knows she left and never came back, but that's pretty much it.

I want to be doing anything other than having this conversation. Siobhan snaps her fingers in my face.

I say, "Did anybody ever tell you that's annoying?"

"What's annoying is people who zone out and don't come back when their best friend is talking to them."

"Sorry. I'm preoccupied. I have to do physics lab."

"Not due until Friday. What's wrong with you? Why are you changing the subject? Is that your mom or not?"

I do not, in the worst way, want to be doing this, but I don't see a way out.

My dad says that most human misery can be staved off by a deep breath followed by ten seconds of rational thought. I don't actually believe this works, but I take several deep breaths while Siobhan sits there staring at me, anyway.

I say, "All right. The thing is that she's dead."

"Shit!" Siobhan says. "I can't believe you didn't tell me. Why would you do that to me?"

"The way it happened—really personal."

She starts punting eucalyptus pods, shooting up clouds of dirt. "Like I haven't told you *personal*? Like I didn't tell you how Missy Rogers tried to kiss me in the locker room?"

She storms down the path toward the stable, and I go after her.

"Why would you *hide* things from me?" She faces me, damp tendrils of hair sticking to her forehead. Her fingernails dig into the flesh of my upper arms through my blouse. "You're *supposed* to be my *best friend*! Do you want to be or don't you?"

But Missy in the locker room is an after-school special. My parents' marriage gone bad, gone worse, and gone, is an oldie-but-goodie film that melts off the reel as soon as it starts running.

It begins as flaky girl meets buttoned-up guy, opposites attract, springtime in Montreal, cue the French music. Except that, in my parents' case, it didn't exactly work out.

Probably it would have helped if the flaky girl hadn't been clinically insane.

It would have helped if the guy hadn't been her psychiatrist.

Because psychiatrists are *not* supposed to get it on with their patients. They are *not* supposed to fall in love and have a baby. And, when they do, all hell breaks loose and there's a giant scandal.

The outcome of the scandal was me.

Not to mention, the fact my mother liked drugs better than me (despite all the free, on-site psychiatric help from my dad) was a disaster. And it's not reassuring to know she stayed clean through the pregnancy because that's how much she loved me.

How much she loved me before she left me.

Even when my mom died—which I don't remember, not her, not her dying, not having her and then not having her—people didn't feel sorry enough for my dad to save what was left of his completely wrecked career. She was gone, I was a screaming baby, and he was the embodiment of bad judgment, well-known as a screwup all over the province of Quebec.

You read *The Scarlet Letter* in ninth grade. You write a paper about poor, ostracized Hester Prynne who screwed up and produced baby Pearl, evidence of all her badness. Not whining, but try being Pearl. Only Hester OD's and you end up with the buttoned-up dad whose goal in life is to keep you from turning out anything like her.

Like Fabienne.

That was her name.

I look exactly like her. Blue eyes, auburn hair, everything.

Possibly explaining why the Lazar clan is stomping around Canada, unhappy I exist. And no amount of repairing the world, good deeds, and candle-lighting will make them see me as anything but a *shiksa*, a *goya*—which means a girl who's not a Jew, but coming out of their mouths sounds like *dirt*, or *worthless*, or *spawn of Fabienne*.

As for my dad, any move I make that reeks at all of Fabiennishness—a bottle of Corona at a Fourth of July party in Chicago, a vintage Bob Marley T-shirt with a faintly stenciled ganja leaf in Washington, D.C., or any hint I might have what my dad quaintly calls unsavory friends anywhere—and he has visions of me morphing into *her*. Wandering off into adulthood in a substance-induced haze. Saved only by the all-purpose parental unit, squelcher of all hints of rebellion, fully capable of making everything fine.

What part of this is fine?

It's as if he's blundering though life in the misguided belief that she's missing in the fine-and-dandy-let's-burst-into-song way the Little Mermaid's mom is missing. As if he overlooked the fact she's missing in the succumbed-to-craziness, OD'd-behind-a-strip-mall-in-Ottawa, shot-up-and-left-me-behind-without-saying-good-bye, it-hurts-to-think-about-it kind of way.

"I can't believe you were keeping that from me," Siobhan says, rooting around in the pocket of her blazer for a cigarette. "Sorry I got weirded out."

I wipe my face against my sleeve. Siobhan smooths the long grass and sits down next to me.

"No wonder you can't piss off your dad," she says. "The whole rest of your family sucks. Excuse you for being *born*. Don't forget to leave your country and your language and your freaking religion at the door on your way out. And by the way, if you don't stay corked in this magic lamp, you're going to turn into a dead addict."

I can't stop crying. I say, "And my name at the door, too."

"What?"

"My name. Amélie." I can hardly say it. "My *name*. It got turned into Amelia in St. Louis and Emmy in Philadelphia and Emma in D.C."

"You didn't even get to keep your *name*? It's not like you're in fucking witness protection, *Amélie*."

Hearing the name in someone else's mouth makes me crack open, when all I want to do is close back up. I say, "*Don't* call me that. It's like she's someone else."

In the knowing-exactly-why-I-picked-her-for-my-friend department: because she gets it in five minutes. Whereas sixteen years later, some people still don't.

Siobhan lights a Gitanes, a French cigarette that smells like rotting garbage. "It's not that bad. My mother is a crazy slut and I turned out great."

"Don't call Nancy a slut."

"She gets new ones before she gets rid of the old ones. How slutty is that?"

"Well, it's not like she's going to die with a needle in her arm behind a mini-mart in Ottawa."

Siobhan pauses, the cigarette halfway to her lips. She says, "Do you want me to tell Miss Roy you have cramps and go to my house?"

We spend the day sitting in Siobhan's Jacuzzi, sunning ourselves on top of a wall of river rocks, immersing ourselves in steaming, bubbling water, cooking ourselves, eating Cheetos, and drinking. The skin on my fingers wrinkles in exact inverse proportion to the unfolding of the furrows in my brain where all the sludge has lodged, until my mind is a blank plane that stretches like the flat blue California sky, all the way to the almost invisible horizon.

CHAPTER TWELVE

"IS THERE ANYTHING YOU WANT TO TELL ME ABOUT school?" my dad asks when I'm sitting in my room with chlorinated hair before dinner. "Such as why you weren't *there* today?"

He could pass for eerily calm if he weren't punching his left hand with his right hand.

I say, "I had cramps." I lie without even planning to or thinking about it. I keep reaching new lows without even trying.

"I know that. Two phone calls. Since when do you leave school and go to a friend's house and not call me?"

Once I start to lie, there is no limit to my creativity. "When I need Advil? If I had my own car, I could have just run home."

"Not a wise moment to ask for a car."

I wonder if being slightly drunk at lunchtime still shows after dark.

I say, "Please let this one go."

"Should I let yesterday go, too? When your best friend tells me she sold Adderall in grade school!"

"She was joking! I don't know why she acted like that."

He shouts, "You know exactly why she acted like that! You know why you were drinking and why you walked out of school and you know if you ever planned to tell me." He shoots me a look of pure parental devastation. "Did you?"

The slippage of Emma the Good into the gutter of parental disappointment is painful to watch. I look at my feet. I think, What would Emma the Good say?

The moral compass, spinning in horror, squawks, *She wouldn't have to say anything, moron. She wouldn't be found in a hundred-yard radius of shit this deep.*

"No."

This is supposed to make me feel good: moral victory.

It doesn't.

My father looks at me with massive, unjustified relief at that one brief, honest syllable.

He says, in a much gentler voice, "Ems, is there anything you'd like to tell me about school? Which is the only place you're going outside this house, by the way."

"How long?"

"Until you're forty. School, Ems. We're moving into honor-your-father territory here. Now."

"Please don't slam me with the Ten Commandments. Please!"

"Now."

"All right, but it isn't pretty."

But who wants to tell her father that she's outside the mainstream of human interaction except for a scary best friend and a lunch table of boys weirdly attracted to the friend, given that she spends lunch abusing them and eating their chips?

And what would I say about Dylan? How when he says, "So, Emma, did Napoleon win?" as I hand him my notes, I want to fall over, preferably into his arms?

How it takes a great deal of restraint and jamming my fingernails into the palms of my hands to keep myself from pressing my face against his chest?

How Dylan says, "Thanks. You've saved me from watching the Battle of Waterloo on the History Channel."

This is not a conversation my dad would appreciate.

I tell my dad the highly-edited-for-parental-consumption saga of Chelsea Hay.

He looks pained. "Is this Chelsea *bullying* you?"

I patiently explained this isn't bullying, this is normal life at Latimer Day.

"High school is a hard time for a lot of kids," he says.

I patiently explain that it is not a hard time for me because my best friend has my back and if he did anything to separate me from my best friend, I would no doubt curl up in a sad, depressed ball.

In homeroom, Siobhan won't look at me.

"What?"

She does not look up.

"What?"

"Way to not return my texts last night," she says.

"I was busy spending three hours getting yelled at and grounded."

She twists to face me. "Shit."

"Yeah."

"You *didn't* tell your dad we cut out, did you?"

"Of course not! School called him. I thought they weren't supposed to do that."

"Shit," Siobhan says. "What's the point of being attendance-*totally*-optional if they call home? Not that Nancy would care."

"Well, he cared. A lot. I feel like swallowing ground glass."

Siobhan clamps her hands over her ears. "Like I forced you to cut school and now you want to die a slow death—really? You sat in a hot tub and you didn't go to Physics. Big fucking deal. You have no sense of proportion!"

It occurs to me, in what could be a complete making-excuses-and-deluding-myself moment (or *could* be a breakthrough of reasonable thought), that I *might* not have that great a sense of proportion.

Siobhan says, "I am so mad at your dad!"

"Keep your voice down."

Siobhan yells, "Stop screaming at me! *I'm* not the one who made you want to swallow ground glass! *I'm* the one who wants you to have *fun!*"

She storms out of class in the direction of the hill, pulling a cigarette out of her pocket before she's out of sight.

I start to get up, but I slam into Dylan, standing behind me by Arif's desk. A full body blow. He catches me as I'm bouncing off him, his hands on the back of my head and on my arm.

I just stand there, blushing, with a bruised head.

Arif, looking distractingly good even to someone who just got hit on the head, says to Dylan, "After you almost run her over, you might want to get her some ice."

Dylan makes a face at him and takes my arm.

"I'm sorry if I almost ran you over," he says, when I'm sitting in the deserted cafeteria looking like an idiot (across from the person to whom I least want to look like an idiot) with melting crushed ice, wrapped in napkins, on my forehead.

"It's possible I almost ran *you* over."

"Either way, I won this round," he says. It almost feels buddy-like. Although buddy-like is so not what I have in mind.

There is a long silence as I try to mop up the rivulets of ice water running down my face. I keep repeating to myself, Do not act embarrassed. It will be so much more embarrassing if he knows you're embarrassed. Make conversation. Talk.

I say, "I have a question for you. You've been at Latimer forever, right?"

"Since I was five. Nothing I can do to get out of it. I spent middle school desecrating the uniform, carried a fifth of Johnnie Walker Black around in my backpack, plus a roach clip instead of a tie tack, and I'm still here."

Oh.

"How did that work?"

"They kept saying, 'Mr. Kahane, do you *want* to attend Latimer?'

I kept saying, 'No, I don't.'" He shrugs, the palms of his hands flipping upward, almost as if he were reaching for me, except he isn't. "Maybe they kept me here to spite me. That and my brother was Mr. Three Varsity Sports, most valuable asshole. They were probably hoping I'd develop team spirit and become a slimebag."

"No sports?"

"Also no slime. And no school spirit."

"So you would know," I debate asking him and then I just ask him. "When you cut out of school, when do they call home?"

"They phoned home on you?"

"Not my best evening ever."

He walks over to the ice machine and scoops up ice chips with a paper cup. He says, "At least this won't leak."

I realize my collar is soaked in front, sticking to my chin and dripping down the navy blue sweater that's such plasticky synthetic, it's virtually waterproof.

He says, "Did you sign out?"

"Sib signed me out."

"If you sign yourself out, they don't care."

This makes no sense whatsoever, but is nevertheless very good to know.

He tilts his head. "So. Are you planning to stop attending? Are you and your evil twin planning to become full-time horse thieves?"

"Do you take a special interest in my life of crime?"

"Ballerina by day, felon by night. Sometimes I wonder if we're on the same misguided path."

"Still not a ballerina. And what path would that be?"

"Trying to get out of here."

"I'm not!"

"Then you might want to rethink your life of crime."

And then his hands are in my hair, pulling out a hairpin. He says, "Your bun is coming down." He works his fingers from the nape of my neck up to the sides of my face, and I'm pretty sure he's going to kiss me. He runs his fingers down my forearm from the elbow to the wrist, until his hands cover my hands.

He says, "Are you going to be okay?"

I nod. I bend my face toward him, my mouth toward his mouth.

He gets up and he walks out of the cafeteria, saluting me from the door.

I am in a state of did-that-just-happen, and what the hell, and I want him, and what was that? In a state of acute longing, sandbagged by something that has to be what temptation feels like, except that the object of temptation has left the building. And even if I were to succumb to that temptation, which I totally would, there's no point because he's not here to be tempted by.

> **Megan:** Some guy did what?
>
> **Me:** I know. I don't want to see him again until I stop blushing. Which could take years. No idea what to make of it.
>
> **Megan:** Do you want me to ask Joe?

Joe is the boyfriend Megan only ever gets to see at mixers presided over by hypervigilant nuns. There is some chance that Joe is somewhat less perfect than he seems to be, given the extremely small amount of time they've actually spent in the same room.

Me: NO!!!!!!

Megan: You wanted him to right?

Me: Still do.

Megan: This is the guy you do the notes for?

Me: Same guy.

Megan: Why doesn't he take his own notes? He's not stupid right?

Me: Not.

Megan: You could always ask him.

Me: NO!!!!!!!!!!!!!!!

Megan: Isn't Siobhan supposed to be the world's expert on men? Ask her.

Me: NO!!!!!!!!!!!!!!!!!!!!!!!!!!!!

Megan: You might need to breathe into a paper bag.

Me: I'm going to pretend it never happened. Maybe I should just wear the bag over my head.

Me: Even Siobhan's starting to think our chance for normal human life around here is nil.

CHAPTER THIRTEEN

WHAT WE DON'T KNOW IS THAT LATIMER MEAN girls have simmering feuds that boil over with infighting and constantly shifting alliances, meaning there's always a popular suddenly left out, shunned, or tortured. And that this has an upside. For us.

It's kind of terrible for everyone else.

Siobhan says, "What's with these skanks? People are crying in the bathroom. It's embarrassing to pee."

The first popular reject we get is Kimmy.

"Do you mind if I sit here?" she says. "If I have to sit with that *god*awful pack of bitches and watch them drip venom off their big, ugly *god*awful canine incisors, I won't be able to keep down this *god*awful mystery meat."

She says this loud enough for the godawful bitches two tables over to hear.

"You should be a poet, Kimmy," Siobhan says.

Kimmy, too distraught over being shunned to notice much else, doesn't even care if Siobhan is being sarcastic.

Mel Burke, passing our table, gapes. "Seriously, Kimmy?"

Kimmy locks eyes with Siobhan. "I don't see how anyone can stand transferring into this *god*awful place," she says. "Were you someplace better? Has to have been. Were you at Spence?"

Siobhan says, "Eastside Episcopal. You can't imagine how much better."

This would be the crap school Siobhan hated.

"And Roedean," Siobhan says. This would be the boarding school Siobhan says was a penitentiary. "In *England*. That wasn't half bad. Except they play field hockey like a pack of crazed hyenas."

Kimmy says, "I'm getting frozen yogurt. You want something?"

She walks past Chelsea, Mel, and Lia, who says, "Hey, Kim," and is instantly shut down by a look from Mel so cold it could freeze Hell on impact.

I lean across the table toward Siobhan. I hiss, "Be nice. She's going to cry."

"She deserves to cry," Siobhan says. "Where was she when we got here—making out with Chelsea?"

"She said hello in Physics. The first day."

"I'm *soooo* impressed. Let's kiss her feet."

I'm thinking that if someone with Kimmy's assets can land in Social Siberia, we are permanently consigned to the gulag. Kimmy has a *Teen Vogue* face; a horse that people carry on about like addled fan girls; and a pack of older brothers who like her well enough that after school, they yell, "Hey, Kimster, you and your friends want a lift to Westwood?" Or wherever they're going to carbo-load.

Also, having grown up in a house full of boys, Kimmy has a bunch of male buddies and looks perfectly comfortable climbing all over them, socking them, and showing them up in Physics. You get the feeling that Kimmy could watch boys light farts on fire and maintain her composure.

"You know," Kimmy says, "my parents are going to a wedding in Houston and my brother, Kenny, is having a party Saturday."

"Is that the water polo one?" Siobhan says.

"The soccer one. The water polo one is in college."

"Maaaaybe," Siobhan says. "Actually, very likely."

"And it won't be like one of those *god*awful back-to-school keggers, either," Kimmy says loudly for her not-that-distant audience.

Then she looks at me. I am holding up a french fry that is dripping ketchup onto my tray. There is no possibility whatsoever that my dad will agree to a high school party in a house with no parents home. This is in the you-can-go-when-pigs-fly range of not happening.

"Oh, *her*," Siobhan says, glancing over. For a minute, I'm afraid that she's dumping me for Kimmy. "No offense, Kimmy, but Emma doesn't *do* high school parties. Em can't *stand* immature boys."

Which makes me sound a lot more interesting than saying my dad won't let me go unless her mom, her dad, and a large contingent of precision-trained chaperones imported from Victorian England are swarming the place, and by the way, I'm grounded forever, so even that won't work. I give Siobhan a thank-you kick under the table.

"I *really* appreciate the invitation," I say.

"You and Dylan Kahane," Kimmy sighs. "Ever since his *god*awful brother Aiden graduated, he hardly goes anywhere either."

This is not, strictly speaking, true. I know this because now that I'm too embarrassed by the kiss that didn't happen to talk to him directly, I'm stuck somewhere between straight-up Facebook-stalking Dylan and merely being very, very interested in everything he ever did, does, or will do.

He would appear to have spent the better part of the summer in resorts on the Mediterranean with Arif, who does a lot of waterskiing on an unidentified European lake, Dylan (literally) in tow, and eating dinner with twenty-seven other people somewhere that houses have extremely large dining rooms. Somewhere the women wear Chanel or hijabs. Or both.

There he is in London with an arm around Arif and his other arm around a woman wearing a dress so short the jacket she's thrown over it falls below the hem. Dylan and Arif look quite pleased with themselves, and the girl looks to be ecstatic. There he is in Mexico with Sam Sherman, eating taquitos.

Lately, he is tagged all over Westwood with a recurring set of girls in UCLA sorority tees covered with interlocking triangles, one feeding him a Diddy Riese cookie. You can't see who she is, only her arms, and hands, and manicure.

Kimmy smiles at me. "Well, I hope you come anyway."

CHAPTER FOURTEEN

SIOBHAN SAYS, "I *TOLD* YOU IT WAS GOING TO GET better."

"For you!"

"Come on. You *have* to find a way to come to this stuff."

"It's never getting better. My life completely sucks. You can't even call my life a life."

Siobhan says, "We just have to get you out of here. Big-time. That's all it would take. For starters."

"Not happening."

She says, "It's completely happening. You want a pact? Okay, here goes: *If* things aren't looking a whole lot better for both of us by the end of the year, we should jump off a tall building."

"Sign me up."

"You're in," she says. "Pact."

I say, "Sure, whatever, pact. If it doesn't get any better than this, we should light each other on fire."

"That's not the pact. It's acrobatic, not incendiary. If things still suck."

Things do suck all weekend.

While Siobhan is at Kimmy's party and at a club on the Strip with Wade, the tennis guy from Burton's club, my only recreational activitiy is playing with Mutt and Jeff, the dogs from next door. Then it turns out that I wasn't supposed to venture into the backyard, as "grounded" means locked inside the house. My dad says if I keep testing the limits, this really will last until I'm forty.

I say, "I was *trying* to cooperate. It's not like I was sitting in the house thinking, 'Hey, when he goes to the grocery store, I'm going to test the limits by petting some bulldogs.'"

My dad says, "Very funny. I believe you. Now get in the house."

Megan: He said until you're 40???
Me: Yes maam. I might have screwed this up.
Megan: Asking for a car while drunk? You might
have. Why were you drinking anyway? You shouldn't
drink.
Me: Don't rub it in.

Siobhan: U won't believe where I am.
Me: Where?
Siobhan: Skybar. Kid at Crossroads party knows
someone having other party on the roof.
Me: What Crossroads party? What happened to

Kimmy's party? I otoh am spending my Sat night
studying for SAT.
Siobhan: U cd be here. Studying for life of fun.
Me: Don't rub it in.

On Monday, after school, Siobhan is sitting on my bed, bouncing. She's not supposed to be here, I'm supposed to be languishing in solitary. But I feel as if, having shown no attitude (seriously: none) all weekend, I deserve some minor bending of the rules. And I didn't get to see her at school because Nancy took her to get hair extensions instead, which is evidently time-consuming.

"I *finally* get why this godforsaken place doesn't just sink into the ocean," she says. "Parties!"

I say, "It was that good?"

"Compared to what I was expecting: legendary. And this was *Kimmy's* party. This is what their *average* parties look like. Because then Grey Burgess, this kid from Crossroads, took me to this other party in Santa Monica with these other Crossroads kids. OMG, as we say in L.A. It was like metrosexual youth on steroids. Not actual steroids."

"Do not say OMG," I say. "I mean it. Next you'll start wearing headbands."

Siobhan is bouncing on my bed and off the walls.

I say, "Sibby, are you all right? Did you, like, take something?"

"Don't be such a baby! If I'm happy, I must be on coke? Is there a hole in my septum? Are my nostrils bleeding? Oh no, I'm having a heart attack!"

"I never said coke."

"Listen to me. Latimer is *famous* for parties. Constant parties. Holiday parties. Beach house parties that defy description. And an afterparty in the spring that *beyond* defies description. Oh my God. This afterparty. Last year it was in a warehouse in the toy district. There was a bar at the center of a maze. It was smoking. Actual smoking, special effects."

"There's a *toy* district?"

"It's industrial. It's downtown. It was incredibly cool. Until the police closed it down, but by then it was four a.m., so no one cared anymore. Don't you get it? I finally found something *good* for us to do!"

Siobhan holds up her phone and shows me a fuzzy YouTube video of flashing lights and smoke and dusky glamour, almost like a riff on the unspeakably romantic black-and-white nightclubs in old movies.

"This is from Grey, from last year," she says. "You *have* to get out of this house. The entire Strip is down the street from you. We *have* to go to Afterparty. This will be so good for you! Your coming-out party of cool. We can go in an all-girl limo, and we can pregame, and then we can dance in a circle and guys can fall over dead crawling to get to us."

"Dream on. I'm never getting out of here." It's pretty clear that the magnitude of crackdown following my foray into, all right, *moderate* badness, but still no boys or drugs or parties or orgies or arrests, precludes any fun whatsoever.

I'm not even allowed to go to the food bank, where by now

the computer has probably shut itself down in protest against being abused by well-meaning volunteers. And no amount of going, "Dad, wait, what about 'Enter the gate of the Lord, if you've fed the hungry'?" "What about 'You shall leave the gleanings of your fields for the poor'?" gets any response beyond, "You shall keep your kid safe, even over her protests," which I'm pretty sure he made up.

But still, that video, the pulsating bursts of light, the hints of music and the kids all in each other's arms, the limo and dancing in a circle in a dress that refracts light like a prism . . .

Siobahn says, "Think of this as a math problem. How hard can it be to get you from point A to point B in a field of moving taxis?"

"How about impossible?"

Siobhan starts shaking my shoulders, bouncing higher and higher on the bed, which has more trampoline potential than I'd ever realized. She yells, "Wake up! Look at this window! It's perfect. Opens out, no screen. We need a pact. We have to get you party-ready by Afterparty. We are *so* going—and you're completely unprepared. Do you want to be the lamby at a wolf orgy? You like lists; we'll make a list. Make out. Do shots. Get stoned. Climb out window. Go to many, many parties. Hook up. Hook up all the way. Finish and we go to Afterparty."

"You are seriously losing it."

"Get a pen. We'll make this list right now. The Afterparty prep list. Let's go in a limo and you have to stand up through the sunroof and scream."

This sounds quite tame.

"But before then, check marks. Many, many check marks. We'll start slow and work up. Do you have kissing on there?"

"Top of the list."

"Okay. Beer pong. It's disgusting, but you're the last kid in this country who can't play. And you have to win. And you have to flash someone, and you have to smoke some weed and you can go harder from there."

"Siobhan, I might possibly want to avoid the pharmaceuticals."

"Jesus. Not heroin, coke. One little line of coke and some itty-bitty pills. And sex, obviously. And you have to get totally shitfaced. At a party. And you have to dance and you have to take off some major clothes and sext."

"Siobhan, are you all right? You might be getting a little bit hyper."

"I'm psyched! I'm hyper-psyched! Have you got anything to drink? I might need something to calm down."

"Iced tea. This is Chez Lazar House of Detention, remember? I can't even have you over."

"Jailbreak! Say you'll do it! Say 'pact'!"

"You dare me to go out this window?"

"I don't *dare you* to do anything. A pact is something you *want* to do. Dares are stupid. Pacts are when you want it and you say 'Screw it' and do it. Don't you want to have fun? We'll work out all the details later. Say it."

"Sib—"

"You should be more enthused! " she says. "You're going to

thank me later. This pact could save your life. There you are in college, getting it on with some total loser—"

"There's something to look forward to."

"After endless kissing, he whips off his clothes. *Just* when you're about to jump into his naked arms, you get a good look at him and you pass out from shock. Oh no! You collapse! You hit your head on the corner of his desk on the way down, and you die a virgin."

"This keeps getting better and better."

"Be that way," Siobhan says, "but you can't keep up Emma the Good forever. This Afterparty list is the ultimate pact."

"A pact to drug my dad's tea?"

"Admit he's asleep by eleven," she says. "Picture this: You wait a whole *year*. You're *seventeen* in this exact spot with cobwebs hanging off your body. Nice?"

I can see it. Me turning into Megan Donnelly only without the boyfriend (no tiny image of Joe waving from *my* iPhone), alone in my room Facebook-stalking Dylan, permanently grounded, playing Angry Birds for an entire year.

"You're coming with," Siobhan says. "And soon. This is for your own good."

"Because my dad will never notice."

"Out the window, missy," Siobhan says. "Pact!"

"Sib—"

"Will you freaking say it?"

I'm so wound up, I'm on the verge of saying it, I almost say it, when there's the horrifying sound of the front door opening.

My dad, having skipped out on his afternoon meeting at Albert Whitbread, no doubt to check up on me, is home. (Not that I get to moan about this in the don't-you-trust-me vein of moaning, given that, obviously, he can't.)

Siobhan says, "I was dropping off notes."

Our sweaters, shoes, books, and remnants of a two-person, two-plate snack are all over my room. By the time she gathers up her stuff and leaves (quickly), my dad is pacing around, all but throwing things.

He says, "I take it being grounded didn't suit?"

I don't even know how to answer this. I mean, yes, but what would happen if I *said* yes. I stare down at my shoeless feet.

He says, "Look up. I cannot believe you'd do this. You were supposed to be home *alone*. You know that."

He's scanning the room as if it were strewn with AK-47s and the spoils of my most recent bank robbery. The Afterparty prep list is wadded up in plain sight in my wastebasket.

I say, "I know this looks bad—"

"*Looks* bad? How can I hope to keep you safe if I can't trust you? Help me out here, Ems, because I'm mystified."

"All right, this is really bad."

He is so anguished when he looks at me, I want to hit myself on the head with a hammer. I'm back to watching my toes squirm.

He shakes his head. "Give me your phone."

I feel around in my bag for the phone, terrified he's going to find a way to read my deleted text messages and trashed email. I hand it over.

"I want your laptop and your iPod and everything that has

a battery, a charger, or a plug except a reading lamp. I want your house keys and your keys to my car and the garage opener. And the credit card."

"Geez, dad, do you want my *shoes?*"

He says, "Does this amuse you?" Oh God, in French. So I apologize in French, which is a lot more dramatic, involving regret and begging pardon and a certain amount of groveling.

He says, "You've become untrustworthy. Crying and apologizing aren't going to make you trustworthy."

Then he says something else with the word "disappointed" featured prominently: how disappointed he is, how disappointing I am, how painful and heartbreaking it is when your kid is so disappointing, and what do I have to say for myself?

I shake my head.

He says, "Then you'd better stay out of my sight while I cool down."

I curl up on the floor of my closet, waiting for some kind of epiphany to propel me to a higher plane of consciousness, or at least for some state of being in which I don't feel like total crap, but it's hard to achieve spiritual enlightenment between a pile of unwashed leotards and the hems of vintage skirts.

The moral compass spends a full twelve hours chanting, *Shame, shame, shame.*

Me: What the hell? My best friend came over when I was grounded. People are rarely guillotined for this.

Compass: *Decent human beings are rarely banished to their rooms because their dads can't bear to look at them. Think about it.*

I try to think about it. Because, okay, how hard would it have been to ignore Siobhan banging on the front door? But I couldn't even do that one small thing. I am completely incapable of being the girl I'm supposed to be.

This is when I reach the opposite of spiritual epiphany, a moment of wrung-out clarity: I don't want to be the girl I'm supposed to be.

Duh.

Not being her was the point of California. All right, it was perhaps incompatible with keeping my dad happy. But given that a roasted chicken breast, green beans, and heirloom tomato slices were just slipped through my door, as if I were a prisoner whose crimes are so appalling that her gourmet jailer can't stand to see her face, how realistic an option is Good Girl?

Afterparty, on the other hand, sheathed in glamour and Hollywood noir and decadent sophistication, glittering slightly in the darkness, sparkling as I turn it over in my mind's eye, is beckoning and dreamy and alluring.

That is who I want to be, a not-afraid, cool, glamorous person, who yields to temptation on purpose and is happy about it.

The list of all the strange and scary things I have to do in order to become that person is crunched into a ball in the gilded Florentine wastebasket, tucked under my desk. If the choice is feeling like this versus being Afterparty girl, crushing the compass under my four-inch heels, it's Afterparty all the way.

Because I just can't do this anymore.

At breakfast, my dad says, "Can I trust you to stay at school?"

"Obviously not. I'm the worst person in the world. Why don't you chain me to the piano?"

In a cold, increasingly familiar voice, he says, "Fine, stay here."

"Dad! I'm sorry! It's school! I have to go to school."

"And where were you again last Wednesday?" He walks over and unplugs the TV, purely a symbolic gesture, but I get it, and he leaves for work. I'm stranded here, not sure if it's okay to turn on the den computer to do homework, or what I have to do to make this end, and no doubt talking back was yet another poor choice.

I say, "Screw it," and I go outside to lie in the grass with Mutt and Jeff. I look at the sky, which is brilliant, blue and cloudless. But I feel too guilty to enjoy it.

When he gets home from work, I say, "Seriously. Please. Is this how you tell people to treat their kids?"

He says, "You're *my* kid. It's a different situation."

"What about: 'Don't do to others what you wouldn't want them to do to you'?"

He says, "Nice try."

I feel terrible, but not terrible enough to want to deal with much more of this.

By Monday, at school, I say, "I'm no doubt going to regret this forever, but I fished that list out of the wastebasket and it might be the new story of my life."

Siobhan intones, "You have used your dungeon wisely, grasshopper. Reject the path of Emma the Good and hop out the window." Then she hands me a prepaid cell phone.

I say, "It's not just that. It's everything."

Because enough disappointment, restriction, confiscation, punishment, confinement, and paternal rage can wear a person down. Tucked away in the hills, shielded from Sunset only by the treetops in the canyon, and the path from point A to point B can get a whole lot easier to navigate.

Also, it's the only slim shot I've got for even one single unsupervised evening of something resembling normal teen life.

I say, "Pact."

PART TWO

mini-mall, and curl up and die between two Dumpsters with a needle in my arm?

If he were honest, he would say *yes* to that one.

That stepping across the threshold of a party-lit tennis court can make a girl succumb to fatal carelessness. That the minute my kitten heels slide out the window and touch down in the wet grass, I'm lost.

No. Just no.

The compass says, *Yeah, you just tell yourself that.*

But even in fairy tales, princesses climb out windows, shimmy down vines and dance all night in diamond shoes. Hot princes vault their castle walls and climb their hair, all to spring them from their parents' lockdown hell.

Seriously, if a fairy-tale princess had lived in a one-story Spanish house with a screenless bay window in the Hollywood Hills, would she have sat there pondering whether she should have a guilty conscience?

I unlatch my window. It's so fast. First I'm inside, and then I'm ankle-deep in a bed of impatiens, and my kitten heels have sunk into the planting soil.

I leave my bag inside.

The moral compass is re-energized: *Could this be a message from your highly moral, totally non-functional conscience calling, Go Back? Hmmm? Well, is it?*

I ignore this. I'm an analyst's kid. I was raised on this stuff, and I'm not climbing back through the window, peeling off my jeans, and retreating into bed.

CHAPTER FIFTEEN

SO THIS IS IT.

A clear, cloudless night with big, fat stars and hazy light rising in glaring whiteness from West Hollywood. The cries of coyotes in the canyon and horns honking down on Sunset.

My dad whispers, "Night, Ems," to the pillows arranged under the covers of my uninhabited bed. The moral compass rotates toward the pillow where the longitude and latitude of where my head should be converge.

I'm in the closet.

The compass mocks, *Night, Ems,* watching me slide into the dark unknown. I've heard my dad say *no* a hundred times to the specific geography I plan to explore, the land of unchained kids doing their thing under the watchful eye of no one.

But it always comes back to the unasked question: Dad, do you think if you let me out of your sight, I'm going to score some heroin, develop an incurable addiction, find myself a

I grab the bag and streak across the lawn. Siobhan keeps texting: *Where ru? RU still coming? U didn't chicken out did u? Where the hellllllll r u???*

I silence my phone.

Suddenly illuminated houses (no doubt with girl-sensitive motion detectors) signal my descent into civilization. Cats meow, dogs bark, and I imagine that somewhere along the way, there's a chatty talking parrot that's about to rat me out to his suspicious owner. By the time I reach the Strip, I'm convinced everyone my dad has ever met is, at this moment, driving down Sunset and speed-dialing him.

Naturally, the Chateau Marmont is flanked by paparazzi. I think, Really bad plan. Why didn't I go to the Standard? But the Chateau is the plan and I'm too wigged-out to cross the street.

I ask one of the guys in the motor court if he could get me a cab. I wait for him to look me over—so much mascara my eyes threaten to seal closed, kitten heels slightly caked with mud— and go, "Who the hell are you?"

But he doesn't. He looks me over and gets me a cab.

It's on.

The streets near the top of Beverly Hills are pitch-black and empty.

"You're not going to regret this!" Siobhan says. She's standing at the bottom of Roy Warner's driveway, shivering in jeans and Nancy's gold mesh top. She smiles into the taxi while I pay the driver. Cash isn't a problem. My credit card might be confiscated, but I haven't spent one cent of birthday money for sixteen years.

She says, "Of course, you're *you*, so you might a little."

"Are you sure this is okay? I don't even know Roy Warner."

"Doesn't matter." Her necklace catches light from the cab's open door. "He's so trashed, he wouldn't recognize his sister. I mean, she's here and he didn't."

Roy Warner goes to Winston and this party seems like a better plan than staging my first adventure in normal teen life at a Latimer party where I could end up acting bizarre around people I know. Still, I'm shaking so hard, Roy's driveway starts to resemble the trail up Mount Everest.

"I want to throw up."

"Breathe," Siobhan says. "Don't geek out on me. Everyone will think you're cool because you're with me. Don't blow it."

She pushes me up the driveway toward the house.

"Roy's parties suck," she says. "It's only stoners from Winston. You can throw up all you want."

By now, we are standing outside the front door, which is hanging open; there are fumes. I'm thinking, What was I thinking? How could this even vaguely be a good idea, there must be something seriously wrong with me.

Siobhan pulls notebook paper folded into origami squares out of her bag.

"Kiddie pool," she says brightly. "I even brought the list. You're going to drink a beer and take a reasonable number of hits on a joint and you're going to hook up with a guy. A half hour from now, you'll have three things checked off."

She sounds like a cheerful camp counselor explaining how

much fun it's going to be to rappel down a cliff when, to me, the whole idea of rappelling down a cliff has a lot in common with jumping off the cliff.

"I'm hooking up with a random Winston stoner? Think again."

"He won't even remember; they're comatose. Some of them might be dead."

"I thought I was *observing* the first time."

"Noooo, you're going to participant-observe, like a cool anthropologist participant-observing in the wilds. Like Jane Goodall if she got it on with apes."

There's the sound of something crashing inside, and someone saying "Shit," but not sounding that upset about whatever it was.

"Do you ever worry something bad could happen?" (Because even Totally Bad Emma can't get all the way away from the images of looming danger I've been raised to entertain.)

In the yellow porch light, Siobhan's pupils are so dilated, they fill her irises, and her lipstick is smudged. She does not look worried.

"Sib, how much did you pregame? Want to wait out here for a minute?"

"I've been here for a while," she says. "I *gamed*. And now you need to game."

In the powder room off the front hall, there is a gold sink with faucets in the shape of scary swans, and wallpaper with flowers that look like Venus flytraps.

Siobhan says, "Frightening, right? No wonder Roy gets loaded."

She spreads the list on the counter. "Oh, I might have updated it," she says. "Don't freak. 'Shrooms is a joke. I might have gotten carried away."

"Seriously? A threesome? And *LSD*?"

"I was just having fun. Don't be a baby."

"What did you do to my list? Where's beer pong? Wait, a *biker* bar? Have you ever *done* any of this stuff?"

"You have no sense of humor. Why would it be so bad if I had, anyway?"

I am staring at this bucket list of bad high school behavior, starting with baby steps and working up to an assortment of sex acts in settings other than a bed.

"Complete joke," Siobhan says. "Look at the easy column. Check mark for passing a joint. You don't even have to take a hit."

"I'm supposed to find *Ecstasy*, is that what this *x* is supposed to be?"

We head down the massive hallway into a rec room where maybe thirty kids are sprawled on big, low couches. A couple of kids are playing pool in slow motion.

The weird thing is, I knew Siobhan partied. My phone is full of little video reminders of how much fun she was having and I wasn't. But her in Roy Warner's rec room is not what I'd visualized. Not thirty glazed-over kids passing a joint around, too far gone to even hook up effectively.

Siobhan leaves me sitting on the arm of a sofa and disappears into a knot of kids who might or might not be dancing. She comes back with a red cup in one hand and a joint in the other. She is completely gleeful.

"Worst party ever. Even if you get *très* wasted and throw up *on* one of these kids, *tant pis*! You could get your freak on here, and no one would look up."

"I don't have a freak to get on. Can we go home now?"

I wait thirty minutes with a frozen smile, holding a red cup of warm beer. Occasionally, I pass a joint to the guy next to me. In slow motion, he tries to nuzzle the left side of my face. I flick him away. It doesn't even seem sexual. He just seems to have an unnatural interest in the taste of human skin. I wait until he tries to stick his tongue in my ear, not getting a single check mark except for passing the joint.

Sib says, "All right. This one sucks. I just wanted to ease you into it, you know, kind of gradually."

"Thanks anyway."

"It's going to work, all right?" Sib says. "We have a *pact*."

"You want to share my cab?"

She says, "I'm giving it another hour. It can't get worse."

I make the taxi drop me off at the Chateau and I climb the hill to home. Everything happens in reverse: the barking dogs, the stalking cats, the security lights triggered by me walking past, Mutt and Jeff going doggie-berserk.

My house is dark and quiet, with no sign of the FBI or a canine search-and-rescue team or the entire juvenile division of the LAPD camped out in front. I push the window open, quietly, quietly, trying not to squash any more impatiens blooms than absolutely necessary to climb back into my room.

I strip down as fast as I can, and put on the big tee I left under one of the many pillows lined up in the shape of me under the covers. When I pull out my phone to recharge it, Megan (who, when I told her the plan, was surprisingly entranced) is texting.

Megan: Are you having fun yet?
Me: Why are you up?
Megan: Are you?
Me: Parties suck. You have no idea how not fun. So not worth it.
Me: Bunch of stoners too wasted to move.
Megan: Cheer up. It can only get better.

Maybe.

And it was *so* easy. I'm not even close to being in extra trouble.

Then there's Siobhan's text: *Next week. On Mulholland.*

The time stamp says 3:00 a.m.

Five hours later, I text back: *Maybe.*

Siobhan: What took u so long?

Chapter Sixteen

I STUDY ALL DAY SUNDAY AND I AM COMPLETELY good.

But inside the good girl, sitting at the desk poring over excessively detailed history notes, is the kernel of a slightly different girl. The thing is, I can't tell if the different girl is the bold fairy-tale princess who sneaks out and dances all night in diamond shoes (all right, didn't dance, sat in a room full of comatose stoners), or if she's Little Red Riding Hood, recklessly skipping through the woods (okay, Beverly Hills) just before the wolf eats her.

I creep down the hall with the pot-scented laundry basket. I dump the entire contents of a bottle of Febreze into the wash with everything I wore to Roy's in case my clothes reek. When the contraband phone vibrates with a text message, I dive back into my room.

Siobhan: Say yes.

Me: Busy being grounded.

Siobhan: Unground yourself. U know you want to.

Only this time we have to pregame together.

Me:????

Siobhan: Don't panic. Not substances, hair. Nails.

We'll pick out your outfit.

Siobhan: Not that same jacket.

Me: Jacket just fell apart. I put it in the washer.

Siobhan: Come on. I'll put pink streaks in your hair.

So, all right, I want pink streaks.

I study some more. I outline two chapters of the truly awful AP European History book and email the fruits of my industrious guiltfest to Dylan.

My dad is eating on the patio. Mutt and Jeff are circling the table, having figured out that we have better food at our house than they get at their house.

I say, "May I come outside?"

My dad pulls out the other chair. I am actually choked up. It would probably be better if I'd felt some shred of guilt last night so I wouldn't be hit with it so hard right now.

My dad is playing an ancient, scratchy recording of guys from Nova Scotia singing sad, monotonous folk songs. I do not complain. Instead, I get him more coffee.

I plow through the most incomprehensible unit of French poetry I've ever seen, which is pretty damned incomprehensible given that I speak French. I take even more notes. For hours. I think, How reckless can I be, sitting at my desk making insanely perfect notes?

The compass says, *You're kidding, right?*

My dad brings me a sandwich. I thank him like crazy. I do not act like a resentful person who is grounded until snow falls on the Hollywood sign. (Hint: Snow never falls on the Hollywood sign.)

Megan texts: *Are you okay? The secret is secret?*

> **Me:** No lightning bolts. No toads. No boils. No killing of the firstborn child.
> **Megan:** You're my hero. You didn't get drunk right?
> **Me:** You sound like your mother
> **Megan:** Kill me now. I wish I had a magic portal.

I am almost making it through the weekend. I think. When Dylan texts: *You weren't lying about notes with footnotes.*

First text since the cafeteria.

It's so much easier to pretend that nothing happened in writing without my voice, or face, or weird choppy breathing to give me away.

> **Me:** You're welcome.
> **Dylan:** You're thanked. OCD outline very handy. Amazed you have time for footnotes and bad parties.

Me: Don't remind me how bad. Wait. How do you even know?

Dylan: Hard to picture you baked. Curled up with a joint outlining sidebars. Being entertained by Roy.

Me: My household is devoid of joints and entertainment.

Dylan: I cd come by with magic tricks.

And your lips.

Me: Hard to picture you pulling a bunny out of a top hat. Is that where you got this number?

Because it's Siobhan's prepaid, the one I'm not supposed to have, the cheap untraceable kind that normal people don't have.

Dylan: Got it from your partner in crime.

Me: Disappointing. I was hoping for a rabbit.

Dylan: Maybe I should go for it. Beef up my resume for Georgetown.

Me: I thought you didn't care about such things.

Dylan: Crap. Slacker image shot to hell by bunnies.

Me: You must be one genius slacker to pass. You're never there.

Dylan: Excuse me Seed. I'm beating my bro's GPA by .2 and he was top ten. Hell I cd be valedictorian if I'd off Arif and Mara. And maybe Lissi.

Meaning that, basically, Dylan is getting better grades with my notes than I am. And is a lot more into school than I gave him credit for.

He's an ad for the benefits of constant cutting.

My dad would so not like this. The best grades ever, yes; the sticking his thumb in Latimer's eye while getting the best grades ever, no.

My dad calls and I slide the phone under my pillow.

I return to the home life of Emma the Good.

I fold all my clean clothes before going to bed early. I get up in the morning. I eat a waffle. I look out at the ocean past Sunset, past Century City. As we drive down the hill, I read my notes for a French poetry quiz.

Me: Do you get the French?
Siobhan: Sorta.
Me: OK first break outside the caf.
Sib: It's just a bunch of shit about Algeria.
Me: I might need more details.
Sib: OK but it's stupid.

My dad says, "Are you texting Siobhan from this car? You're supposed to be using that phone for emergencies only."

(As of this morning, I have my actual phone back because he's concerned that if there's a natural disaster, I'll need it when foraging for freeze-dried snack packs.)

"It's about French. See for yourself. Me: *Do you get the French?*

Siobhan: *Sorta.* Me: *OK first break outside the caf—*"

"Do you think that qualifies as an emergency?" The car slams to a stop in front of Latimer in urgent punctuation.

"I thought the point was no recreational texting. This is *far* from recreational."

All I can think about is how ridiculous my life is, tap-dancing around texting my friend in preparation for a quiz on a French poem about the oppression of colonial Algeria in blank verse. How the ridiculousness of my life is what's going on in this car, not how I'm pursuing happiness under the cover of night.

Twenty-seven weeks to Afterparty.

There's not a chance in hell I'm bailing on this pact.

Chapter Seventeen

"NO WAY," KIMMY SAYS TO ME WHEN I'M SITTING with Siobhan in the caf on Monday. "You won't come to my parties but you go to *Warner's?*"

Chelsea says, "Poor Emily. You should try to get yourself invited someplace a few steps up from Warner's. Maybe a crack house."

Chelsea turns on her heel before I can deliver a comeback.

Then Arif and Dylan stop at our table, presumably not to admire our so-called salads, studded with dried-out sprouts.

Arif says, "I heard you ladies had an issue with your GPS."

"Please," Siobhan says. "One L.A. party is as bad as the next."

Dylan sighs. "It hurts me to argue with anyone slamming L.A., but even here, Roy stands out."

I say, "Come on, it was bad, but it's not like we caught leprosy. He didn't have any problem drawing a crowd."

"Such as you two," Dylan says.

"Play nice," Arif says. "And for the record, there were arrests last Christmas."

Dylan says, "Yeah, some stoner ran over a reindeer."

"It was a bush," Arif says. "There were several bushes. Trimmed in the shape of reindeer. Very festive."

"There was a car-versus-reindeer-bush collision in Roy Warner's front yard?"

Three of us laugh. Siobhan walks away.

"Why do you even talk to them?" she says when I catch up to her. "One more person messes with me about that freaking party, as if I couldn't *tell* it was a loser party—"

"They were trying to be helpful."

"You think that was *helpful*? And Chelsea sneering at me was *helpful*? Because, surprise, it wasn't helpful. When we hit Mulholland on Saturday, we'll see who's helpful."

Megan: Roy Warner is famous. Girls at St. Bernadette know who he is. Guinness World Record for weed consumption. Joe says avoid him.

Me: Now you tell me.

Megan: Where's the next one?

Me: I can't believe you're encouraging me.

Megan: Sacrificing you on the altar of vicarious thrills.

Me: Someplace more glam. Now that I survived my starter party.

* * *

My dad, not incomprehensibly, is reluctant to let me out of his sight. But it's been two weeks, and it's Saturday, and he's not immune to the allure of the girly. He knows I want it, and he knows he can't exactly share a girly salon moment with me. So Nancy offering to take Siobhan and me to Beverly Hills for manicures seals the deal.

"Just no zebra stripes," he says after I more or less beg to go.

"Leopard spots with rhinestones on the cuticles."

"Nothing that glows in the dark."

"Dad! You're taking all the fun out of it!"

"I'm very unhappy with you, Ems," he says. "You might have to go with that clear pink one."

"No! You wouldn't make me do that, right?"

"Never. Go have a nice time."

"And I swear you won't hate it. Too much."

He smiles and pats my shoulder on my way out the door. "And Marisol is chaperoning later?"

"She's going to tuck us into bed."

Clearish pink nail polish isn't even on the table. Literally.

Nancy—who's in on the pink-streaked hair and the party where I plan to wear it—is well known at Lumiere, where we take our scraggly fingernails. She has a long, serious talk with her manicure artist about which of their more glittery colors my nails ought to be. We go for something called Bold Aqua Ice.

I start counting the bottles of polish that contain blue, or contain sparkles, or are some variant of Day-Glo whenever the subject of deceit comes roaring back into my head.

Siobhan picks silver. Nancy says, "I know better than to tell *you* what to do."

Siobhan says, "You've got that right."

I find myself wondering if Fabienne and I would be getting manicures together, if she'd be weighing in on my nail color.

Then I go: Stop it. Stop it, stop it, stop it, stop it. Until I stop it. Because maybe some people can do that and just keep having a normal day, but I'm not one of them. I'm not even close to being one of them.

"Are you listening to me?" Siobhan asks in a voice suggesting that she's on the verge of snapping fingers in my face.

I say, "Sorry, I'm obsessing about nail color. Nancy was right, right?"

"Like if she told you to get some crap color, I wouldn't say anything? Em? You look like you're going to cry. You must really hate aqua. Come on, what?"

"All right, I was thinking about my mom. You and Nancy . . ."

Siobhan puts her arms around me. "That sucks."

When our nails dry, we walk down Little Santa Monica half draped around each other, eating cupcakes from Sprinkles, while the foot reflexology person at Lumiere goes to town on Nancy.

We spend the rest of the afternoon putting pink streaks in my hair with William watching from Switzerland. His roommate, Gunther, who wakes up and shuffles across the screen in drawstring pajama bottoms, says, "Are those real girls? When does she take the robe off?"

William yells at him in German. I tell him he's a pig in French.

Siobhan says, "I'm done with you. *Ciao*, William. Get some sleep."

William says, "*Ciao*, Sibi," and closes his eyes.

Four hours later, we're ready to go.

CHAPTER EIGHTEEN

THE HOUSE HAS A DRIVEWAY THAT PLUNGES OFF Mulholland, as if in enticement to drive off solid land into the city lights. It requires a leap of faith to cross the threshold. Marisol drops us off at the edge of the precipice, and we walk down toward a sprawling house shining with white light below.

There are kids everywhere, food everywhere, music everywhere, drinks everywhere. I have clicked my heels three times and here we are in Party Oz, not even in the same world as Roy Warner and his slow-motion friends.

"Nice birthday party, right?" Siobhan says.

She takes my hand and we wind through the main hall toward the back of the house, to a deck that surrounds a long, rectangular pool, illuminated through the blue-green water. Where a bunch of guys from Latimer football are decimating a ten-foot table of refreshments. These are guys I talk to every day at lunch, and here we are, and there's even a food theme (although with classier food), and the only thing I can think of to do is eat.

I can barely make eye contact, or smile, or chew.

Ian Heath, who has a girl I don't know under his arm, literally drops her as he turns to Siobhan, who's in a tight green dress that matches her eyes, and he says, "Whoa," and he touches her hair.

Siobhan, so quickly that I almost miss it, whispers, "Watch this." Then she puts her hands on his butt and draws him toward her. If Siobhan had a list, Ian Heath would be a straight shot to all the check marks a person could possibly need.

I stand there behind her, half hidden. I don't know where to look or what to say when he kisses her, partly a hello kiss, partly something else.

I grab what looks to be a tiny éclair and stuff it into my mouth.

Across the pool, Sam Sherman is talking with Mara, whose hair is now electric blue. *She* can carry on normal conversation with a guy in party world—even if Sam is wearing a school hoodie, drinking beer out of a can, and looks as if he wandered into the wrong event.

I scoop more éclairs onto my napkin.

Everyone is here. Arif is here, eating skewered fruit. I grab a bottle of microbrewery beer out of a tub of ice and drink it very, very quickly.

I say, "Hey, Arif."

"Hey."

I say, "So you know Strick? Who is he, by the way?"

"Over there," Arif says. "Aspiring biker."

There is actually a kid with a pack of cigarettes tucked into the short sleeve of his T-shirt, with hair combed back like classic James Dean.

I say, "Holy shit."

Arif says, "You drink. You swear. You attend dreadful birthday parties. Your prognosis for fitting in just improved astronomically."

We stand there, watching Sam try to drag Mara in the direction of the food and abandon her in favor of eating his way across the table toward goblets filled with what might be chili.

"Bar mitzvah redux," Sam says. "All we need is DJ Jim and his seizure lights."

I ask Arif, "So where's your boy?" Because here I am in Nancy's pale pink dress and earrings that twine through my earlobes like gold ropes.

"Dylan only hangs at UCLA," Sam says. "He's been otherwise engaged all year."

"And last year," Arif says.

"Kahane is a dog," Mel shouts over the music, loading up on more éclairs.

Lia says, "He's an *aspiring* dog. He's sniffing around after Aiden's castoffs like a puppy is what I heard."

Thank you, Lia Graham, for that arresting image. I'm so far gone, the only part of this I care about is that he's going after somebody who isn't me.

I go off in search of Siobhan, which is a challenge since more people are pouring in and Security isn't doing much to stem the tide. There are kids standing up on the living room couches singing something unrelated to the piped-in music.

Siobhan is standing outside a bathroom off the industrial-sized kitchen. She says, "Did you get any check marks? I told you this would be good."

"I drank, I talked to Sam and Arif, I ate éclairs. I think I can call it a night."

Siobhan puts one finger on her chin. "Let me think. No. Drinking doesn't even count. You already drink. Come on. I'm getting you a giant check mark."

She pounds on the bathroom door with both hands.

She yells, "Come on! Share!"

The door opens. Two guys, one fiddling with white powder on the counter, the other snorting cocaine off the stainless steel soap dish.

I slam the door closed.

"What's wrong with you! I'd have a mother if not for this shit!" I'm screaming at her over the music, holding the door closed until she pulls my hands off the doorknob and I turn around, running, and she follows me down the hall.

"Stop yelling!" she says. "You're going a little crazy."

"I'm *not* crazy!"

She pulls me into a vacant room lined with books, a tiny office, and she locks the door. She says, "Breathe! You're flipping out."

We sit on a love seat between bookshelves. She slips a party napkin out from under a drink on the desk and hands the napkin to me.

She says, "Here's how it works. There's drinking and there's alcoholics. Not the same. Are you listening? And there's heroin and everything else. Heroin is *here*, with maybe that synthetic shit you get at gas stations that kills you." She waves her right arm, her hand cupped, her fingers curved upward, apparently to demonstrate the exact location of the heroin and the deadly gas station synthetic. "Coke and everything else is *there*." *There* being her similarly cupped left hand. "Just because somebody likes to get amped occasionally—*occasionally*—doesn't make her a burnout with holes in her septum."

I say, "Shut up."

"You should listen to me! I know what I'm talking about. That Just Say No assembly? Bullshit. That would make milk a gateway drug to crack."

"That's not that reassuring."

She stands up and pulls on my wrists. "Get up. I shouldn't have left you alone for so long. We're going back out there and get you some check marks."

This party is so overflowing with kids in various states of impairment, they don't even notice someone being dragged toward the yard crying. Except for Chelsea, who says, "What's the matter? Is baby all upset that everybody else has a boyfriend and everybody else is having a good time and everybody else gets it?"

Siobhan says, "Shut the fuck up, Chelsea. How would you even know if Emma has a boyfriend? She *has* a boyfriend. A very *serious* boyfriend. She's crying because watching all these immature bimbos grind makes her miss the real thing."

"So, where is he?" Chelsea holds her hand at a right angle to her forehead and pretends to search the crowd, her lower lip protruding in a big fake frown.

"He's in *Paris*," Siobhan says.

"For the weekend? Just so he could miss Strick's party. I'm sure."

I blurt, "He lives in Paris."

There, now I'm lying to pretty much everyone I know.

"And no one's ever heard of him." Chelsea rolls her eyes. "That's rich."

"Possibly because her father wants to cut his balls off," Siobhan says.

"A French lowlife," Chelsea says. "How nice for you."

I can't even believe this is happening, and I just helped it happen. I break away from Siobhan and stumble through hordes of happy people toward the far end of the pool, where it's darker and quieter than everyplace else.

I stretch out on a pool chair and look toward the city lights. The view from behind my house is a tree-shrouded slice; this is the panorama.

Kimmy walks by with Max Lauder, kicking his legs. He doesn't seem to mind. She is soaking wet, wearing a sports bra and a thong, a wet braid down her back.

She says, "Emma! You came to the party! Awesome!" She is not being sarcastic. "You should go in the water. It's ninety degrees."

I pull Nancy's dress over my head and fold it over the back of the chair.

One hundred and eighty-two days to Afterparty and already I'm removing significant pieces of clothing in public; there's a check mark for sure. I'm wearing a bra and panties and the dangly earrings. Kimmy swims by, giggling. I float on my back in the warm water. I stare up at the half-moon and the stars.

Here I am, half naked, buzzed on microbrew, and wondering if my mom first saw smack in a bathroom at a party. If she liked cocaine. If I would like cocaine. How much I would like it, and if I started to like it, could I stop?

Kimmy taps on my arm. I'm so startled that I almost gulp pool water. She says, "Come on. They're making us get out."

There's a security guy standing by the edge, gesturing with his thumb. I swim slowly to the side of the pool where my dress is and start to boost myself up over the edge. Only the dress isn't there. Perfect.

It feels like I'm climbing into a bad teen movie, although it's hard to see even Chelsea tiptoeing away with Nancy's dress. I wonder what I'm going to do, because walking around in my soaked bra, panties, and earrings is a nonstarter. I'd sooner hide behind the pool cabana for as long as it takes to weave an outfit out of fern fronds, like Insane Challenge Day on *Project Runway*.

Sam is almost passed out on a lounge chair, next to a six-pack.

I call, "Sam! Hey!"

He lurches up and bends over the side of the pool.

I say, "Give me your hoodie. Please."

His hoodie is cozy and falls to mid-thigh. I thank him forty or fifty times as I wring out my hair. He laughs at me, but the embarrassment of walking around in an extra-large Latimer hoodie that smells like Budweiser is nothing compared to the potential embarrassment of walking around in my underwear or in a jumper made of woven plant life.

Siobhan says, "Shit, can't take you anywhere."

We look for Nancy's dress, but it's nowhere.

Siobhan walks up to Strick, who is standing on the lawn smoking weed, and says, "Hey, my friend lost her dress. It's pink. Go make your security guys find it."

Ten minutes later, we're standing in Strick's kitchen with him and his two stoned friends and Nancy's dress, which is soaking and no doubt shrinking to the size of an oven mitt before our very eyes.

Siobhan, who didn't bother to introduce herself back when she was ordering Strick around, says, "Sib," and sticks out her hand.

"Strick," he says. He looks very pleased to meet her. She's about to phone Marisol, but he makes a security guy give us a lift to her house. Where I discover that not only was I standing around dripping wet in Sam's hoodie and Nancy's Jimmy Choos, but the pink streaks ran (which shouldn't be a big surprise, they were supposed to wash out, that was the point of them) and my head is covered with leopard-print-looking pink spots. I have to wash my hair twice, the second time with laundry detergent, to get most of the pink evidence out.

Chapter Nineteen

SUNDAY MORNING, I WILL MYSELF NOT TO LOOK guilty. I will myself to breathe. I will myself not to say one word about the slightly pink hair until my dad notices the slightly pink hair.

The moral compass says, *Aha! Pink hair! You wanted to get caught. Maybe there's an infinitesimally tiny ray of hope for you.*

Me: Did not.

My dad is looking at me strangely. "Is there something you need to tell me?"

Yes, there is, only I can't.

Because I thought about her all day yesterday.

Because I wondered what color nail polish she'd like.

Because when I saw some guy snorting cocaine off a soap dish, I couldn't stop crying.

Because I took off most of my clothes without regard to modesty, good choices, or what anyone would think of me. I swam around the shallow end of a pool until a security guard made me get out, and oh yeah, I semi-inadvertently entered into a pact to lose my virginity. And it would be nice if I had an actual parent to talk to about this whose heart wouldn't get destroyed by knowing who I actually am.

"Did something happen to your hair?" he says, and I can tell he's making a strenuous effort to remain calm.

"Yeah, I put in what was supposed to be a temporary pink rinse, but it won't come out. I might have to use rubbing alcohol or something."

My dad looks as if he's trying to figure out whether to be upset with me, and if so, just how upset.

I say, "I know it looks weird, but this is really a my-body-belongs-to-me thing. This is in the henna-tattoo-wears-off, tweezing-my-eyebrows, and having-green-toenail-polish column—not in the stud-through-my-tongue one."

"You want a stud through your tongue?"

We have had multiple discussions about how putting a stud through your tongue is a medical disaster, creating a tiny bacterial sewer in your mouth; of course I don't want a stud through my tongue after that.

My dad says, "*Ma princesse*, don't cry. I'm sure we can find a way to get it out. It's very slight, the faintest tint."

"So," Dylan says on Monday when I'm about to fork over another week of history notes that are completely handwritten because, in a moment of compulsive frenzy, I made charts. "All this time I thought you were a mild-mannered bad seed, but turns out you're Juliet. Imagine my surprise."

I say, "All this time I thought *you* were an underachiever. What are you raving about?"

Dylan imitates what appears to be a swooning girl. "Oh Rosalind, it's just like Romeo and Juliet!"

"Do we even know anyone named Rosalind? What are you talking about?"

"From fair Verona, where we lay our scene?" he says, misquoting *Romeo and Juliet*. "Big family feud. Older French boyfriend. Clashing tribes. Sword fights. Your dad wants to mutilate him. Is any of this coming back to you?"

Oh shit. What Siobhan said to Chelsea. What *I* said to Chelsea.

Only bigger.

Arif, who has been watching this whole thing, leaning against the bank of lockers, slightly shaking his head, says, "Is this lout bothering you, Miss Capulet?"

Dylan says, "Shut it."

Arif swats him. "You should bypass him and give those notes straight to me," he says. "At least I know enough not to return them coated with cheese and pepperoni."

"Pepperoni envy," Dylan says. "Not halal. You would smear those notes with pepperoni if you could."

"No," Arif says. "I wouldn't. And let me point out that it's not kosher, either. Or even arguably healthy."

"If Jews had Hell, I'd be going straight there," Dylan says. He looks down at me. He's a good eight inches taller than me. "As are you, Juliet. A disgrace to your tribe."

Arif says, "Are you dissing this girl's tribe?" He is fake-incensed. He says to me, "You're Moroccan, right? Would you like me to go get him kicked out of school for cultural insensitivity? They're very keen on that."

"I'm *part* Moroccan. How does everybody suddenly know where my grandmother comes from and my family feuds and how my tribe's pissed off about my boyfriend?" There, I have completely accidentally said it out loud. "My boyfriend." In front of Dylan, who must think I come in a slightly rosy pink color given that I'm in a constant state of blushing in front of him.

"Too bad," Dylan says. "If you were *whole*, he probably could have gotten me booted out of this swamp."

Siobhan says, "Calm down. If you don't want a cool French boyfriend, we can always kill him off. He's an interim measure. It's not a big deal."

It's a pretty big deal.

I'm suddenly a mysteriously tragic figure, languishing in California, texting the increasingly hot Jean-Luc, my romantic absentee imaginary boyfriend. One day after conception, he's up and running and pining for me on the banks of the Seine.

Poor Jean-Luc, from whom Siobhan's imagination has separated me because I'm a Capulet and he's a Montague. Sort of. Jean-Luc and I have passionate yet heartbreaking trysts when he lurks in the forests of Canada tossing pebbles at my cabin window, evading death at the hands of my dad, who—our family elevated to the status of the somewhat Moroccan Kennedys of Quebec—is into dynastic feuds.

I say, "No one is going to buy this."

Siobhan and I are sitting in the student lounge, eating candy bars from the vending machines. Siobhan says, "Are you questioning my brilliance? You're not, right? Because I already told Kimmy, and she's a broadcasting tower."

A highly effective broadcasting tower.

Chelsea says, "How do you know this guy isn't stepping out with a French model?"

I say, "Really, Chelsea. We are *so* far beyond that. He's not a *child*."

Siobhan and I exchange a quick glance, a fast, private, motionless high-five and set up Jean-Luc's Facebook page.

CHAPTER TWENTY

"FACE IT," SIOBHAN SAYS. "JEAN-LUC IS COOL, BUT this whole Afterparty prep list is only going to work if you find someone *not* imaginary that you think is hot and get going. Wasn't there one single guy at Strick's you wanted?"

"You want me to cheat on Jean-Luc with a drunk guy I don't even know?"

"What about Kimmy's water polo brother? He's at Stanford, you'd never have to see him again."

"No!"

"You're too picky. There has to be someone you could try out your training wheels on."

And I'm thinking, What the hell. I've been mad about him since Day One, and if Siobhan has some sort of mysterious how-to for casting spells on boys, this would be the moment for her to dish up the instructions.

I hold my breath. I say, "Dylan Kahane seems kind of interesting."

Siobhan frowns. "That's random."

"You don't think he could like me?" This sounds a lot more heartfelt than intended.

Siobhan pantomimes silent screaming. "Kahane thinks he's above doing high school girls, all right? He's probably saving it for some artsy college bitch who writes incomprehensible poetry. You should lose it with some willing man-slut so *then*, when you get it on with a complicated, arrogant asshole like Kahane, you'll know how things work."

All I want in life is five minutes of romance with the complicated, so *not* arrogant Dylan Kahane. I don't care how things work.

"And there's his whole fucked-up thing with Aiden."

"Aiden?"

"The creep older brother. You need to pick out someone else."

I want to know more. I want to ask five hundred questions. I want to shake her and demand to know why this not-uninteresting topic never came up before. Unfortunately, there's a limit to how crazed and ridiculous I want to look in front of her on the boy front or I would have told her about Dylan way before now. But at first I was afraid that if I revealed the true extent of my geekiness with boys, she'd go find a cooler person to be friends with. And now it's too late.

"You could have anyone you want," she says.

Anyone except Dylan.

I say, "Am I missing something? Have you noticed guys following me around?"

"Because you don't come on to them. You're gorgeous."

"Maybe I'm not that gorgeous."

"You think I'm a gorgeous girl with an ugly-ass best friend to make me look better? And you're the ugly-ass friend, so even if you put it out there, jerks are going to throw up in trash baskets? Because that's not what's going to happen."

She pushes me toward the round mirror that hangs over her dresser. "Look at you," she says. She runs her fingertips along my eyebrows, arching them a little. "I don't see projectile vomit in your future."

I say, "I'm sure Jean-Luc will be very happy I'm not cheating on him with jerks."

Siobhan sighs, "I'm so bored. You want to go to Century City?"

No.

I say, "Could we just go shopping? And not mall shopping."

We head down to Third Street, where I find a cream silk blouse that looks exactly like Ingrid Bergman's in *Casablanca* at Party Like It's 1949, and Siobhan tries on a cigarette girl outfit.

I say, "Does Ian smoke?"

"I am *so* over him," Siobhan says. "I'm going out with Wade the Tennis Pro, and there's nothing Nancy can do about it. Tonight. I told him to come get me and Nancy can just suck it up."

Given my life experience, the concept of a parent sucking it up doesn't compute.

And Nancy doesn't.

When Sib and I get back to her house, Nancy is all but sitting in Wade's lap on the living room couch, and one of her high heels is dangling from her toe.

Siobhan hurls her shopping bags toward them. Phillip Lim ankle boots fall out of their box and skid across the floor.

"He's too *old* for you," Nancy says in a weirdly level voice as Wade sprints back to his car.

I hear Siobhan screaming, "I can't believe you!" when I'm upstairs in her room with a pillow on my head. "What kind of excuse is that? You let my boyfriend grope you for my own good? What's wrong with you!"

"I don't want to see you with one more boy past high school!" Nancy yells. "I mean it Siobhan! No grown-ups."

"You're supposed to be a grown-up?" Siobhan screams. "On what planet do grown-ups do this?"

I don't hear what Nancy says next, but it involves a lot of shrieking.

"There you have it," Siobhan says, yanking the pillow off my head. "My mother is officially the world's richest trailer trash."

"Sibby, Wade is a jerk! Wade has an old-person fetish. Wade is crap."

"It's not *Wade*," she says, "it's her sorry ass. She probably made a video of it for Burton."

"That's disgusting."

"You know what? Screw Wade! It's you and me, babe. We're spending the entire weekend partying like it's 1949—you can wear the blouse, just without the top button. We're going to Missy Roger's thing on Friday and we're going to Kimmy's Saturday, and then we're going to this thing at Strick's beach house in Malibu Sunday."

"Kimmy's thing is *this* Saturday? Is there a continuous party over there?"

"Yeah. Late. I could pick you up on Sunset, like at Pink Taco."

I say, "I can't do it. I have a dinner with my father on Friday, and Saturday I'm keeping Megan company while the parents go to a fund-raiser."

"Is your dad, like, dating the Donnellys?" Siobhan is ranging back and forth across her room, swiveling in her desk chair and getting up again. "Can't you ditch her? Ditch her."

"We could hang out during the day Saturday, but I can't get out of any of this. Come on. You know I want to go with you."

"Yeah, yeah," Siobhan says. "A likely story. And you're not coming to Malibu Sunday either, and why would that be?"

"Food bank, it's my first day back. Inventory, and it lasts forever. And I have to do homework sometime."

Siobhan is out of her chair, yelling. "I can't believe you! You'd rather count jars of peanut butter than go out with me! I'm supposed to be your best friend and you don't even *care*. It was supposed to be a *pact*. I can't count on *anyone*!"

I'm watching to see if she's joking, but there's nothing resembling a joke here.

I say, "Sib, I'm sorry. You know you can count on me. I completely love you. But I have to keep my grades up or he'll brick up my window."

"Oh," she says. Not even looking at me. "That's right. You're the good one and I'm the wild one. Except that—what was that? *Right*—you can count on *me*."

At school, she will barely look at me, and all weekend, it's as if she lost her phone, or my number, or any interest in talking to me.

CHAPTER TWENTY-ONE

IT'S NOT THAT I DON'T ENJOY MY WEEKEND, I DO, it's just that with twenty-four weeks to Afterparty—my list composed of low-hanging fruit, ready to fall into my hand if I'd just reach out the window—it's hard to be locked into good-girl propriety until Monday.

"You don't think I'm a terrible person, do you?" I say to Megan, when our parents are gone and we're alone at her dining room table, staring at stacks of college brochures she's been accumulating since she killed her PSAT.

"Maybe you should check your texts—*I* was the one egging you on." Megan sighs the sigh of doomed Rapunzel. "Think about it. I can't even get that close to Joe at dances. The nuns will break his fingers if he slides them too far down my back."

I say, "This might be weird, but what do you think about losing your virginity on purpose in advance?"

"In advance of what?"

"Real life. College. Not being the last one standing."

"You mean like with *anyone*, just do it? You're kidding, right?"

"Not a random stranger."

Megan hands me her laptop. "Show him to me."

I am so not ready for this.

I click onto Dylan's Facebook page. His status is: "Not here, in preparation for not being here."

"That's a bit cryptic," Megan says. "He's not affected, is he?"

Megan starts clicking through his photos. "Are you sure he's your type?" She keeps scrolling through, clicking, expanding, examining. "I admit he's smoldering, but who's that girl falling out of her dress? Is that in London? Wait, is she a hooker?"

"Is this your mother speaking?"

"Just shoot me," she says absently. "Look at him. How tall is he, anyway? Does he only smile when drunk? He kind of smirks. He doesn't smirk at you, does he? Is this the stupid one who uses your notes?"

"Megan! I'm not in love with some stupid guy who smirks at me, all right?"

Megan says, "You're *in love* with him?"

Oh God.

"You should go for it," Megan says. "You should go out with this guy."

"He hasn't asked me."

"You should make him ask you."

"Did you make Joe ask you?"

Megan shakes her head. "I have that so-near-yet-so-far unattainable pure thing going. He'd kill to get within a hundred yards of me."

"This guy thinks I'm making mad love to an imaginary older guy from Paris. The ship has sailed on the pure thing."

I sigh.

Megan sighs.

There's something so lame about the two of us sitting here among the college brochures, having a purely theoretical conversation about boys.

I say, "You should invite Joe over."

"Now?"

"Why not? I showed you mine, now show me yours."

"A *picture* of yours!" Megan says. "Why don't we ask *yours* over?"

"Maybe because yours would kill to come over—you just said so—whereas so-called mine doesn't even kiss me when he has the chance."

"You need to encourage him more," Megan says.

I hand her her phone.

Joe, it turns out, is sitting with a bunch of guys, post–basketball game, at the Los Feliz House of Pies. Which is maybe five minutes from Megan's house. Megan is somewhat terror-stricken, except she can't stop grinning.

"I'm just born to be wild," Megan says. "Which in my case has Joe sitting in my living room, eating Rice Krispies Treats. With a chaperone."

"I could hide in your garage! You could completely be knocked up before Doctor, Doctor, and Doctor get to the dessert course."

"Stay!" she says. "You should check him out in case he's awful and I missed it."

But when he gets here, when he gets out of his car and comes up the walkway, I might as well not exist. Megan is one happy Rapunzel and Joe is quite well suited for his role as smitten prince. Smitten *normal* prince. Compared to Dylan, he has a Twitter feed of his every thought and feeling embedded in his forehead.

I have seen Joe on the tiny screen of Megan's iPhone, but apparently gawking, mad love is easier to discern in person. Also, tall, dark, and handsome don't come across in this much glory on a three-inch screen.

Megan jumps up to get him a glass of water and crashes into the coffee table.

I say, "I'll help you carry," and follow her into the kitchen.

Arranging the Rice Krispies Treats on a plate with some difficulty, she says, "He's great, right?"

"Come on! You've got Prince Charming waiting on your sofa. Let him climb your hair, already."

"That was a different prince," she says over her shoulder because she's charging through the louvered doors into the living room.

So I sit there in the kitchen trying to concentrate on math. All I can think is, Why can't I sneak Dylan into *my* living room and make out on *my* living room couch?

Oh yeah, because Dylan doesn't idolize me.

Even when he would appear to be about to kiss me and I'm sitting there in a fully cooperative state of complete longing and receptiveness, leaning forward so he could accomplish this feat by moving his lips maybe six inches, he doesn't.

Does he check *my* Facebook every day? Is he even, in a rudimentary way, stalking me back? I think not.

Siobhan doesn't even think that he's a realistic check mark. If Siobhan is even thinking about me at all. She hasn't texted back for two days.

I listen to Megan giggling on the other side of the louvered doors, and I'm thinking, This is truly pathetic. I'm jealous of Megan's love life.

CHAPTER TWENTY-TWO

ON MONDAY, IT'S CLEAR AND COLD. FOR HERE. Driving in the hills toward school, we pass a misplaced maple tree with leaves that have turned colors and are falling to the ground, all yellow and red, among palm trees and birds of paradise.

"Autumn in California," my dad says.

I say, "I like it. I like endless summer."

My dad says, "I do too, I admit it."

"Oh no! What's next? A pair of shorts?"

My dad swats at my arm, but we're both smiling.

"How did I raise such a fresh kid? It's California. I'm getting you to Lac des Sables at winter break."

"In the cabin?"

"Of course the cabin." As if the nightmare aspects of the cabin are forgotten, the way dreams disappear from memory when you're jolted awake, bolt upright in bed, with no recall of the wretched hunchbacked thing that was just chasing you.

"I thought we were building a shelter in Oaxaca. You know, 'You shall take the poor into your house'? Repair the world? Emma gets a nail gun."

"I was with you right up to the last sentence," he says. "No nail gun." Then he says how much he respects my commitment.

I'm not even sure if my commitment is to world repair or to staying the hell, yes, "hell," I use the world advisedly, hell, hell, hell out of the unadulterated Hell that is the Lazar family cabin at Lac des Sables. Siobhan had better be talking to me, because no way will my dad have an honest conversation about this.

She's sitting there in homeroom, looking great. Unusually great. Unusually calm and unusually pleased with the world.

I say, "Hey, Siobhan. Lost your phone?"

"It was one weekend," she says. "To quote Miss Goody-pants."

"Because we have to do the carbon footprint assignment."

"This is bullshit," Siobhan says. "Why is homeroom even allowed to assign homework? My house has solar panels. Marisol drives a Prius. We don't own a plane. How small is my carbon footprint supposed to get?"

"Wow. No plane. You might have been at Latimer too long."

"One day was too long."

I say, "I would seriously die here without you."

"Slain by the evil Chelsea in the flower of her youth, when still a virgin. Pathetic."

"Could you please yell 'virgin' louder?"

She opens the lid of the old-timey wooden desk, a historical artifact that helps give Latimer its movie-set, classic prep-school feel, and lets it fall with a bang. Everyone turns around.

She says, "There. That was loud."

Loudness is the theme of the day.

Siobhan and I are sitting in the snack bar at the Beverly Hills Public Library, where we can't find the references we need to prove our environmental sensitivity.

Siobhan looks disgusted with the entire operation.

A woman who is making a great deal of noise crinkling a giant newspaper, and anyway, this is a snack bar, says, "Shhhhhh!"

Siobhan says, "Don't you want to know about my weekend?"

I am keeping myself awake with coffee. I can barely focus on anything other than not falling off the chair. The food bank took beyond forever on Sunday, and then I had to finish Monday's homework. Which was voluminous. Latimer, in addition to its other charms, is hard.

I say, "I already know about your weekend. You went to awesome parties while I was prisoner of goodness."

The woman turns in her seat to glare at us.

"Madame," Siobhan says, "if you continue to make a racket with that newspaper, I will be forced to ask Security to escort you from the premises."

She waves as the woman scurries back into the library proper.

"People suck," she says. "Have you noticed that? I can't even get William to call back, which, unless his phone got run over by a car, means he'd better be dead."

"Maybe he's in a Swiss canyon. No reception."

"No, he just sucks." She takes a long drag on the straw in her iced coffee. "And this coffee sucks."

I say, "You suck."

She says, "No, you. And about my weekend, don't freak out on me, but I test drove Dylan Kahane for you, and *he* sucks."

She goes back to sipping her iced coffee as if this were just a fun, ordinary, ho-hum conversational gambit. As if it were nothing.

"You *what?*"

"I know. It was Kimmy's party, and this one didn't have Kent and his Stanford boys, and Strick didn't show. If you'd have come, it never would have happened."

"This happened *two nights ago?*"

I look at her and it's as if I'm seeing someone else, as if my actual friend has disappeared and I'm sitting in the snack bar, shaking and completely friendless. As if I'm standing on the bottom of the ocean and there's no one else here.

"Say something," she says.

While I'm figuring out what I can possibly say, she says, "It's not like I was sober at the time. I doubt he even remembers because I don't think his mommy ever told him beer has alcohol in it. Or that the *boy* brings the condom."

It's as if Siobhan is gone and Dylan has turned into someone else, because the Dylan I've wanted since the first day at Latimer doesn't fall down drunk on top of Siobhan in Mandeville Canyon.

How could this even happen?

But what comes out of my mouth is "Whatever. It's not like I'm hooking up with him."

And then I'm looking at her through a landscape of dark water. I'm pushing away long strands of kelp, pushing through beds of rubbery green seaweed. I am remote and cold and flailing and alone down here.

She says, "I know. I'm just saying."

Just saying the hell *what*?

I say, "Get real. It's not like I'm on his speed dial."

Completely true, although it leads to the completely wrong conclusion. But there's no way I can say out loud, can formulate the sentences, can send out into the universe, how much I want him, and I kind of told her, I more than somewhat kind of told her, that he was the one. And yet she took him.

She says, "Are you sure?"

I shake off the salt water that is stinging my eyes, and the cold, and the ropes of kelp, and the sensation of drowning, and I outright lie to whoever she is.

I say, "He's yours, for all I care."

And Siobhan says, "*Quel* relief. Because it wasn't anything, but turns out, he's nice. I wouldn't mind some nice. You have excellent taste in childhood crushes."

I am close to losing it completely.

It wasn't childhood, it was yesterday, and also this morning. "That's all it was," I lie. I will myself not to feel or think.

I keep trying to convince myself that it wasn't anything, and that I'm fine, and that it doesn't matter, and I'm happy for her. I tell myself I never totally told her, I actively hid it from her, and that time he almost kissed me, there was no kiss, proving he never liked me that way. I tell myself it would be stupid to be gutted, and no self-respecting girl would be gutted, it's drama-queenish to feel gutted, and I Am Not Gutted.

It doesn't work.

CHAPTER TWENTY-THREE

MEGAN SAYS, "NO WAY."

I am sitting in her room, eating an entire tin of chocolate chip cookies.

I say, "Oh yeah. They're at a classic film festival she thinks is crap. Tuesday, they went to Stravinsky. He takes her to hear a band and dance in Silver Lake, and she totally doesn't get how cool it is. She wants to be on the roof at Skybar."

"No way," Megan repeats. "And how can she even pretend she likes Stravinsky? I don't even like Stravinsky, and I like classical music."

There's nothing to say. Siobhan is telling him she longs to sit with lavender-haired ladies who beam at them while they listen to Firebird because they look like such an adorable young couple. One of whom likes Firebird. (Hint: not Siobhan.) She is going on my weird dream date and pretending to like it. I don't even get it.

Siobhan: Why do people like this shit again?

Me: Read the program notes.

Siobhan: And y is there a line around the block for the ladies room?

Me: Why don't you just tell him you're not up for this?

Siobhan: I might hv told him I like it. So stupid.

Me: Why did you tell him that?

Siobhan: Stop interrogating me. Duh. Bc I like him.

When you consider the fact that she couldn't even stand him right up until she started dancing her way across L.A. in his not unwilling arms, it's completely breathtaking. In the hardball-hits-you-in-the-chest-and-knocks-the-breath-out-of-you kind of way.

"Have you considered dumping her?" Megan asks. "Everybody knows that girls can't do this to their friends. It's an axiom of high school."

"This is my best friend."

She looks at me.

"You know what I mean, my best friend *at school*. It's different with someone you go to school with every day."

"Different like you get to see her making out with your boyfriend every day."

"He's not my boyfriend! It's not like you can call dibs on someone."

"Yes you can. Isn't there anybody else you could hang out with over there?"

I catalog the junior class, as if I could conjure up someone exactly like Siobhan (except not with Dylan) and make her manifest in homeroom. But I just end up thinking about how Siobhan is stuck to me like gum under a desk.

"At least he's not nibbling her in public, which might actually make me have a heart attack and die. And get this, she keeps telling me all about how nice he is and how she's still planning to marry William when she's thirty."

Megan says, "Yeah, and I'm planning to run away with Joe to Barbie's dream house on the Magic School Bus."

I say, "I don't think she's joking."

"You just sit there and listen?"

I pretty much do. While pretending that I never wanted him.

"Do you still *like* him?"

I do my sick-lamb noise in the form of a "yes."

Megan, who almost never swears, says, "Damn."

"What am I going to do?"

"A whole lot of homework. Sort cans of tomato paste. You know, sublimate."

Sublimating, for those who lack a psychiatric parent, is when instead of getting in touch with your debilitating longings, misery, and sexuality, you throw everything you've got into things such as overstudying for Precalc, competitive ice-skating, and sorting cans of tomato paste. It's what our parents want us to be doing at all times, day and night.

I ask, "Will you come sort with me?"

"Sort canned goods in the basement of a temple?" She sounds quite enthusiastic. "I think I could get out of my house for that."

Siobhan, of course, wants to talk about him. A lot. It is difficult to pretend I don't care, to make myself nod attentively and eat salad at the same time.

"You could eat lunch with *him*," I say as casually as possible, in the interest of extricating myself from a thicket of misery. "You don't have to babysit me."

"He's at Religious Convo lunch."

"He goes to *Convo lunches*?" Only people who are actually *into* Convo, aka Religious Convocation for Interfaith Dialogue (as opposed to people who just want Convo on their college applications in the brotherhood-of-man category) go to Convo lunches. How did I not know this about him?

I've been obsessing about him since the first day I got to Latimer, yet she knows more about him than I do after like five minutes.

My whole semester is turning into a series of awful little shocks.

I take a deep breath and try to look amused. "He can't be that religious."

I try to visualize Dylan, two buildings away, holding hands with Arif and Lissi in a circle with all the Religious Convocation kids, watching documentary shorts about the Dalai Lama and singing "Let There Be Peace on Earth." Every time I get to the place in the circle where I visualize him sitting, the image evaporates.

"Why can't I be with a religious guy?" Siobhan says, dipping her carrot stick into my ranch dressing. "He's not half as Jewy as William."

"Wait a minute! William is Jewish? I thought his grandpa was a Nazi count."

Now that I'm letting pretty much everything slide, I'm letting "Jewy" slide. Even though I'm feeling madly and protectively Jewish myself in the presence of "Jewy." Even though according to some people with the same last name as me, I'm not even.

Who the hell says "Jewy," anyway? People from Aryan Nation compounds? My best friend?

"That's his other grandpa," she says, again as if it's nothing, as if it's just how people chat while eating carrots. "William is Gramps-spent-World-War-Two-hiding-out-in-the-attic-of-a-monastery-in-Pisa-type Jewy."

All right. Can't take it.

"You have to stop saying that word. You're going to get us kicked out of school for being anti-Semitic. Also, a tad offensive."

"How can I be anti-Semitic if I'm going to marry William?" she says, stirring the lumpy dressing with a celery stick. "Think about it."

Reflexively, almost on autopilot, I say, "What if he's already married?"

"Then he'll have to dump the bitch. It's a pact. He can't walk away from a pact just because he hooks up with some Eurotrash."

Perfect. She's still planning to marry an insomniac Swiss boy, while she's sleeping with Dylan. While I pretend to be cheerful and unconcerned and made of freaking construction-grade rebar.

"I can't believe you're seriously planning that." Just to say something.

"Why wouldn't I? I mean, he was my first. How romantic would that be?"

"Wait! You had sex with William? And I'm just now hearing about this, too?"

"Is this the Spanish Inquisition? We were super-young and I wanted to see what it was like. Are you happy now? It's not like it's the first time I saw one. Remember Paolo?"

Paolo was the pervy stepfather two stepfathers ago, who only lasted a couple of weeks because he pranced around naked in front of eleven-year-old Siobhan.

"I thought that was just once when he did that thing with the bath towel and you barely noticed anything."

"Until Nancy noticed anything. Then she checked us into the Grand Hotel Swankissimo and divorced his ass and took me out in gondolas and bought me charm bracelets and bread to rip up for the nasty pigeons in Piazza San Marco."

"Yay, Nancy."

"Yeah, she has completely bad taste in men, but she's not a total failure as a mom."

Which is the polar opposite of Siobhan, who is turning out to have perfect taste in men but to be a total failure as a best friend.

CHAPTER TWENTY-FOUR

EVERY TIME I WALK PAST DYLAN, I IMAGINE HIM with her.

Stop it, stop it, stop it is highly ineffective. There are still tiny little heart-stopping flashes: their fingertips, their lips, their hair against a white, starched pillowcase.

He keeps treating me as if everything is exactly the same.

Nothing is the same.

I can hardly bear to look at his face, even when he's just one row over and completely absorbed in staring out the window. I want to jump into my locker to avoid having to deal, at the same time I can't stop stealing glances.

I can hardly stand to watch his mouth move when he talks or how he shoves his hair behind his ear when it flops in front of his face when he's drawing instead of taking notes due to the fact that *I'm* taking the notes. Except that whenever Mr. Auden calls on him, he sounds smart.

I can hardly stand it when Mr. Auden says, "That's a very Hegelian take on it, Mr. Kahane."

And Dylan, who is not very forgiving, says, "Yes, I'm almost as Hegelian as Aiden."

When Dylan goes, "Hey, Emma, do you have something that could pass as review notes on the origins of Communism?" as if what happened in the cafeteria never happened, as if he weren't completely stepping out of character and, say, sleeping with my best friend, I can hardly get the rings of my binder to open.

Siobhan still wants to hang out after school.

"Don't you want to hang with, you know, the boyfriend?"

She says, "What's wrong with you? You never told me to hang out with Wade or Ian Heath or Strick or anybody. I'm the girlfriend, not the lapdog."

I don't know why I agree to it, but I'm so into pretending everything is fine that we go back to her house. I almost can't bear to step into her bedroom, to see the bed where I'm pretty sure he's been. I turn around and lead us back downstairs to the screening room without a word.

Twenty minutes into the movie, during an endless interlude of seabirds flapping around a depressed French couple, she says, "You know, he's not the funnest person ever born. It's not like I'm going to sit there and do worksheets while he practices violin or whatever."

Another hideous image of togetherness.

"If he wants to be the boyfriend, he's going to have to step it up. Just because he hates L.A. so much and he hates Latimer so much and he hates his asshole brother so much, I don't see why he can't put on something nice and party."

"Have you thought of asking him?" Said with only the slightest hint of edge.

She says, "Okay, we have to keep this Afterparty prep pact going or you're going to stay single and clueless, and Afterparty is going to kill you. You don't go, 'Hey jerk, why are you so rumpled, have you ever noticed signs that say "dry cleaner," and why are you such a freaking drag?' and stay somebody's girlfriend. Too bad we can't double with Jean-Luc. You'd see what I mean."

"I thought we were going to kill off Jean-Luc."

"No! Why would you want to be the pathetic single girlfriend, when you *could* be the International Girl of Intrigue? It would be like going backwards."

I almost can't contain how much I want to slap her. Naturally, the film we're mostly not watching has a tousled, brown-haired guy who pushes his hair behind his ear. Right then.

And it's not as if I'm the only one who notices the novelty of them being together. Everyone who's even marginally nice thinks it's swell that Siobhan and Dylan have taken up with someone semi-normal, even though the two of them might not, at first glance, appear to be the same brand of semi-normal.

"You must be so happy!" Kimmy chirps. By this point, I can admit she's a completely nice person whose horse I never should have touched, and if she finds out and hates me, I would, strictly speaking, deserve it. Kimmy is, as usual, all horse-sweaty and enthusiastic. "Who'd have thought her and *Dylan?* Pretty strange, huh?"

I say, "It's not that strange."

Kimmy looks at me sideways. "Come on, it's strange."

I say, "It's not strange, Kimmy!" As if ordering it not to be strange and ordering her not to think it's strange would work.

"All right!" she says. "Sorry! I'm not saying it to insult her. It's just that she usually goes for these big, macho lacrosse guys and that guy from Crossroads with the really big Harley—"

"Strick?"

"Fake biker, yeah. And Dylan's so kind of *alternative.*"

I snap my head back. I don't even mean to.

She says, "Don't say you don't know what I mean. He doesn't throw, kick, or catch balls except for pickup basketball, and he has Kurt Cobain T-shirts. More than one."

"Tell me you're not serious."

Kimmy shakes her head, and her braid whips over her shoulder. "It's just that he's never interested in anyone our age. When he came to my party, it was kind of a shock. He never parties. He never hangs with us. He never likes anyone that Aiden didn't check out first."

Does everyone know more than I do?

Kimmy looks away. "It's just nice that he's all happy. He *is* all happy, right?"

"You don't think he looks happy?"

"You know what I mean," Kimmy says. "Hard to know what Dylan's thinking, except that he doesn't want to be here."

"How would I possibly know what he's thinking?" I am, perhaps, shouting at her. She takes a tiny step back, as if preparing to bolt.

I say, "Sorry. I'm just having a weird day. Sorry."

"Every day's a weird day at Latimer," Kimmy says. "But at least it's the best-of-the-best-of-the-best weird day. . . . Are you all right?"

"I am spectacularly and outstandingly all right," I lie. "I've never been better."

Kimmy says, "If you say so."

After school, when Siobhan wants to go down to the Strip for iced coffee, I tell her I have to be at the food bank. Lie, lie, lie. Then I actually take the Latimer bus that goes into Hollywood to the food bank, and I help Mrs. Loman, who is too old to be lifting more than one can of tomato paste at a time, but is very gung ho. When my dad calls to find out where I am, since, obviously, I'm not at home dutifully studying, and I tell him I'm at the temple working and I lost track of time, he think's I'm a wonderful, world-repairing person.

I don't have the heart to tell him that I'm not.

CHAPTER TWENTY-FIVE

NOW THAT I'M TRYING TO SUBLIMATE MY LITTLE heart out at the food bank (without a whole lot of success), I'm filled with ideas for repairing the world through acts of subversion.

Megan says, "This isn't going to work," but you can tell she's in love with the idea. I feel like the Sacajawea of girls who need to be led out of oppression.

I check Joe in at the student volunteer desk. When he rolls the *r*'s in "Gutierrez–Ortega" and says that he goes to Loyola, the place goes (very subtly) batshit crazy over the arrival of more interfaith cooperation.

I guide him back to Megan, where, according to plan, she says "Wait, don't I know you? Haven't I seen you at a mixer at Saint Bernadette?" Just in case she's so knocked out she can't completely pretend she's never met him before.

"Why, yes indeed, I have been to a mixer at Saint Bernadette," Joe says. You can see why he's in Model UN and not drama club.

Also, you can see he wants to grab Megan right there in the canned fruit aisle.

I whisper, "I am such an evil genius," and they grin like crazy.

Only then, when I go back to get a box of crunchy peanut butter jars to distribute in the outgoing grocery bags and I see them standing there, very close together, and he's stroking her hair, I start to cry and I can't stop.

I've held out through weeks of shrinkish concern from my dad regarding my rapidly plummeting mood, which apparently even my clever methods for covering up the sound of crying (running water, online concerts by Stanford's Japanese taiko drumming team, Beethoven's Ninth) can't disguise. I have faked cheer through a litany of shrink questions designed to see if I'm planning to off myself anytime soon:

Did you *enjoy* anything today?

Did you *sleep* though the whole night?

Are you by any chance harboring persistent thoughts about *hanging* yourself? (All right, slight exaggeration.)

But after he finds me trying to stop crying in the middle of the boxed pastas, I have to come up with a well-edited version of reality in parent-digestible form.

When I try, when I say in truncated sentences that Siobhan is with a guy I like and I don't know why it bothers me so much but it does, my dad is flabbergasted. You might think a rigorously trained psychoanalyst would have figured out that his daughter might someday like a boy, but apparently this is shocking news.

We are huddled in the car, in the parking lot, and I keep dabbing my eyes and blowing my nose, creating a huge wad of Kleenex.

I moan, "Dad?"

He looks angry, which isn't in the range of things I can even think about coping with.

He says, "Okay, boiling it down, Siobhan is keeping company with someone you like?"

And the way he says her name, you can tell that she's the one drawing his wrath. He turns the key and guns the car out of the parking lot.

"Nobody says *keeping company*." Sob, sob, sob.

My dad could just as well have a thought bubble over his head, with him throwing a party because he might have the rope he needs to drag Siobhan out of my life.

"I've noticed you've been a bit down lately," he says.

"I don't get to complain. I told her it was fine." We're zipping down Sunset, and I'm glad we're in the car and he has to watch the road.

"You told her it was fine because . . ."

"Do not, I mean it, do *not* go all shrinkish on me."

It's not that I don't know the because.

Because telling her how much I like him and how I've been hiding it from her since Day One seems like the ultimate humiliation. Because being her best friend is complicated, and because (other than this) she completely gets me.

He says, "It was the beginning of a sentence. Ems, you also told her that you like him. Doesn't some kind of girl code come into play here?"

"*Girl code?* Is that what your patients tell you?"

"Trying again. If you like him, and you told her that you like him, and it *wasn't* fine for her to go with him, why do you think you told her it *was* fine?"

"I don't know." At this point, I'm wishing that I hadn't told him anything, because he won't let go

He says, "Sure you do."

"No I don't."

"Yes, you do."

I just want to reach over and honk the horn, or pull the wheel out of his hands and steer into something loud and crunchy, and drown out the conversation.

I say, "I know you hate her. I know you want me to say this is the end of life as we know it, but that isn't it. She was drunk. He was drunk. She probably didn't even realize it was *him* the first time."

I don't expect him to respond to the "you hate her" part. Which he doesn't.

He says, "That paints a very attractive picture."

"Megan thinks I should wash my hands of both of them."

"Sensible girl, Megan. Who is this boy?" He says the word "boy" as if it's a federal crime to be one.

I try to think of how to reframe Dylan as the teddy-bearish kind of harmless boy who doesn't scare the shit out of your father, the sweet, respectful kind who wears a tie *without* the roach-clip tie tack, but I don't make much progress. So then I pick out the upstanding citizen bits. Music lover! Religious Convo! Really high GPA!

"I know what you're thinking," I say.

But it turns out, I don't.

"I'm thinking how unfortunate your best friend fell for him too."

A clear invitation to a complete losing-control moment.

"Unfortunate! It's a fucking disaster! I don't know how I'm going to live through it."

"Emma!"

"Sorry! A total disaster. A total unmitigated *freaking* disaster."

He says, "It was the living-through-it part that struck me."

"Stop it! I don't have suicidal thoughts and I sleep through the night and I enjoy eating cheesecake, all right? I am not clinically depressed or suicidal or insane. I just want to kill Siobhan, is all."

CHAPTER TWENTY-SIX

ALL I WANT TO DO IS HIDE, AND ALL ANYBODY ELSE wants to do is keep talking.

Megan calls to apologize. Repeatedly. "That was so insensitive of us!"

"No it wasn't."

She says, "Maybe you're right. Because it will totally cheer you up to see Prince Charming stick his hand down my blouse."

"Joe stuck his hand down your blouse?"

"Of course not," Megan says. "Your dad was there. Those two cute middle-school girls and a rabbi and fifteen women dying to talk to authentic Catholics were there."

"Like Los Angeles isn't crawling with large numbers of Catholics."

"That's not what I mean. You're so argumentative. I called to say sorry."

"I don't want to argue. I want to scream."

Megan says, "You just have to ride it out. How many people has she been with already this semester? How long do you think she can keep this up?"

I say, "Yeah, and I don't see how it can actually get worse."

"I'm sorry about the food bank. You're the genius who got us there together. I didn't mean to upset you like that."

I say, "I'm fine. Just don't tell me how cute and adorable Joe is for a while."

"Whatever you want."

Siobhan, meanwhile, calls to complain. "Does he really think I want to go listen to that bitch Mara and her goth girl band sing in a bowling alley in the Valley?"

I put the phone down and start hammering a pillow.

"What am I supposed to do?" she says. "He's sweet, but he's so demanding. And he doesn't want to go anywhere nice."

"Isn't Disney Hall nice?"

"Not nice like a nice building, nice like *fun*. Nice like cool. Nice like everyone there isn't fifty years old and they drove in from Anaheim. And do you know how long it takes to get out of there when you refuse to use a handicap placard? While listening to his incessant complaining."

"He's an incessant complainer?" I can't stop myself.

"Oh yeah," she says. "Although for someone who hates school and everyone at school so much, he spends a lot of time hanging out with juveniles in Lakers hats."

He goes to basketball games?

She says, "It's not like I want to break his heart. I just don't want to eat someplace three steps below Koo Koo Roo and dance someplace that smells funky. He's got ID. He could go anywhere, but nooooo."

"Don't break his heart!" I say, in a brief, stunning appearance of Emma the Good, popping up through the muck, sincere but with mud in her hair.

I am deathly afraid that somewhere down there, in the least admirable corner of myself, I want my best friend to break the heart of the boy of my dreams, whom I don't even know, apparently.

"What about my *bored* heart?" Siobhan says. "You should come out with us, Em! You'll see what I mean. I could tell him you're pining away for Jean-Luc and you need male attention or something. I'll tell him you won't eat at dives, so at least you won't have to pretend you like pita at some crap falafel place."

I like pita.

The moral compass intones, *Screw pita! Do you seriously want to drown in muck? Say no and walk away. Running would work, too.*

I spend so much time trying to formulate an answer that will satisfy both the (completely rational) compass and my (hot mess) desire to sit next to Dylan at a dinner on a date, even if it isn't, strictly speaking, *my* date, that soon it's too late to answer.

To make things even more excruciating, Dylan starts cornering me at school in his quest for inside info I don't have. He arches forward, his hand above my head, pressing against the locker above mine.

"Do you know what your friend has against Mara's band?"

"Not ever having heard them play, how would I know?" This conversation is at once innocuous and surreal. "Are they bad?"

"They're an acquired taste."

"Like olives?"

"Like tone-deaf Dixie Chicks risen from the grave."

"That could explain it."

And I'm thinking, Dylan Kahane, do you have no idea I like you? Is this some form of torture being meted out by the Universe?

And it goes on. There's no end to how useful I could be in deciphering the mysterious and ever-fascinating ways of Siobhan. He wants to know if she ever tried to give up smoking and why, given her professed love of Gershwin, she can't recognize *Rhapsody in Blue*.

I say, "Was it a culture quiz?" I feel so loyal, yet so sick to my stomach.

He says, "Oh. That's not how I meant it. Do I strike you as someone who gives culture quizzes?"

He stalks off without waiting for the answer, and I think, Yeah, Kahane, you do.

Then he finds me taking a book up on the hill. He's with Arif, but he peels off, and Arif keeps going.

"*Here's* a quiz," he says, following me up the path into the trees. All right, Dylan Kahane is following me into the trees. He probably wants to know Siobhan's favorite restaurant now that he's discerned she hates falafel. All I have to do is stay calm and not trip on a pinecone.

Before I can more fully develop the fantasy of me twisting my ankle on a pinecone and Dylan carrying me away (a scenario in which twisted ankles require a tourniquet, so Dylan has to tear off his white shirt and rip it into strips), he brushes against my arm. I am riveted to the absolute present, preoccupied with the issue of getting a grip.

I say, "Okay, are we moving on to Aaron Copland? I can do quizzes on anybody who ever composed a ballet. Hit me with Tchaikovsky."

Dylan says, "What does your Canadian boyfriend think of your dynamic duo?"

I say, "What?" Then I say, "Why?" Then I say, "He's French."

Dylan says, "That's not on the quiz."

I want to reach up and touch his face, he's standing so close to me, and I'm thinking, *What are you doing?* This is your so-called best friend's boyfriend and you should probably take a pass on this quiz and stop considering creative uses for his shirt involving shirt removal.

I am so not the moral-high-ground, compass-compliant person of this situation.

I say, "He's never met her."

There are very few true things to say about Jean-Luc, whose impending death is becoming more urgent by the second, but I've managed to find one.

Dylan nods. "Probably a wise move."

Then he pats me on the shoulder. He. Pats. Me. On. The. Shoulder. Perhaps I could audition to be mascot of his True

Romance with Siobhan, whom I'm pretty sure he hasn't been patting on the shoulder all that much.

What is this, anyway?

Is he just shooting the breeze, only after years of total indifference to people at school, he's really bad at it? Is he, even slightly conceivably, looking out for me, and if so, is this some weird paternalistic thing where he and Jean-Luc protect me from his bad, bad girlfriend, who happens to be my best friend, and if so, am I just a magnet for paternalistic weirdness?

My thoughts are in chaotic disarray.

I check my heart.

Still broken.

CHAPTER TWENTY-SEVEN

BY THE MIDDLE OF DECEMBER, I AM ACTUALLY looking forward to break. Which is saying a lot, in light of the dystopian bloodbath otherwise known as vacation in the Lazar family cabin at Lac des Sables, in a foresty part of Quebec, north of Montreal.

Usually, by Thanksgiving, I'm imagining scenarios in which Canada seals its borders, possibly as a result of a twenty-first-century plague. Which is what it would take to get me out of spending two weeks being reminded that I'm daughter of the messed-up, out-of-control, wrong-religion, wrong-French-accent woman who catapulted my father out of Quebec and into the wilds of the States. No wonder I can't do anything right—including speak French. Not that they speak French anymore; my aunt married a guy from Toronto. By the time I (not politely) tell my aunt Geneviève to put a sock in it, precipitating the annual name-calling jamboree, the damage is already done. My dad gets us out of there, roaring off to a dingy lodge on the other side of the lake. We always come home early. I always feel entirely beaten up. And we never talk about it.

This year is no different. By the time the red-eye we take to get out of Quebec begins its descent into L.A.—after I've spent six hours in near-silence sitting next to my dad, who feels the need to protect me from the plane's R-rated movie but not his sister's mastery of insults—my need to talk with someone who'll get it more than outweighs how upset with Siobhan I am.

"No way," she says when we're sitting in her Jacuzzi comparing vacations, and hers wins. Even though all Burton did in Barbados was sit in a chair and sleep, which made life in the villa less than amusing.

"Explain to me why you go back to that lake," she says, plying me with screwdrivers.

"Because my dad is a glutton for punishment?"

"You have to stop going there," she says. "They call you *names*. Is *shiksa* like the n-word?"

"Not really, not *that* bad, but from them, it isn't good. It's like, 'We're *us* and you're *you*, and you could run the food bank at Beth Torah and be Good Emma forever, but you'll *never* be good enough to be one of us, because your mother sucks and your dad doesn't even think you're good enough to take to temple.'"

"So it's like a religion thing?"

"It's like a my-dad-isn't-in-Montreal-anymore-and-it's-all-my-fault-for-existing-and-my-mom-was-Satan thing."

"You can tell they're stupid bitches, right?" she says, peering at me. "And you're trapped in a cabin with them *why*?"

"Because my dad is a glutton for punishment! All right?"

"He's the one *sleeping* through the punishment. You're the one he's *subjecting to* the punishment. Just say no."

I point out that we cut those assemblies.

"Not *all* of them." Siobhan shrugs. "We *could* do a pact where you yell at him. You know you want to."

I *do* want to yell at him. I've wanted to yell at him from the moment he chucked my duffel bag through the door of that cabin right up to now. I have to force myself not to slam around the house and yell at him when I get home from Siobhan's, and I don't do that well with the not-slamming.

"Ems," he says. "That's bordering on rude. Do you have something to say?"

I say, "Sorry," in a tone of voice that's bordering on even ruder. And then I can't stand it. I follow him into the kitchen.

"All right. I have something to say." He looks up, perfectly attentive. I wish he'd just keep glazing the chicken and not see my face, which is pretty far past just bordering on anything he generally tolerates. "I don't want to go to Lac des Sables again. Ever."

I stand there during the second of silence, waiting for the ground to open up and swallow me whole.

He says, "Are you sure?" He looks pained. If he says a word, one single word, about disappointment, I'm going to burst into flame and explode in a fiery ball.

"Completely sure. I've been completely sure for *years*."

"For years?"

"Please don't repeat what I say back to me, and don't ask me if I'm exaggerating, and don't ask me how I feel. I feel like, if you want to go, I'll stay with Megan. Because I'm not going."

He does not look back down at the chicken. "What I was going to say is, I wish you'd told me. I know Geneviève is difficult."

"She's a freaking *witch*! She *hates* me! Have you never heard what she *says* to me?"

He says, "That's enough. I've heard. It's done. We'll go to Saint Barts instead."

That's it?

I am having a surreal, my God, why-didn't-I-ask-for-a-pet-monkey-and-a-solid-gold-tiara moment.

He rests his head in his hands. He says, "I'm so sorry, Ems. I wish you could tell me these things before years go by."

I say, "But you *heard* her. You know what she calls me. You were *there*."

But apparently I have stumbled into no-talk territory. He goes back to glazing the chicken.

Me: I did it!!!!! I yelled at him.
Siobhan: Shit. R u walled in your room? Shd I call 911?
Me: Stop it. He was nice. Never going again. Going to St Barts next time!!!!!
Siobhan: No fucking way. You so owe me.
Me: I know.

The next day, in the parental-guilt-so-deep-that-the-kid-gets-the-pet-monkey vein, he gets me a car.

It's the oldest Volvo still running in Los Angeles County. It belonged to Mrs. Loman-from-the-food-bank's late husband, and it's been on blocks in her garage for fourteen years. It's canary yellow, a very poor color for sneaking around. The mechanic says it appears never to have been driven over forty miles an hour, or further than Ralphs market.

Mrs. Loman hugs me and tells me to drive it in good health.

My dad has me drive him home, to prove I can, and then back to pick up his car. We have a lengthy conversation during which I mostly say "Thank you" and he mostly says, Watch the road; no driving other kids for six months; no tickets or you're toast; it's a privilege; it's 3,000 pounds of surging metal; it's a canary-yellow instrument of death.

I cannot wait for him to get out of my car.

All I want is to drive all the way down Sunset to the beach, all the way up the coast to Point Dume. I want to drive up and down canyons with the windows open and the radio blasting. I want to lean toward the window so the wind messes up my hair, like a happy hound with windblown ears.

None of which is actually going to happen unless I somehow get a tool for jimmying odometers.

My dad sits in the passenger seat while I demonstrate how well I can drive back and forth to school. Twice.

On the first day of second semester, I get my car a parking pass. I put it on the windshield, and I have a half hour of pure joy.

Until I see Dylan and it starts again.

He nods at me with perfect neutrality, the kind that makes you wonder if you're supposed to say hello or just walk by.

I say, "Hey. How was Vail?"

I know how Vail was. Okay, it was like sticking pins in the back of my hand, but when I was in Lac des Sables texting Siobhan in Barbados, I sandwiched in asking how Dylan was. And she texted back: *Complain complain complain.*

He says, "Not great. Apparently I was so surly to Aiden, the prodigal son went back to college early."

"Wow. Surliness of biblical proportion. Impressive."

"Thank you. I aim to impress. Yours?"

"I filled in at the food bank at Beth Torah. I got battered by relatives I'm never going to see again in Canada. Oh! I got a car!"

"Welcome to L.A." he says "You've gotta have a car. Don't tell me. It's a fancy French car with bulletproof windows."

"It's a fourteen-year-old Volvo."

Dylan says, "That's very proletarian of you."

"I love that car. Don't dis my car."

No, no, no. I stop dead in the middle of reaching out to touch his arm. I can't be reaching out and touching his arm.

I say, "I forgot something in my car, sorry," and I walk away.

Siobhan says, "You wouldn't think so to look at him, but Kahane is clingy."

I don't want to know, but I so want to know.

"How clingy is he?"

Second day back.

The compass says, *This is getting creepy and your motives are highly suspect.*

Me: Shut up.

We're sitting in Siobhan's Jacuzzi, which has the advantage that if I feel my face turning colors and freezing into a fake, horrified smile, I can slide under the hundred-degree water, simmer, and hide.

"I don't know what shit his mommy did to him in Vail, but he wants to sit around and do homework together. He wants me to come with when he walks his dog. And it *smells*."

I say, "I think that's normal boyfriend-girlfriend stuff."

"You think I'm not *normal*? How would you know about normal boyfriend-girlfriend stuff, anyway? Let's think. Oh. From me."

I regroup quickly. "I think you're not *average*. Seriously. Do you?"

"Why's he even with me if he wants a dog-walking kind of girl? I mean, he totally wants me. So why is he all whining that I'm not walking his dog when I'm Skyping William, which is, news bulletin, a lot more interesting than walking a dog? Why is he all whining that I want to go to a party instead of listening to some sucky Bulgarian string quartet or some band that isn't even signed yet?"

"What string quartet?"

"Why would that possibly matter? Do I care? That's the point. I went to Disney Hall how many times last semester? It's a new year! Could we have some reciprocity and go to a decent club or some kind of a party?"

"I thought the whole essence of his being is, he doesn't do high school."

"It wouldn't have to be a high school party. It could be a college party. It could be any party that isn't in Mara's garage."

I'm really trying hard here. "Maybe you'd like Mara's garage."

"I was already friendly to Lia-freaking-Graham and Paulina at the Lakers game. I am not going to torture myself listening to some hideous girl band with people who look down on me and I couldn't care less about. Not happening."

Trying, trying, trying. "Maybe they're good."

"He says they're laughably horrible. He says you have to strain to keep a straight face. And he wants to play *chess*."

"But you like to play chess." Chess is the only activity Siobhan cops to liking with Burton. She likes creaming him.

"With a hundred-year-old man who's too infirm to get out of his chair without hanging onto the armrests. Why are you fighting me on everything I say? Stop criticizing me! There's nothing wrong with me!" She stretches out so that she's floating on the surface. "Maybe I'm just not the traditional girlfriend."

I give up. I slide under the water.

When I have to come up for air, she says, "He's just going to have to get used to it."

The jets turn off, and Siohan climbs out of the Jacuzzi to turn them back on. "And he wants to talk about you," she says.

I say, "Sib! The welcome-back assembly is ending in ten minutes. I can't miss Physics! Get dressed!"

Because if I said, "Huh?" or "What did he say?" or "Tell me every detail of this conversation immediately so I can I hang on every syllable, inflection, and pause," I would have to hide underwater so long I might drown.

CHAPTER TWENTY-EIGHT

I MANAGE TO AVOID DYLAN FOR THE REST OF THE week. Greatly facilitated by the fact that his New Year's resolution appears to be never to attend a full day of classes ever again.

Then there he is. Coming up from behind the gym, where he plays pickup only when there's no class, team, uniform, or coach involved.

(Siobhan says, "Really? He's standing on principle by not joining a team? *I'm* on a team. Do I seem 'overregimented, overcompetitive, and stupid,' to quote him? I mean, he's completely into me, so how is that even logical?")

He says, "Where's your friend?"

"Her name is Siobhan." I so don't want to sound this irritable. But I don't want to sound too chummy. I want to sound friendly yet distant. Charming yet unattainable. Irresistible yet . . . all right, just irresistible.

He says, "She says you don't think men and women can be friends."

"What?"

"Yeah, because Jean-Paul Sartre said so."

We're walking through the patio by the cafeteria, and he sits down at a table. He just sits and I'm standing there, clutching my books.

"Excuse me?"

"That men and women can't be friends. According to her, you're a big fan of Jean-Paul Sartre, and he says they can't."

I say, "I'm pretty sure that's from an old movie and not a French philosopher. Maybe she got confused."

No way she got confused. He wants to be friends with me and she used a fake quote from Jean-Paul Sartre to talk him out of it. Then I think, Stop jumping to conclusions. Who was completely there for me over vacation?

This has gone so far beyond too far, all I want is to grab him, for the buttons to pop off his white, untucked shirt. I want to stop imagining her grabbing his shirt, and I especially want to stop imagining him grabbing her.

Dylan is paying a great deal of attention to the french fries on the next table. He says, "Do you want some?"

I say, "Sure."

I think, This is Siobhan's boyfriend. You do not want to be having a slightly suggestive conversation about whether men and women can be friends with Siobhan's boyfriend, no matter what starkly stupid thing she told him you said.

But he wants to be *friends.* There's no biblical injunction that says you have to turn down *friendship.*

I think, Give it up, you don't want to be his friend—you know what you want from him, and it isn't just friendship.

I think, You are a crappy friend and a horrible best friend.

Dylan slides a box of fries across the table, with a fistful of ketchup packets.

I think, Say something.

"If Jean-Paul Sartre did say that, he was wrong," I manage. "Look around."

All over the patio, people who've been together since kindergarten, and are too brother-sister close to hook up, are crawling all over each other. Kimmy is in Max Lauder's lap, trying to steal his milkshake. "Unless that's Kimmy's way of seducing Max, Sartre was clueless. Anyway, I don't think it was him. Wasn't he friends with Simone de Beauvoir and any other intellectual girl he could get? We got the censored version of this in French, which, not amazingly, you missed."

He says, "Isn't she the one who thought men and women shouldn't inhabit the same apartment? She was hooking up with Sartre for decades across town."

Perfect, he knows everything there is to know about Sartre's private life, and I don't.

"So are you planning to marry a woman who lives across town?"

"I'm not the one who believes this crap. My parents have been together having the same fight for twenty-five years. You're the one into statutory rape with a boyfriend five thousand miles away."

"Did you just say that?"

He smacks himself on the head. "I'm an idiot. Sorry." He does, admittedly, look sorry, and kind of freaked-out. For him.

"You think that covers it, Kahane?" I'm trying to stay as light and casual as possible under the circumstances. Which is not all that light or casual.

"Douchy, inappropriate, none of my business?"

I don't have the slightest clue of what to say that wouldn't make this worse.

He says, "You want a fry?" He holds one out. To eat it, I'd have to take the death grip off my books. It hits me that I am not only conversing but—as my dad would say—outright carrying on with my best friend's boyfriend, who has now moved into the realm of the explicitly suggestive and possibly insulting.

Then I notice that Dylan is looking at me, expectant and kind of emotional for Dylan, and I think, What the hell?

I take a fry.

Then I take another fry.

Then I eat all his fries while he *smiles* at me, presumably because he's so relieved he hasn't unhinged my mental balance by commenting on my (nonexistent) sex life to the point that I can't eat fries. By the time I've finished off the container, it's clear that I've shed the last vestiges of Emma the Good the way a molting newt sheds skin, and if I don't stop myself, I'm going to do something seriously bad.

I sit there sipping his root beer in a state of complete moral collapse. It's hard to comprehend how a person could experience such extensive ethical decay, could ditch all scruples and the girl code, in the time it takes to polish off a box of fries.

I grab my books and run into the girls' bathroom. I sit in a locked stall through the rest of the period. When the bell rings at the end of the period, I am still in a bleak state of *huh???* So I sit there through half of French, where M. Durand is so overjoyed to see me, a person who reads the books in French, that he doesn't even care if I'm twenty minutes late.

CHAPTER TWENTY-NINE

AFTER SCHOOL, SIOBHAN IS WAITING FOR ME, PER-
fectly happy.

I feel nothing but dread.

She says, "What's wrong with you?"

We were right out in the open. Everyone could see us, so it's
not like I was sneaking around. We were just eating fries and
having a theoretical discussion about friendship. I was making
things up about French philosophers in an effort to sound as if I
knew what I was talking about. How bad could that be?

Bad.

Siobhan says, "Here's something to cheer you up. Kahane was
talking about you some more."

A wave of nausea radiates out from my sick stomach through
the rest of me.

I say, "Siobhan—"

She says, "I know. Pretty twisted. You think he's interested in some three-way action?"

"No. Way." I have no idea where this is going, but I'm completely sure I don't want it to go there.

"Oh yeah," she says, "he wanted to talk about if I thought we could all be friends. Now he wants to be *friends* with you." And by the way she says "friends," it's clear she means friends with three-way benefits.

"No!"

She snorts. "Of course *no*. Like that's going to happen?"

"I just don't think that's what he meant. At all."

"How would you know? Were you there? No. You weren't."

I go home and sit in the closet. I sit there and all I want is for the image of Dylan and Siobhan, together, in her room, to go away.

I want her to stop texting me every ten minutes to tell me how annoying he's getting and expecting me to commiserate.

> **Siobhan:** Party Friday?
> **Me:** Aren't you going out with the boyfriend?
> Or is this the fun threesome in which case no
> thank you.

It almost kills me to type this, but I have to say something.

> **Siobhan:** Dylan doesn't wanna party. So tough.
> **Me:** So do something else.

Siobhan: Like I really want to hang out downtown
and listen to Bach on xylophones when we could go
to this Marlborough girl's blowout? Girl school girls
gone wild.

Me: What about Dylan?

Siobhan: What about him? I don't need a
permission slip to have fun. Are u in? Your window
must be so sad and neglected.

Me: My window is fine.

Siobhan: Are u in?

Me: Fine.

How hard would it have been to go, "Nope, nuh-uh, not me,
won't go help you party without your damned boyfriend? We
both know what's going to happen." But it keeps getting harder
and harder to be even slightly direct with her about anything. As
if she's gone from being my perfect other to being my unpre-
dictable, high-strung Doberman—the kind you love and take on
walks, but bottom line, you don't want to be within lunging dis-
tance when it bares its teeth.

The moral compass quivers with indignation: *Does the lunging-
dog image not tell you something? Walk away!!!*

Me: I'm not walking out on my best friend. You can't just
walk out on people. She wants me with her, and I'm going with.

The pissed-off, unleashed moral compass croaks, *Feel guilty.
Feel very, very guilty. Feel guilty as hell.*

Me: Okay.

CHAPTER THIRTY

ABOUT THE MARLBOROUGH GIRL'S BLOWOUT.

I shoot out the window as if it were just another door to our house. I taxi from the Chateau Marmont, no longer worried that everyone my dad knows in L.A. has chosen this moment to cruise Sunset and is speed-dialing him.

I can hear her party from a block away.

Apparently, her parents are on their annual trip to Hong Kong and she thinks that they won't notice she's appropriated the entire contents of their liquor cabinet, and that the neighbors won't tell them how they called the cops at 2 a.m. because it was the most noise they'd heard in Hancock Park since last year's blowout.

It gets very bad very fast.

It starts with this guy, home from Penn for the weekend, who kisses the back of my neck when I'm standing by the keg, and I don't actually hate it. He's very drunk and he thinks my name is

Merilee, so clearly he thinks he's kissing the neck of an entirely different girl.

This is so not my idea of what's supposed to feel nice.

I go, "Dude, I'm not Merilee. You're really drunk."

He stumbles toward the tennis court where people are setting off firecrackers because, hey, that doesn't draw any unwanted attention in the middle of the night in Hancock Park. I think, I've come a long way since the hair-nuzzling, repulsive guy at Roy's. Now I have a neck-kissing cute guy from Penn who thinks he's kissing someone else, and I'm not all that unhappy about it. Check mark for me.

I fill a red cup with thin, sour beer.

Sib is trotting around the yard. She is flapping her arms like a kid wearing a cape for Halloween, only there's no cape.

She says, "I am so high!"

I say, "High on life, right?"

"Shut up, Em." She is looking around in the darkness. "Where the hell is Strick?"

"Why are we looking for Strick?"

"Strick is *cool*," Siobhan says. "Strick doesn't have a stick up his ass."

Someone staggers by, sloshing beer out of his cup.

"Oh, damn." Siobhan wipes beer off her leg, spins around, and heads toward a table dragged out of the house, the mahogany surface wrecked by liquid and cold bottles and a bowl of cracked ice with big silver tongs. There are half-full, giant-sized bags of corn chips and canned bean dip.

I stand there, drinking my drink.

When I look up, Siobhan is kissing the Penn guy. He has her leaned back as if they were dancing the tango, and he's extricating a rose from her teeth with his tongue, only there's no rose. Then he tilts her up and she leads him toward the house, toward the back door she came flying out of, flapping her arms.

I call, "Hey, Sib!"

He gnaws at her cheek as if he actually plans to eat her up.

I put my hand on her arm. "Sib, I have a headache and I think we should go home. Come on. I'll get a cab."

She says, "You want to go, go," shaking off my hand.

"Siobhan. Are you sure you want to go inside?"

"There's a freaking signed informed consent form in my bag, all right? I want to go inside."

"Come on. *Think* about it."

"Who are you, my slut-shaming sidekick? Go be Good Emma somewhere else." And they stumble off.

I walk up to Larchmont, thinking, Here's a real good choice, walk around in the dark in the middle of the night in a translucent blouse and slightly teetery knock-off Chanel shoes I can't run in.

I fall through the front door of the first open restaurant, a fancy Thai place. The bartender wants my ID. I say I'm waiting for my ride and there's a weird guy outside. Lie, lie, lie, though no doubt there are weird guys lurking all over outside if you look for them. I call a cab and sit there wishing I were picking up take-out and not in the ridiculous situation of wanting to cheat with my best friend's boyfriend while watching her cheat on him with some Penn guy who kissed my neck, too.

And when I sneak home and fall into bed and see my phone lit up and roll over, it's from Dylan and it says: *Sartre was wrong. They can and we should.*

I lie there staring at the message in the dark, and I feel, in equal measure, jubilation and happiness-defying guilt.

Me: Let's.

CHAPTER THIRTY-ONE

NATURALLY, CHEATING BEING A FASCINATING TOPIC that captivates the entire population of Latimer and possibly all high schools everywhere, Monday is a fascinating day; Sib and I weren't the only people we know to attend the blowout, while Dylan was off listening to Bach on some instrument other than what Bach intended with Mara and Sam and an empty seat.

Dylan is walking around his usual opaque self, only somewhat stormier around the edges. Arif looks straight through Siobhan in homeroom, so you have to figure he knows, and if he knows, then Dylan knows too.

"Fun," Kimmy says, plopping down next to me in English. "A shitstorm."

I don't even pretend not to know what she's talking about. I say, "Please. The guy was trying to chew *my* neck before I pushed him over. It didn't mean anything."

"Frank Gart!" she says. "He played soccer with my brother Kirby." This girl has a never-ending supply of older brothers. "He's in his fraternity at Penn. He should join Polysubstance Freaks Anonymous and call it a day."

I say, "He put the moves on me, too, and it's not like I was asking for it either."

I'm thinking, There, see how loyal I am? Here I am, lying my head off to defend Siobhan from what appear to be completely true rumors of cheating.

Kimmy says, "Get real. Like anyone thinks you cheat on Jean-Luc? But Frank Gart is Frank Gart, and she's her."

"Kimmy, I was there, it never happened."

"If I ever need an alibi, you're my girl," Kimmy says. "But no way were you there during the good parts."

Not knowing that the only good part of the entire night was me lying in bed with Dylan's text message.

We should.

At lunch, Siobhan is alone in the middle of the patio, and it's like she's Typhoid Mary.

She says, "I'm out of here."

"Right now?"

"Mental health day."

All right, I promised my dad, with no crossing of fingers, that I wasn't going to keep taking off whenever I felt like it. But I look around at all that empty space. I say, "Hey, I'm all for mental health. You want to sign out?"

She says, "I'm just leaving."

"Wait for me. I'm just going to the office to tell Miss Roy how sick I am."

When I get back, Siobhan hasn't moved from the center of the big empty space. We walk to the parking lot. She doesn't say a word. I drive us over to Doheny and roll down the long driveway, parking under a canopy of trees by the garage, climbing out onto the warm hood of the car.

She says, "What a hypocrite!"

I feel as if I just got sucker-punched. I have to remind myself that she can't read my text messages. "What?"

"Like he isn't still texting that Montana bitch?"

"A bitch in Montana?" I don't actually care. All I care about is that the text bitch isn't *me*.

"A bitch *named* Montana," she says. "Aiden's ex. The one Dylan broke up with just before Kimmy's party."

Some days, there's no news and if someone sends me a video of a dog that nods his head in time to jazz guitar, I watch it sixteen times. And other days, there's too much news for a person to take in without sawing open the top of her head.

I say, "Dylan just broke up with his brother's girlfriend?" (Which kind of makes the snide gossip fit together.)

"Before Kimmy's party. I just *said*. So he gets shitfaced, and he *deigns* to show up somewhere people are having fun—not that *he* has fun, except for being with me."

I keep nodding my head and trying to look sympathetic.

She says, "That's it. I'm *so* done with Dylan Kahane. I need somebody cooler and not boring. Wrong brother. Think about it:

Aiden plays soccer at Saint Andrews. Prince William and Kate went to Saint Andrews. Dylan walks his smelly dog around the block in 90210." She puts her index finger on her chin. "Hmmm. Hard choice."

I say, "Maybe meet the guy before you get engaged."

Siobhan says, "I did. I *told* you. Right after Nancy dragged me to L.A. last summer. The guy was everywhere. At Burton's club; he plays tennis. Buff guy who doesn't have some kind of a vendetta against team sports. Which, guess what, I play. Fuck Dylan."

I say, "Even Kimmy says Aiden's an asshole."

"Can he help it if he attracts psycho clingers? Dylan scoops up the wreckage. To prove he's *so* much better than Aiden. Never works out. So who's the asshole?"

She shakes out her hair behind her, closing her eyes and shuddering a little, as if she's trying to shed the last vestiges of Dylan.

"God," she says. "You should see yourself. Like you feel *sorry* for him. I never said he wasn't surprisingly nice. But you're the one who liked him. I never even would have touched him if you hadn't pointed him out. I need someone with more edge."

It is impossible even to keep nodding my head after she says this.

The thing sandwiched between how nice he is and how he doesn't have enough edge. The middle thing, the thing at the heart of everything.

She touched him because I pointed him out. Because I'm the one who liked him.

My desire to push her off the car is lost in my desire to go find Dylan.

But he finds me.

Because, in the realm where two negatives make a positive, where the girl code and common sense and what you expect is going to happen all float off past the horizon in the absence of gravity and reason, Siobhan has gift-wrapped him, tied him with a bow, and delivered him to me.

> **Dylan:** Hey Juliet.
>
> **Me:** Hey Kahane.
>
> **Me:** You ok?
>
> **Dylan:** I've been better
>
> **Me:** Sorry.
>
> **Dylan:** Not that I don't enjoy all the updates about where Gart's dick has been.
>
> **Dylan:** Shit
>
> **Dylan:** Do I sound surly?
>
> **Me:** You sound kind of unhinged.
>
> **Dylan:** Also stoned
>
> **Dylan:** So baked
>
> **Me:** If you're somewhere with a bed, you should lie down on it.

A half hour later, my phone vibrates: Arif.
No phones at dinner.

I say, "Dad, it's a kid from Physics. Would you mind?"

He says, "I bow to modern life."

I run into my bedroom, out of range of the aroma of the flaky pie crust, and cheese, and dishes cooked from scratch without one single compromise to modern life.

"Did D.K. just text you?" Arif says.

In the background, Dylan is shouting, "Hang up the phone!"

This sounds a lot like a rhetorical question, but I say, "Yup."

Arif sighs. "Did he make a fool of himself?'

"Sorta?"

In the background, Dylan again: "I'm still capable of hearing, asswipe."

Arif says, "Shut up, D.K."

I say, "Bye, maybe?"

There's some sort of a scuffle and Arif says, "Emma. Come back in twenty-four hours. What's the half-life of weed?"

I say, "Not covered in tenth-grade chemistry. And not a ton of personal experience."

"Or it could be permanent brain damage," Arif says.

It isn't brain damage.

Three hours later—when I'm lying on my bed, obsessing about what's going on—he's back.

> **Dylan:** So. Apparently I texted in a state of
> incoherence.

Me: Not that bad.

Dylan: Just so you know, not my m.o.

Me: Just so you know, I heard about you and the comp sci AP exam last yr. Baked and yet a 5.

Dylan: Just so you know, that was comp sci. I'm not planning to do that for physics.

Dylan: God my shirt smells like moldy weed

Me: I hear there's this thing called the washing machine.

Dylan: I heard Romeo is old news

What?

Dylan: Rolled up in a ball in Uganda nursing his wounds.

Me: ?

Dylan: For once good timing.

What?

Me: Rumors of Jean-Luc being eaten by leopards are greatly exaggerated.

Dylan: I heard you left him bleeding in a ditch

Me: Maybe?

Dylan: Cutting to the chase. We should talk. You like the Griddle right? Siobhan says you do.

Dylan: She says you grade men there.

She grades men there.

Me: I always enjoy a nice pancake after hacking
people up.
Dylan: So I heard. We should discuss your violent
proclivities. Now that we're in a mutual state of
broken up.
Dylan: Griddle at 7
Me: Junior assembly vs pancakes?
Dylan: Say pancakes

Siobhan: Do it.
Me: wtf?
Siobhan: Don't be a baby.
Me: What did you just do?
Siobhan: Whatever do u mean my pretty?
Me: Do you know what just happened?
Siobhan: He called me up to rant before his nanny
took the phone away. That's what.
Me: Not enlightening.
Siobhan: So I told him you and French face were
over. No reason one of us shouldn't get some use
out of him.
Me: You told him to take me to the Griddle! You
told him I went after Jean-Luc with a machete!
Does Kahane think I flew to Kampala and cut out
the guy's liver?

Siobhan: OK Jean-Luc is doing some kind of medical shit in Uganda. And I said if I wasn't geeky enough for him he should buy you pancakes.
Me: !!!!!!!!!!!!!!!!!!!!!!!!!
Siobhan: He's just a check mark not a row of exclamations.

It is difficult to hate her for long.
Griddle.
Tomorrow.
Seven.

Chapter Thirty-Two

IT'S 7:05 AND I'M WALKING TOWARD THE GRIDDLE. My car is parked in the lot behind Rite Aid on Fairfax, and I'm walking along, sucking on Tic Tacs. I am counting the squares in the sidewalk between the corner and the restaurant. I am attempting to calm down.

Dylan is sitting at an outside table, facing west. I'm walking toward him from behind. I have half a block to change my mind as long as he doesn't turn around.

Although my mind has been made up since that first minimalist semi-smile.

I get to the table, and I lean down to him because apparently I'm incapable of seeing him without starting a slow descent into his arms. He turns to me, resting his hands on my shoulders. I smell his shampoo. Almonds.

"You came," he says.

"You wanted me to, right?" In the spirit of not crawling into his lap and moaning *Take me!* which I'm pretty sure boys don't find that appealing.

He says, "Friends?"

There is something open-ended and inviting there, in that long, single syllable that suggests *maybe* something more than friends. And I'm thinking, take it. Even if he was your best friend's boyfriend five minutes ago; even if she tossed him to you four minutes ago; even if he doesn't know the first true thing about you: Take it.

I say, "Of course, friends."

"Apologies for yesterday. Making fun of your breakup with that Canadian guy? F in commiseration."

I say, "French," completely without thinking. As if my not-thinking default position now is lying. And I think, He is being so nice, he is comforting me for something that never happened. This is bad.

"You're not heading off to drink poison, are you, Jules?"

I say, "I'm fine! It was nothing." God, he has no idea how much nothing. "Listen, Dylan—"

A waiter drops a pot of coffee on the table, takes our order, and disappears into the restaurant.

I say, "I'm sorry. This is nine ways complicated. You and Siobhan and the whole thing about the French guy—"

And I swear, I am absolutely on the verge of explaining that Jean-Luc never existed. I am sipping my coffee and trying to pull sentences out of the air that are true that I can nevertheless bear to say out loud to him, when he reaches across the table, and he puts his index finger to my lips, and he says, "I don't need explanations. I've got a handle on it. I know you don't ever fool around except when Gart fell in your hair—"

"I did not fool around with Gart!"

He says, "I know. And I know you don't like high school guys and I know your dad has warden-like tendencies."

"Siobhan told you all that?"

"You overlook my powers of observation. Emma. I've been borrowing your notes and staring at you all year, and you never once gave a sign that you were interested. Everybody knows you go for older guys. And you don't flirt. Not even close."

"Maybe I just didn't flirt with *you*. Given that you were with my *best friend*."

"No. I'd know. Latimer's a cesspool of gossip. So unless you're secretly getting it on with Siobhan, we should probably do this."

"Don't go casting aspersions on Siobhan! Siobhan was your girlfriend until yesterday! If not for her, we wouldn't be *together*!"

"She was not my girlfriend yesterday. My new thing is, girls who go down on other guys and lie to me about it aren't my girlfriend."

"Don't tell me this!"

"I'm done with the bullshit," Dylan says. "No one who's seeing someone else. Or in love with someone else. Or engaged to someone else. No one who's touched my brother, is with my brother, or wants to be with my brother. Just so that's clear."

I say, "Completely clear."

He tilts his head. He looks at me with the trademark intensity.

He leans forward, his fingers hooked over the edge of the table. He says, "So. We're together?"

I can hardly hold my voice together. I can hardly hold myself together.

I say, "And by 'together,' you mean—"

Dylan shakes his head slowly. "Come on, Seed."

I say, "Yes."

The boy of my dreams and my make-believe self.

Dylan is grinning his punch-drunk, plastered-in-London face, which I've only ever seen before on Facebook. At least I think he was plastered in London. Maybe he had just eaten a delicious plate of pancakes.

I say, because I have to know, "You wanted me to flirt with you?"

Dylan looks at me sideways over his largely devoured stack of red velvets. "Is this a trick question?"

"No."

"Yeah. Even when you were with the *French* guy and I was busy: yes."

The compass screeches, *Are you stupid AND morally impaired? Stop pledging undying devotion and tell him!*

But my whole body is vibrating, and this demands attention.

"But that time in the caf. Your hands . . ."

His hands are in my hair.

"Like this?"

Exactly like that.

I say, "Hold still." I wipe a drop of syrup off his cheek with a fresh napkin.

I am staring at his lips. He walks around the table and sits next to me, and I know what's about to happen. I lean toward him and this time, he kisses me. At first, only our lips, just barely, just brushing, and then he is out of the chair, he's pulling me to my feet, his hand is at the back of my head, and something that must be the tip of his tongue would seem to have caught fire.

First kiss with Dylan, right on the sidewalk, with traffic whizzing by on Sunset. It goes on and on, but I don't think that there actually exists enough on and on in the world to suit me.

Dylan says, "So we're good?"

I am completely I don't even know what.

I have to say something: Hello? Thank you? Let's do that constantly forever?

I am undone, done and undone, stripped of resolve and magnetically bent in the direction of Dylan Kahane's lips.

CHAPTER THIRTY-THREE

AT LUNCH, SIOBHAN SLIDES IN NEXT TO ME AT A table in the corner of the patio. "You look unusually smiley, missy."

I hold my head down and try not to look too smiley. "It's on. I told you."

She rubs her hands together over her chef's salad. "Checkmark city. You should be thanking me. Do you want the list? I crossed out LSD."

"No." She looks disappointed. I am trying to keep my voice down and my heart beating at a normal rate. "I think I can take it from here."

"Just get in and out," she says. "He's not as cool as you think."

Siobhan giveth and Siobhan taketh away.

"Weren't you the one who said he was surprisingly nice?"

She frowns and starts stabbing cherry tomatoes, watching their mashed interiors gush out.

"You should listen to me," she says. "He's all, *I'm Kahane and I'm too cool for school*, but he's not. I don't want you getting messed up."

"I thought the whole idea was for me to get a little bit messed up."

Siobhan laughs, and I think, Go ahead. But I've been waiting for this day since I got here. There's too much momentum to stop.

And then there's my ear and my lips and the unhinged, sensation-ridden pit of my stomach.

Siobhan is snapping her fingers in my face. "Are you even paying attention?"

I say, "And listen, Jean-Luc, he can't keep showing up all over."

"Don't look at me," Siobhan says. "Kimmy was all freaked out that he didn't come see you at Christmas, *Yak-yak, I'm Kimmy, why, tell me why, how come, where is he, boo-hoo, why?* What was I supposed to do?"

"He needs to disappear. Like now."

Siobhan says, "What's the big deal? It's not like he's real."

After dinner, Dylan and I spend two and a half hours Skyping.

I say, "How was your day at the office, dear?"

He says, "Who knows? I was unusually distracted."

"I thought that was your general state of being."

Dylan says, "My goal at that place is to achieve distraction. Or get kicked out, but not by doing anything so gruesome that I don't get into college. You made the achievement of distraction easier than usual."

"You're welcome."

Periodically, my dad pops his head in at the door and I yelp, "Working on my physics lab! Group session!"

Dylan, his Latimer tie undone and hanging down in two bands of striped navy-and-maroon silk on either side of his neck, looks amused. His hair falling over his forehead, his cuffs unbuttoned and pushed halfway up his forearms, his shirt sliding around over his torso. Where, dear Lord, there is a tattoo—which my dad is *not* going to believe is an unusual blue-black birthmark in the shape of Chinese calligraphy on one side of my supposed physics lab partner's chest.

He says, "Does your dad always look in on you every few minutes or am I a new guy to keep away from you?"

I say, "You might have to button your shirt really fast."

Dylan does a twitch-at-the-left-corner-of-the-mouth smile facsimile. "My father hasn't stuck his head into my room that many times since I was six."

"Don't get too jealous. He's protective on steroids."

He says, "I am jealous." He buttons up his shirt.

"And he's not going to be aware of any guy. In the interest of me ever leaving my house again."

"This is so medieval, Jules!"

"That's me, bringing medieval times to the Sunset Strip."

"What if I *were* your physics lab partner?" he says. "Could you get in your car and come over?"

I say, "You have a very limited understanding of the concept of medieval. You're male and it's not broad daylight."

"Would it be broad enough daylight Friday after school?"

"The old going-to-the-Beverly-Hills-Library-when-I'm-really-someplace-else gambit."

"You have this down to a fine art," he says.

"I have to."

"So. I'm the beneficiary of all your cloak-and-dagger with the French guy? I should thank him."

He makes a face. He says, "Don't look at me like that." He hold his hands up to the screen. "Not trying to upset you. Very poor Skype strategy. But how do I get you out of your cell?"

Tell him, tell him, tell him.

I say, "I'll think of something."

Chapter Thirty-Four

MAYBE I'M THE ONLY PERSON ON EARTH NEVER TO have picked up on this, but school with a boyfriend is completely different from school without one. It takes me a couple of days to realize this isn't just the novelty effect. Dylan materializes next to me all the time. If I see him across the quad, there's an obvious invitation to get over there.

It's quite nice.

Even if people are shooting me odd and judgmental glances.

Siobhan says, "Don't look now, Dorothy, but there's a scarecrow and a tin man looking for you. It's like you're about to start singing with Toto." She doesn't say this as if it's a desirable state of being, either.

"Excuse me, but whose idea was this, anyway?"

It's as if I've developed amnesia where she's concerned, where betrayal, being shot through the heart, and fury used to be. Now that I'm with him, all is forgiven. Almost.

"Can't you just do it and get it over with? You're so cutesy, it's embarrassing."

"It's been *two* days. This is destined to be longer than a two-day relationship."

"It's a *relationship*?" Her head jerks back in a dramatic rendition of annoyance. "What about 'quick in and out' sounds like a relationship?"

"Unfair! I put up with you and how many guys?"

"At least nobody was lapsing into sugar shock because I was skipping around singing. Kahane, too. He was bad enough before. This is pathetic."

I put my hand on her shoulder, but she pushes it away. I try to think of what I can say that will get her off this particular tangent and calmed down, and I say, "Sib, if I could do this stuff quickly, we wouldn't need a list."

Which has so little to do with why I'm with him, it's ridiculous.

She says, "Could you at least show some restraint? You are way out of character."

Next in line, we have Kimmy.

I am reading on the terrace by the publications suite when Kimmy comes up behind me, reeking ever so slightly of horse.

I say, "Hey, Kim, you here for newspaper?" Kimmy is the features editor, resulting in a column written from the perspective of Loogie, called "Horsing Around." Kind of like *Gossip Girl* meets *Mr. Ed*, which for people whose dads don't force them to watch classic TV with talking horses because classic TV is supposedly more wholesome than shows from, say, the twenty-first century, will make no sense. So if *Mr. Ed* means nothing to you, consider yourself lucky.

Kimmy, of course, knows who Mr. Ed is, and also National Velvet, My Friend Flicka, Misty of Chincoteague, and the Water Horse.

Kimmy says, "O-kay. You and Dylan?"

I say, "Uh," which sort of gives it away.

"Oh. My. God." Kimmy, sweaty in her jodhpurs and a dirt-streaked polo shirt, sniffs the air and frowns, I assume due to the fact that she needs a shower and not because of the me-and-Dylan thing. "Twenty-four-hour turnaround, why don't you?"

This is the exact moment it occurs to me that this might not look good to people besides Siobhan. People who are somewhat reasonable.

And that beyond not looking good, it might not *be* good.

That twenty-four-hour turnaround with your best friend's boyfriend might look, be, and feel weird because it *is* weird.

Kimmy looks devastated. "Okay, it's none of my business and you know I have *god*awful taste in men, but isn't your other boyfriend in love with you? Think about the camellias. And the UN is heroic. It's not like he's in Afghanistan on vacation."

Afghanistan?

"Kimmy, oh God, I just remembered something."

Such as I might look like, or possibly *be*, a girl code violator of epic proportion. And that I need to go smack Siobhan.

She is on the hill, smoking in the rocks.

"Why is Jean-Luc in Afghanistan? First you stuck him in

Africa as some kind of a joke. Well, ha-ha, five minutes later, he's in Afghanistan! And what's with the camellias?"

Siobhan says, calmly and slowly, as if talking to a child, "He's on a UN mission in the Khyber Pass. You should be proud. And he's been sending you camellias every Tuesday since Christmas."

I say, "I'm not proud because he's not *real*."

She rolls her eyes.

"Why are you doing this?" I am determined not to raise my voice, not to shout or grab her. "What am I supposed to say to Dylan?"

"I know!" she says. "Why don't you tell him you made Jean-Luc up? Now that you have a *relationship*."

"Don't you think I know I have to tell him? But if Jean-Luc becomes prime minister of France over the weekend, it's going to make it a lot harder."

"Get real. You'd *better not* tell him. I'm not going down over this. Just shut your mouth and hurry it up. He looks obsessed."

"You told him I was in mad love with him! What did you think was going to happen?"

Siobhan shakes her head in a pantomime of disbelief and bug-eyed shock. "You were just supposed to make a check mark with him. I was done with him, and he was the only guy in North America you were willing to make check marks with."

"That didn't tell you something?"

It comes out with an edge, the sharp kind of edge that can cut right through your flesh, your friendship, to the breach in your friendship that left you with a somewhat gutted heart.

"Oh shit," Siobhan says.

At first I think, *no* way, not going there. But I've already said it, I can't take it back. "Yeah, it was kind of a problem."

"So the whole time I was hooking up with him, you were hating on me and you didn't *tell* me?"

"That's putting it in the extreme."

Sort of.

"You have murky depths," she says.

But I'm thinking, No, it's more on the clear and predictable, follow-the-arrows-to-the-exit side. That when your best friend is locked in romantic embrace with the man of your dreams, you might reconsider naming your firstborn child after her.

"Did widdle Megan know you hated me?" she asks in a baby voice, pursed lips and poison. "Does she hate me, too? I bet your daddy hated me."

"Nobody hated you."

"So nooooobody knew you were upset?"

"He's a freaking psychiatrist. The man can tell when people are upset."

"He has no idea when you're upset! I couldn't tell and I know you way better than he does." Her voice is pressured and insistent. "I know you better than anyone, right?"

I say, "Of course you do."

All I know is that I have to say it or she'll lose it, and I have to fix it. I don't even know if it's true or false or all of the above.

I don't seem to have fixed it all that well, either. Because when Dylan walks by, looking at me quizzically when he sees I'm standing with her, even though he's seen me standing with her like this every day since my first day at Latimer, she pushes me toward him, yelling, "Hey, lovebird bitches, why don't you go share some freaking worms?"

I stumble toward him and he catches me in flight.

Dylan says, "Jesus, Seed, what's wrong with *her*?"

I look down, trying to figure out how to summarize the parts of this that don't include Jean-Luc. Or how much I liked Dylan from way before I knew him well enough to like him that much, and how it killed me that he was with Siobhan. And how Siobhan is massively ticked off that I'm in girlfriend mode and not emotion-free checkmark collection mode.

There's not a lot left over to tell him.

But when I look up again, he's smiling at me. And without comment, I watch Siobhan and all that drama slouch away until she's out of sight.

He says, "You going to History?"

"Can you live without my brilliant notes?"

"Your OCD notes? Maybe this once." We are walking toward the path leading onto the hill. It is sunny, cold and clear, and you can smell the pine and eucalyptus from the edge of the quad. "Do you have gym shoes?"

Which seems like an odd question, as I kind of thought we were headed onto the hill to make out, as opposed to shooting hoops. But the fact is, I do. In the trunk of my car, with my earthquake preparedness kit full of packets of water-purifying chemicals, nutrition bars, and waterproof matches.

I say, "I'm prepared for everything."

Everything involves driving west on Sunset and into a neighborhood where houses are far apart and hidden in foliage. At the end of a cul-de-sac, a hiking trail leads back into the hills, a dirt path that widens and narrows through canyons of wild grass and the occasional jolt of wildflowers.

Fifteen minutes up, there's a clearing with some metal picnic tables and a view straight across to the ocean, turning slate blue as the afternoon darkens.

He says, "Hike much?"

"Franklin Canyon. Hollywood sign. Nothing major."

We're sitting on the picnic table closest to the edge, alone except for the occasional hiker with dog, and a woman with a cat on a leash that pauses, snarls at us, and continues up the hill.

"You've never been here?"

"Nuh-uh."

"Major make-out spot."

"If you don't mind attack cats."

He says, "After dark, very few attack cats."

"I take it you've been here after dark. Is this an invitation to ask questions, or are you just planning to torture me with curiosity?"

"It was a different kind of invitation. But ask. Unlike some people, I'm an open book."

"You are so not an open book!"

He says, "Ask."

"All right, rumor has it that you were running around town with some elderly college girl."

Dylan looks surprised, and then impenetrable.

"You didn't just say that to Lia Graham to look cool, right?" This is supposed to come out jokey, but it doesn't. I regret it as soon as it's out of my mouth.

"I never tell anybody anything so I'll look cool. Again, that would be my brother. Face next to the word 'liar' in Wikipedia." He stretches himself out on the picnic table. "Not me, I don't fuck with people."

"Sorry."

"Your lack of gossip is shocking."

More like no one ever tells me anything.

"I'm shockingly virtuous that way. You know, *lashon hara*. This Jewish thing with not gossiping. My dad is way into it; precludes most forms of interesting conversation."

Dylan says, "I know what *lashon hara* is."

Complete brain freeze. Of course he knows what it is, he reps Judaism at Religious Convo. Probably his idea in coming to a major make-out spot wasn't to have a discussion of my dad's completely cherry-picked precepts of religion.

Dylan says, "So. I could be making up a torrid affair with an older woman and you wouldn't know the difference?"

Yikes.

"Were you having a torrid affair? If only I gossiped continually."

Dylan blinks, which would appear to be his version of an eye-roll. "I hate to disillusion you, but guys in high school rarely get to have torrid affairs with older women."

"Have you met Nancy?"

He closes his eyes. "Special case."

"So what *have* you been doing while failing to meet your obligation to socialize at Latimer?"

"Aren't you the girl who's been with some bi-Continental guy that sends her French perfume and who probably doesn't know where to find junior assembly?"

What French perfume?

"Have you ever noticed I was wearing French perfume?"

Dylan says. "Okay. When Aiden was a senior, he went out with this girl, Montana Gibson. She wrote a poem about him in *Latimer Rambles* that compared him to God. Roughly. Lasted all year. Then he left without saying good-bye."

"Literally?"

"She went to Jackson Hole with her family in July. When she got back, *Rambles* was in the trash and Aiden was in Scotland. She went nuts. Came over and screamed at my mom. But this is Aiden we're talking about. If Montana took his name in vain, no wonder he blocked her number."

"He just left for college? He didn't actually break up?"

"Moot point. Even when he's with someone, he's not with them. They can be at the same party, the girl is waiting for him to get back with her drink, and he's locked in the bathroom with some whore who likes muscles."

He peers at me. "Oh. Sorry." He slaps his face. It's not much of a slap. "I know. Don't call women whores. Shit. Did I just finish us off?"

All right, so he's not allowed to say the word "whore" ever

again. But we are so not finished off. Because if it were dark, and if the hikers going up the hill weren't going to come down eventually, and if I didn't have to get back to school, what would I do? There are dark waves of urgency. Are un-whorish girls even supposed to feel like this? God knows, I'm not supposed to feel this or anything in the same general classification as this. I'm supposed to be up for a lovely picnic on the banks of the Thames wearing a flowered sundress from 1956, *not* for naked grappling in the hot, lush jungle where the Amazon veers off into rain forest.

Or on hiking trails fifteen minutes off a cul-de-sac near the 405 Freeway.

Not *this*.

Dylan is saying, "Yeah. I hung out with Montana a lot after that. Last year and this fall."

I am trying to sound civilized, cool, and moderately under control. "Were you, like, her boyfriend? How old is she?"

"I was the Aiden substitute. Aiden was not happy. He comes home from Scotland for summer, he's all over her. Then he breaks up with her for the second time in case the first time wasn't bad enough. Montana starts hooking up with this other guy. And me."

"Wow."

"Aiden's not a very nice guy. I was the revenge fuck. Not that I'm complaining. But it would have been considerate of her to tell me."

"I'm no doubt going to be struck by lightning for gossiping like this, but your brother is a jerk."

Dylan says, "Girls seem to like it."

"Explains where your aversion to bullshit comes from."

"Explains why I like being with someone *honest*, with no interest in running off with my brother. You have no interest in running off with my brother, I assume?"

I put my arm around him. "Let's see. He lives in Scotland, so I could never actually see him, and he's not a very nice guy. Bring it on. I'm hot for one of those."

"I thought you *had* one of those," Dylan says.

Holy shit.

I have officially lied to my dad about everything; to my best friend about how much I didn't want her boyfriend; to everyone at Latimer about my nonexistent boyfriend; and now to this guy—who apart from calling women whores is kind of perfect, and who (hint) likes honest girls—about practically everything.

I say, "As long as you brought it up—"

He sits up. He raises his hand. He says, "I'm done hearing about bad absentee boyfriends."

"But that's not what it's about!"

He says, "That's never what it's about."

He pulls me back down with him to the surface of the picnic table. My cheek seems to be resting on the remnants of potato chips or some other crunchy thing I can't identify. He moves his hand so it's under my face, and he tilts my face toward his. I don't care if the snarling cat sees me.

I kiss him for a very long time.

He says, "Friday."

Oh yeah.

Chapter Thirty-Five

Siobhan: Did u fall off the planet?

Siobhan: I texted like five hours ago. Are you MIA?

Siobhan: Don't be like that

Me: Like what? Like the person you shoved?

Siobhan: Boo hoo. Tough love. U need to speed it up.

Siobhan: Where were you?

Siobhan: Oh. Do Emma and the boy toy have a widdle secret?

Me: Shut up. We were hiking.

Siobhan: Well don't. You're not in this to hike. Quick in and out. Check. Just hurry up and get there.

Siobhan: Before he finds some trivial thing he doesn't like about you and you're toast.

Me: I'm trying to tell him about Jean-Luc first. Takes time.

Siobhan: I TOLD U NOT TO! You'll be fucked and I'LL be fucked.

Siobhan: U can screw up your life all u want but u can't mess me up! I'm not going down w yr boat! Like I want the horse bitches to know I made you up? I don't think so.

Me: This is between me and him. It's not even about you.

Siobhan: It's about me and you. And if you're thinking about fucking me over don't.

CHAPTER THIRTY-SIX

FRIDAY, EVERY TIME I'M NEAR SIOBHAN, SHE WALKS away.

Friday, Dylan attends an unusually high number of classes and keeps looking over at me (which I know because I keep turning around to look at him, and there he is with this laser gaze trained on me).

In English, he says, "So. Have you thought of something? Do you have a sudden need to pretend you're at the library?"

So after school, when I am supposedly lost in the stacks at the BHPL, I follow his car to his house, a giant pseudo–country mansion with ivy growing all over it. He is waiting in the driveway, and he takes my arm and nods toward a small shingled building behind an oleander hedge.

"Guesthouse," he says. "I live in there."

I'm good with this for about thirty seconds. The coolness of the cottage is immediately apparent. Then, as I walk toward it, every terrifying thing I've ever been warned boys do to girls blows through my mind in a gale-force hurricane of paranoia. Until the guesthouse, which is sweet and has blue-painted French doors and shingles and a welcome mat, starts looking like a human-trafficking dungeon for careless girls.

Dylan says, "What's wrong?"

Panic is what's wrong. Well-indoctrinated, no-basis-in-reality fear of the known. Because I know him. And it's the middle of the afternoon. And it's the flats of Beverly Hills.

Dylan says, "Emma? Hey. Seed. You want to walk the dog?"

The dog is a large, unclipped Airedale named Lulu, rolling around on the lawn beyond the guesthouse, chewing a high-top sneaker. She has to be chased because she thinks that Dylan wants the shoe. He looks so goofy loping around the backyard, grabbing for her collar, that I come fairly close to calming down.

Then, once he has the leash on her, she lies down and barks at him, and has to be dragged toward the driveway.

He says, "So. What was that?"

"It was really nothing. Please."

He says, "Did I do something?"

"No, totally not."

"Then what?"

"Let's just walk, okay, please? Take a walk. Walk."

But Lulu doesn't get the concept of a walk. She doesn't get that she's supposed to travel in a straight line, that it isn't good to sit while crossing the street, and that walking up to a car with people getting out of it and peeing against the tire is frowned upon. Dylan pauses for her to sniff grass and other dogs. Lulu is very popular with other dogs.

I say, "How long does it take you to go around the block?"

"Hours." I really wish he'd grin or something, because I can't read how much I freaked him out. "If it gets too bad, I carry her home."

We are standing on the corner while Lulu digs a hole on what would be the front lawn of a house that is being torn down and has gone to weeds and dirt.

I say, "Have you always lived here? It's beautiful."

He says, "My dad grew up in this house. Then he stuck my grandma in a nursing home and took it over."

He is absolutely blank. No emotion at all.

I wait for him to say something else, to enlighten me about what's going on between him and his dad, but nothing happens.

"And you moved here from Montreal?" he says. "You don't seem like an L.A. type."

"I don't seem cool enough to walk around your block?"

"You don't seem nasty enough to go to the same school as Chelsea, okay?"

"Okay." I give him the extremely expurgated version of my life, which covers moving a lot, but not much else.

He says, "Siobhan said something about your mom?"

"Jesus! Is there anything about me that she didn't tell you?"

He says, "I asked. I wanted to know."

He holds my hand. It would be a sweet, romantic moment if Lulu weren't pooping over as wide an expanse of front yard as the leash will allow, and also howling, apparently for fun.

Lulu is now wriggling in the dirt on her back, squealing and barking. I say, "We have English bulls next door that play dead when you pretend to shoot them."

"Cool. Do they have an agent?" He sounds pissed off and not as if he's kidding. Then he slaps his cheek. "That was surly, right? Shit. I probably shouldn't maul you if you criticize my dog."

"Who says you're surly?"

Dylan shakes his head. "My father and I have a limited set of repeating conversations."

"That sucks."

He has nothing more to say on this subject. I retreat.

He says, "We have radically different family lives. I can go for days without seeing my parents, let alone being told what I can't do."

"Literally for days?"

"No. But I probably could if I tried."

"That's sad."

He says, "You wouldn't think so if you knew them. Emma, did I do something to scare you before?"

We are leaning against palm trees along the curb while Lulu eats grass that's growing through cracks in the sidewalk. All this time of wanting to hold him, wanting to grab him when I couldn't, and now here we are, on this quiet street with the occasional decorous dog jogging by with a power-walking human, and I actually could, but I can't.

I hear Siobhan's voice going, *You know you want to. Your turn: Make a move.*

I know I want to.

I walk from my palm tree to his palm tree; he is discernibly pleased. I reach for him, and he pulls me in, and we disgrace the Latimer uniform some more by engaging in more public kissing until, when my hands are in the small of his back, under the untucked tail of his shirt, Lulu's howling gets so loud we have to take her home.

He leans back against the blue French doors, the doorknob in his hand.

He says, "Coming in?" Very carefully. There's a chance that he's figured it out.

I say, "I have to be home for dinner. On time."

He says, "Saved by the bell."

I spend the weekend in a state of crazed longing.

I don't go out the window to Malibu on Saturday with Siobhan. In a flat voice, she says, "You wouldn't. Have fun taking sample SATs and reverting to type."

I don't say "What's that supposed to mean?" because I already know.

Restocking the shelves at the food bank on Sunday, Megan says, "Are you sure being with this guy is good for you? You're acting kind of bizarre."

"Like you didn't act bizarre when Joe first showed up here?"

"That's not a fair comparison. You have lunch with a table full of football players dripping testosterone on their burgers. I have lunch with Sister Mary Eunice. It isn't the same."

At the food bank, I am actually dropping things, even though, apart from being consigned to PE (as opposed to actual) ballet, I'm not generally known for klutziness. After I land a twelve-pound bag of rice on his foot, Joe tactfully suggests that I go log things in, or put food into grocery bags, or get a drink of water.

Megan leads me out into the parking lot. She says, "Well?"

"Well, nothing. We're walking around Latimer staring at each other and nothing. We kiss all the time."

"That counts."

Except I want to jump him all the time.

Megan leans against the hood of Rabbi Pam's car. She says, "You don't have to do anything you're not ready to do."

Oh God, I'm getting romantic advice from Megan. "Is this where you tell me where babies come from?"

She says, "You're tripping over things."

"Tell me something new. Now I have to start working on getting to his house so I can trip over things there. Like at night. I thought Siobhan would cover, but she's acting weird."

"Siobhan acting weird is something new? You are way too forgiving." Megan sighs. "Have you considered telling your dad that you *like* like this guy and seeing where it goes?"

"Really?"

"All right, I realize that I'm living in a similarly tangled web, but what a tangled web we weave—"

"It's getting so I can't keep it all straight."

"At least you're done with Jean-Luc."

"I wish! Dylan is obsessed with him, and half the people at

school are pissed off that I broke his heart. People are looking at me funny."

"Maybe that's because you're dropping things."

Or maybe it's because they've never seen me acting like such a love slob, faux French boyfriend notwithstanding.

CHAPTER THIRTY-SEVEN

IN A SHAMELESS ATTEMPT TO MAKE UP FOR ALL MY weirdness and confusion, I bring Dylan a slab of Sunday night's dense flourless chocolate cake on Monday morning. He says, "You might not be that bad a seed."

There's nothing like the combination of extreme lust and constant guilt to make a girl unusually nice to her boyfriend.

I say, "You have no idea."

Chelsea, who naturally pops up at the exact moment I'm feeding him cake, says, "Interesting. Disgusting, but *interesting*."

Dylan looks her up and down. He says, "Disgusting and uninteresting."

She flounces away.

In English, he doodles me in the notebook he doesn't take notes in. Large enough to be visible to Ms. Erskine, standing, beady-eyed, in front of the room, making William Shakespeare less intriguing than an ad for auto parts. Who says, "Mr. Kahane, we all know Ms. Lazar has a lovely profile, but we're focused on *Henry the Fifth* if you'd care to join us."

Dylan looks up, recites the "Once more unto the breach, dear friends, once more" speech, and looks back down to my penciled profile.

It is one of the weirdest, most humiliating, most satisfying moments of junior year.

Siobhan sticks two fingers down her throat and makes a face, and it's not because Ms. Erskine's take on Shakespeare is making her ill.

Then, when I'm sitting outside the music room during Dylan's orchestra practice, Arif slides onto the bench next to me.

He says, "So, you're with Dylan now."

I try for a she-didn't-miss-a-beat kind of a grin, but my face feels more or less frozen. I say, "Yeah, guess so." I'm going for cheerful here, but my tone of voice is also moderately frozen, because this is so clearly the opening line of an interrogation.

"You *guess* so?" Sitting this close to him, it's hard for even a nervous, frozen person who's obsessed with someone else to miss what his allure is all about. "That won't do. I don't know that I can let him wander around walking into walls over a girl who *guesses* so."

I'm being checked out by the best friend, who wants to be certain I'm besotted.

"Just want to make sure you ladies aren't passing him from hand to hand like lip gloss."

"Arif, nobody shares lip gloss."

"Aren't you supposed to be engaged to some guy twice your age in France?" he says. "Are you still seeing him?"

I find myself wondering if Siobhan has actually told people that Jean-Luc got down on one knee and proposed by Skype from Jalalabad. Or Kampala. Or someplace I don't even know she's put him.

And I think, All right, diversion. Right now.

"What are you, the breakup police? Is your boy still seeing Montana?"

"He told you about that?"

Dylan sticks his head out of the music room and does the Dylan equivalent of a double take, which involves blinking.

"Arif," he says. "What are you doing?"

"I told you I was going to look her over."

"From afar," Dylan says. "Like in class, you can look over the back of her head."

I say, "Give him a break. He just wants to make sure I'm not two-timing you."

Arif grimaces.

I say, "Well, I'm not. Maybe you'd like to share that with the world at large. I'm not cheating on anybody, I'm not engaged, I'm not a bad friend, and I'm not" (ripped from my dad's vocabulary) "a tart. Anything else?"

Arif looks as if he deeply wishes he were somewhere else, and Dylan is snickering.

Arif says, "No, I think that covers it."

Dylan, in front of everyone, says, "Do you want to come to my house again after?"

I, in front of everyone, say, "Yes."

So after Orchestra, when I'm supposed to be at the library again, I'm lounging in Dylan's garden in Beverly Hills. This time he doesn't even lead me toward the door, he gestures to the wooden lawn chairs, and we sit there, side by side, looking back through his mother's fruit trees to the wall of pine trees at the far end of the property. Drinking lemonade from a glass pitcher. Lulu stretched out in the grass, chewing her neckerchief.

The whole scene, the early sunset, the darkening afternoon, the long shadows and unseasonable heat, Dylan pouring lemonade into a heavy, cut glass tumbler (as apparently these are the only kind of glasses they own) is so sweet that the sweetness of it actually aches.

Dylan says, "Sorry about Arif."

"Demerits at Convo. I think that constituted interfaith interrogation."

"Don't laugh at Convo. Arif and I are riding Convo into Georgetown, and it can't happen soon enough. We're pillars of interfaith dialogue. Ask Miss Palmer. Arif wants to quit, but his dad will kill him."

"His dad should meet my dad."

"I like his dad. I spent elementary school at his house. My Superman sheets are on the top bunk of his bunk bed."

"I knew you guys were close, but your sheets on his bunk bed?"

"I lived there. I speak conversational Arabic."

"What was wrong with your house?"

"My brother lived at my house. Funny thing about that."

"He was *that* bad?"

"My parents thought we should work things out between us. Not the best approach when one kid outweighs the other kid by fifty pounds and thinks strangling people is fun."

"You couldn't tell them?"

"The last time I told them, Aiden told the whole third grade at Latimer I peed in the school pool. And . . . other things. Didn't go over well."

"All the same people, age eight?"

"It was brutal. You don't want these people getting dirt on you. Pretty soon, I was barely there." He shrugs. "I'm still barely there."

I think about what my dad would have done if I'd zoned out for eight years, and it does not involve me moving into someone else's house.

"My dad's a director," Dylan says. "Commercials. But he likes to direct everything, and I don't take direction well. They had me evaluated for learning disabilities, deafness, blindness, a conduct disorder, and juvenile psychosis. But the Saads like me fine. Where would *you* live?"

"On my best friend's top bunk."

He reaches over and touches my hand. "So now are you going to tell me?"

"What?"

"Arif said you got all weird when he mentioned French Face. Has he been kidnapped by Al Qaeda or something?"

French Face? Oh God, Siobhan, what did you say?

"Would that be funny for you?"

"Hilarious." He looks over. "Wait. Is something happening with you and him? You have to be honest with me. Once burned. All that."

I'm thinking, Tell him. *Tell him, tell him, tell him.* But he looks so fond of me. And even though I know how wrong/weak/bad/stupid/morally backwards/shortsighted it is to want to keep that—to not want to jeopardize that by being, all right, honest—I don't.

I say, "There's nothing there." How much I hate myself for this is almost totally eclipsed by how much I want him.

He touches my face and pulls me toward him. Oh God. The kiss. I say, "I have to go. I have to be on time for dinner."

"Phone your dad. You might be unavoidably detained."

"Dylan, he's old-school. Really, really old-school. I can't."

"How does this work? How do you go out at night? Do I need written authorization to pick you up or old-school dad comes after me or what?"

I say, "You have no idea. Later," and kiss him some more.

I drive up the hill wondering how this actually is going to work. Wishing that I could morph into the kind of girl he thinks I am. That I were her for real. Wishing I'd stayed.

Siobhan says, "He's taking up *all* your time, you don't answer texts, and you're not getting check marks. Kissing? Seriously? What are you even doing with him?"

She is slouching around my bedroom at her sulkiest. It's 9:00

at night, I'm pretty sure my dad is lurking in the hall, and I'm not sure why she appeared at the front door.

I say, "Come on. This was your idea. You set it up. I still see you all the time. Such as now."

This placates her, but not enough.

I say, "How is it you can't comprehend that I might want to hang out with the person you told me to hang out with? And do you ever look back at the shit you text me? Come on."

"You should come to this Malibu thing Friday," she says. "Bring the boy toy. I don't care. It's in the Colony. Better than last time, no one will freeze up and die between the water and the house."

It is unseasonably hot, it's all over the news; the beach is not out of the question. But the three of us at the same party, somewhat together, somewhat not?

I say, "I don't know."

She bangs the palm of her hand against the wall. "Am I your ninth priority now?" She is pacing, picking things up, tossing them down. "After Dylan and homework and Megan and feeding the poor and conditioning your hair? Do *I* ditch *you* when I'm with a guy? Uh, *no*. When I was with Kahane, I went to parties with you."

I don't even know how to respond to this one. I say, "I'm not ditching you."

"Here's a news flash! This is what ditching people looks like!" And she storms out, slamming my bedroom door, the front door, the gate to the courtyard, and her car door.

Siobhan, when she's annoyed, doesn't keep it to herself.

In the morning, the slamming theme extends to her locker, books on desktops, and snack trays at break. When she talks to me, I (and everybody else within a hundred yards) can tell she's seething.

Dylan says, "Should I avoid dark alleys and homeroom? Eat lunch with me. I'll protect you if she creeps up and tries to hit you with a lunch tray. But you'll have to brave the music room."

I say, "I like music."

Dylan is sprawled on the redwood bench on the far side of the library, framed by vines that no doubt got confused by sudden summer weather and are covered with small, waxy flowers. He looks all earnest, and also to die for.

"Prove it," he says. "Come out with me at night. I'll even demonstrate how chivalrous I am by meeting old-school dad. Maybe he'll like me."

No he won't.

Dylan lives in a guesthouse without parental interference. Dylan smolders and looks through people. There is something about even his posture, the way he stretches his arms out in front of him with his fingers laced together, the way he scowls at the world, and the intensity of the way he looks at you, the way he looks at me, that says Scary Indie Guy You Can't Take Home.

I say, "Dylan, you don't know him."

"A problem easily solved by an introduction. He must have *hated* your French guy."

"Why does my dad even have to know? We can meet late. I have a heavily used window."

"Restaurants," he says. "Movies. The LA Phil. The Bowl. They tend to be public events. Anything between the hours of eight and midnight. Afterparty. Siobhan said you were hot to go to Afterparty. Crown turd of Latimer shit, but maybe a seed from Saskatoon would find it amusing."

"Too bad I don't know anyone from Saskatoon you could go with."

He ignores this. He says, "Well?"

When how wonderful this is hits me: Candy Land on a stick. "You want to? All that?"

Dylan says, "What I want to do, given that *you* can distinguish the brass from the strings, is go hear some music. Like normal people."

"Like normal people with their parents' season tickets. Have you noticed any normal people doing that around here?"

"I hope they crank up the drawbridge as soon as I leave the state," Dylan says.

"I'm going to figure this out. You know I want to go, right?"

Dylan repeats, "Prove it."

My dad says, "You want to study at a *boy's* house?"

This was, I swear, not intended to produce cardiac arrest.

"He's in orchestra. You might have seen him. Kind of geeky. Plays the violin." (This is an accurate description of several guys in orchestra. Just not Dylan.)

"I'd feel a lot better if I knew the family."

"This isn't the twentieth century! People don't look over each other's families like that anymore. And it's weirdly creepy if I can't do homework in Beverly Hills in the middle of the afternoon."

My dad crosses his arms.

I say, "I guess I could study with Siobhan, but she doesn't always focus."

My dad is not immune to the allure of me studying with someone who isn't Siobhan. "Would you be in his bedroom?"

I sound exactly like the self he wants to think I am, the one that would ask first—not the one that has already been at Dylan's virtually every day I'm not at the food bank and who knows the code to the gate at the end of his driveway.

"This isn't a rave in the Mojave Desert!" (True.) "This is *home-work*." (Partly true.) "And his mom works at home. She designs baby clothes." (Completely true, not that I've ever seen her.)

"All right," he says. "Go be normal. I'm convinced. By all means, let's avoid weird creepiness." He throws up his hands, like a person who's surrendering, but I can tell that it's all right with him, which is good, given that I'm going to do it anyway.

As it turns out, I'm going to do a whole lot of things anyway.

CHAPTER THIRTY-EIGHT

Siobhan: After school. My house. Physics. Makes no sense.

Me: Can't after school. My house after dinner.

Siobhan: I know yr schedule. Yes u can.

Me: Dylan after school. Why not after dinner?

Siobhan: Physics demands screwdrivers. No screwdrivers chez Lazar.

Me: Come on. I'll get cupcakes at Buttercake. 8:30?

Siobhan: This is shit.

Me: Come on.

Me: Are u still there?

Me: Siobhan?????????????

Me: This is ridiculous.

Me: Oh come on

Me: OK bye.

She doesn't show at school and she doesn't return texts. And when I'm on a lawn chair behind Dylan's guesthouse, sipping lemonade, barefoot in the weirdly hot winter afternoon, my left leg making a bridge from my chair to Dylan's chair, she is not one of my top ten thoughts.

Dylan says, "What did you say to get here?"

"That you're a eunuch."

"Slumming with a eunuch? Great."

"At least eunuchs were musical."

"They were missing some important parts."

I gaze back through the acres of backyard. "I don't know that I'd call this slumming. You might be in the one percent."

He says, "You know. Siobhan said you wanted to go slumming with a slobby high school boy."

"She said I wanted to go *slumming* with you, and you were *slobby*?"

"Roughly. I'm paraphrasing."

I put down the lemonade, willing myself to not snort it out through my nose or throw anything. "Why did you even want to be with me?"

He says, "You know I like you. You're cute when you're insulting."

"That's so insulting!"

"Was I cute?"

Maybe it's that it's so hot that roses are screwing up and blooming at the wrong time, and the backyard smells like summer. Or because the sole of my foot is touching his calf. Or because he reaches out, and after all that carrying-on to Siobhan that I want to be swept up in the romance of the moment, I *am* swept up in the romance of the moment. Or because when I trust that someone actually likes me and is not, in fact, about to slip a rufie into my lemonade, the ice cubes clinking against the inside of the glass sound like bells.

But thirty seconds later, I'm out of the chair and we've made it through the French doors, past the kitchen and into the bedroom, and my blouse is unbuttoned.

Which is when I notice my ability to go from zero to sixty in ten seconds alone with him.

How one minute, it's a kiss, and how all I want is more lips and more tongue and more heat, and one minute later, I'm inside and my blouse is on the floor.

As is his shirt.

How sentences like "I'm not ready" and "Let's wait" and "Let's slow this down" and "I'm not sure yet" and the whole array of things good girls say (sentences I was pretty sure I would one day be saying, back when we examined all those sentences in detail during all-girl It's Your Choice day in Modern Living) don't seem relevant to modern life or human life or, more specifically, to my life.

Dylan says, "You want to? Not that we have to—"

"I want to."

The compass rolls under the bed as Dylan reaches for the button on my skirt.

I blurt, "I've never done this before."

"*What?*"

This kind of breaks the mood, Dylan standing there in boxers, holding a wrapped condom, looking seriously confused, as if virginity were an alien concept.

I pull the sheet up to my chin. "Yeah. First time."

He says, "So you never . . ."

"First time," I say. "Wait. Aren't guys supposed to be happy about this kind of thing? Yay, a virgin. Like that?"

"Sorry." Dylan sits down beside me on the bed. "I get it." He is looking at me as if I'm breakable. "Does this entail bleeding?"

"*Bleeding!* There's a romantic thought."

"Not that you have anything to compare it to," he says. "But that was a very romantic question."

"For a vampire."

He moves in closer. "Vampires have nothing on me."

"Yeah, prove it."

He does. He pushes my hair back behind my left ear and starts kissing the ear very gently. "This, over here, would be your earlobe."

Who knew that ears could even do that. Oh God.

"And this is the back of your neck." More kisses down toward the side of my neck. I have returned to an advanced state of urgency and, all right, it's romantic.

"And oh look, those are toes. Let me make sure." Oh God, oh God, oh God.

"And this is the back of your knee."

"That tickles!"

"Then I'll stop that."

"Do not stop that!"

He doesn't.

"And hey, look over here, what's this?" Oh God!

And there's no blood.

So it was all about romance with maybe some lust thrown in, but in one afternoon, I have vanquished a large section of my to-do list. Not only the actual list, but the things that I wanted that I didn't even dare to put on the list.

And all it took was a complete failure of impulse control, and proximity to Dylan Kahane.

Protracted eye contact with Dylan Kahane: check.

Find out if I'm so repressed by my bizarre upbringing that I fall over, maybe hitting my head on the way down and sliding, dead, to the floor, in the presence of a naked boy. Well, I'm not: check.

Sex with Dylan Kahane. In Dylan Kahane's bedroom. On Dylan Kahane's bed. Following a long conversation with Dylan Kahane during which he acts as if he is sincerely—I'm not even slightly exaggerating—crazy about me: check.

Lie there with Dylan, acting like I own his room because we both know I'm going to be back there.

A lot.

Check.

CHAPTER THIRTY-NINE

MY DAD SAYS, "HOW DID THE HOMEWORK GO?"

I am an unfortunate cross between Dylanesque smirking and panic. "Good."

So good.

My dad is looking at me. And I think, Oh God, my blouse is on backward, my makeup that he doesn't even think I'm wearing is wrecked, my sweater is inside out and I'm wearing my bra over it. But when I glance down, I am, in fact, dressed like a normal person.

My dad says. "You really like this boy, don't you?"

Say yes, and he really will chain me to the piano.

I say, "Is that lamb stew?" He makes great lamb stew. With rosemary and mint and wine.

"It is lamb stew."

"I love lamb stew. See how cooperative I am when you let me out of my cage?"

"I'm doing the best I can," he says. He puts his arm around me and gives my shoulders a little squeeze. "And you seem to be turning into a pretty solid citizen, so I can't be blowing it too badly."

And I think, Damn, I really am a bad person.

The compass, for once in complete agreement, says, *Yes. You are.*

> **Dylan:** U OK?
>
> **Me:** Exponentially beyond ok. Stratospherically super-ok. You?
>
> **Dylan:** Not bad
>
> **Me:** NOT BAD???
>
> **Dylan:** Also super-ok. OK?
>
> **Dylan:** Tomorrow?
>
> **Me:** Food bank.
>
> **Dylan:** Friday?
>
> **Me:** Shabbat dinner. Early sundown. Guests at 5:30.
>
> **Dylan:** U want to take Lulu to the dog park before?
>
> **Me:** Totally. Right after school.
>
> **Me:** What about Saturday? I'll say I'm shopping or something.
>
> **Dylan:** Saturday, study marathon with eunuch. And Emma, you might want to go out the front door all the time soon. This is getting ridiculous.
>
> **Me:** I told you. I'm working on it.

Dylan is waiting for me outside homeroom, leaning against the building. He hugs me and some male voice behind me goes "Aaaaaawwww" and I don't even care.

Dylan says, "Have you recovered?"

"From what?"

He says, "Come here. I'll jog your memory."

We slide around the corner of the building where we engage in the best of the best of the best kiss.

When we walk into class, Dylan runs a finger between my shoulder blades. His face is cool and blank as always at school, but we might as well just tear off our clothes. That's how obvious we are.

Siobhan says, "Jesus, Emma. Really?"

Between classes, she links arms with me. "You have to knock it off. Tell Mr. Goo-Goo-Ga-Ga to man up. Five more minutes of this and your whole backstory crumbles. The International Girl of Intrigue wouldn't be going with a labradoodle."

"He is not a labradoodle."

"Maybe you have that effect on men. Reduced to licking, and panting, and wagging their widdle tails." She starts to make loud slurping sounds, trailing me toward English.

Arif says, "It looks like you're hungry for Emma's cardigan."

Siobhan glares at him but doesn't stop.

I say, "Stop it. Right. Now."

"Maybe she's hungry for Emma," Chelsea says. Lia giggles into her hands.

Dylan says, "Nice, Chelsea." He sounds so caustic; if she were anyone else, she'd dissolve on the spot. But she just wriggles her hips into class.

Siobhan says, "Maybe you're the one who needs to stop it.

Maybe you need to put the public fondling on hold before people start strewing your path with barf."

I grab Siobhan and pull her toward the lockers. I whisper, "But it's all going according to your plan. What are you doing?"

"This wasn't my plan."

I whisper in her ear, "But I did it. Emma the Good is history."

"You slept with my boyfriend?" she yells. We are visible and audible and no doubt highly entertaining.

"But you told me to!" I'm going for an emphatic whisper.

But she seems to be enjoying the scene she's creating.

"You slept with my boyfriend! Who are you, my mother?" She has me by the wrist and for a moment I'm outside of myself, as if I'm not even here, as if I don't feel her nails biting into my skin.

She glares at me, her eyes are slits, but what I notice are the blackened lashes and how tears are balling up in them as if they were Astroturf. She seems to be living in some alternate reality, and I can't get her back.

"Let *go* of me. You all but bought me the condoms. *Let go.*"

"I told you to try out your learner's permit on his tiny dick. I did not tell you to *fall* for him. I did not tell you to go all Dylan, I *looooove* you, all I can think about is *youuuuuuuu.* I did not tell you to ignore a text for *eighteen hours.*"

"Is that what this is about? I didn't return your text fast enough?"

And there I am, in front of everybody, running after her.

"I'm the one who set you up," she says. "So you liked him first blah blah but it's not like you did anything about it. Do you think you'd be with him if not for me?"

"Why are you doing this? I thought you'd be happy for me!"

"You were supposed to be my *friend*. Only now you're too busy turning into Stepford Girlfriend, and guess what? It isn't going to last. He finds out one bad thing about you, and you're done."

There it is. The thorn at the center of my beating heart of fear: that he will see me, and he won't like what he sees.

"I changed my mind," Siobhan says when I've followed her into the ladies' room. She's staring into the mirror behind the row of sleek stainless-steel sinks, twirling her bangs. "I made you and I could undo you in three minutes. Two online."

"This makes no sense. You're the one who didn't want to go down with me! You said to keep quiet."

"Yeah," she says. "But that's not why you kept quiet. You kept quiet because he's a jerk and you're chicken. And now, chicklet, you're going down."

I am thinking little pieces of thoughts: She'd never do this. I'm her only friend. How stupid would it be to wipe out your only friend? Except that Self-Destructive is her middle name. What am I doing with a best friend with Self-Destructive for a middle name?

"Don't you think someone will remember *you're* the one who made me up?"

Siobhan says, "Nope. I mean, Tweet-tweet. Who cares who started it?" She points at me. "Uh-oh. You didn't tell him *anything*, did you? You are so screwed."

I want to rip a sink out of the wall and throw it.

"I could just stop making you up and you'd be over," she says. "Jesus. You didn't figure out you have to tell him? Do I have to do everything?"

I have to force myself, my airless lungs and ashy mouth, to look irrationally calm and unrealistically in control of my life.

I say, "Why would you do that? I was doing what you *said*."

"Not saying I *would*. Just saying I *could*. If I felt like it. You just tell him, then see how *in looooove* he is."

I'm thinking, I'm five kinds of doomed.

I'm thinking, Who are you, and how is it I didn't notice until now?

I say, "Sib, put down the iPhone. No evil texting. You sound like you've been smoking crack and watching *Mean Girls*."

"You think I'm mean and evil?" She sounds worked up and insulted.

I'm thinking, All right, un-insult her fast, because her finger's on the texting icon and she could wreck your life before you make it out of the ladies' room.

"Sib," I say. "You're saying you could undo my life in under three minutes. What am I supposed to think?"

I'm thinking, fix this. Apologize. Turn cartwheels in the ladies' room. Do anything you have to do to fix this. You can kill her later.

This is possibly the world's worst ladies' room situation that doesn't have a mugger in it.

I say, "Remember me? Best friend and big-time sidekick?" Lie lie, flatter flatter. Except that until now, it was mostly, at least intermittently, intensely and undeniably, somewhat true. "Unless we have some kind of a pact to be evil, and I don't remember that one."

I'm watching her face to see if she looks like a person who's about to push "send" on an evil tweet.

She looks like a girl who is brushing her hair.

She says, "Fuck this. I have to go to Econ."

My lungs start to fill. I should immediately join the UN and broker peace in Sudan, the Middle East, and Chechnya.

I have an extreme need for candy.

I want chocolate so much, I am willing to enter the small space where the vending machines are, off the student lounge, with Chelsea, whom I plan to ignore while scarfing down a Kit Kat bar.

"Aren't you unexpectedly interesting," she says, blocking the swinging door. "Running around school screaming. Classy."

I say, "Excuse me."

Chelsea extends her leg so the toe of her shoe is pressed against the wall opposite, like a railroad crossing gate by Tory Burch.

Ambush.

"Are you seriously trying to trap me here? Because I'm leaving."

This is wishful thinking because Chelsea seems determined to establish that she can intimidate me.

"Nobody likes what you're doing," she says.

"So you decided to trap me here? That's helpful."

"How do you get off being this big, better-than-everyone holdout?" she barks. "First you won't even go out because we're too boring for you. Then you'll go out but you're too good to *do* anything because you're so devoted to this French guy—"

I interrupt, "That's over."

Chelsea has escalated from barking to snarling. "You can't just lose your old boyfriend and take your best friend's boyfriend like that."

"That isn't what happened!"

The glass door of the candy machine is slick against my back; I imagine myself sliding to the floor and crawling out under Chelsea's leg.

"Please," Chelsea says. "She was all giggly and unslutty with him. For her. Didn't you notice that?"

"Are you seriously calling her a *slut*? What century do you come from?"

Chelsea scuffs the wall, planting her foot on the floor. She swings her backpack over her shoulder, and for a second, I think she's going to smack me with it.

"Maybe you spent so long being vintage vanilla, you finally cracked," she says. "Maybe you were a bitch all along. Who cares? But you should look at her because she's not fine, and you're all over school sucking his face. Who do you think you are?"

Am I walking around school sucking his face?

Maybe this is the one time in her life when Chelsea Hay has a point.

Chapter Forty

DYLAN SAYS, "ARE YOU OKAY?"

It's only lunchtime and the day is stretching into a horror show, starring me.

He says, "You look like shit."

"Oooookay . . ."

"Let me rephrase. You look extremely upset, not like shit."

I say, "Semi-okay." Then, in a semi-suicidal moment of confessional daring, I say, "I might need to talk to you before somebody else does."

"Somebody else already did," he says. "Sam said he heard I should watch out because you're a backstabbing bitch. I am, once again, confused as fuck." He is pulling me into him, which is both perfect and clear confirmation of Chelsea's Emma-is-a-big-bitch-and-girl-code-violator hypothesis. "I hate high school."

"*You* hate high school? Is Chelsea Hay ambushing you? Is

Sam Sherman running around telling everybody you kill puppies and pummel your best friend?"

Dylan says, "Want to walk out of here?"

"Physics. I'm barely getting a B in Physics. I can't skip again."

"After. Pancakes. I'll buy."

Only after school, the Griddle is closed, and nothing else will do. He says, "Or. We could go to my house." Where, it turns out, I'm addicted to frequent, impulsive acts of extreme lust, and very good at imagining future acts involving more of the same.

When we're about to get dressed, he says, "So we're good, right? You're okay with the crap at school."

I roll over. "Yeah. Except for the part where I stole you from my best friend and destroyed her life and I'm a bitch, everything's great."

Dylan starts to rub my shoulders. "Who said that?"

"Everyone."

Dylan gets the clothes and drops them in a heap at the end of the bed, dragging along the dog, who is chewing my shoe. He says, "Drop it, Lulu!"

Lulu ignores him.

He says, "So. It seems kind of churlish to talk about her. Now."

"Churlish?"

"Inappropriate, crappy, bad . . ."

"I get it, Kahane. I know what 'churlish' means."

"I was never with her like this."

Oh.

I say, "She might have thought you were. With her like this."

Dylan is looking away from me, putting on his pants. "Do you want to talk about this? Because I'm not proud of it."

I say, "Just tell me why. How did it even happen?"

"Because it was a party," he says, pulling my shoe out of Lulu's mouth and handing it to me by its slightly chewed strap. "Because we were drunk and opportunity presented itself and it wasn't supposed to mean anything. It sounds worse out loud. And then she was just there and it kept going."

"I don't even know what to say." Or feel. If what he's describing is a good thing or a bad thing, relative to something like, Oh, I was in love with her.

"I *said* I'm not proud of it. And for what it's worth: Strick and Gart. She tells me nothing is happening. She lies to my face. Then, after I break up with her, she decides no, she's breaking up with me, and she all but gives me a road map to—shit—she made it clear she knew I liked you, and it was okay with her. And now she's *offended*?"

"Sorry."

"The only person I can stand besides you is Arif, and everyone makes such a big fucking deal over how we don't kill each other, he thinks we ought to stage a fistfight at Convo."

"Bye-bye, Georgetown."

"Not letting that happen. He's more on the bored side. I just want out. No more fakes, no more palm trees. I'm going East and I'm not coming back."

"You'll never see your family?"

"They picked Aiden. They can keep him." The coldness of

this, of having a live mother just across the yard and walking away, is almost unbearable. He says, "What did I say?"

I think of my father and lamb stew. "Your mom. I can't even imagine having one and tossing her. Sorry."

Dylan says, "Emma. If they wanted me in their house, I would be living in their house. Okay? Can we stop there?"

I'm looking over at the stack of folded cloth napkins, all the clean, color-coded laundry, the cash in an envelope, and the grocery bag of fresh fruit.

Dylan clears his throat, but his voice remains choked and still harsh. "Seed, that was the maid, I'm on her list of chores. Not my mom."

I am suddenly sadder for him. "Just me and Arif?"

Dylan stretches his arms over his head. "Sam Sherman before he thought you were Cruella de Vil. Mara. Kimmy's horse. Kimmy. I'm not completely antisocial. I've been tested for that."

"But not Siobhan?"

By now the sun is behind the pine trees in his backyard, and it's suddenly chilly, and my father is texting about where I am and when I'm getting home.

He says, "No, you. It was always you."

There is nothing in that moment—the lamplight in the room, the sound of Lulu thumping her tail on the bedspread, my fingers woven between his fingers, the smell of his hair and the tone of his voice—that isn't imprinted on my heart, like the afterimage of a burst of light, under your eyelids when you close your eyes.

CHAPTER FORTY-ONE

IN THE MORNING, AT SCHOOL, SIOBHAN STARTS texting me as if nothing happened, as if I somehow forgot that she chased me around screaming the day before.

Siobhan: Where were u after English? Are u Stepfording 24/7 now?

Me: Licking my wounds.

Siobhan: What wounds?

Me: Seriously? Do you ever apologize for anything?

Siobhan: I said I wouldn't tell. Chill.

Me: You melted down on me.

Siobhan: When I melt down, you'll know.

Me: You're not slightly sorry are you?

Siobhan: Get over it. I'm slightly sorry. Is your boat all floaty now?

Siobhan: At least I don't cuddle with the enemy.

Siobhan: What were u doing with Chelsea? Are u in the pony club now?

Me: Right. She's my bestest friend.

Me: She cornered me by the candy. Weird but true. She thinks me being with Dylan sucks for you.

Siobhan: WHAT????

Siobhan: You're making that up.

Me: Swear to God. Go check. There's a Tory Burch scuffmark three feet off the floor behind the door.

Siobhan: Not buying this. Walking there now. That horse bitch feels sorry for me???

Siobhan: There was a shoe on this wall!!!!!!! Did u do this?

Me: Go roll somebody for a Tory Burch flat and go all CSI on it. It was Chelsea.

Siobhan: U shd fuck him on the quad.

Me: Not if you're going to hit me in the ladies room.

Siobhan: OK but you're still a bimbo when u have a boyfriend.

Me: Get me an Almond Joy.

Siobhan and I sit there in the student lounge eating our Almond Joys.

"I'm going to fix this," she says. "Like people think I let you screw me over? I don't think so."

Chelsea looks over at us and shakes her head. Then Dylan shows up with Arif and Sam on an Orangina run, and I want to crawl into a dark tunnel that leads away from Latimer and ends in my backyard.

A desire even more acute when Siobhan starts waving her arms at Dylan.

He looks understandably reluctant to come over, which makes sense given that she's offered him nothing but grief since he's been with me. But by the time he makes his way across the room, he has returned to big-time blankness.

"Hey," he says to no one in particular.

Siobhan says, "Kiss her."

Dylan and I start to splutter simultaneously.

Siobhan says, "You should listen to me. I'm doing you a favor."

Dylan starts to say something, but Siobhan interrupts him. "Not a favor for you, jerk. Her. I don't do favors for *you*."

Arif says, "Do it." And to Siobhan: "Assuming you're not going to start screeching, which would be less of a favor."

Siobhan says, "Fuck you."

Dylan leans down and we establish that we can engage in a completely mechanical prolonged kiss with no feelings. It goes on and on, emotionless as Dylan's face.

Arif clears his throat.

Siobhan says, "You're lapsing into get-a-room."

We come up for air, Dylan resting on the arm of my chair.

Chelsea and Lia walk back toward the door. The set point on their faces is contempt. Siobhan keeps smiling beatifically at them, offering the grand finale to our spectacle with a two-handed flip off, waving her forearms from the elbow.

"*Nobody* feels sorry for me," Siobhan says.

Sam keeps shifting his weight from one foot to the other. "And from this fascinating piece of guerrilla theater, we take away—?"

I am still reeling from the non-kiss kiss. Still, I'm pretty sure I'm no longer the stealth bitch who leveled Siobhan; I'm now just some theatrical form of weird.

Dylan says, "Can we go now?"

"Oh, you're excused," Siobhan says.

I follow him out—no holding open of the door, no hand-holding, no PDA of any kind—into the quad and up onto the hill.

I say, "That was maybe the most awkward moment of my life."

I say, "I think she was trying to be nice."

He says, "Don't bet on it."

CHAPTER FORTY-TWO

Dylan: I'm making up for before. Issuing formal invitation. Very romantic.

Me: By text?

Dylan: This is as formal as I get. Valentine's Day. Are you in?

Me: Duh.

Me: I'm going to facetime you right now. I want details and sappiness.

Dylan: I'm not that sappy

Me: Try

Dylan: Cheesy cupid decorations and an open bar with pink mixed drinks?

Me: Yes please!

This Valentine's Day party is a producer's insanely over-the-top annual extravaganza, complete with his revolving girlfriends and exciting gown malfunctions. To which said producer always asks Dylan's parents to bring Dylan, as he's the same age as his kid. When they were little, it gave his kid something to do, other than watch assorted women run into the house for more denture cream to hold up their dresses.

"You should know up front, I'm embarrassed to take you," Dylan says.

"Thanks a lot. I can see why you left that out of the formal invitation."

"That came out wrong. You don't know what my parents are like until you've seen them in action."

"What is it they do?"

"You have a dad who cares if you drink all your milk. I'm not sure you're going to get this." He just looks at me, and even on the tiny screen of my phone, I get that whatever it is, it's not a fun topic. "Are you sure you don't mind going anyway?"

Dylan and Valentine's Day and a lavish, over-the-top extravaganza complete with drama yet such a large contingent of parents and so-called responsible adults (blasted out of their minds) in attendance that my dad couldn't possibly say no—how sure can a person be?

And instantly, without thought or analysis, I want to tell Siobhan. That's my first impulse. All these weeks of crazy and I still want best friendship without the complications.

I want the impossible.

Me: Physics?

Siobhan: Don't you have to sit at boy toy's feet day and night?
Me: Screwdrivers. Cheetos. Electrical fields. Come on.

We're in Siobhan's dining room, trying to figure out our lab reports. Nancy rolls her suitcase by on her way to the airport.

She says, "That school is screwing up your lives but good. Why don't you ladies take a break and have some fun?"

Words that would wither and die on my dad's lips.

Siobhan eats a Cheeto and doesn't look up until Nancy is out the front door.

I say, "Are you ever going to talk to her again? It's been a while."

"I'm just keeping her guessing. It results in lots of shopping. I need all new shoes."

"I just want a Valentine's Day dress. A perfect red one."

"Not vintage."

"Yes, vintage. Like Old Hollywood, maybe?"

"Jesus. I'm coming with, or you're going to end up looking like a drag queen."

On Saturday, we head down Melrose and up La Brea.

She says, "If you still think you're going to Afterparty vintage, think again."

We're shopping, we're having fun, we're picking out each other's clothes and making scathing comments about bad dresses that we rifle through. She threatens to shoplift an extremely large bag (but doesn't) just to freak me out.

I feel as if I've got my friend back.

As if.

Now, if I can just hold it together long enough to talk to Dylan about one or two things and he goes, "Meh, that's not so bad," everything will be perfect.

Right.

Seventy-three days before Afterparty, and I'm delusional.

CHAPTER FORTY-THREE

I TRY TO TELL HIM, I SWEAR I DO, BUT DYLAN'S NOT in one of his better moods.

Aiden is in town for their cousin's wedding, and Dylan can't avoid him. This is their first cousin Bess, from Aiden's class at Latimer, marrying her supervisor from her summer investment banking internship due to the fact that she's slightly pregnant. Half their class is in L.A. for this, whooping it up all over town.

Dylan offers up tidbits from Kahane familyland. "We had to spend hours at Wilshire Boulevard Temple draped around pillars for the wedding pictures. I had to *gaze* at Aiden. The photographer demanded gazing. I had to put my arm around my dad and look son-like. I could feel him cringe."

"It'll be over soon," I say, touching his face. "I'll make you heart-shaped cookies."

"Thanks. You're a credit to your—what are seeds?—your phylum? Your genus? Your gender?"

We're sitting, fully clothed, on his bed, supposedly studying.

I say, "I'm not that much of a credit to anything. Maybe we should talk—"

"No, we should eat. Want to order pizza? My mom has taken to cooking for the Scottish prince. There's only so much charred sea bass a person can take."

"Blackened sea bass? Like with a pepper crust?"

"You don't get large-scale family dysfunction, do you? She burns it, we eat it."

"Excuse me, I get—"

He pushes me onto the pillow. We don't study.

After school, Siobhan and I search for antique stockings with seams down the back to go with my (vintage) dress, which turn out to be the Holy Grail of vintage shopping.

Siobhan is texting Strick, who has some form of the flu. "I don't care if he has to OD on cough syrup. We're clubbing on Valentine's. You aren't the only person with the perfect dress."

"You didn't take me shopping for your perfect dress?"

"Nancy," Siobhan says. "I have to throw her a bone once in a while."

I wonder if my mom liked vintage. If she would have liked it on me. Or if she would have been so rational about teen girl attire that vintage wouldn't have had to be my fallback when my dad rejected any garment associated with modern fashion.

Within seconds, I am deep into the realm of Stop It, Stop It,

Stop It, with Siobhan snapping her fingers six inches from my face and telling me not to sulk.

"I hate to burst your little bubble," she says, "but this Valentine's Day party you're going to: lame. A bunch of Hollywood burnouts with Botox. *Burton* got invited."

"There are going to be kids there."

"Kids who get dragged there. Do you know how cool the Strip is going to be on Valentine's Day? Think: Lame. Awesome. Lame. Awesome. Obviously you and the labradoodle should come with us to Awesome."

"Me and you and Strick and Dylan and three IDs?"

"You could be Birgitta from Malmo. I got her ID in Barbados. And who the hell knows about Strick? I might have to round up Wade."

"*Wade?*"

"Or whoever. It's me. It isn't going to be a problem," Siobhan says. "You just don't want to go with me, do you?"

"It's not that."

"It's *completely* that. I can read you. You're going to an octogenarian yawnfest instead of doing something that actually might be fun? And why is that?"

She is looking at me with the angry, hooded eyes of those Australian toads that squirt poison at their enemies.

I say, "I'll ask Dylan. All right?"

I won't ask Dylan.

"Cause widdle Emma can't make up her own mind," she says. "You should listen to me. You won't survive five minutes in the real world without me. You'd be fucked if I didn't have your back, and you don't even get it! Go to your lame party! I don't even care!"

I pull into her driveway and she slams the car door on her way out.

I am in a state of damn-what-just-happened? Because whatever it was, it's not good.

Chapter Forty-Four

TWO DAYS AND THEN I HEAR FROM HER.

> **Siobhan:** You have to get over here.
> **Me:** Why?
> **Siobhan:** Just do it. Tell DrLaz a friend in need is
> a friend indeed. Tell him you have to borrow my
> earrings. Get over here.
> **Me:** Why?
> **Siobhan:** Tell him I'm jumping out the window if you
> don't talk me down.
> **Me:** Is something actually wrong?
> **Siobhan:** Get over here
> **Siobhan:** I mean it.

My dad is in the living room, reading a journal and drinking brandy. It's like a scene out of the Analyst's Home Companion;

all we need is a black lab and an artsy mom who makes jewelry or hooks rugs or something. I'm wearing jeans and a pajama top and a Latimer hoodie and Bert and Ernie slippers. I figure, how can anybody dressed like this possibly be up to no good?

I say, "I need to go over to Siobhan's for a little while."

He looks at his watch.

I say, "I know, but she sounds upset and it's not like she calls me over there in the middle of the night all the time."

"If anything is going on that you can't handle, you'll call me. No secrets if it's dangerous."

I say, "I know. I will. Thank you."

"And Ems, midnight."

"Midnight."

But as it turns out, there *is* something over there I can't handle. Although phoning home isn't an option.

At first I'm not sure who it is in there with her, submerged to their chins, their heads seeming to bob, disembodied, on the frothy surface of the Jacuzzi, steam rising off the foam, obscuring their faces. I can't tell if he and Siobhan are wearing anything, but they seem to have achieved a level of coziness that makes you wonder why a third person, such as me, would even be invited.

Siobhan says, "Hey! This is my friend." She reaches out of the steaming water to throw a bathing suit at me.

The guy says, "Hey, Siobhan's friend!" He sounds friendly but slightly stoned. I recognize his voice immediately. Then I recognize him. His torso rises from the water, his elbows splayed back over the fieldstone rim of the Jacuzzi.

The profile and the brow. Jesus, the guy from the beach club, still gorgeous in the dark.

It is completely clear he has no idea who I am.

Siobhan says to him, "You're quite the piece of work, aren't you?"

He says, "That I am." He sounds quite taken with this idea.

"How drunk were you at that beach club, anyway?" Siobhan says. "You assaulted this girl outside the ladies' room. Your tongue has been in this girl's mouth."

The profile becomes even more beautiful when all the other details blur into shadow. "Oh. You! Polka dots, right?"

The dress.

I say, "Siobhan—" Because I want him not to remember. I want the whole thing not to have happened. I want to not know him and for him not to know me.

She says, "International Girl of Intrigue, meet Mystery Man."

"Amélie!" I say. I don't want the whole idiot episode to come roaring back with me—and a name anyone in L.A. knows as me—in it.

He says, "Amélie? Pretty. I'd ask you if you're French, but your footwear . . ."

I say, "Seriously, Sib? What are you doing?"

"Oh yeah, *Amélie*," she says. "Get in here. Or do you want me to call up you-know-who and make it a foursome?"

"No!"

"You-know-*who*?" the guy whines. "Don't you like me?"

I say, "Siobhan, could I talk to you for a minute?"

She reaches behind her and I see her phone, and she's waving it above the water. "You're such a buzzkill baby! Don't you want to have fun? Because I'm phoning! Nope, not yet. Yes, I'm phoning right now. Not yet. Yessssss I am! You weren't such a buzzkill in the summer, were you? You didn't care who you kissed!"

"Whom," I say.

"Fuck you!" Siobhan yells.

"No, she's right, 'whom.'" Beach Club Boy is at least highly grammatical.

I say, "I'm leaving."

She says, "No. You're not. I know, why don't I call up your ass-hole boyfriend *and* Jean-Luc. Then all five of us can chat about it. But wait, I'll be the only person in here who hasn't had a tongue down your throat. I feel so sad and left out."

The guy says, "You could put your tongue down her throat, Sibby. I don't mind."

This is the point when I know—Good Emma, Bad Emma, Emma with any sense knows—it is the moment to walk back into the house, say good-night to Marisol, and go home. Because even if she calls my bluff, Dylan showing up with me on my way out is so much better than Dylan showing up with me sitting in a Jacuzzi with drunk Siobhan and drunker Beach Club Boy, and I still don't know if they're wearing anything. She could just be strapless.

It is *not* the moment to step out of the Bert-and-Ernie slippers and into the too-tight swimsuit. But what if I can placate her? What if I can give just the smallest bit, what if I just sit in the Jacuzzi like we have a hundred times since summer, and she doesn't call him up, and he doesn't find out everything about me two hours before Valentine's Day, and that's the end of it?

I climb into the water, slowly.

I immerse myself completely. I come up looking at the stars glittering through the blue-black sky and the rusty half-moon, the steam rising all around me off the roiling water, and the gorgeousness of Siobhan and the boy. And then his hand is on my shoulder, only he's kissing Siobhan, and then he turns to me and I am, *I swear*, pulling away, I am recoiling, I'm thinking, get up, get out, abort, stop, don't. I'm climbing out, my shoulders are out of the water, but he kisses me. His lips feel unnaturally cold as my body steeps in the hot water, pummeled by the jets. Cold but compelling.

I push out of the water and out of his half embrace, his other arm still around Siobhan. And I shout, "Stop! I have a boyfriend."

Siobhan says, "Sure you do."

CHAPTER FORTY-FIVE

MIDNIGHT.

I am on the floor of my closet, doing the arithmetic of poor choices. I'm in the negative numbers column, not even counting the things that I refuse to guilt myself about but maybe I should, starting with every second I've spent with Dylan. Not to mention every lie I've told to get every one of those seconds with him.

And then there's every second I *want* to erase.

It isn't that hard to differentiate.

> **Me:** How could you blindside me like that?
>
> **Siobhan:** Give it up. He tried, you left. Big fucking deal.
>
> **Me:** You might have warned me it was him.
>
> **Siobhan:** Like u'd have come?
>
> **Me:** That's the point!!!!! Where did you dig him up?
>
> **Siobhan:** Beach club. Thought we could get another taste.

Me: I didn't want another taste.

Me: What am I supposed to say to Dylan? I so suck.

Siobhan: Check mark for killing labradoodle. Time to bail.

Me: I'm not bailing. I'm going to tell him. Obviously. I got in a Jacuzzi with your latest whatever and he tried to kiss me and I left. It's not that big a deal.

Siobhan: Obviously.

Me: He'll understand.

Siobhan: Sure he will. Are u and labradoodle coming to Sunset tomorrow with me or what?

Me: You're delusional. You did that to mess with me. Did you think I wouldn't notice?

Siobhan: Nobody fucks with me grasshopper. Even u.

CHAPTER FORTY-SIX

THE GENERAL UN-FUNNESS OF NOT GETTING ready with a best friend is getting to me. Siobhan is as incommunicado as you can be when you're in most of the same classes and capable of communicating volumes with a single scowl. Given that I want to punch her, this is not entirely a bad thing. Clearly, the combing of the hair and the shellacking of the nails, the admiration of each other's exquisite taste in hot dresses, won't be happening

I ask my dad if I can go down to Sunset Plaza to Blushington to get the infinitesimal, minute amount of makeup I plan to wear applied by a professional and get my hair blown out in Hollywood at Je Jeune. I'm not sure if it's that he's so in love with the idea of completely invisible makeup, or if he feels sorry for me, if it's my motherless-girl-in-need-of-arcane-female-knowledge mojo, but he says yes in less than a second.

And even though, thanks to professional help, I finally

achieve something as close to gorgeousness as I will ever hover—glossy hair, perfectly made-up eyes, the to-die-for vintage scarlet dress—I keep thinking about getting ready for parties with a mother, and whether she ever contemplated dyeing *her* eyelashes.

I am tangled up in small, intimate details I will never know.

Even the compass feels sorry for me. It goes, *Buck up. For once, you're in a dress that's not obscene, and you're so depressed, there's a good chance that you'll behave yourself out of sheer listlessness. Yay!*

My dad says, "Just remember –"

"I'll only get soft drinks directly from the bartender, and I won't drink anything that's left my hand, and I won't let anyone who's drunk anything but pop drive me, and if I see drugs or weapons or gang warfare, I'll walk away. And there's enough money in my handbag to fly back to Canada if California has an armed insurrection between now and two a.m."

"This is serious, Ems."

"Dad! I know that you're concerned about me and I appreciate it so much and I'm so happy you're letting me go and thank you. But seriously, I'm not going to get drunk or pregnant or kidnapped or shot. The guy's parents are going to be there."

My dad looks dubious. He says, "How did you get me to agree to this again?"

"Don't I look nice and respectable? This dress comes from the nineteen-*fifties*."

My dad says, "You look stunning. That's what worries me."

But he hugs me, and then he opens the front door, and I walk out in my extravagantly high-heeled red shoes as quickly as a person in such slender heels can walk, before he changes his mind.

I just want to get to Dylan's, and for Dylan to look up and say something like "wow," if not the actual word "wow." Then I want to finally meet his parents, who can admire the vintage dress as well as marveling at Dylan's good taste in girlfriends.

But apparently going to a party with Dylan's parents doesn't mean actually going to a party with Dylan's parents. When I drive up to his house, they've already left for a different party they're going to first. Dylan is sitting outside in the dark, lit by the dim porch light, slouched on a wooden lawn chair, bare feet in Lulu's fur.

I say, "Did something happen?"

"My family happened. My fault, of course." He shrugs. "Aiden stormed off for parts unknown, which is, again, my fault. No one is very happy with me."

"We should go cheer you up with some partying immediately."

Dylan looks at me in the red dress. He does not say "wow." "Probably you're overdressed for Mel's Drive-In. Which was my plan B."

"But your Plan A is so promising. Music, champagne, over-the-topness. A live band I've actually heard of."

"Probably I'm overdressed for Mel's, too," he says, standing up. "But I could change."

"Don't change. You clean up really well."

Dylan shakes his head. "I'm so fucked up right now. You look amazing. You'll probably run off with a guy at Mel's."

He kicks at one of the pseudo-rocks, cast from a glasslike substance, lined up along his driveway.

I say, "It's just, it's Valentine's Day, and we're dressed up, and it's a party. Do you really want to spend Valentine's Day in a diner?"

He says, "When I'm back East and this is all a bad memory from my overprivileged youth, I'm never going to another one of these crap things."

"We don't have to go, but I thought you were inviting me somewhere you wanted to take me. Explaining how I'm feeling."

He sits with his feet sticking out of the driver's side door of his car, putting on socks. "I've been inviting you where I want to take you. I tried to get you to do whatever it takes to get sprung by your dad so we could go hear some real music downtown. But apparently it took this glitz fest."

I wonder how many miles over the Atlantic Aiden has to be for Dylan to stop being so irritable.

"Shoot me," I say, fastening my seat belt, in two-can-play-at-this mode, I-might-be-your-excessively-adoring-girlfriend-but-I'm-not-your-doormat mode. "I thought a party with Hell's Gate playing would be *fun*."

"Hell's Gate is putrid."

"I thought you liked this kind of thing."

"Why would you think I like this? I hate this kind of party. I hate this."

He waves at his house, or maybe at all of Beverly Hills, or at all of L.A. County. Hard to tell.

"Excuse me for not figuring it out, but there are pictures of you whooping it up at glitzfests all over the Internet."

"Maybe you confused me with my brother, hallowed be his name. Ladies' man. Asshole. Liar. Looks a lot like me, only taller. Likes the same girls. He really likes this over-the-top shit."

We wind up to Mulholland. Dylan accelerates into a curve, and there's L.A., lit up below the guardrail.

He says, "Yeah, you two could hit it off."

"Excuse me?"

By this time, we're parked in a turnout, my hands are over my ears, and Dylan is slouched behind the wheel.

He says, "I'm sorry. My fault. No excuse."

We aren't actually looking at each other.

I say, "Do you suddenly hate me?"

"I opposite of hate you. I tend to kick the cat when I feel like shit."

"I get to be the cat?"

"Sorry. Bad week."

"I know," I say. "Sorry I pushed this party so hard. Seriously, let's go back to your house and admire each other's outfits."

Dylan turns his head farther away from me. "So I can be the sulky dud boyfriend who screws up your Valentine's Day and Jean-Luc can be the one who sends you the camellias? No."

"Dylan, there were *no* camellias, all right?"

"You don't have to make things up to make me feel better. Maybe I'm not cool like that."

"Believe me, he wasn't all that."

"Give it up. He was the French god of cool."

"He wasn't what you think. I'm trying to be honest here. We should turn around and talk."

Because this is it, I can feel it coming, I have to do this before we're any deeper into this.

Just not in this car on the way to this party.

Dylan says, "So. What haven't you told me about him?"

"Maybe let's talk after the party if you don't want to turn back. It's already intense."

He says, "Answer. The question."

And here I am with my back to the wall. All right, pressed between a car door and a bucket seat. Seat-belted in and brushed with body glitter, no doubt shedding sparkles in the very spot where I am trapped.

My heart is beating too fast, and I'm so clammy that I'm sticking to the leather seat. We're driving along Mulholland now, at the part where it gets curvy and narrow—we're whipping around and it doesn't feel as if there's any choice.

If I don't tell him, he'll be with someone who isn't actually me—someone he thinks is me, and looks, and sounds, and smells like me, but isn't.

If I don't tell him, I'll hate myself with really good reason.

Even the most morally challenged person could tell what has to happen.

I say, "There is no Jean-Luc."

"Don't play with me, Emma."

"No, literally. There's no Jean-Luc."

CHAPTER FORTY-SEVEN

DYLAN SEEMS TO BE SWERVING OFF THE ROAD, but, in fact, we are turning into the circular driveway of a serious palace. We are on the threshold of what has to be the splashiest Valentine's Day party in the history of the world, in a black suit and a perfect scarlet dress, yet I have just dragged us into the eye of another shitstorm.

Hell's Gate must be taking a break, because the speakers are blaring a hideous reggae version of "I Only Have Eyes for You."

Dylan stands there glaring at me, after which he stomps off and we end up on the side of the house, which is terraced, strung with paper lanterns, and studded with astonishingly well-dressed people of the I-have-a-bazillion-dollars-and-this-dress-is-made-of-spun-gold-thread variety.

Dylan says, "I don't. Fucking. Believe you."

"I'm sorry! I tried to tell you last week, but you were in such a bad mood."

"*Last week!* That's how long it took you to figure out you should stop making a fool of me?"

"I tried to tell you at the Griddle. I really did."

Dylan says, "You should. Have. Tried. Harder."

"Dylan—I know."

"Did you have *fun* when I was fucking jealous of him?"

"Please let me explain."

Dylan leans back against one of the many random Greek pillars dotting the landscape all over the place, festooned with red ribbon and hearts that look a lot like little pincushions. He says, "Great. Explain. This should be interesting."

He looks as if he wants to string me up. And in the absence of a workable lie, I blunder into the unfamiliar truth.

"Okay, this is it. I thought that maybe you'd prefer to be with a girl who wasn't, all right, lying about basically everything. Because you would, right? But when it started to seem as if you might possibly like me, I was just afraid you *wouldn't* like me if you knew. Obviously, I blew it."

I just want to rewind. I want to be back at Strick's party and for Siobhan to say, *Yo, Chelsea, Em has a boyfriend*, and for me to seize possession of my right mind and go, *Good one, Sib*—as opposed to finding Jean-Luc an apartment in Paris with a view of the Eiffel Tower and making him a Facebook page.

Dylan says, "Why?"

There's no way to say it without drowning in humiliation, no way to paddle in the general direction of decent human being without saying it. So I just say it. "At the time, International Girl of Intrigue with the romantic French boyfriend seemed like a better plan than Virgin Geek Girl from the Frozen Tundra."

Dylan whistles. "You think I'm a jerkoff who'd like you better if you're cheating on some guy from Montreal with me?"

"He was from Paris. And I broke up with him before I touched you."

"Great. Paris. That changes everything."

Then we look at each other and I hear the ridiculousness of what I just said and he just shakes his head. "Jesus, Emma."

He sounds so bitter. And angry. And justified. And I have no idea what I can say or do to make this better.

He says, "Every time I talked about him, you stood there and *let* me? Were you laughing at me behind my back?"

"I would never! I just didn't think you'd exactly *admire* me if you knew I was . . ." (This is the place where I don't want to say "lying" again, or "a liar," or "pathologically dishonest," and I just stand there silently until I come up with something slightly less awful yet true.) ". . . making him up."

"You're right. I wouldn't."

I try to touch his arm, but he tenses as if he's repulsed by my fingertips.

I say, "Don't do that. If you're breaking up with me, just break up with me."

"This isn't us breaking up," he shouts. "This is us having a big-ass fight."

We would appear to be heading toward the far reaches of a

patio where we can fight in private when Dylan stops dead and takes out his vibrating phone.

He says, "Not tonight. Aiden. He will not quit."

He holds up the phone; on the screen, there is a text that says, *Look what I've got*, with a photo of Beach Club Boy, dressed up and wrapped around Siobhan with one arm, aiming his phone at the two of them with the other.

"That's *Aiden*?"

"He'd be the perfect man for you. Liar, meet liar."

How much that hurts, how deep that cuts, and how much I probably deserve it is mitigated by my urgent need to get us out of there. Because that's freaking Aiden. *Because why didn't I know that that was freaking Aiden?????* Because why didn't I tell Dylan about last night, say, last night? Why didn't I fix this before what Siobhan set up (only I went along with it, and what kind of excuse it that, anyway?) plays itself out in the form of a train wreck?

Aren't brothers supposed to freaking resemble each other so an unsuspecting girl gets some slight hint of what she's doing when she accidentally kisses more than one of them?

"Let's leave. Dylan! Could we please go? I *really* need to talk to you."

"First we find them," he says. "Then we leave."

"But they could be anywhere." Such as Siobhan could be clubbing with Strick or Wade or anyone but Aiden on the Sunset Strip, and Aiden could be back in Scotland.

Dylan says, "They're in the pool house. I've been there fifty times."

I say, "Could we please talk somewhere? Like *now*!"

Dylan is racing forward, through crowds of tipsy dancing grown-ups. Waiters are trying to waylay us with offers of food and drink. This would be quite the glamorous party if it weren't the end of the world.

I race after Dylan with a skewered jumbo shrimp kebab in one hand and his sleeve in the other. I am trying to slow him down without actually tearing his jacket, to stop him before we reach the pool house, before we reach the point of complete hopelessness and relationship doom.

But we are there.

They are not in the pool house. They are laughing their way down the stairs from the upper patio toward us, Aiden still wrapped around her, Siobhan with huge pupils, and barefoot, and wearing a tiny red dress, hanging off his side.

Even though anyone with half a brain would know in advance that this was going to be a disaster of immense proportion, the actual unfurling of the immense disaster is just as surprising as if I hadn't imagined it so many times, with ever-changing details and a lot of imaginary screaming.

I say, "Dylan, before—"

Aiden says, "Hey, Amélie!"

Even when he's lurching, he's got swagger. Swagger that says, Hello, see this girl under my arm? I own her. I own this night, and this party, and the Western Hemisphere, and you. Or, in the alternative, I'm a completely ridiculous macho drunk guy that you never should have touched, because now you're toast.

My mouth. Dry, bitter burnt toast.

Dylan says, "Shit, Aiden. Do they all blend into each other? This is one" (by which he means me) "you haven't wrecked yet."

Siobhan shakes herself loose of Aiden and gapes at me. I scream at her, "What are you doing here? What's wrong with you? Why didn't you tell me?"

She says, "You stupid bitch, you didn't tell him, did you?"

Aiden says, "Amélie. Where's your Bert-and-Ernie slippers?"

"Her name is Emma and you've never seen her slippers," Dylan says. Then he gestures at Siobhan, and shakes his head. "Drop the girl and get on a plane. I had her and now you've got her. You've made your point with her, now fly away."

Siobhan yells, "I'm not anybody's point!"

I say, "Dylan, we need to leave."

"A-*mé*-lie," Aiden crooks his finger at me. "C'mere. Sibby doesn't mind. She didn't mind before."

People coming down the staircase from the upper deck have to forge a path around us at the foot of the stairs. Make spectacle of self at big, glam party: check.

Dylan turns to me. "Please tell me you don't know what he's talking about."

I don't say anything.

Dylan turns and walks back toward the dark side yard.

Aiden shouts, "D.K.! Don't go over there."

Dylan raises his arm in a one-fingered salute, but doesn't turn around.

I am on his heels, clamoring for attention, like Mutt chasing a macaroon.

"It's my French name. I don't use it. It wasn't anything."

He stops short. "Then what was it?"

God, it's no wonder I haven't been telling the truth all along—beyond my more obvious moral failings and complete tumble off the Emma the Good horse—because it's hard, it's just so hard, and also painful.

"Dylan, it was one random kiss before I even knew you. It was anonymous. It was nothing."

"Is this supposed to make me feel better?"

"I didn't even know it was your brother. You don't look that much alike. Your eyes aren't even the same color, and he's taller—" This is not going well. "And then when I saw him again—"

"When?"

"You have to believe me—"

"No. I don't have to believe you. I don't believe you. *When?*" Followed by a second so long and so painful, it feels as if it's being stretched out on a medieval instrument of torture.

"Yesterday, I'm so sorry!"

"*Yesterday.*" He is shaking his head, as if marveling at how horrible and unexpected this is. "Is there anything I know about you that's true? I don't even know your *name.*"

I grope for a list of true things, hard facts with no spin or shading, but as I'm trying to compile it, he is pulling me along by the arm as we traverse the dark lawn, weaving around plants and the occasional couple, in a shoe-wrecking shortcut to the valet parkers off the circular driveway.

He says, "Hot damn."

We are facing a decades older, exact model of Dylan, presumably his dad, jumping to get his hand off Dylan's mother's ass. And I wonder, in the middle of all this, if his mom is the second wife, because she looks decades younger, as if either she's had the best cosmetic surgery on earth or she had Dylan when she was twelve.

In his I'm-actually-not-here-and-would-rather-eat-dirt-than-speak voice, Dylan says, "And here we have my father."

I stick out my hand, dutiful girlfriend, even though that's going to last for maybe five more seconds. I go, "Hello, Mr. Kahane. Hello, Mrs. Kahane," followed by stone silence.

Dylan's deadpan, it turns out, did not fall from the sky; it was inbred. He and his dad stand there looking at each other without any discernible facial expression between them, essentially without blinking.

"This is *not* Mrs. Kahane," Dylan says. "This would be . . . Who are you?"

And I realize, of course I realize, that as horrible as this evening has been up to now, this is the main event.

I say, "We should go."

Dylan says, "I wish I'd never met you."

I am pretty sure he's talking to me.

"Are you all right?"

"You're the third-to-last person on earth I want sympathy from."

He hands the parking ticket to the valet, not looking at me, not responding.

All I want to do is make him feel better. But the only way to do that would be to turn into someone else, preferably a better person, because, as things stand, all I can do, beyond apologizing, is make him feel worse. Listening to me apologize probably makes him feel worse, too.

In the car, every time I start to form a word, or a syllable, such as the "I'm" of "I'm sorry," Dylan says, "I can't. Talk. About this. While I'm driving."

We're parked just beyond the driveway of his parents' house, having more or less driven through the rock garden, stopping just short of a hedge of white roses.

We just sit there and I watch him fume in profile.

I am waiting for his eyes to narrow in the amused way and not the so-angry-he-can't-even-speak way. I am waiting for some slight indication that he's thinking, okay, well, that's not so bad.

And then I think, Sure, like that's going to happen. Emma the I Don't Even Know What, who did this to him on Valentine's Day, who just couldn't stop kicking his feelings down the road endlessly. The one who every time she had a chance to tell him, didn't. In what universe do you get to lie this much, and then the person you're lying to thinks it's somehow okay because who cares if his girlfriend has been lying to him forever?

I don't mean to grab him, but I grab him, in what is likely the most awkward and unreciprocated hug ever offered to a boy who wasn't dead. He's so stone still, inhaling, exhaling, not holding me back, that it seems even more likely that I'm clinging to the last hug, or, more accurately, half hug, and it's over, and I wrecked it.

My forehead is resting on his shoulder, but he doesn't move.

He says, "Get out of the car."

He turns his head slightly to look at me, to look me over, and it's the kind of look that Emma the Good would never, ever, in the furthest reaches of anyone's imagination, ever have to look back at.

This is us breaking up.

CHAPTER FORTY-EIGHT

I TEXT "SORRY" EVERY COUPLE OF HOURS ALL DAY
Sunday. I entertain brief, tiny delusional moments when I think,
Hey, it'll blow over, so he's had a grudge against his brother since
third grade and plans to cut off his parents as soon as he hits the
Eastern Seaboard, but hey, he'll forgive *me*.

After six "sorries," he texts back, "Good for you."

Over, over, over.

Megan, who is visiting her grandparents in Pebble Beach,
bicycles down the road and calls me from behind a tree in a
scenic overlook.

First I moan, and then Megan says, "Uh, Emma, you get that
lying to him like that was really bad, right?"

"Of course I get it! I get that he's not a shithead for dumping me and I get that I'm a terrible person. Justice is served.
Balance is restored to the universe. It would probably feel better, though, if I hadn't spent every waking minute fantasizing

about him since September and if he wasn't *perfect*."

"If he's that perfect, eventually he'll figure out you're a good person and forgive you."

"He'll never forgive me."

Megan says, "He's probably flattened by the thing with his father. I would die."

"I know. And I can't even help him or talk to him or anything. I'm not even his friend anymore. I completely screwed that up."

Siobhan: Cheer up. He's just some stupid high
school boy who couldn't deal.

Siobhan: Where r u?

Siobhan: It's me. U know u want to talk to me.

Siobhan: Yr nemesis is now in Scotland if u care.

Siobhan: They're both crap.

Siobhan: So he ditched you. Big freaking deal.

Siobhan: U got your check mark. Move on.

Siobhan: Why would you even want to be with him?

Siobhan: I told u he was crap.

Me: U told me he was surprisingly nice.

Siobhan: I told u to bail.

Me: WHY DIDN'T YOU TELL ME THAT WAS
AIDEN???

Siobhan: Are u BLAMING me??????? U think I
screwed u on purpose?????

Me: If it looks like a fish and it swims like a fish and
it smells like a fish.

Siobhan: Quaint. A Canadian proverb. Here's an
American fact. U said u were going to tell him. How
wd I know u wussed out?
Me: You were supposed to be with Strick on Sunset.
And I couldn't tell him about Aiden could I because my
best friend didn't bother to tell me who Aiden was!!!!!
Siobhan: Strick sucks. Strick was supposed to b
home coughing to death but he was at a party in
Encino. Quel loser. Aiden said come I went.
Siobhan: Big freaking deal.

But at the end of all this, at the end of the day, at the end of
agonizing in the closet, which shouldn't have taken more than
two minutes because the truth is so obvious: my fault. Completely.
Not just some joke of a Bad Emma taking a shortcut around an
immovable wall to experience high school hijinks up close. An
actual Bad Emma who hurt someone she proclaimed she loved.

How could I do that to him?

I text him: *Still sorry. Could we please talk?*

Dylan: Go away.

This is what I want to do at school: hide.

I want to find the Latimer equivalent of my closet and sit
in there. I don't want to face Dylan. When we accidentally catch
each other's eye, he looks at me and then, pointedly, looks away.

I like it down behind the stables, where it's quiet, and there's no one there, possibly because even when there's no sun, the air smells ripe and horsey.

I don't want to see Siobhan, hear from Siobhan, or talk to Siobhan.

And nobody else at school seems all that interested in talking with me, except for Kimmy. Who is kind of friend-like, but who more than kind of can't stand not having any and all late-breaking Latimer news.

"You and Dylan," she says as I'm heading away from the candy machines and toward the path into the woods. "What's up with that?"

I say, "Nothing."

"You're not back with Jean-Luc, are you?"

"No! Could we please not talk about this?"

Kimmy says, "But you're MIA. Literally. Siobhan is slamming things, so that's getting annoying. And Dylan is total Dylan, only more so."

"Don't."

"Damn! Kahane didn't dump you did he, because if he did, after you gave up Jean-Luc for him—"

"Kimmy, it's nothing like that! Could we please talk once I figure it out?"

She says, "I guess. But nobody knows where you are and I, like, miss you."

Siobhan, tromping down the hill, says, "You have to stop hiding out."

I have a slice of pizza and I'm sitting on a rock with my physics book.

I say, "Go away. I don't forgive you."

Siobhan says, "Fine. Because I'm not sorry."

"How can you not be sorry? That was a complete and total setup with your signature on it."

"You keep repeating yourself. You're boring me to death. It was a *game*. Man of Mystery and International Girl of Intrigue."

"How far back did you plan this?"

"You are so paranoid," Siobhan sighs. "And Dylan is a jerk. Who cares if you kissed some guy you didn't even know?"

"You were supposed to have my back, not stab me in it!"

"Well, this blows, doesn't it?" she says "You totally fuck up by not telling your stupid boyfriend what you said you were going to tell him, so why not blame your best friend?" She pulls some tall, dry grass out by the roots. "Are you just going to hide out back here forever or what?"

She reaches down. She says, "Come on, missy. Two weeks in time-out is plenty."

It's not completely clear who she thinks was in time-out, her or me.

"Crap," Siobhan says, sitting down. "Bad Emma, bad Emma. Are you happy now? You have to cut it out."

"I'd appreciate it if you'd go away."

And it gets worse. I stop at the caf for a root beer to wash down the awful pizza, and there's Dylan, getting fries. He is as blank as a chunk of white ice, and as warm.

I say, "Hey."

He says nothing.

Siobhan, sitting by the window with frozen yogurt, says, "Give it up, Kahane. Talk to the girl."

Dylan takes the fries, slaps down a couple of dollars at the cash register, and leaves. He never once looks at me.

In English, I glance at Arif, who hasn't said a word to me either, and he is not even slightly smiling back.

I say, "I don't want to embarrass you, but aren't you talking to me either?"

There's a long pause during which he appears to be deciding if the degree of his not talking to me includes not answering direct questions. He says, "I know there are two sides to every story, but—"

"You can stop there. There's one side, and FYI, it's not my side. I don't even *have* a side."

"Really." It's as if Dylan has been tutoring him on expressionlessness. I figure, if I can push Arif over the edge to less-than-polite, I really have strayed beyond the bounds of the civilized world.

"Oh yeah, I'm Satan. It's in my genes."

"Don't say that," he says. Very sharply. "There are very few unforgivable things."

I wonder how many of them I've managed to land on.

I text Dylan. "I get it. I can't get any sorrier. You can stop now."

He doesn't reply.

At the food bank, Megan says, "I'm worried about you."

"Don't be."

She says, "It really is a shame Jews don't have confession. Because you need absolution, and you need it fast."

"How would I even know what Jews do and don't have? My dad doesn't even think I'm good enough to get any higher than a temple basement."

I leave her there. Or try to. She trails me back into the powdered milk.

She says, "You know what delusional depressive thinking that is, right?"

"That's me. Sad and delusional."

"You know what I mean. There are pills for this."

"My boyfriend dumped me because I suck. This isn't a mental disorder."

Megan sighs, "Your dad doesn't want you upstairs because your dad is a raging atheist."

"What?"

"My mom says. Although my mom thinks Cardinal Mahony is a secret atheist. Why don't you just take him at face value that he doesn't want to impose religion on you? Not because he doesn't think you're good enough. Aren't you supposed to *want* to impose religion on people who aren't good enough?"

"I think Dylan might have noticed that I wasn't good enough."

"This is classic depressed thinking," Megan says.

I wave her away and duck deeper into the back of the food supply.

This time, it's Rabbi Pam who finds me behind the cheese.

"Come on," she says, "let's go upstairs." I freeze for a second, and she says, "I understand that your dad doesn't want you within ten miles of a prayer. I promise I'll respect that."

So there I am in Rabbi Pam's office. Just barely inside the door of Rabbi Pam's office. She is gazing at me with a whole poor-motherless-girl-let-me-make-you-a-sandwich look, which is alarming. Also, there isn't a single object in her office without a Star of David, a Hebrew letter, or a picture of a Torah on it. Even the plant pot has Hebrew lettering. The whole place freaks me out, possibly because I haven't been allowed anywhere near anyplace like it for sixteen years.

She says, "Would you rather take a walk?"

I wouldn't rather take a walk. I'd rather run out the door and get an In-N-Out burger. But I don't want to insult her, so I follow her across the parking lot.

"You haven't been your usual cheerful self for a while," she says.

I'm somewhere between a state of kill-me-now and just wanting to talk to someone who doesn't know me well enough to disapprove of me. And as long as I've got a person with a graduate degree in morality, no doubt a lot more familiar with the Word of God than I am, standing in the parking lot with me, and because I want to change the subject, I say, "What's unforgivable in Judaism?"

She runs her hand through her hair. She says, "Not much, if you're sorry and you try to fix it." We are walking down toward Hollywood Boulevard. She says, "Do you want to get some soda? We got rid of the soda machines, and I'm craving a Coke."

Which gives me hope that this might be an actual conversation and not just rabbinical probing for teen angst.

I say, "You want to go to In-N-Out?"

We head down the block. She looks a lot more like a normal person when you get her away from the ten-foot-tall religious symbols and the massive stacks of prayer books.

She says, "You do know that the holiest day of the year is about atonement and forgiveness? Which includes forgiving yourself."

"Not that I've ever been in a temple for Yom Kippur, but yeah. 'We have committed evil, we have acted abominable, we have totally gone astray.'"

A lady passing us on the sidewalk gives me a look as if I'm a guy with a sign that says the world is ending, with the biblical location of the chapter and verse to prove it.

"Close. Your dad's not big on candy-coating, is he? But you don't think you've personally gone totally astray, do you?" She gives me an appraising look, but "yes" isn't the answer she's going for, and who lies to a rabbi who's taking her to In-N-Out? "Remember, 'This is the gate of the Eternal. Enter into it, you who have fed the hungry'?"

I say, "Don't even. It's not like I can bag beans twice a week and that makes me a good person."

Rabbi Pam says, "You don't experience yourself as a good person?"

"Sometimes it feels like the world would be a better place if I'd stay in my closet."

"Is that what was going on when you stopped coming a while back?" Even though I'm looking straight ahead, I can feel her eyes scanning my face.

"That wasn't completely my choice." In the spirit of total honesty because she's a rabbi, even if she does want to be called Pam, I say, "Although probably my fault. Overboard in the breaking-of-rules department."

"What kinds of rules are we talking about?" We are paused, standing just outside of a shoe repair shop with cracked leather handbags and old boots hanging in the window, and she's half blocking my path, as if she can tell that the harder I'm trying to tell her the absolute truth, the more I want to run.

"Rules," I say. "Honor your father. Tell the truth occasionally. Stop on red. Go on green. Thou shalt not murder." Her facial expression suggests that hyperbole was a poor choice. "Not that I murdered anyone."

Which is kind of a bad example, anyway, in the forgiving-yourself-because-you-tried-to-fix-things department. Because, seriously, how do you un-murder someone? How do you un-hurt people and undo months of unwise choices and take back conversations you wish you'd never had, but you had them, and now you're stuck with them?

So what if you've tried to cobble things back together, made restitution, cleaned up your act, chatted with a friendly rabbi who's racking her brain to make you feel better without any real understanding of what you've done?

"Maybe just asking the questions puts you on the right track," Rabbi Pam says. She smiles, but her attempt at good cheer is betrayed by her eyes. "And there's your conscience."

My conscience is nothing to smile about.

Where was it when I needed it?

Then her cell phone rings, and she goes searching through her bag looking for it. I wave while she's saying she'll call back and nodding her head at me to stay.

I whisper, "It's okay. You should talk to them," and I run back toward the food bank before any exploration of my conscience can happen.

I finish my shift and I drive home and I dive into the closet.

CHAPTER FORTY-NINE

Siobhan: U and boy toy have a lot in common, u know that?

Siobhan: Don't you want to know what?

Siobhan: All right I'll tell u what. You both don't ever forgive people.

Me: Excuse me. You're not sorry. You said so.

Siobhan: Why should I have to be sorry for you to forgive me?

Me: Excuse me????

Siobhan: Not much on LOL these days are we?

Siobhan: I'm sorry. R u happy now?

Me: That was sincere.

Siobhan: No I'm really sorry.

Siobhan: R u coming over?

At school, Siobhan keeps pulling on my sleeve and I keep turning away.

In homeroom, she says, "You have to get your dad to give you Prozac or something. I'm not kidding. Because everything sucks, but you have to last until Afterparty or the whole year was pointless."

There. Something Siobhan and Megan can agree on: my need for medication.

I say, "Thanks. Because lasting to Afterparty is my goal in life."

"It's not?"

I start counting the minuscule pleats in Miss Palmer's skirt. I take notes on the morning announcements, which pertain mostly to carpool-line policies and other similarly compelling topics.

Before English starts, Siobhan is talking to William via her iPad. She is moaning, "I'm bored, I'm bored, I'm bored. I'm trapped in the smog belt, or the sunbelt, or whatever the hell belt this is, and you're going to freaking Rome."

William starts singing "Party All the Time" in German. He says, "Sibi, you should come."

She says, "I wish."

Then, to me, she says, "See. *We* should party all the time. Aren't you bored yet?"

I never want to go to another party again, say, forever.

"Just one short walk to the Chateau Marmont, one giant step for mankind." she says.

"I'm done."

"You can be as severely deluded and mad at me as you want," she says. "But if you think you're getting back at me by eating pizza on a compost heap, guess what, you're not. And if you think your asshole boyfriend is going to like you better if you mope for the rest of the year, he doesn't notice."

"Excuse me while I write this down."

"There's a Winston lacrosse party in the Palisades Saturday. Why don't you cut back on Scrabble with daddy to six nights a week?"

"Party with degenerates. Perfect."

"I'm not talking about Winston water polo." Overblown sigh. "It's not like I keep a rape kit in my car. But it's a law of nature that Winston lacrosse is hot and has good parties. Even you know this. This *is* perfect."

"I'm not up for it."

"Do you want to get over this or not?" Siobhan says. "And if you don't go with me, who are you gonna go with? Chelsea?"

I shrug like there's no way in hell.

Eye-roll. "You're just too perfect for me. Because I'm sure you stood up for me when Kahane talked trash about me. Which there's no way he didn't." She crosses her hands over her mouth and raises her eyebrows in perfect "gotcha" position. "You must be the perfect friend."

Well, there you have it. I'm now just as bad as she is in the friend-I've-got-your-back department. I suck, which I already knew.

She stalks off in the direction of the lounge. "I don't even care!" she calls back. "Text me if you change your mind, and maybe you can come with me."

In English, Arif leans forward and pokes me. It hurts.

I say, "What? Are you coming after me with a pitchfork now?"

Arif says, "Listen, are you planning to say something to him ever? Because he's still leveled."

Bullet to the heart, but I realize it's a you-made-the-bullet-riddled-bed-now-lie-in-it kind of situation.

"The deal is, he's not talking to me. His last communication was, 'Go away.'"

"Really?"

"Yes, really! Did he not mention I've apologized fifty times? How sorry can I be? I'm telling his best friend I'm sorry—that's how sorry."

"What did you do to him, exactly?"

"Arif," I say, "he talked to you about the other thing, right?"

Arif says, "What other thing?"

I can't tell if he's being tactful or if Dylan really isn't talking to anyone about his dad, which makes me even sadder, and also a far worse person for putting him in a position of being alone with something that bad.

"Maybe ask him about the party."

Now Arif is glaring straight at me. "Forgive me if I don't take your advice at face value."

I gather up my pad, my pen, and my entirely synthetic cardigan, and walk out.

And I think, all right, I can tell that Siobhan set me up, I'm not a complete idiot. But it's not as if I'm Snow White and I get to reject the morally deficient as potential companions because I'm just so ethically superior. Maybe she and I are even more perfect for each other than I'd ever imagined, because look at me.

Me: The Palisades. It's on.
Siobhan: I knew it.

Then I text Dylan my fifty-first apology.

PART THREE

PART THREE

CHAPTER FIFTY

THE COMPASS SAYS, *DON'T GO.*

To which I reply: Go torture a nice, salvageable girl. Which (hint) would not be me.

I say to my dad, who is, by necessity, oblivious to everything that's been going on, "I'm sleeping over at Sib's, all right?"

My dad says, "Doesn't Siobhan go wild Saturday nights?"

"Not this Saturday, she doesn't." Not really caring, because going wild is sounding slightly attractive and not entirely inconsistent with what I've turned myself into.

He says, "Okay."

I pack my overnight bag while telling myself, This is what Kimmy does when she says she's going to take pictures of Hoover Dam and stay with Declan Hart's sister at UNLV, when, in fact, she's going camping with Declan. I say to myself, I actually am sleeping over at Siobhan's, so the actual sentence that came out of my mouth was true. See how improved I am now that I've stopped skulking around with Dylan Kahane in the wonderful world of teen contraception so as not to accidentally turn up on a future season of *Teen Mom*?

The compass says, *Cool, a new form of lying. Unpack. Play a nice round of French Scrabble and call it a night. Repent. Repair. Make your dad tea.*

Part of me wants to, but the part with legs is out the door.

Siobhan is completely antsy, chanting, "Party, party, party." She turns up my car radio, and dances around in her seat.

I look over at her, bouncing around as if everything is swell, and I think, Why am I doing this? Pretending we can still have a Girls Just Want to Have Fun night after everything that's happened? What am I even doing in the car with her?

We are driving through a tract of giant houses at the far end of Sunset. On the list of things my dad objects to in the U.S., these houses aren't anywhere near the top, but I still can't drive past them without hearing him go, "Ah, the marriage of bad taste, ostentation, and money."

I do not, at this moment, want to be hearing my dad's voice in my head.

Or the compass saying, *Turn around.*

Siobhan says, "You're awfully quiet, missy. Don't you want to have a widdle fun?"

The party house is on a wooded knoll. I can't tell if the electricity is overloaded and flickering out, or if this is weirdly intentional.

Siobhan is out the door before I've even parked, running toward the house, up through the ivy on the steep bank because there's no way to squeeze between the cars crammed in the sloping driveway.

She yells, "Come on!" above the blasts of music.

By the time I get there, she's disappeared. The band is so loud, it hurts to be in the same room with them. The loudness vibrates into the part of the brain that produces headaches in bursts of pain behind the eyes. I head outside. The backyard smells like weed and vomit.

The first person I see that I know, and who looks to be enjoying things even less than me, is Arif. He's in a gazebo with Kimmy, who doesn't look as if she's in much of a party mood either.

She's sitting on a white bench, her hand on Arif's arm. I can see her mouth move, but the music is so raucous, she might as well be in a silent movie, all the colors washed out in the blinking lights, her white top and Arif's shirt glowing like phosphorescent fish dead on the beach at night.

She yells, "Emma!"

I climb through more ivy, up to the gazebo.

She says, "Did you come with Dylan?"

And I'm thinking, Maybe I should have told her something about that, back when she wanted to know.

"With Siobhan."

"Can you drive?"

"What?"

She yells louder, "Can you drive? Are you sober? Your stupid boyfriend or whatever is trashed and someone has to get Arif out of here."

I yell, "What's going on?"

"The Winston assholes parked Arif's car in, and he's sick."

In the green light, his skin looks ashy.

I yell, "Are you drunk?"

Kimmy says, "Hello. This is *Arif*. He doesn't do alcohol. It's against his religion. Literally."

Arif moans something about nachos. Bad, nasty poisonous nachos.

Here it is if I want it, served up on a bad-nacho platter: a way out of here. Sib can taxi if she wants to stay, no big scene, sick friend. Arif could throw up in my car, but sitting on blocks for fourteen years makes a car smell like a sweat sock, so the risk is less hideous than in a normal vehicle that smells either new or like a cedar-scented car deodorizer.

Then I register Dylan, who is indeed trashed—you can see it in his walk as he lopes toward the gazebo. I register the extreme, imminent awkwardness of being in my car with trashed Dylan and sick Arif, in front of whom Dylan and I couldn't actually talk about anything, not that I want to.

All right, I want to.

I say, "Okay, I just have to tell Siobhan."

Kimmy says, "Try upstairs. It's pretty insane up there."

Siobhan is on the landing with her shirt mostly unbuttoned, barefoot on the deep pile of the Persian runner, deep blues and jewel greens and wet spots. I only find her because I hear her laughing, louder and louder and louder.

I call her, but she doesn't turn around. I touch her and she's shivering, but her skin feels hot.

I say, "Sib, we need to go."

"But Mommy, we just got here."

"Yeah, but I'm sober and Arif needs a ride. He's sick."

She looks over the banister at the party below, teetering over the railing. She says, "Who elected you nanny?"

I say, "Come on, he's really sick. Kimmy can't take him because she's plowed."

"Oh no!" Siobhan says. "Not Kimmy! Maybe you should go try to button up *her* shirt and take her home too. Or you could stay and get some check marks. Don't you want some cocoa-puffs? Little bitty blow? You know you do."

"Sib, we're going. I can't play with this stuff: bad genes."

She gives me a little-kid-pout face. "You're already *half* her. Don't you even want to know what would happen?"

A completely trashed boy I don't know comes out of a bed-room and says he'll take Siobhan home.

"Fuck off," she says. "Like *this* is taking me home? You go, I'll taxi. It's not like I never went to a party and got home fine without you before."

She looks like the girl who gets into a taxi and is never seen again, not the girl who is going to get home just fine.

At this point, Charlene Perry, who appears never to drink but does a damn good impersonation of a totally drunk girl, comes down the hall. "I'll take her home. I'm not, you know, incapacitated."

Siobhan is already heading into another bedroom, leaning on the guy's bigger, cuter friend.

Charlene says, "Don't worry. I'll take care of her. This is a Winston party. I have pepper spray."

Someone is making noise about flamethrowers. I say, "What's that?" And Charlene says, "Cigarettes with smack sprinkles. These people have *everything*," as she heads downstairs. "And I won't forget Siobhan, get out of here."

The walk from the party house to my car is completely silent except for Arif groaning and thanking me. The drive to his house is silent except for the voice of my GPS lady taking us into the stratosphere of Bel Air. I am hyperaware of Dylan sitting next to me, of the proximity of his elbow, but he might as well be a crash dummy.

Arif's house is a giant concrete fortress, built into a hillside, looking out at the city. We are at the gated end of a long driveway flanked by rows of conical trees.

I say, "It's so modern."

Dylan, slightly slurred, says, "You were expecting minarets?"

Arif moans for Dylan to shut up, and rests his head against the window.

Dylan says, "Reef, where's your key?"

"Didn't need it," Arif says. "My car opens the gate."

There is a very serious fence. "Great security," I say.

"Just buzz," Arif says.

Just buzzing doesn't seem like that great an alternative. I have a vision of my dad's face if some unknown person in an ancient

Volvo unloaded me in that kind of shape, but I can't think of any other way to get Arif into his house.

I punch the buzzer, the shortest buzz humanly possible, and drive in as the gate swings open.

Arif's dad is at the front door in pajamas and a striped bathrobe. He looks upset, but not homicidal. This is good. I don't want to be responsible for Arif being the object of parental rage.

Dylan does the drunk equivalent of helping Arif exit the backseat, and I sit there feeling useless and still worried I'm about to witness Arif getting creamed.

But his dad, fumbling around with his glasses, just kind of hugs him and looks concerned as Arif tells him about the bad nachos.

And then Arif's dad says to Dylan, "Have you been drinking, D.K.?"

Dylan says, "Not Arif. He's sick."

"I can see that," Arif's dad says. "What about *you*?"

"I have a designated driver," Dylan says. "I'll be fine. She's driving me home."

Arif's dad peers in at me. He says to Dylan, "There's a young lady in that car."

Mr. Saad leans down toward me. "I'd be happy to drive both of you, and you could come get your car in the morning." He pushes his glasses along the bridge of his nose, as if he's trying to get a better look at me. "Or Mrs. Saad could drive you."

Mr. Saad looks approximately as happy as my dad would be with the idea of me driving a drunk guy around in the middle of the night. The Saads and my dad and the Donnellys are no doubt all in a secret support group for the militantly overprotective. But the last thing in the world I want to have happen—just before being struck by giant bolts of lightning—is to lose the opportunity to be alone with Dylan.

I say, "Thank you so much, but I told my dad I needed to drop two friends off"—lie, lie, lie, even Arif seems to be jolted out of his nauseated, half-dead state by my creativity—"so I'll be fine. But thank you. That's very nice of you."

Mr. Saad does not look convinced, but before he can throw himself in front of the Volvo, Dylan jumps back in and I'm rolling down the driveway toward the open gate.

And I'm pretty sure, I'm almost certain, that Dylan wants to be here with me, too. Which, except for the fact that he makes me pull over before we get back down to Sunset so he can throw up in the gutter, could be somewhat romantic.

Maybe.

Chapter Fifty-One

DYLAN GETS BACK IN THE CAR, SMELLING DISGUST-ing, and we roll down Sunset, not talking to each other. Dylan hangs on to the door handle and stares into the street, as if fascinated by oncoming headlights. Then he closes his eyes.

A stunning reconciliation with a guy who first throws up and then falls asleep, or worse, simulates sleep, seems less than imminent.

In a maybe slightly louder-than-normal voice, I say, "Are you asleep?"

Dylan makes a show of stretching, which is difficult for a tall person in my car. He pushes against the roof. He says, "I'm up now." He does not sound very happy about this.

I say, "Could we please talk?"

"Isn't that what you said the last time you were trying to bull-shit me? No."

He closes his eyes again.

I slightly poke him.

"Emma," he says. "Please. I feel like shit."

"Can't you cut me five minutes of slack?"

"No."

All I had wanted in life was to be alone in the car with him and for him to go, *Hey, that was pretty bad but now I'm past it,* hug, hug, hug, and basically acknowledge my existence. But whatever there was before is clearly gone. All that longing followed by what felt like the opening chapter of endless bliss and then, welcome to this.

The car might be jerking a little, or possibly a lot, and Dylan puts his hand on the steering wheel and he barks, "Let me out!"

We are sitting in front of a lit-up house on Alpine.

"I get that you're just in my car to get home. Go ahead."

Quietly, Dylan says, "Why are you being like this?"

"*Maybe* because you dumped me on Valentine's Day, which was totally justified, I get it, but now you won't even speak to me and you look right through me and I hate going to school." This is punctuated by me splattering tears all over like a showerhead that somebody went after with a hammer.

"Aren't you leaving out the part where you *lied* to me and made a *fool* of me?"

"Is it impossible for you to believe I might be sorry?"

"*And* made it very clear you'd rather be with Aiden?"

"What are you talking about?"

"I know you went over to Sib's to hook up with him, okay?"

What?

"*Who told you that?*" I am pretty much screaming. "*That's not what happened!*"

"I don't want to hear this," Dylan says. "I don't want to listen to you trying to get out of it."

"How do you get from *I'm sorry* to I'm trying to get out of it? Do you just stay mad at people permanently?"

"At least I don't lie about myself!" he shouts back. "Unlike you. I stayed away from you for how long out of respect for a nonexistent French guy? What an idiot! And then, February *thirteenth*, you decide it's a good day to cheat with my brother? Hey, be my Valentine."

"I did not cheat with him!"

"Why should I believe anything you say?"

"Dylan! I kissed some random guy at the beach club, and then six months later Siobhan all but orders me to come over or she might jump out the window, and there's the guy in the Jacuzzi with her. And all right, I got in out of cowardice. The things she was threatening to tell you if I didn't: all true. You can call me nine kinds of bad person for that. But I didn't want Aiden, hook up with Aiden, cheat with Aiden, or *anything* with Aiden other than push him away when he came at me, all right?"

Dylan pauses. "Oh Jesus, Seed."

I dig around in my bag for a box of Tic Tacs and I give him a whole handful.

I say, "Well, are you ever going to stop it?"

He shakes his head. I can't decipher if this is Dylan saying no or Dylan being rueful. "Maybe I'll send you a one-word text message fifty-two times," he says.

"I'm sorry!"

In a flatlined voice, Dylan says, "That fixes everything."

I turn the key in the ignition.

"Nothing ever fixes anything, does it? Everything just gets hopelessly broken, and then we're all permanently stuck with it."

He says, "That's your philosophy of life?"

"Like it's not yours, too? Show me some evidence to the contrary. It seems remarkably accurate."

This is when he brushes back the hair at my temple and he kisses the side of my forehead.

And when we get there, when my car has made its loud approach to his house, crunching toward the guesthouse on the part of the gravel that's probably supposed to be a walkway, when he opens his eyes and his hand is covering my hand, when he walks around and opens my car door and takes my hand again, I rest my head against him for a minute.

Then I follow him inside.

A light from the bed of white roses outside the bedroom window is the only illumination in the room.

He has his arms around me, and he says, "Could we fast-forward to being okay? Skip the long emo conversation with crying and be okay?"

I sink into his desk chair, and he spins me around.

I say, "Probably not."

"What would I have to do?"

"Two sappy sentences, maybe? One with a lot of clauses Massive reassurance?"

He sits behind me on the bed. "I don't do sap. Last time I tried to do sap, I invited you to that party. How did that work out for you?"

Dylan swivels my chair until I'm facing him. "Shit. You don't stop crying, do you?" He grabs the back of the desk chair and rolls me through the darkness into the guesthouse's tiny kitchen. "I'll give you sap. I have half your chocolate duck left over from Valentine's Day."

"You bought me a chocolate *duck*?"

"Okay, it was a swan and it came in a silver bag. Is that sappy enough for you? But it's missing its head and neck."

"You decapitated my swan?"

"I was hungry."

Dylan opens the refrigerator, which is completely filled with international take-out. Pizza, and tacos, and Indian, and Chinese rice boxes.

"You *were* hungry. Have you been ordering snacks every night?"

Dylan says, "This is dinner. I don't eat with them. When Aiden's not here, family life grinds to a halt. Not that I mind."

I touch his sleeve. "Your dad's still . . . here?"

He says, "We're not going to talk about my dad. Ever. Suffice to say, he's still here; Aiden's not here; neither is my mom, mostly; and I'm leaving. Nothing has changed."

Dylan roots around in the refrigerator, behind what looks to be a quart of take-out Chinese soup, and pulls out an extremely wrinkled foil bag covered in silver mesh. He reaches in and breaks a wing off my swan and he sits on the kitchen table and feeds it to me. Establishing for all eternity that the universe, or at least Beverly Hills north of Santa Monica Boulevard, is not completely fucked.

I say, "I got you the best valentine. It came from the fifties. It went with the dress."

"We're also never going to talk about that party."

"Fine, just answer this one question: Did Siobhan flat-out tell you I went over there to get with Aiden?"

He groans, "Yes. And we're not talking about how I fell for that, either." He raps his forehead against the door of a kitchen cabinet.

Which is not—despite my complete sorry-ness and sopping up of all possible responsibility for everything I ever did—entirely inappropriate. Even though she's the one I want to slam, Siobhan, the person formerly known as my best friend. As my any kind of friend.

I say, "Christ, Dylan. If I want a list of things that I can't talk about, I'll stay home."

He says, "Shut up and eat." He breaks off another piece and he outlines my lips with it. Withholds it a few inches from my mouth, very briefly, and then feeds me tiny, sweet splinters of dark chocolate.

"I'm afraid if I keep teasing you with this duck, you'll bawl again," he says.

"What if I gave you the valentine?"

"What if I teased you?"

At which point, he rolls the chair back into the bedroom.

CHAPTER FIFTY-TWO

I WAKE UP TO BIRDS CHIRPING, AND A ROOM FILLED with pale gray light. Which would be charming except it's 9:40 in the morning and I'm still at Dylan's house. My car is still parked in his driveway. My head is on his pillow, and my clothes are draped over his desk chair.

I'm wearing a T-shirt with Kurt Cobain on the front, no doubt the universe's way of saying, Off yourself immediately and get it over with, because you are monumentally dead.

On the other hand, we are so back together.

My head feels spongy and I don't even remember how I ended up falling asleep here. Which is, I guess, how falling asleep works. Wham, you're down. Other than the imminent deadness part of it, sleeping over here was nice. Waking up to rain on the shingles and Dylan spread over three-quarters of his bed.

Nine forty. Brunch with the Karps. Oh God.

"I was supposed to be home from Siobhan's at nine!"

Dylan hands me my phone. Four missed calls. Which I slept through.

And then there's the exciting prospect of Dylan being reminded of my improvisational skills when I tell my dad some fairy tale all about how his (slightly debauched) princess is over at Siobhan's house. Not how I've been cuddled up all night with the world's most restless sleeper. Who seems remarkably calm under the circumstances, given that unless I fix this, he's going to be executed by my dad.

My only slim ray of hope is that if my dad tried to reach me on Burton's landline, nobody over there is up before noon on weekends.

My dad opens with: "Why aren't you here?"

I am feeling a confusing combination of dread, guilt, and extreme happiness. "I slept through your calls!" (True.) "I didn't set the alarm on my phone." (True.) "I've never been this late in my whole life!" (True.)

He tells me how rude and inconsiderate I am in French, which is somehow more appalling than in English, although it no doubt beats being nailed with whatever term applies to girls who spend the night in boys' beds.

I apologize in French, as Dylan looks on, making faces at me. I politely motion that I'm going to cut his throat and he disappears into the kitchen.

My dad says, "I'll meet you there. Two cars."

"But all I have with me is jeans."

Jeans would be completely all right with the Karps and everybody else we know, including the Donnellys, but count as wardrobe disrespect with him when visiting anyone other than bears at the zoo.

He says, "Can't you borrow something from Siobhan?"

Oh God.

I say, very quietly, because it's not true yet, but it will be if I ever talk to her again, "We just had a fight."

My dad is too overjoyed about this to stay that annoyed. Or maybe I'm reading too much into the fact that he stops yelling at me.

Dylan is rummaging around in the kitchen. "You want something before you go?"

"Could I borrow a shirt?" The overnight bag is at Siobhan's. All I have is the spaghetti-strap tight thing from last night and, in my car, a Latimer tee that's cut off (actually cut, with scissors, not my best fashion experiment ever) three inches above waist level, and is not debuting at the Karps'.

Dylan's closet smells like him. Not in a bad way. I take a white linen shirt, and I roll up the sleeves and look in the mirror to see if this could in any way pass as something a girl would wear when not desperate. I take the little metal belt from last night and try to get it to sit in the right place. The result isn't strikingly horrible.

I hear Dylan rummaging around in the cupboards. "You want a jelly doughnut? It's the only breakfast food I've got."

"No time! I'll just snort the powdered sugar off the top."

"Bad joke, considering who I used to go out with."

I say, "There's another thing we're never going to talk about."

Mrs. Karp admires Dylan's shirt and wonders if I got it at Fred Segal.

CHAPTER FIFTY-THREE

BY THE TIME I'VE (BARELY) SURVIVED BRUNCH—THE first hour of which my dad spends glowering at me while Mrs. Karp flutters around saying how happy she is to have me, no matter *what* time I arrived, in possibly the world's least helpful effort to be helpful—things are back to (mostly) normal.

My return to my dad's good graces is greatly assisted by the youngest Karp child, who quietly spreads peanut butter on the Karp dachshund. Reminding my dad of his own amazing success in raising a daughter so repressed that she never, ever so much as considered coating a dog with peanut butter *or* jelly.

And when he walks me to my car afterward, if I weren't wearing my boyfriend's shirt, I would be the picture of goodness. Which is when I tell him how I left my overnight bag at Siobhan's (true) because I was racing so fast to get out of there (not).

Now I'm tooling down Sunset in my own gumdrop-yellow car,

windows open, radio blasting; this was the Candy Land dream, for a second at the beach club that first day when I first saw Siobhan. When Montana Gibson was no doubt down on the beach toasting a marshmallow while I was in the clubhouse kissing Aiden, and Siobhan was bagging him, and I had no idea who they were, or what I was actually seeing, or how all that confectionary sugar was going to melt and get sticky and rank.

I turn up Doheny toward Burton's house, with its fake-pond Jacuzzi, and I'm thinking, Quick in and out. No confrontation, no screaming, no drama. Just bye.

I'm thinking, One forty-five, she could still be asleep, this could be completely painless.

But Siobhan is not asleep. She doesn't look as if she slept that much earlier, either. She just looks wasted.

This couldn't be completely painless. We've already had the big-ass fight a dozen times; this is us breaking up.

"Look who finally showed," she says, rolling over on her black and white quilt, setting down her book.

I feel weirdly defensive, as if what I think is the final betrayal hadn't already happened. As if we were still the Dynamic Duo and this was just a rocky patch in Gotham City.

I say, "I fell asleep. It was kind of unplanned. Sorry if you were worried."

"I thought you went off with some forty-year-old perv who asked you to help find his lost kitten."

I say, "Yeah, well, I told him I was boss of my body."

She is sitting on the edge of her bed now, in the same short little skirt and unbuttoned shirt as when I left her at the party. "Didn't get much sleep, did we?" she says.

"Could I just have my bag? I have to go."

She says, "Where were you?"

"You know where."

"He broke up with you for no good reason!" she half shouts. "He broke your heart and then you slept with him? Did you wake up stupid yesterday?"

At the center of me, there is something so hard and cold and icy, it's as if my body temperature has plummeted to absolute zero and I don't even have feelings left, because my heart is ice.

I say, "Forget it. I'm done. I can't even listen to you."

"What's wrong with you?" She's off the bed and in my face.

I'm dodging her, I'm behind the rocking chair, and I yell back. "What's wrong with *you*? You pretend we're friends and then you tell him I came over here to hook up with Aiden! Are you out of your mind?"

She's grabbing at me and I'm holding up my arms and she has me.

I can't twist out of her grasp. When I try to pull away, it just gets tighter. Her mouth is all blurred lipstick and her pupils are so dilated, her irises have almost disappeared.

I say, "Shit, Siobhan, did you do flamethrowers back there?"

"Who told you I do flamethrowers?" she screams, her face six inches from my face.

"How high are you right now?"

"Flames don't last that long," she says. "Because. If they did. I wouldn't feel like this. And *I'm* not the one obsessed with heroin, grasshopper, *you* are."

Then she curls up in a ball, and she closes her eyes, and I can tell from her breathing that she's asleep.

At school, on Monday, Dylan says, "Look what I brought you."

Two slightly melted chunks of chocolate swan wing, which he procedes to feed me during break.

He says, "Does this satisfy your lust for sappiness, Seed?"

Arif says, "Do you two want privacy?" Only he says it with a soft *i*, and it sounds British and adorable.

"I'll just drag her into the bushes for that," Dylan says.

Arif slaps his hand to his forehead. "If you don't stop trying to impress her with your feeble attempts at humor, she's going to race back to her ex."

"Thank you for not telling him about my so-called ex," I say to Dylan when we're walking to class, his hand at my waist, which Latimer has now banned as inappropriate intimate contact. We are no-public-displays-of-physical-affection-and-joy violators.

Dylan says, "Once again, reminding you that I'm not Aiden."

"You are the model boyfriend."

Dylan puts his hands to his throat and demonstrates strangling himself.

He does, however, spend the next two weeks demonstrating model boyfriend behavior.

I barely miss Siobhan.

Barely.

When I think about her, I am either so sad or so angry or such a confusing combination of sad and angry that I go into Stop It mode. I do a lot of counting.

She seems to get it. There are no texts and no IMs and no tripping me in the hall or hauling me into the bathroom for drama. Or maybe she's too high to care.

I keep wondering why Nancy or even—half-blind as Siobhan says he is—Burton doesn't notice. Because Siobhan arrives at Latimer high, and she leaves even higher. At least Marisol is chauffeuring her around.

The hair isn't perfect, and then, in English, when Ms. Erskine says something typically, monumentally stupid (unless you actually think that Shakespeare was an early feminist and *King Lear* proves it, which it doesn't), Siobhan laughs out loud. Very loud. Normally, she distracts herself during moments like this by chipping off her nail polish. I look over, and no nail polish.

She says, "Oh fuck this," and she runs out of the room.

I wait maybe three seconds to follow her, but I can't find her.

Dylan says, "Drop it. She's not your problem anymore."

"Dylan, she's constantly high!"

"Like you never noticed that before? Weren't you at the same parties?"

I say, "This isn't parties, this is school."

He says, "You never noticed at school?"

"I didn't notice at school because she was straight at school."

After lunch, French tests get passed back and she's sitting

there with a red D. Which is essentially impossible to get unless you accidentally stumbled into the room when you were trying to find Russian II.

After orchestra practice, when I meet Dylan and Arif in the caf, Arif says, "You should have seen your friend in Econ. Not a pretty sight."

I say, "What?"

Dylan says, "Her former friend."

"Oral reports," Arif says. "Ordinarily she's a big fan of the free market. Eats socialists for lunch, actually. Today—hard to tell what she was even talking about."

I remember telling my dad how we were staying up late making suits of armor out of tinfoil for our Joan of Arc oral report, the night we went out riding Loogie and Sir Galahad. Eons ago. A few months ago.

Dylan says, "You can't fix her. You already tried."

I say, "Not hard enough. Look at her."

Dylan intones, "Once again sucked into the vortex of bullshit."

Arif says, "D.K., get off her back! You know it's the right thing to do."

"Do you want to get frog-marched back to Convo, where someone *wants* to hear you ranting about the right thing to do?" Dylan says.

It's like hanging out with ten-year-olds. Really smart ones, but still.

I say, "Did anyone ever mention that you guys don't exactly bring out each other's mature sides?"

Arif says, "All the time."

Dylan says, "Never."

"Prepare to be amazed by my extraordinary maturity come September," Arif says.

I ask, "Why?"

They both look at me. They both look slightly stricken.

Arif says, "D.K.?" Then he says, "Maybe I'll go polish my shoes and learn Greek." Latimer doesn't have Greek, and he's wearing Adidas made of shiny cloth and suede. He picks up his backpack and gives Dylan a withering look.

I say, "What?"

Dylan says, "I was going to tell you. But I wasn't sure if it was going to be a parade or a funeral."

At the pit of my stomach, something curdles. I put down my shake.

"*What?*"

"Do you want to walk?"

I have the feeling that, basically, he doesn't want to tell me whatever this is in the caf and then be treated to me throwing food at him.

The quad is almost empty by now as we walk around its perimeter. "Just tell me."

He says, "I got into Georgetown."

I am just above us, in the trees, watching us. I am watching him evaporate into thin air as I reach out my arms and find them flapping in an unpopulated space.

"But you're a junior. You can't get into Georgetown."

"I have enough units," he says. "A junior from Loyola got in last year. Palmer just has to get Latimer to fork over a diploma. But they will, just to get rid of me."

I am watching myself be a good friend and a decent person, and not having the clingfest that I feel like having.

I say, "That's great! Congratulations."

I am trying to be completely happy for him. Because it's a big deal and it's wonderful and he wants out so much—such as every few sentences, ever since I met him. I'm thinking about how the only things he'll miss in L.A. are me and Arif and Lulu. How staying would mean one more year in a guesthouse he hates, at a school he hates, with parents who only make cameo appearances to tell him that he's surly.

I say, "You have to go. Dylan! It's amazing."

He says, "You don't look happy."

"I didn't realize that we had an expiration date that soon. That's all."

He says, "So. Here's the thing. I don't do sap. But where else am I going to find somebody that enthused over a half-eaten chocolate bird?"

"Excuse me?"

"We could still be together," he says.

We are sitting on the bench on the far side of the library, my back against his chest, my head lolled back against his shoulder.

And I want to believe this, I do, but even in my smitten state, it's not all that believable. "How would that even work?"

He says, "I can fly back all the time."

"Don't promise me things that you're going to regret. Don't. You're not going to want to. You'll be in *college*."

He says, "I'll want to."

We walk to the parking lot, holding hands.

He says, "So. This is going to be good, right?"

I'm pretty sure that if I got into Georgetown, I'd get home and my dad would have frosted cupcakes in the school colors, and there'd be streamers in the living room. And I realize, he is going home to that cool, completely solitary guesthouse, clean laundry and fruit left by the housekeeper—not to people jumping up and down and going, Yay! Boy genius! Hug, hug, hug.

I say, "We're going to celebrate. This weekend. We're going to completely whoop it up."

He says, "You don't look like you want to celebrate, Seed. You look miserable."

"I'm going to miss you, what do you think? But this is *Georgetown*, it's not like I don't know how much you want it. You want to picnic Saturday? Or I could take you to brunch? Or I could drive you up the coast. We could play miniature golf at that dorky place in Ventura."

"*Brunch?*" He looks aghast. Then he says, "Yeah, that would be nice."

He stands over me as I get into my car. It doesn't hit me how much I'm shaking until he walks away.

CHAPTER FIFTY-FOUR

I SPEND THE EVENING IN AVID CELEBRATION MODE, as opposed to wallowing in the fact of Dylan's somewhat imminent departure. I find the Georgetown colors (blue and gray) for purposes of cake decoration. I do not make a playlist of women wailing blues songs to accompany this activity. I order a Hoyas sweatshirt for him online. I consider putting on his white shirt that I haven't returned yet, but don't, due to the pathetic-ness factor. I make a congratulatory card in which a kinetic Airedale resembling Lulu tap-dances.

I don't much feel like tap-dancing.

My dad sticks his head in and says, "Are you crying in there?"

It's hard to deny, when there are tears dripping down your face, and you're not dicing raw onions or watching *Bambi*.

He says, "Should I be worried?"

"Nope. It's just stupid. I'm trying to do a ton of work instead."

My dad says that this sounds quite mature, but walks away looking confused.

Mature or not, I am determined to jump around and say "Yay" all over Latimer in the morning, in a masterful display of my unclinginess.

But Dylan isn't there. Not that that's entirely unheard of, but usually he makes an appearance in homeroom, or he shows up in the music room. Or somewhere.

> **Me:** Where are you?
>
> **Dylan:** Taking the day off. Taking Lulu up to Tree People Park.
>
> **Dylan:** Want to come?
>
> **Me:** Some of us have to go to class from time to time.
>
> **Me:** Some of us still have to worry about our GPA.
>
> **Dylan:** And some of us don't!
>
> **Me:** Go be smug with your dog Kahane.

And I'm fine, completely fine. I eat lunch with two ballet girls that I barely know, and they're kind of friendly. At the end of it, Kimmy sits down, takes her burger apart, and eats the bun, tomato slices, lettuce, and patty separately, all with ketchup.

She says, "Disgusting, huh?"

I'm not sure if she means the burger or her eating habits, but I agree.

I feel like master of the universe, like a person who can actually cope, in a riding-for-a-fall kind of a way.

I don't have a clue.

Siobhan is still walking around entirely un-made-up, entirely hostile, although somewhat cogent when called on. I'm wondering if a former best friend can ever mount some sort of intervention that the other former best friend listens to.

I head up to the rocks to find her, but nothing.

I leave for home, the back way through the hills, and there she is, sitting cross-legged on the hood of Burton's DeLorean, with a box of Gitanes on her lap, smoking something that doesn't look much like a Gitanes.

I roll down my window.

I say, "You want a ride?"

"Sweet," she says, "are you *supporting* me? Because no thank you."

"Shit, Sib, you can't drive like that!"

"Why not? Don't you know how officially sober I am? Nancy found my stash. Ask me about home drug testing kits. Fuck my life."

"So Gitanes is selling undetectable weed now?"

"Nancy's take on it is I'm too young for major pharma, so I should stick to drinking."

She takes a long drag on the joint.

"Siobhan! We're ten yards from school!"

"So what? If you weren't completely obsessed going *Ooooooh, Dylan, baby, delude me some more,* you might notice that they don't actually care."

She crooks her finger at me. "You want to talk to me, c'mere. I have something to *shoooooow* you."

I pull up in a no-parking zone and climb onto the hood of the car. Siobhan takes out her phone, and I'm seriously waiting for this to be a horrible picture of me doing something embarrassing. But it's not. It's William and a beautiful, emaciated girl walking along the street in Milan. Shot after shot after shot.

"Her name is Elisabetta," Siobhan says. "And he claims that she's his other half. Does that bitch look like half of him?"

They do look remarkably similar to one another, rich and emaciated and half asleep.

"He can't just walk away from me and take up with a piece of Eurotrash!" she yells. "We have a *pact*! He can't just walk away!"

But there he is, walking away down the Via Montenapoleone, carrying Elisabetta's shopping bags.

"Sucks. I'm sorry."

Siobhan stares at the photo. "Doesn't she look trashy to you?"

"Totally."

"Elisabetta von Koppenfels," she says. "Sounds like some famous Nazi's girlfriend."

"She could actually *be* some famous Nazi's grandchild," I say. "Look at her."

"This makes me feel so much better. You think he can be happy with a blatant Nazi but not with me."

"That's not what I said."

"You think I'm not good enough for your widdle boy toy and I'm not good enough for William." She is drumming on the hood of the car. "You think Dylan broke up with *me*."

Which I do, obviously, because he did.

She grabs my arm. "Admit that's what you think."

I yank my arm away from her and end up jabbing her with my elbow. She steadies herself against the windshield so as not to fall off the car.

"You pushed me!" she shouts.

"It was an accident. Be rational!"

"I'm irrational and you are such a damn rocket scientist! Stop feeling sorry for me!" She is glaring at me with a level of rage not commonly seen on the faces of even former best friends. Not that I've had that many of them. "You've never been my real friend!" she yells.

Before she can come at me again, I'm off the car and standing in the street.

"What do you think is going to happen when your boy toy *leaves*?" she asks.

"You knew about that?"

"Duh. Why don't you ask him who he was doing when he was pissed at you?" she hisses. "You are *so stupid*!"

I get into my car, and I turn the key, and I just sit there for a minute watching her kick Burton's car before I head down the street.

CHAPTER FIFTY-FIVE

I CALL MY DAD AT ALBERT WHITBREAD. I SAY, "I can't come home now."

He says, "Why not?"

"This is the complete truth. I'm alone. I'm really upset. And I just want to drive around for a while."

"Ems, I don't want you driving around upset. What if I don't come home until you phone me, and you have the house all to yourself?"

I say, "Wow. That's so nice. But I just want to sit in my car."

He says, "I don't suppose you want to talk about it?"

"No! I mean, no thank you. But no."

My dad sighs, "All right. But Ems, ten o'clock, or I'm tracing you with LoJack."

"Or the GPS chip you had implanted in my scalp when I was sleeping."

He laughs. "That's not the worst idea."

I drive up to a turnout on Mulholland. I watch the sun set, pink and orange, and then I watch the city lights go on, and the clouds fade into the blackening sky. I stare up at that black sky, and at the airplanes trailing through it. Whenever I think a single thought beyond L.A. turning to night, I just go, Stop It.

Then I drive home over Laurel Canyon.

My dad is waiting. Of course he is, with raisin bread and tea.

He says, "If there were some way I could keep you insulated from all this high school angst, believe me—"

"I know."

I am deep in postponing-the-inevitable territory, hacking through the underbrush of nighttime conversation, not hacking all that quickly because I'm not all that sure I want to know what I'm about to find out.

I say, "I have to call someone."

"It's so late, Ems." (It's 10:05.)

I say, "I'm in high school. No one sleeps."

I close my door and I crank up Beethoven's Ninth. Loud. Eardrum-shredding, fingernails-in-palms-of-hands loud.

I say to Dylan, "If this is nothing, I apologize in advance, but I was just talking with Siobhan."

Very carefully, he says, "And?"

"And when did you hear from Georgetown?"

Even more carefully and evenly, he says, "Just before I told you."

"When?"

"I was deferred, then I got off the list." He pauses. "Why is this important?"

"My God. You're messing with me so you won't have to flat-out lie to me!"

Dylan says, "You should know."

"*What?*"

"Not what I meant to say."

I say, "Was it before or after we made up? And here's a hint, the right answer is *after*."

Long pause.

He says, "It wasn't after."

I wish I had the kind of old-fashioned landline where you can slam the earpiece into the receiver.

"So Siobhan knew before I knew? Were you *with* her?"

He shouts, "Jesus Christ! I cannot believe she told you about that! The second installment of the Siobhan Lynch setup and she tells you?"

Not what I was expecting. Not what I want to know about, hear about, process, or deal with.

He says, "We were broken up. It was bad. I was shitfaced. It was once. She's evil."

I say, "I've gotta go."

My dad pops his head in. He says, "Ems, do you want to talk about it now?"

I do, but obviously, I can't.

I can't talk to anyone about anything.

CHAPTER FIFTY-SIX

NOT THAT DYLAN DOESN'T TRY. HE PHONES, BUT I don't pick up. Then he texts.

> **Dylan:** The texting isn't meant to be ironic. But I'm sorry.
> **Me:** No irony taken.
> **Dylan:** And?
> **Me:** And I just wish you'd have told me. But we were broken up. It's not like we were married so technically you weren't coloring outside the lines.
> **Dylan:** It wasn't OK. I get it.
> **Dylan:** Emma?
> **Me:** I know I don't get to play the you-shoulda-told-me-card with you. But you were back with Siobhan.
> **Me:** And you didn't once think to say you applied to college?

Dylan: Maybe I'm hardwired to treat women like shit

Me: You didn't treat me like shit. This all just kind of sucks.

Dylan: Could we cut to the chase and skip forward to being OK?

Me: I don't want to be mean to you. I just want this conversation to be over.

Dylan: Could I get you pancakes?

Me: Maybe we need a break from pancakes.

Cutting to the chase, my life as Emma the Scourge of God has not left me in the world's best emotional state. I don't have a boyfriend, a best friend, or very good judgment. I seem to be going for an F in navigating moral complexity, not unlike everybody else I know, except for Megan, and she feels guilty about bagging groceries at a food bank with Joe, so that doesn't really count.

I am in my closet, making lists of applicable clichés, in order of relevance. "Chalk it up to experience," "Don't count your chickens (or, for that matter, Candy Land happy endings) before they hatch," and "People who live in glass houses shouldn't throw stones" being the top contenders.

On the other hand, I have completed every last damned item on my Afterparty prep list.

Every. Single. One.

(Minus Siobhan's BS about carrying on in a glass elevator, etc.)

The year was not a total waste.

All right, I was completely in love with the idea of me being a good person in a heart-stopping relationship with another good person, and with a wild but good best friend.

Now, I'm not sure any of us qualifies.

I'm back to flying around solo, a flockless bird, and who even knows if I'll know when to go south for the winter, or even where the south is located.

But I do know how to get to Afterparty.

My dad says, "Have you seen this letter from Miss Palmer about the dangerous party?"

About how going to Afterparty in a limo so you can cut out in style when the police shut down the party doesn't make you safe. How many kids leave in ambulances due to their ingestion of large numbers of shots mixed with their friends' prescription Xanax. And how its reputation as the best party ever held anywhere, ever, gives it an unhealthy allure that parents should counter with vigilant catastrophizing.

I say, "There was an assembly about it."

Not that I attended. I snuck into the library because school is like an obstacle course. Siobhan is staring me down. Dylan I'm avoiding. Chelsea is snorting at me. And Arif keeps looking at me as if he pities me.

"Last year, the theme was Pimps and Ho's!" He is apoplectic.

"Every high school in L.A. has had a Pimps 'n' Ho's afterparty. Except maybe Saint Bernadette. This year it's Beyond the Grave. Do you like that better?"

"You know this how?"

Oh God.

"Common knowledge. Kids in K though 3 know. The secret location is what nobody knows."

It's at the Camden Hotel, a less-than-secret location so people can reserve rooms upstairs in advance, creating even more venues for bad behavior.

He makes me sit there while he shares more scraps of Afterparty lore from Miss P. He says, "I hope your friends aren't planning to do this."

Not that I have friends at school at the moment, but if I did, they would be planning to do this. Even though anyone caught selling, buying, or stashing tickets on campus is automatically punished in some unspecified way that shows up on your permanent record, everybody has one.

I ask Arif, "Are you going to this thing?"

"My mom tore open Palmer's letter, and five minutes later, my father was taking me to a Dodger game that night. In San Diego."

Walking past my locker, Siobhan says, "Just so you know. The limo is full."

I say, "You knew that was never going to happen. Like I could jump into a limo and ride around town, and my dad would buy that I was studying at your house the night of Afterparty?"

She says, "I thought a lot of things were never going to happen. Like my *formerly* best friend wasn't going to mistake me for a burnout."

"That shit makes twelve-year-olds have heart attacks. I get to be concerned."

"Your level of ignorance is awesome. Have fun sucking up to your dad while *I'm* at Afterparty. No all-girl dance at the Camden for you, young lady."

"I'm going to be there," I say. "Just really late."

"Sure you are. Do we even still have pacts? Can I trust you for *anything*? Can I even count on you to do what you said?"

"I do what I say I'm going to do, Siobhan," I say, "whether or not we're BFF's. So yes."

God help me, I say yes.

CHAPTER FIFTY-SEVEN

THREE HOURS TO AFTERPARTY, AND MY DAD WANTS to play Scrabble. I think about hypnotists in old black-and-white movies who go, *You are getting sleeeepy, very, very sleeeeeeeeepy.* As my dad keeps making word after word, I admire those hypnotists' skills.

But eventually he yawns and I pad down the hall to my room in the buttoned-up blouse and prim skirt I'm about to change out of, a girl on the verge of uncorking her own damn magic genie lamp.

Here it is: absolute proof that even without Siobhan coaxing me out of the lamp and into the land of wrong decisions, I am perfectly capable of doing all manner of wrong things all by myself. And I don't need some lame boyfriend by my side to go for it, either.

Capable of planning, prep, and execution.

I bought the dress on sale at Kitson, a filigreed silver skin with a skirt that flares just a little and stops dead mid-thigh. It isn't vintage, but I still feel like a slightly glammed-up version of myself in it. The silver sandals were borrowed from Nancy a long time ago, very high, very glittery. I plan to return them, ignoring the drizzle and the mud just outside my window, and how delicate the tiny silver straps are, and how they need to go to the shoe hospital before I hit Sunset.

I have perfect makeup, the kind that shows.

I don't care if the theme is Beyond the Grave, I'm not going as the Bride of Frankenstein. I bring a bloodred lipstick-liner pencil I can use to draw a couple of drops of blood on my chin if it turns out I'm the only girl there who can't pass as a nonliving creature. I have a cheap umbrella that I plan to ditch as soon as I arrive. No coat because it doesn't sound as if the Camden has a coat-check room or a concierge or a high level of sanitation, organization, or safety.

Which is kind of the point.

The taxi driver says, *"The Camden?"* as if I'm asking to be dropped off at the gates of Hell.

The Camden is built in the style of a make-believe Spanish castle, with giant wrought iron chandeliers, whitewashed walls, and a red tile roof with turrets. It got famous for splashy Hollywood trysts in the twenties and choked-on-barf rock star deaths fifty years later. All these events happened during parties in the dimly lit ballroom, which has balconies and staircases leading to derelict roof gardens, roped off but still in use.

There are celebrity trivia websites that document who blew whom on which Camden balcony. But now the Camden is mostly famous for not checking ID's all that carefully and letting kids rent suites.

It's a place where no one's parents would even dream of going, but not a warehouse in a sketchy part of town where a kid could get mugged between the limo and the front door. And not too particular about hundreds of kids showing up half plowed as long as they can pay for corridors of seedy rococo suites: big musty beds with satin comforters, tufted club chairs missing buttons, and, weirdly, a couple of either feral cats or some guest's hapless lost pets prowling the corridors.

An unexpected doorman with a giant umbrella, the same green as the derelict awnings that extend from the sidewalk to the front door and arch over the ground-floor windows, helps me up to the lobby—grand and too dark to show cobwebs and dust, filled with kids I know, kids I've partied and gone to class with, but who are transformed by the grandeur of the decadence.

I am trying to figure out if the distinct odor of mold and the way it constricts my throat as I step into the lobby is a sign.

The compass says, *Fucking A, it's a sign. Get back in the taxi.*

I don't grace this with a response.

Everyone is slightly off. Without shoes, or with their hair messed up, or with eye makeup bleeding into raccoon eyes, or with a whole lot of bra showing, or with the entirely wrong guy, or with nipples more than shadowed through the near-transparency of tissue-paper-thin tops.

Maybe half the guys hanging on the edges of the lobby look like severely stoned members of the overgrown ten-year-old-boys club, ready to slide across the slick, polished paver floor in their sock feet, ready to slither down banisters and play catch with girls' underwear. But the rest of them look to be slouching through in between doing whatever kinds of drugs have got to be here somewhere and instigating acts of extreme perversion.

Charlene comes through in a semi-formal dress with a senior guy I don't know, his suit jacket slung over his shoulder. She nods to me.

Charlene says, "It's all going on upstairs. Just a bunch of dancing down here."

The boyfriend says, "Except the bar."

"I'm not going in there," Charlene says. And to me, "Don't go in there."

I am so going in there.

There are kids heading in every direction, including toward walls and circling pillars and falling into dark corners, in slightly impaired party entropy. Up on the landing of the staircase, there are shadowed bodies undulating, a leg draping down the stairs, an occasional arm emerging from the huddle, rotating like the blade of an off-kilter windmill. People are sweeping up and down the stairs, wandering past the front desk and down the rank, mildewy hall toward the ballroom, where there is a truly terrible loud band of undeniably cool but musically backward senior guys.

I hand over my ticket, and the back of my hand is stamped with something visible only under the bouncer's ultraviolet light beam. The room is black with intermittent pops of faint light that makes people's faces take on a momentary beyond-the-grave pallor. And everywhere dancing of the too-cool-to-move-much, already-dead-and-no-muscle-tone variety.

There are water misters lodged somewhere overhead, tiny droplets of water drizzling out of the darkness, making everything slick and clammy. There are actors with shredded clothes and makeup suggesting that they would be unspeakably gruesome were the lights to be turned up. They wander through, muttering softly, the living dead, staring out with big, blank eyes. They are the pathetic, pleading kind of living dead, only when they reach out their hands and clamp onto your shoulder, there is a second of terror.

Not fun terror.

Just terror.

And it doesn't feel like Halloween, it feels like a sick ball in a teenage world where living-dead wraiths get their hands stamped with invisible ink.

Declan Hart, who was supposed to be with Kimmy (evidence of her tendency to choose mean players), takes my hand when I'm too distracted by the living-dead hand on my upper arm to resist. Declan starts to dance with me, a riff on stiff seventh-grade cotillion ballroom dancing. Either I'm paranoid or he's sneering at me. Or sneering at the world at large, and I happen to be the one he's feeling up.

I say, "Declan, do you have moves besides the box step?"

Declan calls me a bitch and walks off, leaving me standing there on the edge of the dance floor, where there *is* some all-girl dancing, in a loose circle with a bunch of juniors I recognize and a living-dead girl I don't. Mara is in the middle of it, in costume, and we're not talking a pretty, glam costume; we're talking layers and layers of cheesecloth that are supposed to represent a shroud in a state of postmortem disintegration.

I am in the circle. I am right there. I am sparkly silver After-party girl.

Then Declan walks by and says, "No wonder. Bitch likes girls," and I return to my quest for the bar. Edging along the outer wall and trying not to bump into people, steering away from anywhere that has anything close to the familiar party aroma of barf, or a paid zombie.

Already, someone is being carried out. I say, "Is he all right? Did somebody call 911?"

A guy in a tuxedo T-shirt says, "Ambulance number two. Not to worry." He sounds sober and reasonably credible, so I don't worry.

The bar is in an almost pitch-black room off the ballroom. I hand the bartender my money, and I get a screwdriver. I have developed a taste for screwdrivers.

Behind me, there is a tight circle of kids smoking. Strick, in fact.

He says, "Cocoa puff?"

I start to say I'll pass, but I don't pass. I take it and I take a hit, or a drag, or a puff, or whatever it is when it's a cigarette with cocaine frosting, and I wait for something to happen. Nothing discernible does.

I keep trying. I try and try.

I say, "Are you sure?"

And he says, "Maybe. I'm too wasted to tell. I should lie down. I have a joint, though."

He starts it and hands it to me, and I smoke it until my throat is burning and I'm pretty sure I'm feeling it. I turn to hand it back, but there's nothing left of it.

Then he gestures to a curtain, a heavy brocade curtain, with a coffin jutting out underneath. With feet reaching almost to the end. There are coffins with their lids propped open, people inside, not all dressed, not fully, and some people are lying there, and some people are making out, and in the faint green light they look maggoty, although maybe the deadness motif just brings that to mind.

And when I look down, the coffins are resting in something soft, mounds of loamy-smelling dirt, five coffins resting in dirt, and there are two girls rubbing that dirt on a guy's chest, slowly, as if in a party trance, as he lies there with his hands folded at his throat.

A voice that sounds so eerily like Siobhan's, but isn't, says, "Want to play?"

And I'm gone.

The band starts up with a strange, punkish cover of "Hooray for Hollywood."

There is a blast of light so bright it hurts my eyes. I press my eyelids closed but the outline of shooting flames is visible behind my eyelids. When I open my eyes, Dylan is standing in front of me.

In jeans and a standard-issue white shirt, only one that skims his body, and a dinner jacket not unacquainted with a tailor. He is leaning against a pillar, smoking a cigarette. He doesn't smoke.

He says, "Hey. Not bad for a girl who's home asleep."

I say, "Not bad yourself. For someone who's—where are you?"

"We don't live in the same fucking house," he says. "I'm wherever I want to be. I'm where you wear jeans and a dinner jacket, and a zombie from Screen Actors' Guild hands you a cigarette."

I say, "What are you doing here? I thought you hated this."

Dylan says, "You look beautiful. You always look beautiful."

Straight to the heart. Which is not where I want him.

He smooths his lapels. "I might be overdressed. Paulina's suite is clothing optional. And well stocked. As promised."

Paulina has rented the semi-official junior class suite.

"Well stocked with what?"

"Wine, women, a shitload of pharmaceuticals. It's raining white powder up there."

I say, "Shit, is Siobhan there?" Almost reflexively, that's where my concern goes.

"What do you think?"

I am struck by my remarkable inability to let go. Of her, of him, of Good Emma, of anything I decide to let go of, but don't. Because here I am, right back in it, not dealing with the reality of a boyfriend I should have noticed wasn't perfect and also was leaving town, and a best friend I should have noticed was high all the time.

Dylan groans. "No. Emma. Don't go." It is, despite everything, almost irresistible. "At least dance with me first."

He reaches his hand around the small of my back, the Aiden move, and it feels so good, I let him lead me. He doesn't even have to open his mouth; just him standing there, swaying a little, almost imperceptibly, to the music is a compelling argument. And it isn't that I want to do anything other than dance with him, to cuddle up to that black dinner jacket and those scruffy jeans, to succumb to the bursts of light in the dark room. But I'm backing away.

"Christ, Emma, you're not her keeper," Dylan says. "Are you planning to track her down wherever she's passed out forever?"

"She's *passed out*?"

"Not yet. She's more in her flapping-around, making-out-with-anyone-that-looks-at-her stage, *before* she passes out."

"That is so mean."

"Yet so accurate."

I turn toward the doors, but I'm moving against the tide.

"You should dance with me," he says from behind. "You shouldn't get distant and cold in advance."

We're standing in the middle of the ballroom. Kids are waving their own bottles—the Camden isn't particular—and smoking all manner of things; there are little plumes of smoke all around us. In the dim recesses of the room, people are hanging off the stage and off stairways to balconies, the acrid sensation of mold in my nostrils superseded by perfume and body odor and rum. Up on the stage, the drummer isn't drumming because there's a girl in his lap and they're sharing a bottle and she's whipping his belt around over their heads. It's picking up the light, like a lone streamer.

We are being pushed toward the stage by bodies, elbows and shoulders knocking into us, and I keep moving to the side, trying for the exit door, if I could get to it through the crowd.

"You should stay here and dance with me," Dylan says again. He starts off plaintive, but by the end of the sentence, it's a demand. "Why don't you face it? She's too broken for you to fix." I can't tell if his arms are around me in anger or affection.

"Say what?"

"I said—"

"I know what you said! And if she's so broken, what were you doing with her?"

"I told you why I was with her," Dylan says. "Drunk and an idiot. Both times. Now tell me why you were with me."

"You know why I was with you! I saw you my first day at Latimer. Like you didn't notice."

Dylan says, "That's not what she says. And it's starting to make sense."

I say, "Excuse me?"

"She said I was a check mark. That's what I was to you." Even in the darkness of the ballroom with the flashes of disorienting light, even with the poker face, even with everything, it's hard to miss the sadness. Or the anger. "You might have told me."

His hand on my back feels more like a fist and less like the hand of a guy who has one single good feeling toward me.

"And you believed her, obviously."

He says, "She said I was your learner's permit supervised hours. Care to comment?"

But there's no anger left in me for her; I already know who she is.

I say, "I can explain."

The hand is off my back entirely.

I say, "It wasn't like that." Just a beat too late.

A burst of white light captures the contours of his face, a flash of rage.

He says, "Listen, Emma, high school is about to be over. You might have to hang up your learner's permit and get a license. This is what people do. They fuck and then they leave for college."

"You suck, you know that?" I am pushing him away.

He shakes his head and touches my cheek. It might as well be the cold fingers of the living dead.

I am weaving between people, and he is following, toward the exit door, which is heavy and warped and damp. I brace myself against it, pressing it with my right shoulder and all my weight, but it is slow to give until the moment it bursts open and I fall through it, into a cold, dark hallway, and run back toward the lobby.

Chapter Fifty-Eight

THE ELEVATORS IN THE LOBBY HAVE HAMMERED copper doors, decorated with intricately wrought tree branches and vines. The doors open slowly, the elevator having creaked to a stop six inches below the level of the lobby's tile floor. Death trap, anyone? I head up the wide, curved stairway, which is draped with people sprawled from step to step.

I keep climbing to the penthouse floor, because apparently that is where we all are, nothing but the best of the best of the best of trashy. Hotel-room doors are hanging open on both sides of the hall, with odd assortments of people I know and don't know all over each other. It's hard to imagine that anyone is spending the night cooking up a storm, but there are sour boiled-cabbage smells. And apparently the hookah has made a comeback with smoke that smells fruity, burnt and aromatic, that curls up like a floating shadow of gray paisley.

Kimmy—who is finally making out with Max Lauder, barely

inching down the hall, hugging the wall, with Max working the thin straps of her dress off her shoulders—looks out at me.

I say, "Do you know where Paulina is?"

She pries her head out of the embrace and says, "Charlene has champagne," nodding toward the door over her left shoulder. Where a bunch of kids are sitting on the bed, popping bottle after bottle in rapid succession. Where Charlene's senior boyfriend is pouring champagne into her no-longer-abstinent mouth.

Charlene yelps, "Why didn't anybody ever tell me how good this is?"

Senior boyfriend appears to be deeply perplexed as to why he didn't think to tell her sooner.

Charlene cups her hands under her chin so the champagne won't pour down over her chest. She is a serious good girl, yet someone is trying to lick champagne out of the dimple on her chin. She is now wearing a strapless bra and a tulle skirt that might be a slip.

A guy on the bed waves a bottle of uncorked champagne at me, bubbles frothing from the mouth of the bottle onto the patterned carpeting. Grey Burgess, very cute, and with a crooked smile. I think, Shit yes, Grey Burgess. Drink champagne. Get a buzz. Save Siobhan. This year did not exactly work out as planned, everything kind of sucks, but here I am.

I walk in, Grey Burgess nodding to me, and I sit next to him on the edge of the heavily populated bed. The mattress tilts in our direction. He hands me the bottle and I take a swig. Then he kisses my ear. It isn't the same as with Dylan, nothing is the same as with Dylan, not his chest or the smell of him or his hands under my hair.

I hoist my legs onto the bed, thinking, This is nothing, we fucked and then he leaves for college. Nothing, nothing, nothing. I am so not the lamb at the wolves' orgy, I have so passed the point of no return for lamblike girls with no out-of-control proclivities.

Which is working great until we roll off the bed and Grey is on top of me, kind of crushing me, and it's somewhere between meh and unpleasant. I roll him off, he's not insistent, and I go, "Sorry, Grey, I have to find Siobhan."

Grey props himself up on his side and looks at me.

He says, "You'd have a better time with me."

"I'm sure. Gotta go."

Standing up is hard. I feel light-headed and a little bit elated. I wonder if maybe the cocoa puffs were, in fact, cocoa puffs, and the joint was more than weed, and I've made it over the line to hard drugs. As innocuous and nothing-like as Siobhan claims they are. Or if this is the champagne. Or if this is just how people feel in check-mark city.

I find Paulina's suite. I stand in the hall with the sounds of someone bumping into the door from the inside, muffled music, and the smell of weed and cat pee.

There is the wet-trash smell of Siobhan's French cigarettes.

I bang on the door and people I can't see in rooms I can't see into shout for me to be quiet. They are hoarse and loud and insistent.

Lia Graham, stumbling down the hall barefoot, a champagne bottle in each hand, wants to know if I can zip her up.

I can.

Paulina's door opens inward, whoever opened it no longer in evidence. The girls' lacrosse team, that I usually think of as scary upright creatures who live for sports, are huddled with Siobhan and some guys on the floor, and no one looks all that upright.

Siobhan is half undressed and halfway to oblivion.

I don't even get what they're doing at first; it's like a live reenactment of a semi-abstract painting with limbs protruding at angles that don't make anatomical sense. Missy Rogers and Kyra, who is in so-called ballet with me, are at the center of it, Missy having finally found someone glad to kiss her back. Everyone seems happy to kiss everyone back, sharing what looks to be a monster joint—hash, maybe? Maybe something I don't recognize and probably ought to avoid.

Siobhan extricates herself, a disembodied arm rises from behind her to push her up, and she hands me the joint and watches as I take a hit. It's harsh, and the roof of my mouth feels charred.

I say, "What is this?"

She says, "You don't want to know. I thought you weren't coming."

"I said I was coming. We were supposed to be dancing downstairs. Don't you remember?"

"Just saying."

I say, "I'm here, aren't I? Where's your shirt?"

366

There are people and coats and bottles everywhere. There's a cat eating something off the carpet by the bed.

"Why do you always care about my shirt?" she says. "You're not my mother. Hell, my mother's barely my mother."

"Why is everybody walking around with half their clothes off?"

Siobhan looks puzzled. "Games. Strip poker in Ian's suite. Truth or dare. Fun."

Just then, Paulina, standing on the bed, pops a bottle and jumps up and down until one side of the mattress hits the floor and the pile of coats slides onto the rug. Siobhan says, "Why don't you just—wait! Where are you going with that?"

Assorted pills are the *that*. That thing local news stations say misguided teens do with a jumble of random, unidentified pills in festive candy bowls passed hand-to-hand at parties—that thing that we don't do? Apparently, at Afterparty, we do.

"Do you even know what kind of pill that is?" I bat it out of her hand. Then I go scrambling after it, so I won't be responsible for the death or the out of body experience of the cat.

I'm thinking that I'll get a shirt on her, something over the lavender bra and the black skirt, and I'll get her out of the suite. I'll get a shirt on her and we'll freaking dance. We'll be Afterparty girls dancing that long-planned dance and it'll be freaking fun.

I'm thinking that I have no doubt been rendered psychotic by assorted substances if I think that's what's going to happen.

"Shut up, Mommy," she says in a weird voice. "Look, here comes Daddy in half a suit."

Apparently Dylan is following me up and down the halls of the Camden.

"Aren't you going to kiss your boyfriend?" Siobhan says. "Aren't you going to go, Oh, baby, let's stay together forever and ever. No, let's break up. No, let's stay together. No, let's break up."

Dylan says, "Can we make this stop?" And then, "Shit. Is that guy shooting up?"

There's a guy on the sill of a black, painted-shut window, and unless he's busy staving off a diabetic coma with a whole lot of insulin, yes, he is.

Dylan says, "Emma, you need to get out of here. Will you please, for one second, let me help you out?"

"Stop following me! And you're not who I'd turn to for help."

He says, "Open your eyes."

My open eyes are blinking and they sting a lot.

"What, is the happy couple having a widdle pwoblem?" Siobhan croons.

"Shut up, Sib," Dylan says, and he heads toward a little settee with carved wooden arms in the back of the room. I could resist if I wanted to, I could break free of the loose grasp, but I go with him, sitting pressed against him, aware of my breath, my heartbeat, my pulse, the joint-induced burning sensation at the back of my throat.

He holds my face and he says, "You don't hate me, right?"

"No. But you still suck."

"I know," he says. "You too. You were the virgin and I was the check mark?"

"Fuck and leave for college? That's what was going on?"

"No."

And then yes. In a smoky room with people in it, and the only feeling I feel is the intensity of wanting it, pushed harder against the wooden arm of the settee, no room, and here I am with him, in a completely private embrace, only in public, and on the other side of him, Siobhan, her hands under his shirt, her mouth on his mouth, a hand on my breast, I don't know whose. Crammed against the arm, trying to rise, and Dylan saying, "Shit, Siobhan! Get off me!"

But she doesn't get off until he pushes her off.

"Get over him!" she spits at me. "You can't trust him. I'm the one who made you. Not him. But you just won't listen."

She looks crazy, hysterical crazy. Screaming and grabbing at my arm as I pull away.

Siobhan says, "Nothing got better! Don't you get it? Everything got worse. You can't rely on *anybody*. Stupid William! It was supposed to get better, but everything keeps getting worse. And you *know* what that means." Then she yells, "I'm going on the roof! Who's coming on the roof?"

Paulina pushes open the glass-paned door to the balcony. The air is laced with cold and rain.

I say, "You can't go on the roof."

"Watch me." I almost can't make out the words, it's so noisy. And then she yells, "Pact, pact, pact, pact! You have to come or I'm doing it myself. And what's the point of that?"

I don't remember.

Then I do.

By then she is climbing the cordoned-off stairs to the loft. By then I'm chasing after her. By then I'm yelling "No!"

There are narrow metal stairs, curved in a corkscrew, from the balcony up toward the roof. The staircase ends with a door to a steep passageway that takes you back inside the building, along a corridor with taped-up pipes and discarded cleaning supplies, old brooms and paint cans, just below the roof. At the end of the hall, Siobhan pushes through a door marked ALARM WILL SOUND, but there's just the sound of rain, and the night sky.

The roof is slippery and you can feel the wind, not enough to topple you, but enough that you have to pay attention.

She says, "Come on!"

I reach out for her, but I slip and she gets me by the upper arm. Not to pull me up, to pull me down. I try to steady myself, but my heels are too high and too fragile.

I yell, "Siobhan, stop it! This isn't funny!"

"Pact!" she says. "You promised. So you have to do it. I am totally bombed, I am as mellow as I get, so mellow, and it isn't working, is it? You know it isn't. You're a wreck and it's never going to get any better for you."

"Siobhan, I'm fine! That pact was stupid! We're both going to be *fine*."

"You need me! You know you do, you can't cope without me, and I'm so out of here." She is pulling on my arm, pulling toward the edge where the roof slopes down, across an expanse of tar paper and toward the tiles that are slick with mud and rain.

"No! Siobhan! Stop!"

"You can't live without me," she says, panting, pulling me along the roof, yanking on my wet hair. "Can't live either way." Her breath is labored as we struggle there, pulling and pulling away, pushing toward the edge as I maintain the wholly unrealistic hope that I can somehow talk her out of this.

Because I see where this is going.

This is going over the edge.

I am not going over the edge.

She is pulling me by my arm and by my hair, toward the edge of the roof. Each time I think I'm braced, that I've figured out how to balance myself, how to crouch down and push back with each new surface—tiles, and tar paper shingles that seem to tear like paper, and flat places covered with jagged little white stones, and then a slope that ends in puddled, muddy rainwater—we're on another surface and I'm struggling again to keep my balance.

I yell, "Siobhan, no!" and I keep trying to pull her back, but she's stronger and we go down onto the flat of the roof, crawling over stones. I am pulling away and her nails are cutting into the skin on my forearms as I pull away from her grip. Almost free, not quite. I fall on top of her and she seems to be rolling away. But she's taking me with her toward the edge, where the roof swoops downward and the rows of broken Spanish tile are treacherous, and the surface can't be mastered.

I yell, "Stop it! Siobhan, stop!" But I can't pull away, she has my blouse and my hair and she's on top of me now, rising to her knees and pulling me up with her.

She says, "It's a pact! You said! You can't back out!"

But I do. I back out. I end it.

I grab onto a drainpipe just before we reach the sharp incline of the overhanging eaves, and I hang on.

I'm crouched on the edge of the roof and I'm panting and soaked, and I'm not even cold.

I have been running and running uphill. I have been rolling to the edge of the roof, sliding down a precipice of Spanish tiles and planes of gritty tar paper. Between my fingers, there is slime and a brown paste of decomposing leaves scooped from the rain gutter.

From the rain gutter that saved me.

The rain gutter I grabbed onto, onto the pipe that braced the rusty gutter to the roof, when she rolled over me, when she closed her eyes and grabbed me hard, when she tried to pull me with her, pull me down, down over the edge, and then I couldn't hold her anymore. I couldn't hold her back. Couldn't hold back the dead weight of her, pulling and falling. All I could do not to go over, not to fly down with her, not to plummet through the branches to the awning, down, down to the hard sidewalk, all I could do was to push her off me.

Was to push her over.

Was to brace myself and push her as hard as I could, push her off me, push her headfirst off the roof, before she could pull me down with her.

CHAPTER FIFTY-NINE

THE LAST TIME I SEE DYLAN THAT NIGHT, I AM alone on the edge of the roof, and he is standing by the stairwell. He is coming out of the stairwell. He is pulling himself erect. He is pushing back his hair, but it sticks to his face. Or maybe he has been there, crouching there, just outside the door all along. Maybe he saw.

I'm pretty sure he saw.

Drenched with rain, dark strands of hair dripping down his face.

He peels off the wet black dinner jacket. And I think, Not here, what's wrong with you, not here, not now, not again, not ever. He takes my arms and threads them through the wet sleeves, and he rolls the cuffs up just above my wrists.

I am breathing fog and rain. I am shivering in the cold, wet jacket, and the sleeves hurt where my arms are scraped raw from the elbows to the wrists, my arms encased in gabardine and blood and rain.

He says, "Go, you have to go."

I am nodding my head but there's nothing to say. I am breathing hard, as if I had been running miles and miles, running hard through a ravine of dark inclines.

He says, "Emma. Focus. We're leaving."

I say, "Get off the roof."

There's rain, and there's breathing, and there's the moment when he backs away.

He says, "Do you know what to do?"

"Just go away."

He says, "Go down the stairs and out behind the ballroom. Walk down to Hollywood Boulevard. Turn east. In a couple of blocks, it's the Mayfield. There'll be a bunch of taxis. Get in. Go to the Chateau. Or in front of a club. Are you up to walking?"

I nod my head.

I say, "I have to go get her."

Dylan says, "No. You don't. Hear the sirens? Are you taking this in? I'll walk you to the other staircase. At the bottom, there are people making out. Go out past the doorway, Hollywood Boulevard, east to the Mayfield, don't hail a cab, just get one at the Mayfield. Do you have cash? Walk home."

I say, "Okay." It is hard to climb down stairs, and when I step over the bodies at the bottom, nobody looks up.

There are sirens and flashing lights and running.

I go out the door, I go back out into the night, and I'm not the only person in a wet dress walking through the rain, down to Hollywood Boulevard. When the streetlights hit my dress, it glows. But I am not the only glowing girl walking away.

CHAPTER SIXTY

CONSIDER THE VIGIL: I'M NOT THERE.

Three days after Afterparty. A hard rain is flattening magnolia leaves against my window, the sky is almost white between the branches. White and cold.

Eighty-seven people have said yes to the vigil on Facebook. They are standing outside Cedars-Sinai Hospital, holding hands in hypocritical fellowship with everyone else who treated Siobhan like an expensive form of dirt. They're posting pictures of rain-sodden votive candles, waterlogged teddy bears, and helium balloons with her name on them.

Lia Graham recommends room deodorizer candles encased in pear-shaped glass to stay lit through the downpour, green for pine and yellow lemon zest. She is tagged on the event page in a knot of rain-drenched juniors singing inspirational songs. Waving their candles and praying for Siobhan to live. Waiting for her to die.

I, on the other hand, am sitting on the floor of my closet. The screen of my phone glows through the darkness with all of Dylan's texts that say some variant of *Talk to me*.

And my one text message back that says *No*.

I have watched "Tickle Penguin" on YouTube one hundred and sixteen times. I have watched a goose play with a cocker spaniel. I have prayed for her to live for three days straight, but unless you believe in the saving power of the ratty hotel awnings and the giant hydrangea bush that broke her fall, you are stuck with Occam's Razor, which our physics teacher likes so much: The simplest solution is the likeliest; I pushed her off the roof, ergo, she dies.

And no matter how many times emissaries of Religious Convo lead eighty-seven juniors waving room-deodorizer candles in chanting the Lord's Prayer, it would take a huge number of screwdrivers to wipe out their ability to reason their way to the inevitable conclusion.

If they knew.

Even so, it seems highly unlikely that they're going to start chanting, *Our Emma, who art hiding in her closet, you are so not a walking exemplar of badness, the she-devil of Latimer Country Day, the harlot of the Hollywood Hills.*

Even I wouldn't say that.

Because every bad thing that a person can do, I just did.

My dad, watching me sitting in the closet in the dark, but who knows nothing, is also trapped under the influence of Occam. I am sitting in the closet, ergo, I am sad because Siobhan has fallen.

He offers to drive me down to Cedars to visit her, but how do you visit with a person in a medically induced coma? Do you just stare at her unconscious face? Do you talk to her as if she could hear you, and pretend that she's taking it in? Do you say, Hey, sorry I killed you, bye, but you don't get to take me down no matter what asinine pact I accidentally said yes to?

If things don't get better, we'll jump off a tall building? No.

My dad is making soup: pea soup. Pea soup and French onion soup and chicken curry broth so far. This is as close to a mother as I'm going to get, a soup-making father who doesn't understand a thing. And I think, Well, that's pretty close.

And I start to wish I could tell him, but of course, there's no way.

What happened that night and how hard it was raining and how it didn't seem real and then it seemed like the only real thing in my life.

My dad sits down outside the closet. The door is open a crack; I can see the window and the tree and the sky. I can see a slice of his plaid shirt, and an oven mitt.

He says, "Ems, I know you aren't ready to process this yet, and I understand, but I want you to hear me. Whatever happens to Siobhan, whatever she did and whyever she did it, it's not your fault. Do you hear me? You're a good friend, you've been very kind to her, and sweet, and you're probably the reason she could cope for as long as she did."

Oh God, oh God, oh God. I am so not what he thinks I am, and it just keeps getting worse and worse and worse.

I say, "I'm not Emma the Good anymore, Dad, I'm sorry, I'm not."

More soup.

He says, "Would you like to talk to Rabbi Pam? She's worried about you."

I have visions of my dad trotting out Rabbi Pam and a minister and a priest—like a slightly dirty joke with the same crew walking into a bar—and giving them all equal time.

This is who I am: A person who thinks of semi-dirty jokes in the middle of this. A person who keeps checking the computer, trolling for anything about what happened. For the nothing that means she's still alive. For rumors and gossip and word on the street.

Which is that Siobhan fell off the roof unassisted.

Which is that she was drunk and stoned and crazy and belligerent all night, that she got into a hair-pulling catfight with an unsuspecting girl from Winston over nobody knows what, after which she tried to yank my hair out when I tried to put her blouse back on her.

That she careened up to the roof screaming something incoherent about impact.

That maybe her brain was so scrambled by a smorgasbord of Afterparty substances by then that she thought of her head as that seventh-grade welcome-to-science-class experiment where you toss a padded raw egg off a roof to see if it will crack on impact.

Or maybe she thought she could fly.

My dad says, "I see how difficult this is for you." He is being so kind, he is trying so hard, I don't deserve all of his soup and effort. "Would you like to come out of the closet and lie on the sofa? Give me your hand. Ems? Amélie?"

It's been all French for days.

But I am screaming in English: "Don't call me that!"

He sits out there for hours. It's like a weird pajama party game. He hands me in a pillow and a quilt from Montreal.

I hand him back the quilt and he gives me my yellow comforter and some French *Vogue*s and a flashlight.

He says, "Do you want to play with Mutt?"

I open the door and Mutt squeezes in and falls asleep on my shoes. He wheezes when he sleeps.

We're in the fourth day.

Mutt is circling around my boots as if he's looking for a special place to poop. I open the door and let him out in the backyard, where Jeff is sitting, nose to the back door, looking bereft, missing him.

There is banging on the front door. Not the knocker, a fist.

My dad gets off the floor. He says, "Come on. Maybe it's Megan."

I say, "Is it Megan?"

He shakes his head.

CHAPTER SIXTY-ONE

DYLAN IS STANDING IN THE DOORWAY IN JEANS and one of those extremely cool jackets that isn't quite a sports coat but hovers over his torso as if his tailor just finished perfecting it. He is dressed up. Not that I think my dad will register this fact, given that there's no tie involved.

"I'm Dylan Kahane," he says.

Even though I can only see my dad from the back, I know what his face is doing. I know this is not the genre of boy my dad sees as being in the same story as me.

"The orchestra geek," Dylan says.

My dad says, "The hell you are."

But he lets him come in, and Dylan walks through the front hallway and into the living room. He comes toward me where I've curled up on the couch. I start to get up and he holds me there, against his chest. I've been crying, off and on, for three days—why stop now? I press my face into the dark wool of the jacket, against the lapel, and I feel his chin on top of my head, vibrating, as if he were humming.

Here I am, leading my new, improved, and not imaginary secret life in front of my father, between the piano and the shelves of books on the technical aspects of being insane. I am kissing Dylan, walking past the record player with cabinets with all my dad's historic vinyl, holding Dylan's hand. I am walking into my bedroom and closing the door.

And the oddness of it strikes me, how I feel furtive, like a renegade bad girl, sitting chastely in my closed-door bedroom with Dylan across the room, yet I can sleep with him at his house without one single guilt-tinged scruple.

And from across the killer girl's pale green-and-yellow bedroom, Dylan says, "Hey."

I say, "Hey." I say, "I'm sorry." I say, "Nothing seems real."

Dylan says, "I'm sorry. I know. I keep thinking, if I'd just done something differently—"

"I know."

Because this wasn't one of those quicksand landscapes with an inevitable outcome. The kind where you can tell yourself that there was nothing you could do to stop it, it was a runaway train, it was a stampede of crazed cattle, it was kismet, fate, and preordained.

I could have said no, said maybe, not said yes. All year.

Dylan says, "I know you don't want me over here, but you won't answer the phone. I never should have let you leave there by yourself. I should have gotten you home. I should have figured it out."

"I think I told you to get lost."

"So what. I just stood there. Jesus."

And then I think, Siobhan is comatose, Siobhan is lying there at Cedars-Sinai and no one knows if she's going to live or die, and I'm behind a closed door in my bedroom, engaged in teen romance.

But it's possible that our compatibility lies in him being a similarly bad person, because he says, "This isn't why I came, and we don't have to get into this, but are we still broken up?"

I say, "I don't know, but if I said we are, I take it back."

Dylan gets out of the vanity chair that he's too big for and sits down next to me on the bedspread. "Your dad's not going to shoot me, is he?"

I lean my head against his shoulder.

He says, "Did you tell him what happened yet?"

What they say about soldiers in trenches with their mouths tasting like metal, that's exactly how my mouth tastes. Like metallic terror.

He says, "You're going to have to go public pretty soon. You're going to have to tell him. I've got your back, but we can't just not tell anyone what happened."

Closet, closet, closet. Where it is silent and dark.

"It's already started," he says. "Facebook. YouTube. Pictures of people going up the stairs. The bed collapsing under Paulina is going viral."

"Emma kills Siobhan. How many hits do you think that would get?"

He says, "What are you talking about?"

I just look at him.

"I was up there," he says. "I saw what happened. I thought, God, I'm sorry Emma, I should have figured it out, but you were under her and she was squirming around and I thought—I don't know what I thought. I'm sorry. And then, it was so fast but it was pretty clear she wasn't kissing you. When she was trying to kill you."

I am trying to stay on point. I am trying not to think about the fact that my boyfriend thought I was getting it on with my former BFF when, in fact, something quite different was transpiring.

"She wanted us to jump together."

Dylan straightens up and shakes his head. He looks very grave, completely serious, no irony, no movement at the corners of his mouth, only a thin, tight line where his lips are pressed together.

"She was trying to push you off the roof. If you hadn't grabbed that drainpipe and thrown her off-balance, you'd be dead."

I am dizzy with the possibilities. If this is what he saw, or if this is what he thought he saw, or if this is what he's making up to save me. If he just saw what he wanted to see, which was not me killing Siobhan.

I look into his face.

He is telling the truth. He thinks he is telling the truth.

Maybe it is the truth.

Maybe Siobhan was trying to kill me and I was so down

for being friends for life, I didn't notice just how short a life she wanted me to have.

Maybe my best friend wanted me dead. Maybe she wanted us both dead, or maybe just me.

Maybe my best friend was trying to kill me on the roof of the Camden Hotel.

Maybe I killed her instead.

CHAPTER SIXTY-TWO

MY DAD IS OUTSIDE MY DOOR, AND AS HE OPENS it, Dylan literally jumps off the bed, which makes it appear that we were doing something my dad wouldn't approve of. Beyond sitting on my bed with the door closed.

My dad says, "Emma." He nods toward the living room. "Now."

I get up, smoothing my hair, smoothing my uniform (because I got dressed for school but didn't go), looking incredibly guilty, although probably not of homicide.

My dad nods toward the living room couch and it's pretty clear that now that I'm out of the closet, we're back to the fairy tale with the princess who is expected to do as she's told. My dad looks shell-shocked. I would no doubt feel guilty as hell about this if I wasn't already feeling guilty for so many other, worse things.

He says, "Why is that boy in your bedroom?"

I don't say anything. Surprise, Dad, I'm a killer liar sex fiend and sitting in my bedroom is Exhibit One?

Maybe not.

I sit down on the couch, as far away from him as I can without perching on the armrest. Cradling a cushion in my lap, but I still feel unprotected, as if I'm being showered with embers and my uniform is melting off and here I am, uncovered, with no sign of being a student, or in high school, or the best of the best of the best.

At his end of the couch, my dad says, "Emma, are you pregnant?"

This from the man who wouldn't sign the parental waiver to get me out of Issues in Modern Living, where I was forced to learn to roll a condom onto produce.

"No! Why is it always about girls getting pregnant? Is that why you tried to keep me locked up here, so I wouldn't get pregnant?"

"I take it I didn't do a very good job of keeping you locked up, eh?" It's that Canadian "eh?" thing that gets to me, it still so gets to me. I feel so sorry for him, stuck with me, so sorry for what I am about to put him through.

"Emma," he says. "We've always been very honest with one another. You can talk to me about anything."

It is the moment of truth. Or of no truth. In the moral hierarchy, where does lying stack up next to shredding your father? With the corollary issue of my insides and the shredder, when he knows, and he gives me that look, only gone exponential, and there's nothing left of me but bad genes and poor impulse control.

I say, "No, I can't. We're not honest with each other at all. And everything we don't talk about just exploded."

My dad just looks at me.

I say, "Say something."

I am thinking that this will be the last sentence before I completely expunge any notion he might have of my Emma the Goodness, and how wonderful I am, and his belief that if he's a good enough father, he can somehow prevent me from turning into *her*.

So I just say it: "I'm *her*. You might as well have stayed in Montreal and let everyone throw things at me, because I deserve it."

From his end of the couch, my dad says, "You know that we left Montreal because of me. Not you, Ems. And no one wants to throw anything at you."

"Have you *been* to Lac des Sables? Where I never have to go again."

My dad is leaning toward me now, but not actually touching me, as if I might be a stick of some volatile explosive. Which I might be.

He says, "Ems, this is a difficult moment. I understand that. Siobhan is in the hospital. You have something going on with this boy. I'm not sure where Canada comes into this, but I'm going to sit with you until we sort it out."

"Do. Not. Go. Psychiatric. On. Me."

"Ems! Look at me. Look up. This is what *parental* looks like."

By now I'm shouting at him and I can't stop. "Don't you get it? I'm her! No matter what you did and how far from home you stashed me, I'm a total fuckup. Look at *me*! I look exactly like her!

I just go around doing whatever I feel like doing and I don't even feel guilty enough about it to stop."

My dad, who is by this point three inches away from me and white, pretending that he's still calm, says, "Don't you ever, for one moment, blame a single decision you've made on who your mother was." He shakes his head. "And I think you might be exaggerating. Just a little."

"No I'm not! You know I'm not or you wouldn't have kept me locked up here!"

"Ems, if I've been inflexible, we can discuss it. But it's because the world is a dangerous place. Here especially. No other reason. Not because I don't think you're wonderful."

"I'm not that wonderful."

Compass: *You are a master of understatement.*

My dad says, "You're wrong." He sounds so sure and uncomprehending. "Teenagers have lapses in judgment. It's expected. I don't know what you possibly could have done that makes you feel this way about yourself, but I know you, and it's not going to change what I think of you. I love you."

I scream, "Even if I killed Siobhan?"

"Even if you did *what*?"

This is when Dylan comes out of the bedroom, when my dad stands up and says, "You need to go home."

Dylan, who is backing toward the door, stops and says in extremely bad French, "Sir. Dr. Lazar. She didn't. You need to hear this. She thinks that she did, but she didn't."

My dad says, "Of course she didn't."

On his way out the door, Dylan calls back, "And she's not anything like her mother!"

My father follows Dylan out the door.

When my dad comes back, he is teary and ever so slightly furious.

I say, "Before you even say anything—"

He says, "Tell me what happened Saturday night."

Deep breath.

Then I tell him.

I tell him everything in gory detail. The window, the taxi, Dylan leaving Latimer, Paulina's suite, the all-girl limo that I wasn't in, the rooftop and the rain. And every time I say another true sentence, I feel as if I'm punching him in the face.

He is pacing in front of the couch. He says, "We can deal with this." It sounds as if he's brainstorming, not as if he actually believes it. "You were frightened and you took off. We'll talk to the police. We'll talk to Siobhan's mother. We can deal with this."

I say, "She's going to die, isn't she?"

"What happened on that roof is not your fault. *Entendu?*"

"Yes it was! What was I even *doing* there?"

"*That* we have to talk about. Parties, taxis, drinking, drugs." He is ticking it off on his fingers. "What am I leaving out? But this we have to handle first."

"Boyfriend," I say. "You left that out."

He frowns. Then he says, "I'm a sucker for anyone who says my baby girl didn't commit capital murder."

This is so extremely not funny that I think he might have snapped.

He says, "This is the one you've been studying with?"

I nod.

He says, "Ems, the boy was there. He saw what happened. You were drunk and in the middle of it."

"I wasn't that drunk."

"You were *drinking* and in the middle of it. Either way, that poor girl was trying to push you off the roof. He was a few yards away. He saw. I'm staying with his version."

"You have no idea—"

"I know you."

"You don't even. Weren't you listening? I've been doing things all year. Pacts with Siobhan and all kinds of things."

"You rode a horse down Mulholland," he says. "It's not the worst thing anybody ever did."

I don't even want to know how he knows that. "All I've done since we landed in this state is lie to you. That first day, at that beach club, I kissed some guy I didn't even know."

"In those terrible plastic sunglasses."

I don't know what I have to do to get him to see. "Everybody thought I had a secret boyfriend, and I made that up too."

"Lots of girls have secrets from their parents," he says. "It's part of growing up." You can just hear him saying this in a similarly clueless way to the clueless parents of his pathologically dishonest patients who kill cats.

"Stop making excuses for me! Stop believing I'm this wonderful person who couldn't possibly do anything wrong. Admit you're disappointed."

He says, "I know you." As if this were definitive. "I believe you're a wonderful person who did a lot of things wrong. As did I. That doesn't make you a killer, or Fabienne, or—I regret I ever used this word with you—a disappointment."

"Like you're not disappointed? Please."

"Of course I'm disappointed! You've been sneaking out of my house for six months. I should have listened when you said to chain you to the piano."

"It's not a joke! You should have listened when I said to let me go out. You should have trusted me."

"*Not* the moment to tell me to trust you."

"Sorry."

He looks at me and he isn't scowling, which is good under the circumstances. He says, "I think the boyfriend you *didn't* make up is still in the courtyard."

"No!"

"Do you want to ask him if he'd like to come in?"

"Seriously?"

He nods.

CHAPTER SIXTY-THREE

SIOBHAN WAKES UP.

Nobody thought that she would, but she does.

And when I see her, weeks later, battered and bandaged and hooked up to machines, when they let people in, I can't help it, I love her again.

I see the green eyes, part open and a little crusty, and the ashy blond hair with roots badly in need of some attention, and her unmanicured fingernails, and I know how much she must hate this.

And then I think, I'm in complete denial. She wanted to kill me. This is bad.

"Way to screw up a pact," she says.

I'm so thrown off, it's difficult to form a sentence.

"Yeah, well, if I'd kept the pact, we'd both be dead."

"That," Siobhan says, looking around the hospital room, "was the *point*. The point was not to still be here and damn straight the point was not for me to go to Austen-fucking-Riggs while you're screwing some college geek. This is not how it was supposed to turn out."

Austen Riggs is where kids who ventured over the line from out of control to mental cases went to get better. It's where Courtney Garland went after she tried to gas herself with car exhaust in her father's eight-car garage in October, and she got better. Second semester, she came back, transferred to Campbell Hall, and got onto the cheer squad.

Although it's hard to imagine Siobhan cheering, no matter how mentally shored up.

She says, "It was a pact. You *said* you'd do it."

The fact that I thought it was a joke when she first proposed this pact, the fact that I was so busy overlooking serious craziness and joking when I said, sure, we should do that if things don't improve, that's just what we should do, has evidently evaded her.

"Yeah, but on that roof, it had to be pretty obvious, even to you, that that wasn't what I wanted."

She is breathing so heavily and loudly, I'm afraid that the little jagged lines, the peaks and valleys of her monitor, will spell out "SOS" and bring forth frantic nurses and a crash cart. "What do you mean, *even* to me?"

I say, "You were kind of chemically impaired."

"I knew exactly what I wanted to do," she says, grasping my hand. Her fingers are dry and wiry. "I said what I wanted to do, and you came with me. Like always. I said 'pact' and you came. We had a pact."

"Siobhan, did you not notice I was trying not to?"

Trying not to *what*? Kill, be killed, die together at the age of sixteen because of a misunderstanding, *what*?

I say, "People think you were trying to kill me."

"What!"

"People think—"

"I heard you," she says. "And that's not what *people* think, is it? That's what *you* think. Isn't it? It is! It's what you think!"

There it is. There is no answer that would work for both of us. But this is my answer. I say, "Yes. That's what I think because that's what happened. By the end, it was you pushing me."

She pulls away, gazing past my head and toward the door, to the hospital corridor, past wheely racks hung with pouches of clear liquids, past surfaces of fresh flowers and unopened gift bags from Stella McCartney and Fred Segal. "Never mind," she says. "I thought I could trust you, but obviously not." She is playing with the ends of her bangs, twirling her hair, but will not look at me. "Well, *tant pis*!" she says.

"Siobhan, this is not a 'tough shit' kind of situation—"

"No. I'm sorry, but I don't think we should be friends at all. If I can't trust you, what's the point?"

EPILOGUE

IT ISN'T THE ENDING I EXPECTED.

Standing on the roof in the rain, the colored lights of Hollywood Boulevard blurred in the sky, when I was absolutely certain that Siobhan was dead, and Dylan saw me do it, and that I was evil incarnate and not just some moderately bad good girl who screwed up.

It's the ending that comes after the last scrap of the drama, when life goes on, and even though my life has holes in it where people used to be, I'm still here at the food bank, shelving cans of tuna and boxes of mac and cheese with Megan and Joe.

Also, I go upstairs.

Rabbi Pam says, "Finally! Come in."

I slam the door to her office so hard, a book falls off her bookcase. Then I have a more generalized meltdown about the unfairness of certain key aspects of life. She doesn't disagree or say that God will fix it or try to teach me how to crochet.

For this, I'm grateful.

I say, "So, am I part of this religion or not?"

She shrugs. She says, "I choose it for myself every day. And I suspect that you do, too. I could lend you some books."

We are looking out her window toward downtown. Below, Mrs. Loman is patting an even older man on the shoulder as he sets off, shuffling, across the parking lot with his bag of food.

I say, "Yeah, books would be good."

I am repairing the world, one grocery bag at a time.

And I haven't told a lie in three weeks. That's kind of good, right?

The compass says, *Three weeks. World's record. You are so not out of the woods.*

It's a depressing thought, but does anyone ever get out of the woods? Was there supposed to be a moment of blinding clarity when the path through the thicket appeared, brightly illuminated, and Good, Bad, and Morally Neutral all sorted themselves out, slightly messy but completely unambiguous, like egg yolk and egg white and shell?

If so, I missed it.

So here I sit, deciding for myself. Emma the Tentative. Emma the Previously Unfamiliar with the Truth. Emma Who is Not Fabienne, Emma the Good Enough.

Megan says I'm inspirational.

Joe walked up to her front door and knocked and Megan announced she was going out to dinner and a movie, and drove off in Joe's car to the Arclight, where they shared a giant Coca-Cola and a vat of highly salted popcorn. Her parents stood there in the front hall in Los Feliz with their mouths hanging open. No one died.

It is difficult for me to extract even the smallest shred of inspiration from what I did.

I celebrated the High Holy Days in September. I dragged my dad to Beth Torah, which was weird. I fasted on Yom Kippur, which, if you've never been there, is a total bloodbath of everybody confessing an extensive list of sins in alphabetical order, forgiving other people, and asking God for forgiveness for nine hours straight. And here we are, three weeks later, and I still feel about as morally fit as roadkill.

The moral compass has been shrieking, *Honesty is the best policy! Nothing good happens on the Strip after midnight! Do not unhook your bra in the presence of others!* for years. And did I listen?

I try a do-it-yourself making-amends thing.

I tell Miss Roy I wasn't sick a single time I told her I was sick and signed myself out, and she gives me a week of detention.

I tell Dylan the gruesome details of the Afterparty list and watch him cringe for forty-five minutes.

I tell Kimmy how I rode Loogs in the middle of the night, and he's really a nice horse, and I'm sorry, and she says, "I know, but don't tell Chelsea, or she'll probably kill you."

I feel somehow a lot more secure about my ability to cope if people try to kill me. I am still not that good at coping when they leave.

I miss Siobhan. This is no doubt sick, but I do.

As for Dylan, he insists he hasn't left me. Generally, he is sitting across from me at the Griddle when he says this, wearing a Georgetown T-shirt. I am cutting twelfth-grade assembly and watching him eat a syrupy stack of red velvet pancakes, which apparently do not exist—at least not really good ones—in Washington, D.C., or the entire state of Maryland. He is reduced to IHOP back there.

He says, "Seed. We're here. I miss you. Nothing has changed."

I say, "Note the T-shirt."

But when we are leaning against each other, walking around the corner at Sunset and Fairfax, back to our two cars, me heading to Latimer and him heading home to catch a shuttle to the airport, he says, "You have to have a little faith in people." He is pushing against me and I push back. "You have to have a little faith in yourself."

I put my arms around him and I rest my head against his chest. I hear his heart. And I think, Maybe I will.

Maybe I do.

Acknowledgments

First, thank you to my agent, Brenda Bowen, whose judgment, savvy, and expertise continue to inspire absolute trust, and whose literary sensibility remains awe-inspiring. More than I could have hoped for, and what I hoped for was pretty far over the top.

Huge thanks to *Afterparty*'s two editors—both brilliant, creative, and a joy to work with. Jen Klonsky, who first acquired my novels, is a whirlwind of enthusiasm and a master brainstormer, and I would probably never forgive her for leaving Simon Pulse if I didn't love her so much. I was terrified at the concept of a new editor, but Patrick Price's intellect, energy, and humor bowled me over. Patrick, I so value your ideas, your amazing eye for detail, and the way the manuscript has developed with your guidance. Plus it's really fun to work with you.

Actually, there isn't one person at Simon Pulse who hasn't been wonderful. Bethany Buck, many hugs and thank you. Carolyn Swerdloff in marketing has been holding my hand and doing fabulous things above and beyond for the past two years, now with the help of the dynamic and sweet Emma Sector. Mara Anastas has been kind and darling. Paul Crichton is a truly generous magician, and Lydia Finn the most amazingly effective, proactive, and genuinely nice person. Jacket designer Jessica Handelman is inspired (and also prescient). Michelle Fadlalla, Venessa Carson, and Anthony Parisi have done all kinds of beyond great things right from the start. And Mary Marotta and Teresa Brumm, just wow. Both Nicoles, Ellul and Russo, have been lovely, as has Courtney Sanks, and as for my local rep, Kelly Stidham—I am so lucky. (And, Dawn Ryan, I miss you.)

Many thanks to Professor Amir Hussain and to Rabbi Morley Finestein for sharing your wisdom with so much depth and sensitivity. I am deeply grateful for your help. Thanks also to my dear Mimi Roberts for help on the Montreal front; to Menachem Kaiser for his input on the use of the word "shiksa"; and to super-librarian and horse expert Leslie Chudnoff, who was kind enough not to laugh at me when Loogs acted more like a very large wheaten terrier than a horse. (If I did blow it, the fault is mine, of course, and not that of the experts who tried to save me from myself.)

Thank you, Alethea Allarey, for keeping me electronically connected, technologically semi-competent, and sometimes, also, sane.

To the L.A. branch of the Apocalypsies—thank you for taking me in. The half a clue I finally have, I got from you. And to the LAYAS, you rock. To my critique group, Alexis O'Neal, Caroline Arnold, Gretchen Woelffle, Nina Kidd, and Sherril Kushner for years of support and friendship and wisdom and input: thank you.

To my mom, Lillian Redisch, who is still cheerleading as avidly as when I was a six year old with a black-and-white marbled notebook and a pencil, and to my mother-in-law, Marilyn Stampler, and our dear friend, Jay Markoff, with all my books on permanent display on your coffee table, thanks.

Laura and Michael, you are phenomenally good storytellers

in your own right, and such sage advisers. Thanks. Laura, your notes saved me when I was stuck. I love you both so much. And as for Rick, you read every word of every draft, and offered smart, smart input and endless encouragement. Then there's your complete willingness to share our house with new crews of characters for years at a time, and act as if it's normal to have conversations about them as if they were real. I love you. I thank you. I appreciate you.

Finally, Evan, rescue dog extraordinaire, thank you for reforming and not actually eating any significant pieces of paper, note cards, or paper clips involved in the creation of this book.